HOLLYWOOD STATION

"Exhilarating . . . blisteringly funny . . . colorful . . . a pleasure . . . It has all the authority, outrage, compassion, and humor of the great early novels."
—*New York Times Book Review*

"Astonishing, wildly funny, poignant, and horrifying . . . hands down the best crime fiction I've read this year."
—*Boston Globe*

"Highly entertaining . . . outrageous and hilarious . . . all of Wambaugh's trademark jet-black humor is intact."
—*Washington Post Book World*

"Cops just want to have fun! As you turn the pages of Wambaugh's newest offering on the subject of the foibles and ferocities of the LAPD, you are going to have quite a good time yourself."
—*San Francisco Chronicle*

"Sharp characterization, fine plotting, and irreverent humor that mark Joseph Wambaugh's best work."
—*Dallas Morning News*

more . . .

ALSO BY JOSEPH WAMBAUGH

JOSEPH WAMBAUGH

THE BLUE KNIGHT

GRAND CENTRAL
PUBLISHING

NEW YORK BOSTON

Copyright © 1972 by Joseph Wambaugh
Excerpt from *Hollywood Crows* copyright © 2008 by Joseph Wambaugh
All rights reserved. Except as permitted under the U.S. Copyright Act of 1976, no part of this publication may be reproduced, distributed, or transmitted in any form or by any means, or stored in a database or retrieval system, without the prior written permission of the publisher.

Grand Central Publishing is a division of Hachette Book Group USA, Inc. The Grand Central Publishing name and logo is a trademark of Hachette Book Group USA, Inc.

Hachette Book Group USA
237 Park Avenue
New York, NY 10017
Visit our Web site at www.HachetteBookGroupUSA.com

Printed in the United States of America

Originally published in hardcover by Little, Brown and Company
First Mass Market Edition: April 2008

10 9 8 7 6 5 4 3 2 1

I often remember the rookie days and those who had discovered the allure of the beat. Then I thought them just peculiar old men. Now I wish they were all still here and that they might approve of this book.

WHOEVER FIGHTS MONSTERS

AN APPRECIATION OF
JOSEPH WAMBAUGH

THERE IS A BEDROCK TRUTH that resides in the heart of this book. And that is that the best crime stories are not about how cops work on cases. They are about how cases work on cops. They are not about how the cops work the streets. They are about how the streets work the cops. Procedure is window dressing. Character is king.

This is a truth we learn when we read the work of Joseph Wambaugh. No assessment of this novel or the other work of this policeman turned writer can conclude that he is anything other than one of the great innovators of the crime novel. Wambaugh brought the truth with him when he left the police department for the publishing house.

A century after its first inception the crime novel had moved from the hands of Edgar Allan Poe to the practitioners of the private eye novel. More often than not, these tomes told the story of the loner detective who works outside of the system he distrusts and even despises, who must overcome obstacles that often happen to be the corrupted police themselves. It fell to Wambaugh, with his stark and gritty realism, to take the story inside the system to the police station and the patrol car where it truly belonged. To tell the stories of the men who did the real work and risked their lives and their sanity to do it. And to explore a different kind of corruption—the premature cynicism and tarnished nobility of the cop who has looked too often and too long into humanity's dark abyss.

Wambaugh used the crime novel and the lives of his character cops as the lens with which he examined society. Within the ranks of his police officers he explored the great socio-economic divide of our cities, racism, alcoholism and many other facets of the rapidly changing world. He used cops to make sense of the chaos. And he did it by simply telling their stories. The episodic narrative of this book and those that followed became his signature. And along the way he gave us looks into the lives of characters like Serge Duran, Roy Fehler and Bumper Morgan, full blooded and flawed, and placed them on the sunswept streets of Los Angeles. His first two books, *The New Centurions* and *The Blue Knight,* are perfect bookends that offer the full scope of police life and Wambaugh's power. The former traced three officers through the police academy and their early years on the job. The latter traced a veteran officer's last three days on the job. No one had ever read books like these before. They were the mark of a true innovator.

It is important to note that Wambaugh wrote his first books while still on the job. The detective sergeant did the real work by day while pounding out the made up stuff at night on a portable Royal typewriter. His family had to sleep through the clatter. The results were uncontested as some of the most vivid police prose ever put on paper. Wambaugh opened up a world to the reader, a world no one outside of those who did the real work had ever seen before. Cop novelist Evan Hunter called it right on the money in the *New York Times* when he said, "Mr. Wambaugh is, in fact, a writer of genuine power, style, wit, and originality who has chosen to write about police in particular as a means of expressing his views on society in general."

A hundred years ago the philosopher Friedrich Nietzsche warned us that whoever fights monsters should take care not to become a monster himself. He reminded us that when we stare into the abyss that the abyss stares right back into us. So then these are the poles that hold up the Wambaugh tent. These are the battle lines that every cop faces and Wambaugh so intimately delineates in this book and others. He writes about how cops shield themselves, medicate themselves and distract themselves from the view of the abyss. Think of it in terms of a physics lesson. For every action there is an equal and opposite reaction. So then if you go into darkness then darkness goes into you. The question is how much darkness has gotten inside and what can be done about it. How can you pull yourself back from the edge of the abyss. In this book, and all of his books, Joseph Wambaugh tells us the answers.

—Michael Connelly

WEDNESDAY,
THE FIRST DAY

ONE

THE WHEEL HUMMED and Rollo mumbled Yiddish curses as he put rouge on the glistening bronze surface.

"There ain't a single blemish on this badge," he said.

"Sure there is, Rollo," I said. "Look closer. Between the *s* in *Los* and the big *A* in *Angeles*. I scratched it on the door of my locker."

"There ain't a single blemish on this badge," said Rollo, but he buffed, and in spite of his bitching I watched bronze change to gold, and chrome become silver. The blue enameled letters which said "Policeman," and "4207," jumped out at me.

"Okay, so now are you happy?" he sighed, leaning across the display case, handing me the badge.

"It's not too bad," I said, enjoying the heft of the heavy oval shield, polished to a luster that would reflect sunlight like a mirror.

"Business ain't bad enough, I got to humor a crazy old cop like you." Rollo scratched his scalp, and the hair, white and stiff, stood like ruffled chicken feathers.

"What's the matter, you old gonif, afraid some of your

burglar friends will see a bluesuit in here and take their hot jewelry to some other crook?"

"Ho, ho! Bob Hope should watch out. When you get through sponging off the taxpayers you'll go after his job."

"Well, I've gotta go crush some crime. What do I owe you for the lousy badge polishing?"

"Don't make me laugh, I got a kidney infection. You been free-loading for twenty years, now all of a sudden you want to pay?"

"See you later, Rollo. I'm going over to Seymour's for breakfast. He appreciates me."

"Seymour too? I know Jews got to suffer in this world, but not all of us in one day."

"Good-bye, old shoe."

"Be careful, Bumper."

I strolled outside into the burning smog that hung over Main Street. I started to sweat as I stopped to admire Rollo's work. Most of the ridges had been rounded off long ago, and twenty years of rubbing gave it unbelievable brilliance. Turning the face of the shield to the white sun, I watched the gold and silver take the light. I pinned the badge to my shirt and looked at my reflection in the blue plastic that Rollo has over his front windows. The plastic was rippled and bubbled and my distorted reflection made me a freak. I looked at myself straight on, but still my stomach hung low and made me look like a blue kangaroo, and my ass was two nightsticks wide. My jowls hung to my chest in that awful reflection and my big rosy face and pink nose were a deep veiny blue like the color of my uniform which somehow didn't change colors in the reflection. It was ugly, but what made me keep looking was the shield. The four-inch oval on my chest glittered and twinkled so that after a second or two I couldn't even see the blue man behind it. I just stood there staring at that shield for maybe a full minute.

Seymour's delicatessen is only a half block from Rollo's jewelry store, but I decided to drive. My black-and-white was parked out front in Rollo's no parking zone because this downtown traffic is so miserable. If it weren't for those red curbs there'd be no place to park even a police car. I opened the white door and sat down carefully, the sunlight blasting through the windshield making the seat cushion hurt. I'd been driving the same black-and-white for six months and had worked a nice comfortable dip in the seat, so I rode cozy, like in a worn friendly saddle. It's really not too hard to loosen up seat springs with two hundred and seventy-five pounds.

I drove to Seymour's and when I pulled up in front I saw two guys across Fourth Street in the parking lot at the rear of the Pink Dragon. I watched for thirty seconds or so and it looked like they were setting something up, probably a narcotics buy. Even after twenty years I still get that thrill a cop gets at seeing things that are invisible to the square citizen. But what was the use? I could drive down Main Street anytime and see hugger-muggers, paddy hustlers, till-tappers, junkies, and then waste six or eight man-hours staking out on these small-timers and maybe end up with nothing. You only had time to grab the sure ones and just make mental notes of the rest.

The two in the parking lot interested me so I decided to watch them for a minute. They were dumb strung-out hypes. They should've made me by now. When I was younger I used to play the truth game. I hardly ever played it anymore. The object of the game is simple: I have to explain to an imaginary blackrobed square (His Honor) how Officer William A. Morgan knows that those men are committing a criminal act. If the judge finds that I didn't have sufficient probable cause to stop, detain, and search my man, then I lose the game. Illegal search and seizure—case dismissed.

I usually beat the game whether it's imaginary or for real. My courtroom demeanor is very good, pretty articulate for an old-time copper, they say. And such a simple honest kisser. Big innocent blue eyes. Juries loved me. It's very hard to explain the "know." Some guys never master it. Let's see, I begin, I know they are setting up a buy because of . . . the clothing. That's a good start, the clothing. It's a suffocating day, Your Honor, and the tall one is wearing a long-sleeved shirt buttoned at the cuff. To hide his hype marks, of course. One of them is still wearing his "county shoes." That tells me he just got out of county jail, and the other one, yes, the other one—you only acquire that frantic pasty look in the joint: San Quentin, Folsom, maybe. He's been away a long time. And I would find out they'd just been in the Pink Dragon and no one but a whore, hype, pill-head, or other hustler would hang out in that dive. And I'd explain all this to my judge too, but I'd be a little more subtle, and then I'd be stopped. I could explain to my imaginary jurist but never to a real one about the instinct—the stage in this business when, like an animal, you can *feel* you've got one, and it can't be explained. You *feel* the truth, and you know. Try telling *that* to the judge, I thought. Try explaining *that*, sometime.

Just then a wino lurched across Main Street against

the red light and a Lincoln jammed on the binders almost creaming him.

"Goddamnit, come over here," I yelled when he reached the sidewalk.

"Hi, Bumper," he croaked, holding the five-sizes-too-big pants around his bony hips, trying his best to look sober as he staggered sideways.

"You almost got killed, Noodles," I said.

"What's the difference?" he said, wiping the saliva from his chin with the grimy free hand. The other one gripped the pants so hard the big knuckles showed white through the dirt.

"I don't care about you but I don't want any wrecked Lincolns on my beat."

"Okay, Bumper."

"I'm gonna have to book you."

"I'm not that drunk, am I?"

"No, but you're dying."

"No crime in that." He coughed then and the spit that dribbled out the corner of his mouth was red and foamy.

"I'm booking you, Noodles," I said, mechanically filling in the boxes on the pad of drunk arrest reports that I carried in my hip pocket like I was still walking my beat instead of driving a black-and-white.

"Let's see, your real name is Ralph M. Milton, right?"

"Millard."

"Millard," I muttered, filling in the name. I must've busted Noodles a dozen times. I never used to forget names or faces.

"Let's see, eyes bloodshot, gait staggering, attitude stuporous, address transient. . . ."

"Got a cigarette?"

"I don't use them, Noodles," I said, tearing out the copies of the arrest report. "Wait a minute, the nightwatch left a half pack in the glove compartment. Go get them while I'm calling the wagon."

The wino shuffled to the radio car while I walked fifty feet down the street to a call box, unlocked it with my big brass key, and asked for the B-wagon to come to Fourth and Main. It would've been easier to use my car radio to call the wagon, but I walked a beat too many years to learn new habits.

That was something my body did to me, made me lose my foot beat and put me in a black-and-white. An ankle I broke years ago when I was a slick-sleeved rookie chasing a purse snatcher, finally decided it can't carry my big ass around anymore and swells up every time I'm on my feet a couple of hours. So I lost my foot beat and got a radio car. A one-man foot beat's the best job in this or any police department. It always amuses policemen to see the movies where the big hood or crooked politician yells, "I'll have you walking a beat, you dumb flatfoot," when really it's a sought-after job. You got to have whiskers to get a foot beat, and you have to be big and good. If only my legs would've held out. But even though I couldn't travel it too much on foot, it was still my beat, all of it. Everyone knew it all belonged to me more than anyone.

"Okay, Noodles, give this arrest report to the cops in the wagon and don't lose the copies."

"You're not coming with me?" He couldn't shake a cigarette from the pack with one trembling hand.

"No, you just lope on over to the corner and flag 'em down when they drive by. Tell 'em you want to climb aboard."

"First time I ever arrested myself," he coughed, as I lit a cigarette for him, and put the rest of the pack and the arrest report in his shirt pocket.

"See you later."

"I'll get six months. The judge warned me last time."

"I hope so, Noodles."

"I'll just start boozing again when they let me out. I'll just get scared and start again. You don't know what it's like to be scared at night when you're alone."

"How do you know, Noodles?"

"I'll just come back here and die in an alley. The cats and rats will eat me anyway, Bumper."

"Get your ass moving or you'll miss the wagon." I watched him stagger down Main for a minute and I yelled, "Don't you believe in miracles?"

He shook his head and I turned back to the guys in the parking lot again just as they disappeared inside the Pink Dragon. Someday, I thought, I'll kill that dragon and drink its blood.

I was too hungry to do police work, so I went into Seymour's. I usually like to eat breakfast right after roll-call and here it was ten o'clock and I was still screwing around.

Ruthie was bent over one of the tables scooping up a tip. She was very attractive from the rear and she must've caught me admiring her out of the corner of her eye. I suppose a blue man, dark blue in black leather, sets off signals in some people.

"Bumper," she said, wheeling around. "Where you been all week?"

"Hi, Ruthie," I said, always embarrassed by how glad she was to see me.

Seymour, a freckled redhead about my age, was putting together a pastrami sandwich behind the meat case. He heard Ruthie call my name and grinned.

"Well, look who's here. The finest cop money can buy."

"Just bring me a cold drink, you old shlimazel."

"Sure, champ." Seymour gave the pastrami to a take-out customer, made change, and put a cold beer and a frosted glass in front of me. He winked at the well-dressed man who sat at the counter to my left. The beer wasn't opened.

"Whadda you want me to do, bite the cap off?" I said, going along with his joke. No one on my beat had ever seen me drink on duty.

Seymour bent over, chuckling. He took the beer away and filled my glass with buttermilk.

"Where you been all week, Bumper?"

"Out there. Making the streets safe for women and babies."

"Bumper's here!" he shouted to Henry in the back. That meant five scrambled eggs and twice the lox the paying customers get with an order. It also meant three onion bagels, toasted and oozing with butter and heaped with cream cheese. I don't eat breakfast at Seymour's more than once or twice a week, although I knew he'd feed me three free meals every day.

"Young Slagel told me he saw you directing traffic on Hill Street the other day," said Seymour.

"Yeah, the regular guy got stomach cramps just as I was driving by. I took over for him until his sergeant got somebody else."

"Directing traffic down there is a job for the young

bucks," said Seymour, winking again at the business-man who was smiling at me and biting off large hunks of a Seymour's Special Corned Beef on Pumpernickel Sandwich.

"Meet any nice stuff down there, Bumper? An airline hostess, maybe? Or some of those office cuties?"

"I'm too old to interest them, Seymour. But let me tell you, watching all that young poon, I had to direct traffic like this." With that I stood up and did an imitation of waving at cars, bent forward with my legs and feet crossed.

Seymour fell backward and out came his high-pitched hoot of a laugh. This brought Ruthie over to see what happened.

"Show her, Bumper, please," Seymour gasped, wiping the tears away.

Ruthie waited with that promising smile of hers. She's every bit of forty-five, but firm, and golden blond, and very fair—as sexy a wench as I've ever seen. And the way she acted always made me know it was there for me, but I'd never taken it. She's one of the regular people on my beat and it's because of the way *they* feel about me, all of them, the people on my beat. Some of the smartest blue-coats I know have lots of broads but won't even cop a feel on their beats. Long ago I decided to admire her big buns from afar.

"I'm waiting, Bumper," she said, hands on those curvy hips.

"Another funny thing happened while I was directing traffic," I said, to change the subject. "There I was, blowing my whistle and waving at cars with one hand, and I had my other hand out palm up, and some little eighty-year-old lady comes up and drops a big fat letter on my palm. 'Could you please tell me the postage for this, Officer?' she says. Here I am with traffic backed up clear to Olive, both arms out and this letter on my palm. So, what the hell, I just put my feet together, arms out, and rock back and forth like a scale balancing, and say, 'That'll be twenty-one cents, ma'am, if you want it to go airmail.' 'Oh *thank* you, Officer,' she says."

Seymour hooted again and Ruthie laughed, but things quieted down when my food came, and I loosened my Sam Browne for the joy of eating. It annoyed me though when my belly pressed against the edge of the yellow Formica counter.

Seymour had a flurry of orders to go which he took care of and nobody bothered me for ten minutes or so except for Ruthie who wanted to make sure I had enough to eat, and that my eggs were fluffy enough, and also to rub a hip or something up against me so that I had trouble thinking about the third bagel.

The other counter customer finished his second cup of coffee and Seymour shuffled over.

"More coffee, Mister Parker?"

"No, I've had plenty."

I'd never seen this man before but I admired his clothes. He was stouter than me, soft fat, but his suit, not bought off the rack, hid most of it.

"You ever met Officer Bumper Morgan, Mister Parker?" asked Seymour.

We smiled, both too bloated and lazy to stand up and shake hands across two stools.

"I've heard of you, Officer," said Parker. "I recently opened a suite in the Roxman Building. Fine watches. Stop around anytime for a special discount." He put his card on the counter and pushed it halfway toward me. Seymour shoved it the rest of the way.

"Everyone around here's heard of Bumper," Seymour said proudly.

"I thought you'd be a bigger man, Officer," said Parker. "About six foot seven and three hundred pounds, from some of the stories I've heard."

"You just about got the weight right," said Seymour.

I was used to people saying I'm not as tall as they expected, or as I first appeared to be. A beat cop has to be big or he'll be fighting all the time. Sometimes a tough, feisty little cop resents it because he can't walk a foot beat, but the fact is that most people don't fear a little guy and a little guy'd just have to prove himself all the time, and sooner or later somebody'd take that nightstick off him and shove it up his ass. Of course I was in a radio car now, but as I said before, I was still a beat cop, more or less.

The problem with my size was that my frame was made for a guy six feet five or six instead of a guy barely six feet. My bones are big and heavy, especially my hands and feet. If I'd just have grown as tall as I was meant to, I wouldn't have the goddamn weight problem. My appetite was meant for a giant, and I finally convinced those police doctors who used to send "fat man letters" to my captain ordering me to cut down to two hundred and twenty pounds.

"Bumper's a one-man gang," said Seymour. "I tell you he's fought wars out there." Seymour waved at the street to indicate the "out there."

"Come on, Seymour," I said, but it was no use. This kind of talk shriveled my balls, but it did please me that a newcomer like Parker had heard of me. I wondered how special the "special discount" would be. My old watch was about finished.

"How long ago did you get this beat, Bumper?" asked Seymour, but didn't allow me to answer. "Well, it was almost twenty years. I know that, because when Bumper was a rookie, I was a young fella myself, working for my father right here. It was real bad then. We had B-girls and zoot-suiters and lots of crooks. In those days there was plenty of guys that would try the cop on the beat."

I looked over at Ruthie, who was smiling.

"Years ago, when Ruthie worked here the first time, Bumper saved her life when some guy jumped her at the bus stop on Second Street. He saved you, didn't he, Ruthie?"

"He sure did. He's my hero," she said, pouring me a cup of coffee.

"Bumpers always worked right here," Seymour continued. "On foot beats and now in a patrol car since he can't walk too good no more. His twenty-year anniversary is coming up, but we won't let him retire. What would it be like around here without the champ?"

Ruthie actually looked scared for a minute when Seymour said it, and this shook me.

"When is your twentieth year up, Bumper?" she asked.

"End of this month."

"You're not even considering pulling the pin, are you Bumper?" asked Seymour, who knew all the police lingo from feeding the beat cops for years.

"What do *you* think?" I asked, and Seymour seemed satisfied and started telling Parker a few more incidents from the Bumper Morgan legend. Ruthie kept watching me. Women are like cops, they sense things. When Seymour finally ran down, I promised to come back Friday for the Deluxe Businessman's Plate, said my good-byes, and left six bits for Ruthie which she didn't put in her tip dish under the counter. She looked me in the eye and dropped it right down her bra.

I'd forgotten about the heat and when it hit me I decided to drive straight for Elysian Park, sit on the grass, and smoke a cigar with my radio turned up loud enough so I wouldn't miss a call. I wanted to read about last night's Dodger game, so before getting in the car I walked down to the smoke shop. I picked up half a dozen fifty-cent cigars, and since the store recently changed hands and I didn't know the owner too well, I took a five out of my pocket.

"From you? Don't be silly, Officer Morgan," said the pencil-necked old man, and refused the money. I made a little small talk in way of payment, listened to a gripe or two about business, and left, forgetting to pick up a paper. I almost went back in, but I never make anyone bounce for two things in one day. I decided to get a late paper across the street from Frankie the dwarf. He had his Dodger's baseball cap tilted forward and pretended not to see me until I was almost behind him, then he turned fast and punched me in the thigh with a deformed little fist.

"Take that, you big slob. You might scare everybody else on the street, but I'll get a fat lock on you and break your kneecap."

"What's happening, Frankie?" I said, while he slipped a folded paper under my arm without me asking.

"No happenings, Killer. How you standing up under this heat?"

"Okay, I guess." I turned to the sports page while Frankie smoked a king-sized cigarette in a fancy silver holder half as long as his arm. His tiny face was pinched and ancient but he was only thirty years old.

A woman and a little boy about four years old were standing next to me, waiting for the red light to change.

"See that man," she said. "That's a policeman. He'll come and get you and put you in jail if you're bad." She gave me a sweet smile, very smug because she thought I was impressed with her good citizenship.

Frankie, who was only a half head taller than the kid, took a step toward them and said, "That's real clever, lady. Make him scared of the law. Then he'll grow up hating cops because *you* scared him to death."

"Easy, Frankie," I said, a little surprised.

The woman lifted the child and the second the light changed she ran from the angry dwarf.

"Sorry, Bumper," Frankie smiled. "Lord knows I'm not a cop lover."

"Thanks for the paper, old shoe," I said, keeping in the shade, nodding to several of the local characters and creeps who gave me a "Hi, Bumper."

I sauntered along toward Broadway to see what the crowds looked like today and to scare off any pick-pockets that might be working the shoppers. I fired up one of those fifty-centers which are okay when I'm out of good hand-rolled custom-mades. As I rounded the corner on Broadway I saw six of the Krishna cult performing in their favorite place on the west sidewalk. They were all kids, the oldest being maybe twenty-five, boys and girls, shaved heads, a single long pigtail, bare feet with little bells on their ankles, pale orange saris, tambourines, flutes and guitars. They chanted and danced and put on a hell of a show there almost every day, and there was no way old Herman the Devil-drummer could compete with them. You could see his jaw flopping and knew he was screaming but you couldn't hear a word he said after they started *their* act.

Up until recently, this had been Herman's corner, and even before I came on the job Herman put in a ten-hour day right here passing out tracts and yelling about demons and damnation, collecting maybe twelve bucks a day from people who felt sorry for him. He used to be a lively guy, but now he looked old, bloodless, and dusty. His shiny black suit was threadbare and his frayed white collar was gray and dirty and he didn't seem to care anymore. I thought about trying to persuade him one more time to move down Broadway a few blocks where he wouldn't have to compete with these kids and all their color and music. But I knew it wouldn't do any good. Herman had been on his beat too long. I walked to my car thinking about him, poor old Devil-drummer.

As I was getting back in my saddle seat I got a burning pain in the gut and had to drop a couple acid eaters. I carried pockets full of white tablets. Acid eaters in the right pocket and bubble breakers in the left pocket. The acid eaters are just antacid pills and the bubble breakers are for gas and I'm cursed with both problems, more or less all the time. I sucked an acid eater and the fire died. Then I thought about Cassie because that sometimes settled my stomach. The decision to retire at twenty years had been made several weeks ago, and Cassie had lots of plans, but what she *didn't* know was that I'd decided last night to make Friday my last day on duty. Today, tomorrow, and Friday would be it. I could string my vacation days together and run them until the end of the month when my time was officially up.

Friday was also to be her last day at L.A. City College. She'd already prepared her final exams and had permission to leave school now, while a substitute instructor took over her classes. She had a good offer, a "wonderful opportunity" she called it, to join the faculty of an expensive girls' school in northern California, near San Francisco. They wanted her up there now, before they closed for the summer, so she could get an idea how things were done. She planned on leaving Monday, and at the end of the month when I retired, coming back to Los Angeles where we'd get married, then we'd go back to the apartment she'd have all fixed up and ready. But I'd decided to leave Friday and go with her. No sense fooling around any longer, I thought. It would be better to get it over with and I knew Cruz would be happy about it.

Cruz Segovia was my sergeant, and for twenty years he'd been the person closest to me. He was always afraid something would happen and he made me promise him I wouldn't blow this, the best deal of my life. And Cassie *was* the best deal, no doubt about it. A teacher, a divorced woman with no kids, a woman with real education, not just a couple college degrees. She was young-looking, forty-four years old, and had it all.

So I started making inquiries about what there was for a retired cop around the Bay area and damned if I didn't luck out and get steered into a good job with a large industrial security outfit that was owned by an ex-L.A.P.D.

inspector I knew from the old days. I got the job of security chief at an electronics firm that has a solid government contract, and I'd have my own office and car, a secretary, *and* be making a hundred more a month than I was as a cop. The reason he picked me instead of one of the other applicants who were retired captains and inspectors is that he said he had enough administrators working for him and he wanted one real iron-nutted street cop. So this was maybe the first time I ever got rewarded for doing police work and I was pretty excited about starting something new and seeing if real police techniques and ideas couldn't do something for industrial security which was usually pretty pitiful at best.

The thirtieth of May, the day I'd officially retire, was also my fiftieth birthday. It was hard to believe I'd been around half a century, but it was harder to believe I'd lived in this world thirty years before I got my beat. I was sworn in as a cop on my thirtieth birthday, the second oldest guy in my academy class, the oldest being Cruz Segovia, who had tried three times to join the Department but couldn't pass the oral exam. It was probably because he was so shy and had such a heavy Spanish accent, being an El Paso Mexican. But his grammar was beautiful if you just bothered to listen past the accent, and finally he got an oral board that was smart enough to bother.

I was driving through Elysian Park as I was thinking these things and I spotted two motor cops in front of me, heading toward the police academy. The motor cop in front was a kid named Lefler, one of the hundred or so I've broken in. He'd recently transferred to Motors from Central and was riding tall in his new shiny boots, white helmet, and striped riding britches. His partner breaking him in on the motor beat was a leather-faced old fart named Crandall. He's the type that'll get hot at a traffic violator and screw up your public relations program by pulling up beside him and yelling, "Grab a piece of the curb, asshole."

Lefler's helmet was dazzling white and tilted forward, the short bill pulled down to his nose. I drove up beside him and yelled, "That's a gorgeous skid lid you got there, boy, but pull it up a little and lemme see those baby blues."

Lefler smiled and goosed his bike a little. He was even wearing expensive black leather gloves in this heat.

"Hi, Bumper," said Crandall, taking his hand from the bar for a minute. We rode slow side by side and I grinned at Lefler, who looked self-conscious.

"How's he doing, Crandall?" I asked. "I broke him in on the job. He's Bumper-ized."

"Not bad for a baby," Crandall shrugged.

"I see you took his training wheels off," I said, and Lefler giggled and goosed the Harley again.

I could see the edge of the horseshoe cleats on his heels and I knew his soles were probably studded with iron.

"Don't go walking around my beat with those boots on, kid," I yelled. "You'll be kicking up sparks and starting fires." I chuckled then as I remembered seeing a motor cop with two cups of coffee in his gloved hands go right on his ass one time because of those cleats.

I waved at Lefler and pulled away. Young hotdogs, I thought. I was glad I was older when I came on the job. But then, I knew I would never have been a motor officer. Writing traffic tickets was the one part of police work I didn't like. The only good thing about it was it gave you an excuse to stop some suspicious cars on the pretext of writing a ticket. More good arrests came from phony traffic stops than anything else. More policemen got blown up that way, too.

I decided, what the hell, I was too jumpy to lay around the park reading the paper. I'd been like a cat ever since I'd decided about Friday. I hardly slept last night. I headed back toward the beat.

I should be patrolling for the burglar, I thought. I really wanted him now that I only had a couple days left. He was a daytime hotel creeper and hitting maybe four to six hotel rooms in the best downtown hotels every time he went to work. The dicks talked to us at rollcall and said the M.O. run showed he preferred weekdays, especially Thursday and Friday, but a lot of jobs were showing up on Wednesdays. This guy would shim doors which isn't too hard to do in any hotel since they usually have the world's worst security, and he'd burgle the place whether the occupants were in or not. Of course he waited until they were in the shower or napping. I loved catching burglars. Most policemen call it fighting ghosts and give up trying to catch them, but I'd rather catch a hot prowl guy than a stickup man any day. And any burglar with balls enough to take a pad when the people are home is every bit as dangerous as a stickup man.

I decided I'd patrol the hotels by the Harbor Freeway. I had a theory this guy was using some sort of repairman disguise since he'd eluded all stakeouts so far, and I figured him for a repair or delivery truck. I envisioned him as an out-of-towner who used the convenient Harbor Freeway to come to his job. This burglar was doing ding-a-ling stuff on some of the jobs, cutting up clothing, usually women's or kids', tearing the crotch out of underwear, and on a recent job he stabbed the hell out of a big teddy bear that a little girl left on the bed covered up with a blanket. I was glad the people weren't in when he hit *that* time. He was kinky, but a clever burglar, a lucky burglar. I thought about patrolling around the hotels, but first I'd go see Glenda. She'd be rehearsing now, and I might never see her again. She was one of the people I owed a good-bye to.

I entered the side door of the run-down little theater. They mostly showed skin flicks now. They used to have a halfway decent burlesque house here, with some fair comics and good-looking girls. Glenda was something in those days. The "Gilded Girl" they called her. She'd come out in a gold sheath and peel to a golden G-string and gold pasties. She was tall and graceful, and a better-than-average dancer. She played some big-time clubs off and on, but she was thirty-eight years old now and after two or three husbands she was back down on Main Street competing with beaver movies between reels, and taxi dancing part-time down the street at the ballroom. She was maybe twenty pounds heavier, but she still looked good to me because I saw her like she used to be.

I stood there in the shadows backstage and got accustomed to the dark and the quiet. They didn't even have anyone on the door anymore. I guess even the weinie waggers and bustle rubbers gave up sneaking in the side door of this hole. The wallpaper was wet and rusty and curling off the walls like old scrolls. There were dirty costumes laying around on chairs. The popcorn machine, which they activated on weekend nights, was leaning against the wall, one leg broken.

"The cockroaches serve the popcorn in this joint. You don't want any, Bumper," said Glenda, who had stepped out of her dressing room and was watching me from the darkness.

"Hi, kid." I smiled and followed her voice through the dark to the dimly lit little dressing room.

She kissed me on the cheek like she always did, and I took off my hat and flopped down on the ragged over-stuffed chair behind her makeup table.

"Hey, Saint Francis, where've all the birdies gone?" she said, tickling the bald spot on my crown. She always laid about a hundred old jokes on me every time we met.

Glenda was wearing net stockings with a hole in one leg and a sequined G-string. She was nude on top and didn't bother putting on a robe. I didn't blame her, it was so damn hot today, but she didn't usually go around like this in front of me and it made me a little nervous.

"Hot weather's here, baby," she said, sitting down and fixing her makeup. "When you going back on nights?"

Glenda knew my M.O. I work days in the winter, night-watch in the summer when the Los Angeles sun starts turning the heavy bluesuit into sackcloth.

"I'll never go back on nights, Glenda," I said casually. "I'm retiring."

She turned around in her chair and those heavy white melons bounced once or twice. Her hair was long and blond.

She always claimed she was a real blonde but I'd never know.

"You won't quit," she said. "You'll be here till they kick you out. Or till you die. Like me."

"We'll both leave here," I said, smiling because she

was starting to look upset. "Some nice guy'll come along and . . ."

"Some nice guy took me out of here three times, Bumper. Trouble is I'm just not a nice girl. Too fucked up for any man. You're just kidding about retiring, aren't you?"

"How's Sissy?" I said, to change the subject.

Glenda answered by taking a package of snapshots out of her purse and handing them to me. I'm farsighted now and in the dimness I couldn't really see anything but the outline of a little girl holding a dog. I couldn't even say if the dog was real or stuffed.

"She's beautiful," I said, knowing she was. I'd last seen her several months ago when I drove Glenda home from work one night.

"Every dollar you ever gave me went into a bank account for her just like we agreed at first," said Glenda.

"I know that."

"I added to it on my own too."

"She'll have something someday."

"Bet your ass she will," said Glenda, lighting a cigarette.

I wondered how much I'd given Glenda over the past ten years. And I wondered how many really good arrests I'd made on information she gave me. She was one of my big secrets. The detectives had informants who they paid but the bluesuits weren't supposed to be involved in that kind of police work. Well, I had my paid informants too. But I didn't pay them from any Department money. I paid them from my pocket, and when I made the bust on the scam they gave me, I made it look like I lucked onto the arrest. Or I made up some other fanciful story for the arrest report. That way Glenda was protected and nobody could

say Bumper Morgan was completely nuts for paying informants out of his own pocket. The first time, Glenda
turned me a federal fugitive who was dating her and
who carried a gun and pulled stickups. I tried to give her
twenty bucks and she refused it, saying he was a no-good
asshole and belonged in the joint and she was no snitch. I
made her take it for Sissy who was a baby then, and who
had no dad. Since then over the years I've probably laid
a thousand on Glenda for Sissy. And I've probably made
the best pinches of any cop in Central Division.

"She gonna be a blondie like momma?" I asked.

"Yeah," she smiled. "More blond than me though. And
about ten times as smart. I think she's smarter already.
I'm reading books like mad to keep up with her."

"Those private schools are tough," I nodded. "They
teach them something."

"You notice this one, Bumper?" she smiled, coming
over to me and sitting on the arm of the chair. She was
smiling big and thinking about Sissy now. "The dog's
pulling her hair. Look at the expression."

"Oh yeah," I said, seeing only a blur and feeling one of
those heavy chi-chis resting on my shoulder. Hers were
big and natural, not pumped full of plastic like so many
these days.

"She's peeved in this one," said Glenda, leaning closer,
and it was pressed against my cheek, and finally one tender doorbell went right in my ear.

"Damn it, Glenda!" I said, looking up.

"What?" she answered, moving back. She got it, and
laughed her hard hoarse laugh. Then her laugh softened
and she smiled and her big eyes went soft and I noticed
the lashes were dark beneath the eyes and not from mas-

cara. I thought Glenda was more attractive now than she ever was.

"I have a big feeling for you, Bumper," she said, and kissed me right on the mouth. "You and Sissy are the only ones. You're what's happening, baby."

Glenda was like Ruthie. She was one of the people who belonged to the beat. There were laws that I made for myself, but she was almost naked and to me she was still so beautiful.

"Now," she said, knowing I was about to explode. "Why not? You never have and I always wanted you to."

"Gotta get back to my car," I said, jumping up and crossing the room in three big steps. Then I mumbled something else about missing my radio calls, and Glenda told me to wait.

"You forgot your hat," she said, handing it to me.

"Thanks," I said, putting the lid on with one shaky hand. She held the other one and kissed my palm with a warm wet mouth.

"Don't think of leaving us, Bumper," she said and stared me in the eye.

"Here's a few bucks for Sissy," I said, fumbling in my pocket for a ten.

"I don't have any information this time," she said, shaking her head, but I tucked it inside her G-string and she grinned.

"It's for the kid."

There were some things I'd intended asking her about some gunsel I'd heard was hanging out in the skin houses and taxi-dance joints, but I couldn't trust myself alone with her for another minute. "See you later, kid," I said weakly.

"Bye, Bumper," she said as I picked my way through the darkness to the stage door. Aside from the fact that Cassie gave me all I could handle, there was another reason I tore myself away from her like that. Any cop knows you can't afford to get too tight with your informant. You try screwing a snitch and you'll be the one that ends up getting screwed.

TWO

AFTER LEAVING GLENDA it actually seemed cool on the street. Glenda never did anything like that before. Everyone was acting a little ding-a-ling when I mentioned my retirement. I didn't feel like climbing back inside that machine and listening to the noisy chatter on the radio.

It was still morning now and I was pretty happy, twirling my stick as I strolled along. I guess I *swaggered* along. Most beat officers swagger. People expect you to. It shows the hangtoughs you're not afraid, and people expect it. Also they expect an older cop to cock his hat a little so I always do that too.

I still wore the traditional eight-pointed hat and used a leather thong on my stick. The Department went to more modern round hats, like Air Force hats, and we all have to change over. I'd wear the eight-pointed police hat to the end, I thought. Then I thought about Friday as being the end and I started a fancy stick spin to keep my mind off it. I let the baton go bouncing off the sidewalk back up into my hand. Three shoe shine kids were watching me, two Mexican, one Negro. The baton trick impressed the hell out of them. I strung it out like a Yo-Yo, did some back twirls and dropped it back in the ring in one smooth motion.

"Want a choo chine, Bumper?" said one of the Mexican kids.

"Thanks pal, but I don't need one."

"It's free to you," he said, tagging along beside me for a minute.

"I'm buying juice today, pal," I said, flipping two quarters up in the air which one of them jumped up and caught. He ran to the orange juice parlor three doors away with the other two chasing him. The shoe shine boxes hung around their necks with ropes and thudded against their legs as they ran.

These little kids probably never saw a beat officer twirl a stick before. The Department ordered us to remove the leather thongs a couple years ago, but I never did and all the sergeants pretend not to notice as long as I borrow a regulation baton for inspections.

The stick is held in the ring now by a big rubber washer like the one that goes over the pipe in the back of your toilet. We've learned new ways to use the stick from some young Japanese cops who are karate and aikido experts. We use the blunt end of the stick more and I have to admit it beats hell out of the old caveman swing. I must've shattered six sticks over guys' heads, arms and legs in my time. Now I've learned from these Nisei kids how to swing that baton in a big arc and put my whole ass behind it. I could damn near drive it through a guy if I wanted to, and never hurt the stick. It's very graceful stuff too. I feel I can do twice as well in a brawl now. The only bad thing is, they convinced the Department brass that the leather thong was worthless. You see, these kids were never real beat men. Neither were the brass. They don't understand what the cop twirling his stick really means to people who see him stroll down a quiet street throwing that big shadow in an eight-pointed hat. Anyway, I'd never take off the leather thong. It made me sick to think of a toilet washer on a police weapon.

I stopped by the arcade and saw a big muscle-bound fruit hustler standing there. I just looked hard at him for a second, and he fell apart and slithered away. Then I saw two con guys leaning up against a wall flipping a quarter, hoping to get a square in a coin smack. I stared at them and they got nervous and skulked around to the parking lot and disappeared.

The arcade was almost deserted. I remember when the slimeballs used to be packed in there solid, asshole to belly button, waiting to look at the skin show in the viewer. That was a big thing then. The most daring thing around. The vice squad used to bust guys all the time for masturbating. There were pecker prints all over the walls in front of the viewer. Now you can walk in any bar or movie house down here and see live skin shows, or animal flicks, and I don't mean Walt Disney stuff. It's women and dogs, dykes and donkeys, dildos and whips, fags, chickens, and ducks. Sometimes it's hard to tell who or what is doing what to who or what.

Then I started thinking about the camera club that used to be next door to the arcade when nudity was still a big thing. It cost fifteen bucks to join and five bucks for every camera session. You got to take all the pictures of a naked girl you wanted, as long as you didn't get closer than two feet and as long as you didn't touch. Of course, most of the "photographers" didn't even have film in their cameras, but the management knew it and never bothered putting in real camera lights and nobody complained. It was really so innocent.

I was about to head back to my car when I noticed another junkie watching me. He was trying to decide whether to rabbit or freeze. He froze finally, his eyes roaming around too casually, hitting on everything but me, hoping he could melt into the jungle. I hardly ever bust hypes for marks anymore, and he looked too sick to be holding, but I thought I recognized him.

"Come here, man," I called and he came slinking my way like it was all over.

"Hello, Bumper."

"Well, hello, Wimpy," I said to the chalk-faced hype. "It took me a minute to recognize you. You're older."

"Went away for three years last time."

"How come so long?"

"Armed robbery. Went to Q behind armed robbery. Violence don't suit me. I shoulda stuck to boosting. San Quentin made me old, Bumper."

"Too bad, Wimpy. Yeah, now I remember. You did a few gas stations, right?"

He *was* old. His sandy hair was streaked with gray and it was patchy. And his teeth were rotting and loose in his mouth. It was starting to come back to me like it always does: Herman (Wimpy) Brown, a lifelong hype and a pretty good snitch when he wanted to be. Couldn't be more than forty but he looked a lot older than me.

"I wish I hadn't never met that hangtough, Barty Mendez. Remember him, Bumper? A dope fiend shouldn't never do violent crime. You just ain't cut out for it. I coulda kept boosting cigarettes out of markets and made me a fair living for quite a while."

"How much you boosting now, Wimpy?" I said, giving him a light. He was clammy and covered with gooseflesh. If he knew anything he'd tell me. He wanted a taste so bad right now, he'd snitch on his mother.

"I don't boost anywhere near your beat, Bumper. I go out to the west side and lift maybe a couple dozen cartons of smokes a day outta those big markets. I don't do nothing down here except look for guys holding."

"You hang up your parole yet?"

"No, I ain't running from my parole officer. You can call in and check." He dragged hard on the cigarette but it wasn't doing much good.

"Let's see your arms, Wimpy," I said, taking one bony arm and pushing up the sleeve.

"You ain't gonna bust me on a chickenshit marks case, are you, Bumper?"

"I'm just curious," I said, noticing the inner elbows were fairly clean. I'd have to put on my glasses to see the marks and I never took my glasses to work. They stayed in my apartment.

"Few marks, Bumper, not too bad," he said, trying a black-toothed smile. "I shrink them with hemorrhoid ointment."

I bent the elbow and looked at the back of the forearm. "Damn, the whole Union Pacific could run on those tracks!" I didn't need glasses to see those swollen abscessed wounds.

"Don't bust me, Bumper," he whined. "I can work for you like I used to. I gave you some good things, remember? I turned the guy that juked that taxi dancer in the alley. The one that almost cut her tit off, remember?"

"Yeah, that's right," I said, as it came back to me. Wimpy *did* turn that one for me.

"Don't these P.O.'s ever look at your arms?" I asked, sliding the sleeves back down.

"Some're like cops, others're social workers. I always been lucky about drawing a square P.O. or one who really digs numbers, like how many guys he's rehabilitating. They don't want to *fail* you, you know? Nowadays they give you dope and call it something else and say you're cured. They show you statistics, but I think the ones they figure are clean are just dead, probably from an overdose."

"Make sure *you* don't O.D., Wimpy," I said, leading him away from the arcade so we could talk in private while I was walking him to the corner call box to run a make.

"I liked it inside when I was on the program, Bumper. Honest to God. C.R.C. is a good place. I knew guys with no priors who shot phony needle holes in their arms so they could go there instead of to Q. And I heard Tehachapi is even better. Good food, and you don't hardly work at all, and group therapy where you can shuck, and there's these trade schools there where you can jive around. I could do a nickel in those places and I wouldn't mind. In fact, last time I was sorta sorry they kicked me out after thirteen months. But three years in Q broke me, Bumper. You know you're really in the joint when you're in that place."

"Still think about geezing when you're inside?"

"Always think about that," he said, trying to smile

again as we stopped next to the call box. There were people walking by but nobody close. "I need to geez bad now, Bumper. Real bad." He looked like he was going to cry.

"Well, don't flip. I might not bust you if you can do me some good. Start thinking real hard, while I run a make to see if you hung it up."

"My parole's good as gold," he said, already perking up now that he figured I wasn't going to book him for marks. "You and me could work good, Bumper. I always trusted you. You got a rep for protecting your informants. Nobody never got a rat jacket behind your busts. I know you got an army of snitches, but nobody never got a snitch jacket. You take care of your people."

"You won't get a jacket either, Wimpy. Work with me and nobody knows. Nobody."

Wimpy was sniffling and cotton-mouthed so I unlocked the call box and hurried up with the wants check. I gave the girl his name and birthdate, and lit his cigarette while we waited. He started looking around. He wasn't afraid to be caught informing, he was just looking for a connection: a peddler, a junkie, anybody that might be holding a cap. I'd blow my brains out first, I thought.

"You living at a halfway house?" I asked.

"Not now," he said. "You know, after being clean for three years I thought I could do it this time. Then I went and fixed the second day out, and I was feeling so bad about it I went to a kick pad over on the east side and asked them to sign me in. They did and I was clean three more days, left the kick pad, scored some junk, and had a spike in my arm ever since."

"Ever fire when you were in the joint?" I asked, trying

to keep the conversation going until the information came back.

"I never did. Never had the chance. I heard of a few guys. I once saw two guys make an outfit. They were expecting half a piece from somewheres. I don't know what they had planned, but they sure was making a fit."

"How?"

"They bust open this light bulb and one of them held the filament with a piece of cardboard and a rag and the other just kept heating it up with matches, and those suckers stretched that thing out until it was a pretty good eye-dropper. They stuck a hole in it with a pin and attached a plastic spray bottle to it and it wasn't a bad fit. I'd a took a chance and stuck it in my arm if there was some dope in it."

"Probably break off in your vein."

"Worth the chance. I seen guys without a spike so strung out and hurting they cut their arm open with a razor and blow a mouthful of dope right in there."

He was puffing big on the smoke. His hands and arms were covered with the jailhouse tattoos made from pencil lead shavings which they mix with spit and jab into their arms with a million pinpricks. He probably did it when he was a youngster just coming up. Now he was an old head and had professional tattoos all over the places where he shoots junk, but nothing could hide those tracks.

"I used to be a boss booster at one time, Bumper. Not just a cigarette thief. I did department stores for good clothes and expensive perfume, even jewelry counters which are pretty tough to do. I wore two-hundred-dollar suits in the days when only rich guys wore suits that good."

"Work alone?"

"All alone, I swear. I didn't need nobody. I looked different then. I was good looking, honest I was. I even talked better. I used to read a lot of magazines and books. I could walk through these department stores and spot these young kids and temporary sales help and have them give me their money. *Give* me their money, I tell you."

"How'd you work that scam?"

"I'd tell them Mister Freeman, the retail manager, sent me to pick up their receipts. He didn't want too much in the registers, I'd say, and I'd stick out my money bag and they'd fill it up for Mister Freeman." Wimpy started to laugh and ended up wheezing and choking. He settled down after a minute.

"I sure owe plenty to Mister Freeman. I gotta repay that sucker if I ever meet him. I used that name in maybe fifty department stores. That was my real father's name. That's really *my* real name, but when I was a kid I took the name of this bastard my old lady married. I always played like my real old man would've did something for us if he'd been around, so this way he did. Old Mister Freeman must've gave me ten grand. Tax free. More than most old men ever give their kids, hey, Bumper?"

"More than mine, Wimpy," I smiled.

"I did real good on that till-tap. I looked so nice, carnation and all. I had another scam where I'd boost good stuff, expensive baby clothes, luggage, anything. Then I'd bring it back to the salesman in the store bag and tell him I didn't have my receipt but would they please give me back my money on account of little Bobby wouldn't be needing these things because he smothered in his crib last Tuesday. Or old Uncle Pete passed on just before he went on his trip that he saved and dreamed about for forty-eight years and I couldn't bear to look at this luggage anymore. Honest, Bumper, they couldn't give me the bread fast enough. I even made *men* cry. I had one woman beg me to take ten bucks from her own purse to help with the baby's funeral. I took that ten bucks and bought a little ten-dollar bag of junk and all the time I was cutting open that balloon and cooking that stuff I thought, 'Oh you baby. You really are my baby.' I took that spike and dug a little grave in my flesh and when I shoved that thing in my arm and felt it going in, I said, 'Thank you, lady, thank you, thank you, this is the best funeral my baby could have.'" Wimpy closed his eyes and lifted his face, smiling a little as he thought of his baby.

"Doesn't your P.O. ever give you a urinalysis or anything?" I still couldn't get over an old head like him not having his arms or urine checked when he was on parole, even if he *was* paroled on a non-narcotics beef.

"Hasn't yet, Bumper. I ain't worried if he does. I always been lucky with P.O.'s. When they put me on the urine program I came up with the squeeze-bottle trick. I just got this square friend of mine, old Homer Allen, to keep me supplied with a fresh bottle of piss, and I kept that little plastic squeeze bottle full and hanging from a string inside my belt. My dumb little P.O. used to think he was sneaky and he'd catch me at my job or at home at night sometimes and ask for a urine sample and I'd just go to the john with him right behind me watching, and I'd reach in my fly and fill his little glass bottle full of Homer's piss. He thought he was real slick, but he never could catch me. He was such a square. I really liked him. I felt like a father to that kid."

The girl came to the phone and read me Wimpy's record, telling me there were no wants.

"Well, you're not running," I said, hanging up the phone, closing the metal call box door, and hanging the brass key back on my belt.

"Told you, Bumper. I just saw my P.O. last week. I been reporting regular."

"Okay, Wimpy, let's talk business," I said.

"I been thinking, Bumper, there's this dog motherfucker that did me bad one time. I wouldn't mind you popping him."

"Okay," I said, giving him a chance to rationalize his snitching, which all informants have to do when they start out, or like Wimpy, when they haven't snitched for a long time.

"He deserves to march," said Wimpy. "Everybody knows he's no good. He burned me on a buy one time. I bring him a guy to score some pot. It's not on consignment or nothing, and he sells the guy catnip and I told him I knew the guy good. The guy kicked my ass when he found out it was catnip."

"Okay, let's do him," I said. "But I ain't interested in some two- or three-lid punk."

"I know, Bumper. He's a pretty big dealer. We'll set him up good. I'll tell him I got a guy with real bread and he should bring three kilos and meet me in a certain place and then maybe you just happen by or something when we're getting it out of the car and we both start to run but you go after him, naturally, and you get a three-key bust."

"No good. I can't run anymore. We'll work out something else."

"Any way you want, Bumper. I'll turn anybody for you. I'll roll over on anybody if you give me a break."

"Except your best connection."

"That's God you're talking about. But I think right this minute I'd even turn my connection for a fix."

"Where's this pot dealer live? Near my beat?"

"Yeah, not far. East Sixth. We can take him at his hotel. That might be the best way. You can kick down the pad and let me get out the window. At heart he's just a punk. They call him Little Rudy. He makes roach holders out of chicken bones and folded-up matchbooks and all that punk-ass bullshit. Only thing is, don't let me get a jacket. See, he knows this boss dyke, a real mean bull dagger. Her pad's a shooting gallery for some of us. If she knows you finked, she'll sneak battery acid in your spoon and laugh while you mainline it home. She's a *dog* motherfucker."

"Okay, Wimpy, when can you set it up?"

"Saturday, Bumper, we can do it Saturday."

"No good," I said quickly, a gas pain slicing across my stomach. "Friday's the latest for anything."

"Christ, Bumper. He's out of town. I know for sure. I think he's gone to the border to score."

"I can't wait past Friday. Think of somebody else then."

"Shit, lemme think," he said, rapping his skinny fingers against his temple. "Oh yeah, I got something. A guy in the Rainbow Hotel. A tall dude, maybe forty, forty-five, blondish hair. He's in the first apartment to the left on the second floor. I just heard last night he's a half-ass fence. Buys most anything you steal. Cheap, I hear. Pays less than a dime on the dollar. A righteous dog. He deserves to fall. I hear these dope fiends bring radios and stuff like that, usually in the early morning."

"Okay, maybe I'll try him tomorrow," I said, not really very interested.

"Sure, he might have lots of loot in the pad. You could clear up all kinds of burglaries."

"Okay, Wimpy, you can make it now. But I want to see you regular. At least three times a week."

"Bumper, could you please loan me a little in advance?"

"You gotta be kidding, Wimpy! Pay a junkie in advance?"

"I'm in awful bad shape today, Bumper," he said with a cracked whispery voice, like a prayer. He looked as bad as any I'd ever seen. Then I remembered I'd never see him again. After Friday I'd never see any of them again. He couldn't do me any good and it was unbelievably stupid, but I gave him a ten, which was just like folding up a saw-buck and sticking it in his arm. He'd be in the same shape twelve hours from now. He stared at the bill like he didn't believe it at first. I left him there and walked back to the car.

"We'll get that pothead for you," he said. "He's sloppy. You'll find seeds between the carpet and the molding outside the door in the hall. I'll get you lots of probable cause to kick over the pad."

"I know how to take down a dope pad, Wimpy," I said over my shoulder.

"Later, Bumper, see you later," he yelled, breaking into a coughing spasm.

THREE

I ALWAYS TRY to learn something from the people on my beat, and as I drove away I tried to think if I learned anything from all Wimpy's chatter. I'd heard this kind of bullshit from a thousand hypes. Then I thought of the hemorrhoid ointment for shrinking hype marks. That was something new. I'd never heard that one before. I always try to teach the rookies to keep their mouths shut and learn to listen. They usually give more information than they get when they're interrogating somebody. Even a guy like Wimpy could teach you something if you just give him a chance.

I got back in my car and looked at my watch because I was starting to get hungry. Of course I'm always hungry, or rather, I always want to eat. But I don't eat between meals and I eat my meals at regular times unless the job prevents it. I believe in routine. If you have rules for little things, rules you make up yourself, and if you obey these rules, your life will be in order. I only alter routines when I have to.

One of the cats on the daywatch, a youngster named Wilson, drove by in his black-and-white but didn't notice me because he was eyeballing some hype that was hot-footing it across Broadway to reach the crowded Grand Central Market, probably to score. The doper was moving fast like a hype with some gold in his jeans. Wilson was a good young copper, but sometimes when I looked at him like this, in profile when he was looking somewhere else, that cowlick of his and that kid nose, and something else I couldn't put my finger on, made me think of someone. For a while it bothered me and then one night last week when I was thinking so hard about getting married, and about Cassie, it came to me—he reminded me of Billy a little bit, but I pushed it out of my mind because I don't think of dead children or any dead people, that's another rule of mine. But I *did* start thinking of Billy's mother and how bad my first marriage had been and whether it could have been good if Billy had lived, and I had to admit that it *could* have been good, and it would have lasted if Billy had lived.

Then I wondered how many bad marriages that started during the war years had turned out all right. But it wasn't just that, there was the other thing, the dying. I almost told Cruz Segovia about it one time when we used to be partners and we were working a lonely morning watch at three a.m., about how my parents died, and how my brother raised me and how he died, and how my son died, and how I admired Cruz because he had his wife and all those kids and gave himself away to them fearlessly. But I never told him, and when Esteban, his oldest son, died in Vietnam, I watched Cruz with the others, and after the crushing grief he still gave himself away to them, com-pletely. But I couldn't admire him for it anymore. I could marvel at it, but I couldn't admire it. I don't know what I felt about it after that.

Thinking all these foolish things made a gas bubble start, and I could imagine the bubble getting bigger and bigger. Then I took a bubble buster, chewed it up and swallowed it, made up my mind to start thinking about women or food or something good, raised up, farted, said "Good morning, Your Honor," and felt a whole lot better.

FOUR

IT ALWAYS MADE ME FEEL GOOD just to drive around *without* thinking, so I turned off my radio and did just that. Pretty soon, without looking at my watch, I knew it was time to eat. I couldn't decide whether to hit Chinatown or Little Tokyo today. I didn't want Mexican food, because I promised Cruz Segovia I'd come to his pad for dinner tonight and I'd get enough Mexican food to last me a week. His wife Socorro knew how I loved *chile relleno* and she'd fix a dozen just for me.

A few burgers sounded good and there's a place in Hollywood that has the greatest burgers in town. Every time I go to Hollywood I think about Myrna, a broad I used to fool around with a couple years ago. She was an unreal Hollywood type, but she had a good executive job in a network television studio and whenever we went anywhere she'd end up spending more bread than I would. She loved to waste money, but the thing she really had going as far as I was concerned is that she looked just like Madeleine Carroll whose pictures we had all over our barracks during the war. It wasn't just that Myrna had style and elegant, springy tits, it's that she really looked like a woman and acted like one, except that she was a stone pothead and liked to improvise *too* much sexually. I'm game for anything reasonable, but sometimes Myrna was a little too freaky about things, and she also insisted on turning me on, and finally I tried smoking pot one time with her, but I didn't feel good high like on fine scotch. On her coffee table she had at least half a key and that's a pound of pot and that's trouble. I could just picture me and her getting hauled off to jail in a nark ark. So it was a bummer, and I don't know if it's the overall depressant effect of pot or what, but I crashed afterwards, down, down, down, until I felt mean enough to kick the hell out of her. But then, come to think of it, I guess Myrna liked that best of all anyway. So, Madeleine Carroll or not, I finally shined her on and she gave up calling me after a couple weeks, probably having found herself a trained gorilla or something.

There was one thing about Myrna that I'd never forget—she was a great dancer, not a good dancer, a *great* dancer, because Myrna could completely stop thinking when she danced. I think that's the secret. She could dig hard rock and she was a real snake. When she moved on a dance floor, often as not, everyone would stop and watch. Of course they laughed at me—at first. Then they'd see there were *two* dancers out there. It's funny about dancing, it's like food or sex, it's something you do and you can just forget you *have* a brain. It's all body and deep in your guts, especially the hard rock. And hard rock's the best thing to happen to music. When Myrna and me were really moving, maybe at some kid place on the Sunset Strip, our bodies joined. It wasn't just a sex thing, but there *was* that too, it was like our bodies really made it together and you didn't even have to *think* anymore.

I used to always experiment by doing the funky chicken when we first started out. I know it's getting old now, but I'd do it and they'd all laugh, because of the way my belly jumped and swayed around. Then I'd always do it again right near the end of the song, and nobody laughed. They smiled, but nobody laughed, because they could see by then how graceful I really am, despite the way I'm built. Nobody's chicken was as funky as mine, so I always stood there flapping my elbows and bowing my knees just to test them. And despite the raw animal moves of Myrna, people also looked at *me*. They watched both of us dance. That's one thing I miss about Myrna.

I didn't feel like roaming so far from my beat today so I decided on beef teriyaki and headed for J-town. The Japanese have the commercial area around First and Second Streets between Los Angeles Street and Central Avenue. There are lots of colorful shops and restaurants and professional buildings. They also have their share of banks and lots of money to go in them. When I walked in the Geisha Doll on First Street, the lunch hour rush was just about over and the mama-san shuffled over with her little graceful steps like she was still twenty instead of sixty-five. She always wore a silk slit-skirted dress and she really didn't look too bad for an old girl. I always kidded her about a Japanese wearing a Chinese dress and she would laugh and say, "Make moah China ting in Tokyo than all China. And bettah, goddam betcha." The place was plush and dark, lots of bamboo, beaded curtains, hanging lanterns.

"Boom-pah san, wheah you been hide?" she said as I stepped through the beads.

"Hello, Mother," I said, lifting her straight up under

the arms and kissing her on the cheek. She only weighed about ninety pounds and seemed almost brittle, but once I didn't do this little trick and she got mad. She expected it and all the customers got a kick out of watching me perform. The cooks and all the pretty waitresses and Sumi, the hostess, dressed in a flaming orange kimono, expected it too. I saw Sumi tap a Japanese customer on the shoulder when I walked in.

I usually held the mama-san up like this for a good minute or so and snuggled her a little bit and joked around until everyone in the place was giggling, especially the mama-san, and then I put her down and let her tell anyone in shouting distance how "stlong is owah Boom-pah." My arms are good even though my legs are gone, but she was like a paper doll, no weight at all. She always said "owah Boom-pah," and I always took it to mean I belonged to J-town too and I liked the idea. Los Angeles policemen are very partial to Buddha heads because sometimes they seem like the only ones left in the world who really appreciate discipline, cleanliness, and hard work. I've even seen motor cops who'd hang a ticket on a one-legged leper, let a Nip go on a good traffic violation because they contribute practically nothing to the crime rate even though they're notoriously bad drivers. I've been noticing in recent years though that Orientals have been showing up as suspects on crime reports. If they degenerate like everyone else there'll be no *group* to look up to, just individuals.

"We have a nice table for you, Bumper," said Sumi with a smile that could almost make you forget food—almost. I started smelling things: tempura, rice wine, teriyaki steak. I have a sensitive nose and can pick out individual smells. It's really only *individual* things that count in this world.

When you lump everything together you get goulash or chop suey or a greasy stew pot. I hated food like that.

"I think I'll sit at the *sushi* bar," I said to Sumi, who once confessed to me her real name was Gloria. People expected a geisha doll to have a Japanese name, so Gloria, a third generation American, obliged them. I agreed with her logic. There's no sense disappointing people.

There were two other men at the *sushi* bar, both Japanese, and Mako who worked the *sushi* bar smiled at me but looked a little grim at the challenge. He once told Mama that serving Boom-pah alone was like serving a *sushi* bar full of *sumos*. I couldn't help it, I loved those delicate little rice balls, molded by hand and wrapped in strips of pink salmon and octopus, abalone, tuna and shrimp. I loved the little hidden pockets of horseradish that surprised you and made your eyes water. And I loved a bowl of soup, especially soybean and seaweed, and to drink it from the bowl Japanese style. I put it away faster than Mako could lay it out and I guess I looked like a buffalo at the *sushi* bar. Much as I tried to control myself and use a little Japanese self-discipline, I kept throwing the chow down and emptying the little dishes while Mako grinned and sweated and put them up. I knew it was no way to behave at the *sushi* bar in a nice restaurant, this was for gourmets, the refined eaters of Japanese cuisine, and I attacked like a blue locust, but God, eating *sushi* is being in heaven. In fact, I'd settle for that, and become a Buddhist if heaven was a *sushi* bar.

There was only one thing that saved me from looking too bad to a Japanese—I could handle chopsticks like one of them. I first learned in Japan right after the war, and I've been coming to the Geisha Doll and every other res-

taurant here in J-town for twenty years so it was no wonder. Even without the bluesuit, they could look at me click
those sticks and know I was no tourist passing through.
Sometimes though, when I didn't think about it, I ate with
both hands. I just couldn't devour it fast enough.

In cooler weather I always drank rice wine or hot sake
with my meal, today, ice water. After I'd finished what
two or three good-sized Japanese would consume, I quit
and started drinking tea while Mama and Sumi made
several trips over to make sure I had enough and to see
that my tea was hot enough and to try to feed me some
tempura, and the tender fried shrimp looked so good I
ate a half dozen. If Sumi wasn't twenty years too young
I'd have been awful tempted to try her too. But she was
so delicate and beautiful and so *young*, I lost confidence
even thinking about it. And then too, she was one of the
people on my beat, and there's that thing, the way they
think about me. Still, it always helped my appetite to eat
in a place where there were pretty women. But until I was
at least half full, I have to say I didn't notice women or
anything else. The world disappears for me when I'm eating something I love.

The thing that always got to me about Mama was how
much she thanked me for eating up half her kitchen. Naturally she would never let me pay for my food, but she
always thanked me about ten times before I got out the
door. Even for an Oriental she really overdid it. It made
me feel guilty, and when I came here I sometimes wished
I could violate the custom and pay her. But she'd fed cops
before I came along and she'd feed them after, and that
was the way things were. I didn't tell Mama that Friday
was going to be my last day, and I didn't start thinking

about it because with a barrel of *sushi* in my stomach I couldn't afford indigestion.

Sumi came over to me before I left and held the little teacup to my lips while I sipped it and she said, "Okay, Bumper, tell me an exciting cops-and-robbers story." She did this often, and I'm sure she was aware how she affected me up close there feeling her sweet breath, looking at those chocolate-brown eyes and soft skin.

"All right, my little lotus blossom," I said, like W. C. Fields, and she giggled. "One spine tingler, coming up."

Then I reverted to my normal voice and told her about the guy I stopped for blowing a red light at Second and San Pedro one day and how he'd been here a year from Japan and had a California license and all, but didn't speak English, or pretended not to so he could try to get out of the ticket. I decided to go ahead and hang one on him because he almost wiped out a guy in the crosswalk, and when I got it written he refused to sign it, telling me in pidgin, "Not gear-tee, not gear-tee," and I tried for five minutes to explain that the signature was just a promise to appear and he could have a jury trial if he wanted one and if he didn't sign I'd have to book him. He just kept shaking his head like he didn't savvy and finally I turned that ticket book over and drew a picture on the back. Then I drew the same picture for Sumi. It was a little jail window with a stick figure hanging on the bars. He had a sad turned-down mouth and slant eyes. I'd showed him the picture and said, "You sign now, maybe?" and he wrote his name so fast and hard he broke my pencil lead.

Sumi laughed and repeated it in Japanese for Mama. When I left after tipping Mako they all thanked me again until I really *did* feel guilty. That was the only thing I didn't like about J-town. I wished to hell I could pay for my meal there, though I confess I never had that wish anywhere else.

Frankly, there was practically nothing to spend my money on. I ate three meals on my beat. I could buy booze, clothes, jewelry, and everything else you could think of at wholesale or less. In fact, somebody was always giving me something like that as a gift. I had my bread stop and a dairy that supplied me with gallons of free ice cream, milk, cottage cheese, all I wanted. My apartment was very nice and rent-free, even including utilities, because I helped the manager run the thirty-two units. At least he thought I helped him. He'd call me when he had a loud party or something, and I'd go up, join the party, and persuade them to quiet down a little, while I drank their booze and ate their canapes. Once in awhile I'd catch a peeping tom or something, and since the manager was such a mouse, he thought I was indispensable. Except for girlfriends and my informants it was always hard to find anything to spend my money on. Sometimes I actually went a week hardly spending a dime except for tips. I'm a big tipper, not like most policemen.

When it came to accepting things from people on my beat I did have one rule—no money. I felt that if I took money, which a lot of people tried to give me at Christmas time, I'd be getting bought. I never felt bought though if a guy gave me free meals or a case of booze, or a discounted sport coat, or if a dentist fixed my teeth at a special rate, or an optometrist bounced for a pair of sunglasses half price. These things weren't money, and I wasn't a hog about it. I never took more than I could personally use, or which I could give to people like Cruz Segovia or Cassie, who recently complained that her apartment was beginning to look like a distillery. Also I never took anything from someone I might end up having to arrest. For instance, before we started really hating each other, Marvin Heywood, the owner of the Pink Dragon, tried to lay a couple cases of scotch on me, and I mean the best, but I turned him down. I'd known from the first day he opened that place it would be a hangout for slimeballs. Every day was like a San Quentin convention in that cesspool. And the more I thought of it, the more I got burned up thinking that after I retired nobody would roust the Dragon as hard as I always did. I caused Marvin a sixty-day liquor license suspension twice, and I probably cost him two thousand a month in lost business since some of the hoods were afraid to come there because of me.

I jumped in my car and decided to cruise by the Dragon for one last shot at it. When I parked out back, a hype in the doorway saw me and ran down the steps to tell everybody inside the heat was coming. I took my baton, wrapped the thong around my hand which they teach you not to do now, but which I've been doing for twenty years, and I walked down the concrete stairway to this cellar bar, and through the draped doorway. The front is framed by a pink dragon head. The front doorway is the mouth of the beast, the back door is under the tail. It always made me mad just to see the big dumb-looking dragon-mouth door. I went in the back door, up the dragon's ass, tapping my stick on the empty chairs and keeping my head on a swivel as I let my eyes get accustomed to the gloom. The pukepots were all sitting near the back. There were only about ten customers now in the early afternoon, and Marvin, all six feet six inches of him, was at the end of the bar grinning at a bad-looking bull dyke who was putting down a pretty well-built black stud in an arm wrestle.

Marvin was grinning, but he didn't mean it, he knew I was there. It curdled his blood to see me tapping on the furniture with my stick. That's why I did it. I always was as badge heavy and obnoxious as I could be when I was in there. I'd been in two brawls here and both times I knew Marvin was just wetting his shorts wishing he had the guts to jump in on me, but he thought better of it.

He weighed at least three hundred pounds and was damned tough. You had to be to own this joint, which catered to bookmakers, huggermugger whores, paddy hustlers, speed freaks, fruits and fruit hustlers, and ex-cons of both sexes and all ages. I'd never quite succeeded in provoking Marvin into attacking me, although it was common knowledge on the street that a shot fired at me one night from a passing car was some punk hired by Marvin. It was after that, even though nothing was ever proved, that I really began standing on the Dragon's tail. For a couple of months his business dropped to nothing with me living on his doorstep, and he sent two lawyers to my captain and the police commission to get me off his back. I relented as much as I had to, but I still gave him fits.

If I wasn't retiring there'd be hell to pay around here because once you get that twenty years' service in, you don't have to pussyfoot around so much. I mean no matter what kind of trouble you get into, nobody can ever take your pension away for any reason, even if they fire you. So if I were staying, I'd go right on. Screw the lawyers, screw the police commission. I'd land on that Dragon with both boon-dockers. And as I thought that, I looked down at my size thirteen triple E's. They were beat officer shoes, high top, laces with eyelets, ankle supporting, clumsy, round toes, beat officer shoes. A few years ago they were actually popular with young black guys, and almost came into style again. They called them "old man comforts" and they were soft and comfortable, but ugly as hell, I guess, to most people. I'd probably always wear them. I'd sunk my old man comforts in too many deserving asses to part with them now.

Finally Marvin got tired of watching the arm wrestlers and pretending he didn't see me.

"Whadda you want, Morgan," he said. Even in the darkness I could see him getting red in the face, his big chin jutting.

"Just wondering how many scumbags were here today, Marvin," I said in a loud voice which caused four or five of them to look up. These days we're apt to get disciplinary action for making brutal remarks like that, even though these assholes would bust their guts laughing if I was courteous or even civil.

The bull dyke was the only righteous female in the place. In this dive you almost have to check everybody's plumbing to know whether it's interior or exterior. The two in dresses were drags, the others were fruit hustlers and flimflam guys. I recognized a sleazy bookmaker named Harold Wagner. One of the fruit hustlers was a youngster, maybe twenty-two or so. He was still young enough to be offended by my remark, especially since it was in front of the queen in the red mini who probably belonged to him. He mumbled something under his breath and Marvin told him to cool it since he didn't want to give me an excuse to make another bust in the place. The guy looked high on pot like most everyone these days.

"He your new playmate, Roxie?" I said to the red dress queen, whose real name I knew was John Jeffrey Alton.

"Yes," said the queen in a falsetto voice, and motioned to the kid to shut his mouth. He was a couple inches taller than me and big chested, probably shacking with Roxie now and they split what they get hustling. Roxie hustles the guys who want a queen, and the kid goes after the ones who want a jocker. This jocker would probably become a queen himself. I always felt sorry for queens because they're so frantic, searching, looking. Sometimes I twist them for information, but otherwise I leave them alone.

I was in a rotten mood thinking nobody would roust the Dragon after I was gone. They were all glaring at me now, especially Marvin with his mean gray eyes and knife mouth.

One young guy, too young to know better, leaned back in his chair and made a couple of oinks and said, "I smell pig."

I'd never seen him before. He looked like a college boy slumming. Maybe in some rah-rah campus crowd beer joint I'd just hee-haw and let him slide, but here in the Pink Dragon the beat cops rule by force and fear. If they stopped being afraid of me I was through, and the street would be a jungle, which it is anyway, but at least now you can walk through it watching for occasional cobras and rabid dogs. I figured if it weren't for guys like me, there'd be no trails through the frigging forest.

"Oink, oink," he said again, with more confidence this time, since I hadn't responded. "I sure do smell pig."

"And what do pigs like best?" I smiled, slipping the stick back in my baton ring. "Pigs like to clean up garbage, and I see a pile." Still smiling I kicked the chair legs and he went down hard throwing a glass of beer on Roxie who forgot the falsetto and yelled, "Shithouse mouse!" in a pretty good baritone when the beer slid down his bra.

I had the guy in a wristlock before he knew what fell on him, and was on my way out the door, with him walking backwards, but not too fast in case someone else was ready.

"You bastard!" Marvin sputtered. "You assaulted my customer. You bastard! I'm calling my lawyer."

"Go right on, Marvin," I said, while the tall kid screamed and tippy-toed to the door because the upward thrust of the wristlock was making him go as high as he could. The smell of pot was hanging on his clothes but the euphoria wasn't dulling the pain of the wristlock. When you've got one that's really loaded you can't crank it on too hard because they don't react to pain, and you might break a wrist trying to make them flinch. This guy felt it though, and he was docile, ow, ow, owing all the way out. Marvin came around the bar and followed us to the door.

"There's witnesses!" he boomed. "This time there's witnesses to your dirty, filthy false arrest of my customer! What's the charge? What're you going to charge him with?"

"He's drunk, Marvin," I smiled, holding the wristlock with one hand, just in case Marvin was mad enough. I was up, high up, all alive, ready to fly.

"It's a lie. He's sober. He's sober as you."

"Why, Marvin," I said, "he's drunk in public view and unable to care for himself. I'm obliged to arrest him for his own protection. He *has* to be drunk to say what he did to me, don't you agree? And if you're not careful I might think you're trying to interfere with my arrest. You wouldn't like to try interfering with my arrest would you, Marvin?"

"We'll get you, Morgan," Marvin whispered helplessly. "We'll get your job one of these days."

"If you slimeballs could have my job I wouldn't want it," I said, let down because it was over.

The kid wasn't as loaded as I thought when I got him out of there into the sunshine and more or less fresh Los Angeles air.

"I'm not drunk," he repeated all the way to the Glass House, shaking his mop of blond hair out of his face since I had his hands cuffed behind his back. The Glass House is what the street people call our main police building because of all the windows.

"You *talked* your way into jail, boy," I said, lighting a cigar.

"You can't just put a sober man in jail for drunk because he calls you a pig," said the kid, and by the way he talked and looked, I figured him for an upper-middle-class student hanging out downtown with the scumbags for a perverse kick, and also because he was at heart a scumbag himself.

"More guys talk themselves into jail than get there any other way," I said.

"I demand an attorney," he said.

"Call one soon as you're booked."

"I'll bring those people to court. They'll testify I was sober. I'll sue you for false arrest."

"You wouldn't be getting a cherry, kid. Guys tried to sue me a dozen times. And you wouldn't get those ass-holes in the Dragon to give you the time of day if they had a crate full of alarm clocks."

"How can you book me for *drunk*? Are you prepared to swear before God that I was drunk?"

"There's no God down here on the beat, and anyway He'd never show his face in the Pink Dragon. The United States Supreme Court decisions don't work too well down here either. So you see, kid, I been forced to write my own laws, and you violated one in there. I just have to find you guilty of contempt of cop."

FIVE

AFTER I GOT THE GUY BOOKED I didn't know what the hell to do. I had this empty feeling now that was making me depressed. I thought about the hotel burglar again, but I felt lazy. It was this empty feeling. I was in a black mood as I swung over toward Figueroa. I saw a mailbox hand-book named Zoot Lafferty standing there near a public phone. He used to hang around Main and then Broadway and now Figueroa. If we could ever get him another block closer to the Harbor Freeway maybe we could push the bastard off the overpass sometime, I thought, in the mood for murder.

Lafferty always worked the businessmen in the area, taking the action and recording the bets inside a self-addressed stamped envelope. And he always hung around a mailbox and a public phone booth. If he saw someone that he figured was a vice cop, he'd run to the mailbox and deposit the letter. That way there'd be no evidence like betting markers or owe sheets the police could recover. He'd have the customers' bets the next day when the mail came, and in time for collection and payment. Like all handbooks though, he was scared of plainclothes vice cops but completely ignored uniformed policemen.

So one day when I was riding by, I slammed on the binders, jumped out of the black-and-white, and fell on Zoot's skinny ass before he could get to the mailbox. I caught him with the markers and they filed a felony book-making charge. I convicted him in Superior Court after I convinced the judge that I had a confidential reliable informant tell me all about Zoot's operation, which was true, and that I hid behind a bush just behind the phone booth and overheard the bets being taken over the phone, which was a lie. But I convinced the judge and that's all that matters. He had to pay a two-hundred-and-fifty-dollar fine and was given a year's probation, and that same day, he moved over here to Figueroa away from my beat where there are no bushes anywhere near his phone booth.

As I drove by Zoot, he waved at me and grinned and stood by the mailbox. I wondered if we could've got some help with the Post Office special agents to stop this flim-flam, but it would've been awful hard and not worth the effort. You can't tamper with someone's mail very easy. Now, as I looked at his miserable face for the last time, my black mood got blacker and I thought, I'll bet no other uniformed cop ever takes the trouble to shag him after I'm gone.

Then I started thinking about bookmaking in general, and got even madder, because it was the kind of crime I couldn't do anything about. I saw the profits reaped from it all around me, and I saw the people involved in it, and knew some of them, and yet I couldn't do anything because they were so well organized and their weapons were so good and mine were so flimsy. The money was so

unbelievably good that they could expand into semilegiti-
mate businesses and drive out competition because they
had the racket money to fall back on, and the legitimate
businesses couldn't compete. And also they were tougher
and ruthless and knew other ways to discourage competition. I always wanted to get one of them good, someone
like Red Scalotta, a big book, whose fortune they say can't
be guessed at. I thought all these things and how mad I get
everytime I see a goddamn lovable Damon-Runyon-type
bookmaker in a movie. I started thinking then about Angie Caputo, and got a dark kind of pleasure just picturing
him and remembering how another old beat man, Sam
Giraldi, had humbled him. Angie had never realized his
potential as a hood after what Sam did to him.

Sam Giraldi is dead now. He died last year just fourteen months after he retired at twenty years' service. He
was only forty-four when he had a fatal heart attack,
which is particularly a policeman's disease. In a job like
this, sitting on your ass for long periods of time and then
moving in bursts of heart-cracking action, you can expect
heart attacks. Especially since lots of us get so damned fat
when we get older.

When he ruined Angie Caputo, Sam was thirty-seven
years old but looked forty-seven in the face. He wasn't
very tall, but had tremendous shoulders, a meaty face, and
hands bigger than mine, all covered with heavy veins. He
was a good handball player and his body was hard as a
spring-loaded sap. He'd been a vice officer for years and
then went back to uniform. Sam walked Alvarado when I
walked downtown, and sometimes he'd drive over to my
beat or I'd come over to his. We'd eat dinner together and
talk shop or talk about baseball, which I like and which

he was fanatic about. Sometimes, if we ate at his favorite delicatessen on Alvarado, I'd walk with him for a while and once or twice we even made a pretty good pinch together like that. It was on a wonderful summer night when a breeze was blowing off the water in MacArthur Park that I met Angie Caputo.

It seemed to be a sudden thing with Sam. It struck like a bullet, the look on his face, and he said, "See that guy? That's Angie Caputo, the pimp and bookmaker's agent." And I said, "So what?" wondering what the hell was going on, because Sam looked like he was about to shoot the guy who was just coming out of a bar and getting ready to climb aboard a lavender Lincoln he had parked on Sixth Street. We got in Sam's car, getting ready to drive over to catch the eight o'clock show at the burlesque house out there on his beat.

"He hangs out further west, near Eighth Street," said Sam. "That's where he lives too. Not far from my pad, in fact. I been looking to see him for a few days now. I got it straight that he's the one that busted the jaw of Mister Rovitch that owns the cleaners where I get my uniforms done." Sam was talking in an unnaturally soft voice. He was a gentle guy and always talked low and quiet, but this was different.

"What'd he do that for?"

"Old guy was behind on interest payments to Harry Stapleton the loan shark. He had Angie do the job for him. Angie's a big man now. He don't have to do that kind of work no more, but he loves to do it sometimes. I hear he likes to use a pair of leather gloves with wrist pins in the palms."

"He get booked for it?"

Sam shook his head. "The old man swears three nig-gers mugged him."

"You sure it was Caputo?"

"I got a good snitch, Bumper."

And then Sam confessed to me that Caputo was from the same dirty town in Pennsylvania that he was from, and their families knew each other when they were kids, and they were even distant relatives. Then Sam turned the car around and drove back on Sixth Street and stopped at the corner.

"Get in, Angie," said Sam, as Caputo walked toward the car with a friendly smile.

"You busting me, Sam?" said Caputo, the smile wid-ening, and I could hardly believe he was as old as Sam. His wavy hair was blue-black without a trace of gray, and his handsome profile was smooth, and his gray suit was beautiful. I turned around when Caputo held out a hand and smiled at me.

"Angie's my name," he said as we shook hands. "Where we going?"

"I understand you're the one that worked over the old man," said Sam in a much softer voice than before.

"You gotta be kidding, Sam. I got other things going. Your finks got the wrong boy for this one."

"I been looking for you."

"What for, Sam, you gonna bust me?"

"I can't bust you. I ain't been able to bust you since I knew you, even though I'd give my soul to do it."

"This guy's a comic," said Caputo, laughing as he lit a cigarette. "I can depend on old Sam to talk to me at least once a month about how he'd like to send me to the joint. He's a comic. Whadda you hear from the folks back in

Aliquippa, Sam? How's Liz and Dolly? How's Dolly's kids?"

"Before this, you never really hurt nobody I knew personally," said Sam, still in the strange soft voice. "I knew the old man real good, you know."

"He one of your informers, Sam?" asked Caputo. "Too bad. Finks're hard to come by these days."

"Old guy like that. Bones might never heal."

"Okay, that's a shame. Now tell me where we're going. Is this some kind of roust? I wanna know."

"Here's where we're going. We're here," said Sam, driving the car under the ramp onto the lonely, dark, dirt road by the new freeway construction.

"What the fuck's going on?" asked Caputo, for the first time not smiling.

"Stay in the car, Bumper," said Sam. "I wanna talk with Angie alone."

"Be careful, *fratello*," said Caputo. "I ain't a punk you can scare. Be careful."

"Don't say *fratello* to me," Sam whispered. "You're a *dog's* brother. You beat old men. You beat women and live off them. You live off weak people's blood."

"I'll have your job, you dumb dago," said Caputo, and I jumped out of the car when I heard the slapping thud of Sam's big fist and Caputo's cry of surprise. Sam was holding Caputo around the head and already I could see the blood as Sam hammered at his face. Then Caputo was on his back and he tried to hold off the blows of the big fist which drew back slowly and drove forward with speed and force. Caputo was hardly resisting now and didn't yell when Sam pulled out the heavy six-inch Smith and Wesson. Sam knelt on the arms of Caputo and cracked the gun muzzle through his teeth and into his mouth. Caputo's head kept jerking off the ground as he gagged on the gun muzzle twisting and digging in his throat but Sam pinned him there on the end of the barrel, whispering to him in Italian. Then Sam was on his feet and Caputo flopped on his stomach heaving bloody, pulpy tissue.

Sam and me drove back alone without talking. Sam was breathing hard and occasionally opened a window to spit a wad of phlegm. When Sam finally decided to talk he said, "You don't have to worry, Bumper, Angie'll keep his mouth shut. He didn't even open it when I beat him, did he?"

"I'm not worried."

"He won't say nothing," said Sam. "And things'll be better on the street. They won't laugh at us and they won't be so bold. They'll be scared. And Angie'll never really be respected again. It'll be better out here on the street."

"I'm just afraid he'll kill you, Sam."

"He won't. He'll fear me. He'll be afraid that *I'll* kill *him*. And I will if he tries anything."

"Christ, Sam, it's not worth getting so personally tied up to these assholes like this."

"Look, Bumper, I worked bookmaking in Ad Vice and here in Central. I busted bookmakers and organized hoodlums for over eight years. I worked as much as six months on *one* bookmaker. Six months! I put together an investigation and gathered evidence that no gang lawyer could beat and I took back offices where I seized records that could prove, *prove* the guy was a millionaire book. And I convicted them and saw them get pitiful fines time after time and I *never* saw a bookmaker go to state prison even though it's a felony. Let somebody else work bookmaking I finally decided, and I came back to uniform. But Angie's different. I know him. All my life I knew him, and I live right up Serrano there, in the apartments. That's *my* neighborhood. I use that cleaners where the old man works. Sure he was my snitch but I liked him. I never paid him. He just told me things. He got a kid's a school-teacher, the old man does. The books'll be scared now for a little while after what I done. They'll respect us for a little while."

I had to agree with everything Sam said, but I'd never seen a guy worked over that bad before, not by a cop any-way. It bothered me. I worried about us, Sam and me, about what would happen if Caputo complained to the Department, but Sam was *right*. Caputo kept his mouth shut and I admit I was never sorry for what Sam did. When it was over I felt something and couldn't put my finger on it at first, and then one night laying in bed I figured it out. It was a feeling of something being *right*. For one of the few times on this job I saw an untouchable touched. I felt my thirst being slaked a little bit, and I was never sorry for what Sam did.

But Sam was dead now and I was retiring, and I was sure there weren't many other bluesuits in the division who could nail a bookmaker. I turned my car around and headed back toward Zoot Lafferty, still standing there in his pea green slack suit. I parked the black-and-white at the curb, got out, and very slow, with my sweaty uni-form shirt sticking to my back, I walked over to Zoot who opened the package door on the red and blue mailbox and stuck his arm inside. I stopped fifteen feet away and stared at him.

"Hello, Morgan," he said, with a crooked phony grin

that told me he wished he'd have slunk off long before now. He was a pale, nervous guy, about forty-five years old, with a bald freckled skull.

"Hello, Zoot," I said, putting my baton back inside the ring, and measuring the distance between us.

"You got your rocks off once by busting me, Morgan. Why don't you go back over to your beat, and get outta my face? I moved clear over here to Figueroa to get away from you and your fucking beat, what more do you want?"

"How much action you got written down, Zoot?" I said, walking closer. "It'll inconvenience the shit out of you to let it go in the box, won't it?"

"Goddamnit, Morgan," said Zoot, blinking his eyes nervously, and scratching his scalp which looked loose and rubbery. "Why don't you quit rousting people. You're an old man, you know that? Why don't you just fuck off outta here and start acting like one."

When the slimeball said that, the blackness I felt turned blood red, and I sprinted those ten feet as he let the letter slide down inside the box. But he didn't get his hand out. I slammed the door hard and put my weight against it and the metal door bit into his wrist and he screamed.

"Zoot, it's time for you and me to have a talk." I had my hand on the mailbox package door, all my weight leaning hard, as he jerked for a second and then froze in pain, bug-eyed.

"Please, Morgan," he whispered, and I looked around, seeing there was a lot of car traffic but not many pedestrians.

"Zoot, before I retire I'd like to take a real good book,

just one time. Not a sleazy little handbook like you but a real bookmaker, how about helping me?"

Tears began running down Zoot's cheeks and he showed his little yellow teeth and turned his face to the sun as he pulled another time on the arm. I pushed harder and he yelped loud, but there were noisy cars driving by.

"For God's sake, Morgan," he begged. "I don't know anything. Please let my arm out."

"I'll tell you what, Zoot. I'll settle for your phone spot. Who do you phone your action in to?"

"They phone *me*," he gasped, as I took a little weight off the door.

"You're a liar," I said, leaning again.

"Okay, okay, I'll give you the number," he said, and now he was blubbering outright and I got disgusted and then mad at him and at me and especially at the bookmaker I'd never have a chance to get, because he was too well protected and my weapons were too puny.

"I'll break your goddamn arm if you lie," I said, with my face right up to his. A young, pretty woman walked by just then, looked at Zoot's sweaty face and then at mine, and damn near ran across the street to get away from us.

"It's six-six-eight-two-seven-three-three," he sobbed.

"Repeat it."

"Six-six-eight-two-seven-three-three."

"One more time, and it better come out the same."

"Six-six-eight-two-seven-three-three. Oh, Christ!"

"How do you say it when you phone in the action?"

"Dandelion. I just say the word Dandelion and then I give the bets. I swear, Morgan."

"Wonder what Red Scalotta would say if he knew you gave me that information?" I smiled, and then I let him go when I saw by his eyes that I'd guessed right and he was involved with that particular bookmaker.

He pulled his arm out and sat down on the curb, holding it like it was broken and cursing under his breath as he wiped the tears away.

"How about talking with a vice cop about this?" I said, lighting a fresh cigar while he began rubbing his arm which was probably going numb.

"You're a psycho, Morgan!" he said, looking up. "You're a real psycho if you think I'd fink on anybody."

"Look, Zoot, you talk to a vice cop like I say, and we'll protect you. You won't get a jacket. But if you don't, I'll personally see that Scalotta gets the word that you gave me the phone number and the code so we could stiff in a bet on the phone clerk. I'll let it be known that you're a paid snitch and when he finds out what you told me you know what? I bet he'll believe it. You ever see what some gunsel like Betnie Zolitch can do to a fink?"

"You're the most rottenest bastard I ever seen," said Zoot, standing up, very shaky, and white as paste.

"Look at it this way, Zoot, you cooperate just this once, we'll take one little pukepot sitting in some phone spot and that'll be all there is to it. We'll make sure we come up with a phony story about how we got the information like we always do to protect an informant, and nobody'll be the wiser. You can go back to your slimy little business and I give you my word I'll never roust you again. Not personally, that is. And you probably know I always keep my word. Course I can't guarantee you some *other* cop won't shag you sometime."

He hesitated for a second and then said, "I'll settle for

you not rousting me no more, Morgan. Those vice cops I can live with."

"Let's take a ride. How's your arm feeling?"

"Fuck you, Morgan," he said, and I chuckled to myself and felt a little better about everything. We drove to Central Vice and I found the guy I wanted sitting in the office.

"Why aren't you out taking down some handbook, Charlie?" I said to the young vice cop who was leaning dangerously back in a swivel chair with his crepe-soled sneak shoes up on a desk doping the horses on a scratch sheet.

"Hi, Bumper," he grinned, and then recognized Zoot who he himself probably busted a time or two.

"Mr. Lafferty decide to give himself up?" said Charlie Bronski, a husky, square-faced guy with about five years on the Department. I broke him in when he was just out of the academy. I remembered him as a smart aggressive kid, but with humility. Just the kind I liked. You could teach that kind a little something. I wasn't ashamed to say he was Bumper-ized.

Charlie got up and put on a green striped, short-sleeved ivy-league shirt over the shoulder holster which he wore over a white T-shirt.

"Old Zoot here just decided to repent his evil ways, Charlie," I said, glancing at Zoot who looked as sad as anyone I'd ever seen.

"Let's get it over with, Morgan, for chrissake," said Zoot. "And you got to swear you'll keep it confidential."

"Swear, Charlie," I said.

"I swear," said Charlie. "What's this all about?"

"Zoot wants to trade a phone spot to us."

"For what?" asked Charlie.

"For nothing," said Zoot, very impatient. "Just because I'm a good fucking citizen. Now you want the information or not?"

"Okay," Charlie said, and I could tell he was trying to guess how I squeezed Zoot. Having worked with me for a few months, Charlie was familiar with my M.O. I'd always tried to teach him and other young cops that you can't be a varsity letterman when you deal with these barf-bags. Or rather, you *could* be, and you'd probably be the one who became a captain, or Chief of Police or something, but you can bet there'd always have to be the guys like me out on the street to make you look good up there in that ivory tower by keeping the assholes from taking over the city.

"You wanna give us the relay, is that it?" said Charlie, and Zoot nodded, looking a little bit sick.

"*Is* it a relay spot? Are you sure?" asked Charlie.

"I'm not sure of a goddamn thing," Zoot blubbered, rubbing his arm again. "I only came 'cause I can't take this kind of heat. I can't take being rousted and hurt."

Charlie looked at me, and I thought that if this lifelong handbook, this ex-con and slimeball started crying, I'd flip. I was filled with loathing for a pukepot like Zoot, not because he snitched, hell, everybody snitches when the twist is good enough. It was this crybaby sniveling stuff that I couldn't take.

"Damn, Zoot!" I finally exploded. "You been a friggin' scammer all your life, fracturing every friggin' law you had nuts enough to crack, and you sit here now acting like a pious nun. If you wanna play your own tune you better damn well learn to dance to it, and right now you're gonna do the friggin' boogaloo, you goddamn hemorrhoid!"

I took a step toward Zoot's chair and he snapped up straight in his seat saying, "Okay, Morgan, okay. Whadda you want? For God's sake I'll tell you what you wanna know! You don't have to get tough!"

"Is the number you phone a relay?" repeated Charlie calmly.

"I think so," Zoot nodded. "Sounds like some goofy broad don't know nothing about the business. I been calling this same broad for six months now. She's probably just some stupid fucking housewife, sitting on a hot seat and taking them bets for somebody she don't even know."

"Usually record them on Formica," Charlie explained to me, "then somebody phones her several times a day and takes the action she wrote down. She can wipe the Formica in case the vice cops come busting down her door. She probably won't even know who pays her or where the phone calls come from."

"Fuck no, she ain't gonna know," said Zoot, looking at me. "This shit's too big, Morgan. It's too goddamn big. You ain't gonna bother nobody by rousting me. You don't understand, Morgan. People *want* us in business. What's a guy get for bookmaking? Even a big guy? A fucking fine. Who does time? You ever see a book get joint time?" said Zoot to Charlie, who shook his head. "Fuck no, you ain't and you ain't going to. Everybody bets with bookies for chrissake and those that don't, they like some other kind of vice. Give up, Morgan. You been a cop all these years and you don't know enough to give up fighting it. You can't save this rotten world."

"I ain't trying to, Zoot," I said. "I just love the friggin' battle!"

I went down the hall to the coffee room, figuring that Charlie should be alone with Zoot. Now that I had played the bad guy, he could play the good guy. An interrogation never works if it's not private, and Charlie was a good bullshitter. I had hopes he could get more out of Zoot because I had him loosened up. Anytime you get someone making speeches at you, you have a chance. If he's shaky about one thing, he might be about something else. I didn't think you could buy Zoot with money, he was too scared of everything. But being scared of us as well as the mob, he could be gotten to. Charlie could handle him.

Cruz Segovia was in the coffee room working on his log. I came in behind him. There was no one else in the room and Cruz was bent over the table writing in his log. He was so slim that even in his uniform he looked like a little boy bent over doing his homework. His face was still almost the same as when we were in the academy and except for his gray hair he hadn't changed much. He was barely five feet eight and sitting there he looked really small.

"*Qué pasó, compadre,*" I said, because he always said he wished I was Catholic and could have been the godfather for his last seven kids. His kids considered me their godfather anyway, and he called me *compadre*.

"*Órale, panzón,*" he said, like a pachuco, which he put on for me. He spoke beautiful Spanish and could also read and write Spanish, which is rare for a Mexican. He was good with English too, but the barrios of El Paso Texas died hard, and Cruz had an accent when he spoke English.

"Where you been hiding out all day?" I said, putting a dime in the machine and getting Cruz a fresh cup, no cream and double sugar.

"You bastard," he said. "Where've I been hiding. Communication's been trying to get *you* all day! Don't you know that funny little box in your car is called a radio and you're supposed to listen for your calls and you're even supposed to handle them once in a while?"

"Chale, chale. Quit being a sergeant," I said. "Gimme some slack. I been bouncing in and out of that black-and-white machine so much I haven't heard anything."

"You'll be a beat cop all your life," he said, shaking his head. "You have no use at all for your radio, and if you didn't have your best friend for a sergeant, your big ass'd be fired."

"Yeah, but I got him," I grinned, poking him in the shoulder and making him swear.

"Seriously, Bumper," he said, and he didn't have to say "seriously" because his large black eyes always turned down when he was serious. "Seriously, the skipper asked me to ask you to pay a little more attention to the radio. He heard some of the younger officers complaining about always handling the calls in your district because you're off the radio walking around so much."

"Goddamn slick-sleeved rookies," I said, hot as hell, "they wouldn't know a snake in the grass if one jumped up and bit them on the dick. You seen these goddamn rookies nowadays, riding down the friggin' streets, ogling all the cunt, afraid to put on their hats because it might ruin their hair styles. Shit, I actually saw one of these pretty young fuzz sitting in his black-and-white spraying his hair! I swear, Cruz, most of these young cats wouldn't know their ass from a burnt biscuit."

"I know, Bumper," Cruz nodded with sympathy. "And the skipper knows a whole squad of these youngsters couldn't do half the police work you old-timers do. That's why nobody says anything to you. But *hombre*, you have to handle some calls once in a while instead of walking that beat."

"I know," I said, looking at my coffee.

"Just stay on the air a little more."

"Okay, okay, you're the *macho*. You got the *huevos de oro*."

Cruz smiled now that he was through stepping on my meat. He was the only one that ever nagged me or told me what to do. When someone else had ideas along those lines, they'd hit Cruz with them, and if he thought I needed talking to, he'd do it. They figured I'd listen to Cruz.

"Don't forget, *loco*, you're coming to dinner tonight."

"Can you see me forgetting dinner at your pad?"

"You sure Cassie can't come with you?"

"She sure wishes she could. You know Friday's the last day for her at school and they're throwing a little party for her. She *has* to be there."

"I understand," said Cruz. "What day is she actually going up north? She decided yet?"

"Next week she'll be packed and gone."

"I don't know why you don't just take your vacation now and cut out with her. What's the sense of waiting till the end of the month? That vacation pay isn't worth being away from her for a few weeks, is it? She might come to her senses and ask herself why the hell she's marrying a mean old bastard like Bumper Morgan."

I wondered why I didn't tell Cruz that I'd decided to do just that. What the hell was the secret? Friday was going to be my last day, I never cared anything about the vacation pay. Was I really afraid to say it?

"Gonna be strange leaving everything," I muttered to my coffee cup.

"I'm glad for you, Bumper," said Cruz, running his slim fingers through his heavy gray hair, "If I didn't have all the kids I'd get the hell out too, I swear. I'm glad you're going."

Cruz and me had talked about it lots of times the last few years, ever since Cassie came along and it became inevitable that I'd marry her and probably pull the pin at twenty years instead of staying thirty like Cruz had to do. Now that it was here though, it seemed like we'd never discussed it at all. It was so damn strange.

"Cruz, I'm leaving Friday," I blurted. "I'm going to see Cassie and tell her I'll leave Friday. Why wait till the end of the month?"

"That's fine, 'mano!" Cruz beamed, looking like he'd like to cut loose with a yelp, like he always did when he was drunk.

"I'll tell her today." Now I felt relieved, and drained the last of the coffee as I got up to leave. "And I don't give a damn if I loaf for a month. I'll just take it easy till I feel like starting my new job."

"That's right!" said Cruz, his eyes happy now. "Sit on that big fat *nalgas* for a year if you want to. They want *you* as security chief. They'll wait for you. And you have forty percent coming every month, and Cassie's got a good job, and you still have a good bank account don't you?"

"Hell yes," I answered, walking toward the door. "I never had to spend much money, with my beat and all."

"Shhh," Cruz grinned. "Haven't you heard? We're the new breed of professionals. We don't accept gratuities."

"Who said anything about gratuities? I only take tribute."

Cruz shook his head and said, *"Ahí te huacho,"* which is anglicized slang meaning I'll be seeing, or rather, watching for you.

"Ahí te huacho," I answered.

After I left Cruz I went back to the vice squad office and found Zoot hanging his head, and Charlie downright happy, so I figured Charlie had done all right.

"I'd like to talk to you alone for a minute, Bumper," said Charlie, leading me into the next room and closing the door while Zoot sat there looking miserable.

"He told me lots more than he thinks he did," said Charlie. He was charged up like any good cop should be when he has something worthwhile.

"He thinks you re taking me off his back?" I asked.

"Yeah," Charlie smiled. "Play along. He thinks I'm going to save him from you. Just lay off him for a while, okay, Bumper? He told me he's planning on moving his territory out of the division to Alvarado in a couple of weeks but he has to stay around Figueroa for the time being. I told him I'd talk to you."

"Tell Zoot he doesn't have to worry about old Bumper anymore," I said, getting another gas pain. I vowed to myself I'd lay off the soy sauce next time I ate in J-town.

"Yeah, he'll be a problem for the Rampart vice squad then," said Charlie, not getting my meaning.

"Want me to take him back to Fig?"

"I'll take him," said Charlie. "I want to talk a little more."

"Do me a favor?"

"Sure, Bumper."

"You think there's any chance of something going down because of what Zoot told you?"

"There's a damn good chance. Zoot half-assed copped that he thinks the broad at the relay spot that takes his action is Reba McClain, and if it is we might be able to swing real good with her."

"How's that?"

"She's Red Scalotta's girlfriend. We took her down in another relay about six months ago and she got probation with a six months' jail sentence hanging. She's a meth head and an ex-con and stir crazy as hell. Kind of a sex thing. She's got a phobia about jails and bull dykes and all that. Real ding-a-ling, but a gorgeous little toadie. We were just talking last week about her and if we could shag her and catch her dirty we might get to Scalotta through her. She's a real shaky bitch. I think she'd turn her mama to stay on the street. You bringing in Zoot with that phone number was a godsend."

"Okay, then I'm really going to ask the favor."

"Sure."

"Take her today or tomorrow at the latest. If she gives you something good, like a back office, take it down on Friday."

"A back office! Jesus, I don't think she'll have that kind of information, Bumper. And hell, Friday is just two days away. Sometimes you stake out for weeks or months to take a back office. Jesus, that's where the book's records are kept. We'd have to get a search warrant and that takes lots of information beforehand. Why Friday?"

"I'm going on vacation. I want to be in on this one, Charlie. I never took a back office. I want it real bad, and it has to be before I go on vacation."

"I'd do it for you, Bumper, if I could, you know that, but Friday's only two days away!"

"Just do police work like I taught you, with balls and brains and some imagination. That's all I ask. Just try, okay?"

"Okay," Charlie said. "I'll give it a try."

Before I left I put on an act for Zoot so he'd think Charlie was his protector. I pretended I was mad at Charlie and Charlie pretended he was going to stop me from any future attempts to stuff Zoot down the goddamn mail chute.

SIX

AFTER I got in my car I remembered the friendly ass bite Cruz gave me and I picked up the hand mike and said, "One-X-L-Forty-five, clear."

"One-X-L-Forty-five, handle this call," said the operator, and I grumbled and wrote the address down. "Meet One-L-Thirty, Ninth and Broadway."

"One-X-L-Forty-five, roger," I said disgustedly, and thought, that's what I get for clearing. Probably some huge crisis like taking a chickenshit theft report from some fatass stockbroker who got his wallet lifted while he was reading dirty magazines at the dirty bookstore on Broadway.

One-X-L-Thirty was a rookie sergeant named Grant who I didn't know very well. He wore one five-year hashmark showing he had between five and ten years on. I'd bet it was a whole lot closer to five. He had a ruddy, smooth face and a big vocabulary. I never heard him swear at any roll-call he conducted. I couldn't trust a policeman who didn't swear once in a while. You could hardly describe certain things you see and feelings you have in this job without some colorful language.

Grant was south of Ninth near Olympic, out of his car, pacing up and down as I drove up. I knew it was snobbish but I couldn't call a kid like him "Sergeant." And I didn't want to be out and out rude so I didn't call these young sergeants by their last names. I didn't call them anything. It got awkward sometimes, and I had to say, "Hey pal," or "Listen bud" when I wanted to talk to one of them. Grant looked pretty nervous about something.

"What's up?" I asked, getting out of my car.

"We have a demonstration at the Army Induction Center."

"So?" I said, looking down the street at a group of about fifteen marchers picketing the building.

"A lot of draftees go in and out and there could be trouble. There're some pretty militant-looking types in that picket line."

"So what're we gonna do?"

"I just called you because I need someone to stand by and keep them under surveillance. I'm going in to talk to the lieutenant about the advisability of calling a tactical alert. I'd like you to switch to frequency nine and keep me advised of any status change."

"Look, pal, this ain't no big thing. I mean, a tactical alert for fifteen ragtag flower sniffers?"

"You never know what it can turn into."

"Okay," and I sighed, even though I tried not to, "I'll sit right here."

"Might be a good idea to drive closer. Park across the street. Close enough to let them see you but far enough to keep them from trying to bait you."

"Okay, pal," I muttered, as Grant got in his car and sped toward the station to talk to Lieutenant Hilliard, who was a cool old head and wouldn't get in a flap over fifteen peace marchers.

I pulled out in the traffic and a guy in a blue Chevy jumped on his brakes even though he was eighty feet back and going slow. People get black-and-white fever when they see a police car and they do idiotic things trying to be super careful. I've seen them concentrate so hard on one facet of safe driving, like giving an arm signal, that they bust right through a red light. That's black-and-white fever for you.

The marchers across Broadway caught my eye when two of them, a guy and a girl, were waving for me to come over. They seemed to be just jiving around but I thought I better go over for several reasons. First of all, there might really be something wrong. Second, if I didn't, it looked like hell for a big bad copper to be afraid to approach a group of demonstrators. And third, I had a theory that if enough force could be used fast enough in these confrontations there'd be no riot. I'd never seen real force used quick enough yet, and I thought, what the hell, now was my chance to test my theory since I was alone with no sergeants around.

These guys, at least a few of them, two black guys, and one white, bearded scuz in a dirty buckskin vest and yellow headband, looked radical enough to get violent with an overweight middle-aged cop like myself, but I firmly believed that if one of them made the mistake of putting his hands on me and I drove my stick three inches in his esophagus, the others would yell police brutality twice and slink away. Of course I wasn't sure, and I noticed that the recent arrivals swelled their numbers to twenty-three. Only five of them were girls. That many people could stomp me to applesauce without a doubt, but I wasn't really worried, mainly because even though they were fist shaking, most of them looked like middle-class white people just playing at revolution. If you have a few hungry-looking professionals like I figured the white guy in the headband to be, you could have trouble. Some of these could lend their guts to the others and set them off, but he was the only one I saw.

I drove around the block so I didn't have to make an illegal U-turn in front of them, made my illegal U-turn on Olympic, came back and parked in front of the marchers, who ignored me and kept marching and chanting, "Hell no, we won't go." And "Fuck Uncle Sam, and Auntie Spiro," and several other lewd remarks mostly directed at the President, the governor, and the mayor. A few years ago, if a guy yelled "fuck" in a public place in the presence of women or children, we'd have to drag his ass to jail.

"Hi, Officer, I love you," said one little female peace marcher, a cute blonde about seventeen, wearing two inches of false eyelashes that looked upside-down, and ironed-out shoulder-length hair.

"Hi, honey, I love you too," I smiled back, and leaned against the door of my car. I folded my arms and puffed a cigar until the two who had been waving at me decided to walk my way.

They were whispering now with another woman and finally the shorter girl, who was not exactly a girl, but a woman of about thirty-five, came right up. She was dressed like a teenager with a short yellow mini, violet panty hose, granny glasses, and white lipstick. Her legs were too damned fat and bumpy and she was wearing a theatrical smile with a cold arrogant look beneath it. Up close, she looked like one of the professionals and seemed to be a picket captain. Sometimes a woman, if she's the real thing, can be the detonator much quicker than a man can. This one seemed like the real thing, and I looked her in the eye and smiled while she toyed with a heavy peace medal hanging around her neck. Her eyes said, "You're just a fat harmless cop, not worth my talents, but so far you're all we have here, and I don't know if an old bastard like you is even intelligent enough to know when he's being put down."

That's what I saw in her eyes, and her phony smile, but she said nothing for a few more minutes. Then a car from one of the network stations rolled up and two men got out with a camera and mike.

The interest of the marchers picked up now that they were soon to be on tape, and the chanting grew louder, the gestures more fierce, and the old teenybopper in the yellow dress finally said, "We called you over because you looked very forlorn. Where're the riot troops, or are you all we get today?"

"If you get *me*, baby, you ain't gonna want any more," I smiled through a puff of cigar smoke, pinning her eyeballs, admiring the fact that she didn't bat an eye even though I knew damn well she was expecting the businesslike professional clichés we're trained to give in these situations. I'd bet she was even surprised to see me slouching against my car like this, showing such little respect for this menacing group.

"You're not supposed to smoke in public, are you, Officer?" She smiled, a little less arrogant now. She didn't know what the hell she had here, and was going to take her time about setting the bait.

"Maybe a real policeman ain't supposed to, but this uniform's just a shuck. I rented this ill-fitting clown suit to make an underground movie about this fat cop that steals apples and beats up flower children and old mini-skirted squatty-bodies with socks to match their varicose veins in front of the U.S. Army Induction Center."

Then she lost her smile completely and stormed back to the guy in the headband who was also much older than he first appeared. They whispered and she looked at me as I puffed on the cigar and waved at some of the marchers who were putting me on, most of them just college-age kids having a good time. A couple of them sincerely seemed to like me even though they tossed a few insults to go along with the crowd.

Finally, the guy in the headband came my way shouting encouragement to the line of marchers who were going around and around in a long oval in front of the door, which was being guarded by two men in suits who were not policemen, but probably military personnel. The cameraman was shooting pictures now, and I hid my cigar and sucked in a few inches of gut when he photographed me. The babe in the yellow dress joined the group after passing out some Black Panther pins and she marched without once looking at me again.

"I hear you don't make like the other cops we've run into in these demonstrations," said the guy with the headband, suddenly standing in front of me and grinning. "The L.A.P.D. abandoning the oh so firm but courteous approach? Are you a new police riot technique? A caricature of a fat pig, a jolly jiveass old cop that we just can't get mad at? Is that it? They figure we couldn't use you for an Establishment symbol? Like you're too fucking comical looking, is that it?"

"Believe it or not, Tonto," I said, "I'm just the neighborhood cop. Not a secret weapon, nothing for lumpy legs to get tight-jawed about. I'm just your local policeman."

He twitched a little bit when I mentioned the broad so I guessed she might be his old lady. I figured they probably taught sociology 1A and 1B in one of the local junior colleges.

"Are you the only swine they're sending?" he asked, smiling not quite so much now which made me very happy. It's hard even for professionals like him to stay with a smirk when he's being rapped at where it hurts. He probably just loves everything about her, even the veiny old wheels. I decided, screw it, I was going to take the offensive with these assholes and see where it ended.

"Listen, Cochise," I said, the cigar between my teeth, "I'm the only old pig you're gonna see today. All the young piglets are staying in the pen. So why don't you and old purple pins just take your Che handbooks and cut out. Let these kids have their march with no problems. And take those two dudes with the naturals along with you." I pointed to the two black guys who were standing ten feet away watching us. "There ain't gonna be any more cops here, and there ain't gonna be any trouble."

"You *are* a bit refreshing," he said, trying to grin, but it was a crooked grin. "I was getting awfully sick of those unnatural pseudoprofessionals with their businesslike platitudes, pretending to look right through us when really they wanted to get us in the back room of some police station and beat our fucking heads in. I must say you're refreshing. You're truly a vicious fascist and don't pretend to be anything else."

Just then the mini-skirted broad walked up again. "Is he threatening you, John?" she said in a loud voice, looking over her shoulder, but the guys with the camera and mike were at the other end of the shouting line of marchers.

"Save it till they get to this end," I said, as I now estimated her age to be closer to forty. She was a few years older than he was and the mod camouflage looked downright comical. "Want some bubble gum, little girl?" I said.

"Shut your filthy mouth," he said, taking a step toward me. I was tight now, I wound myself up and was ready. "Stay frosty, Sitting Bull," I smiled. "Here, have a cigar." I offered one of my smokes, but he wheeled and walked away with old lumpy clicking along behind him.

The two black guys hadn't moved. They too were professionals, I was positive now, but they were a different kind. If anything went down, I planned to attack those two right away. They were the ones to worry about. They both wore black plastic jackets and one wore a black cossack hat. He never took his eyes off me. He'd be the very first one I'd go after, I thought. I kept that flaky look, grinning and waving at any kid who gave me the peace sign, but I was getting less and less sure I could handle the situation. There were a couple other guys in the group that might get froggy if someone leaped, and I've seen what only two guys can do if they get you down and put the boots to you, let alone nine or ten.

I hated to admit it but I was beginning to wish Grant would show up with a squad of bluecoats. Still, it was a quiet demonstration, as quiet as these things go, and there was probably nothing to worry about, I thought.

The march continued as it had for a few more minutes, with the young ones yelling slogans, and then headband and mini-skirt came back with six or eight people in tow. These kids were definitely collegiate, wearing flares or bleach-streaked Levis. Some of the boys had mutton-chops and moustaches, most had collar-length hair, and two of them were pretty, suntanned girls. They looked friendly enough and I gave them a nod of the head when they stopped in front of me.

One particularly scurvy-looking slimeball walked up, smiled real friendly, and whispered, "You're a filthy, shit-eating pig."

I smiled back and whispered, "Your mother eats bacon."

"How can we start a riot with no riot squad," another said.

"Careful, Scott, he's not just a pig, he's a wild boar, you dig?" said the mini-skirt who was standing behind the kids.

"Maybe *you* could use a little bore, sweetheart, maybe that's your trouble," I said, looking at the guy in the head-band, and two of the kids chuckled.

"You seem to be the only Establishment representative we have at the moment, maybe you'd like to rap with us," said Scott, a tall kid with a scrubbed-looking face and a mop of blond hair. He had a cute little baby hanging on his arm and she seemed amused.

"Sure, just fire away," I said, still leaning back, act-ing relaxed as I puffed. I was actually beginning to *want* to rap with them. One time when I asked some young sergeant if I could take a shot at the "Policeman Bill"

program and go talk to a class of high-school kids, he
shined me on with a bunch of crap, and I realized then
that they wanted these flat-stomached, clear-eyed, handsome young recruiting-poster cops for these jobs. I had
my chance now and I liked the idea.

"What's your first name, Officer Morgan?" asked
Scott, looking at my nameplate, "and what do you think
of street demonstrations?"

Scott was smiling and I could hardly hear him over
the yelling as the ring of marchers moved twenty feet
closer to us to block the entrance more effectively after
the fat bitch in yellow directed them to do it. Several kids
mugged at the cameraman and waved "V" signs at him
and me. One asshole, older than the others, flipped me the
bone and then scowled into the camera.

"That's it, smile and say pig, you pukepot," I mumbled, noticing the two black cossacks were at the other
end of the line of marchers talking to purple legs. Then
I turned to Scott. "To answer your question, my name's
Bumper Morgan and I don't mind demonstrations except
that they take us cops away from our beats, and believe
me we can't spare the time. Everybody loses when we're
not on patrol."

"What do you patrol, the fucking barnyard?" said one
little shitbird wearing shades and carrying a poster that
showed a white army officer telephoning a black mother
about her son being killed in Vietnam. She was shown in
a corner of the poster and there was a big white cop club-
bing her with an oversized baton.

"That poster doesn't make sense," I said. "It's awful
damn lame. You might as well label it, 'Killed by the run-

ning dogs of imperialism!' I could do a lot better than that."

"Man, that's *exactly* what I told him," Scott laughed, and offered me a cigarette.

"No thanks," I said, as he and his baby doll lit one. "Now that one's sort of clever," I said, pointing to a sign which said "Today's pigs are tomorrow's porkchops."

None of the other kids had anything to say yet, except the shithead with the poster, who yelled, "Like, what're we doing talking to this fucking fascist lackey?"

"Look," I said, "I ain't gonna lay down and play dead just because you can say 'fuck' pretty good. I mean nobody's shocked by that cheap shit anymore, so why don't we just talk quiet to each other. I wanna hear what you guys got to say."

"Good idea," said another kid, a black, with a wild natural, wire-rim glasses, and a tiger tooth necklace, who almost had to shout because of the noise. "Tell us why a man would want to be a cop. I mean really. I'm not putting you on, I want to know."

He was woofing me, because he winked at the blond kid, but I thought I'd *tell* them what I liked about it. What the hell, I liked having all these kids crowded around listening to me. Somebody then moved the marchers' line a little north again and I could almost talk in a normal voice.

"Well, I like to take lawbreakers off the street," I began.

"Just a minute," said the black kid, pushing his wire-rims up on his nose. "Please, Officer, no euphemisms. I'm from Watts." Then he purposely lapsed into a Negro drawl and said, "I been knowin' the PO-lice all mah life." The others laughed and he continued in his own voice. "Talk like a *real* cop and tell us like it is, without any bullshit. You know, use that favorite expression of L.A.P.D.—'asshole,' I believe it is." He smiled again after he said all this and so did I.

"What part of Watts you live in?" I asked.

"One-O-Three and Grape, baby," he answered.

"Okay, I'll talk plainer. I'm a cop because I love to throw assholes in jail, and if possible I like to send them to the joint."

"That's more like it," said the black kid. "Now you're lookin' so good and soundin' so fine."

The others applauded and grinned at each other.

"Isn't that kind of a depressing line of work?" asked Scott. "I mean, don't you like to do something *for* someone once in a while instead of *to* them?"

"I figure I do something *for* someone every time I make a good bust. I mean, you figure every real asshole you catch in a dead bang burglary or robbery's tore off probably a hundred people or so before you bring him down. I figure each time I make a pinch I save a hundred more, maybe even some lives. And I'll tell you, most victims are people who can't afford to be victims. People who can afford it have protection and insurance and aren't so vulnerable to all these scummy hemorrhoids. Know what I mean?"

Scott's little girlfriend was busting to throw in her two cents, but three guys popped off at once, and finally Scott's voice drowned out the others. "I'm a law student," he said, "and I intend to be your adversary someday in a courtroom. Tell me, do you really get satisfaction when you send a man away for ten years?"

"Listen, Scott," I said, "in the first place even Eichmann would stand a fifty-fifty chance of not doing ten years nowadays. You got to be a boss crook to pull that kind of time. In fact, you got to work at it to even *get* to state prison. Man, some of the cats I put away, I wouldn't give them ten years, I'd give them a goddamned lobotomy if I could."

I dropped my cigar because these kids had me charged up now. I figured they were starting to respect me a little and I even tried for a minute to hold in my gut but that was uncomfortable, and I gave it up.

"I saw a big article in some magazine a few years ago honoring these cops," I continued. " 'These are not pigs' the article said, and it showed one cop who'd delivered some babies, and one cop who'd rescued some people in a flood, and one cop who was a goddamn boy scout troop leader or something like that. You know, I delivered two babies myself. But we ain't being paid to be midwives or lifeguards or social workers. They got other people to do those jobs. Let's see somebody honor some copper because the guy made thirty good felony pinches a month for ten years and sent a couple hundred guys to San Quentin. Nobody ever gives an award to him. Even his sergeant ain't gonna appreciate that, but he'll get on his ass for not writing a traffic ticket every day because the goddamn city needs the revenue and there's no room in prisons anyway."

I should've been noticing things at about this time. I should've noticed that the guy in the headband and his old lady were staying away from me and so were the two black guys in the plastic jackets. In fact, all the ones I spotted were staying at the other end of the line of marchers who were quieting down and starting to get tired. I should've noticed that the boy, Scott, the other blond kid, and the tall black kid, were closer to me than the others, and so was the cute little twist hanging on Scott's arm and carrying a huge heavy-looking buckskin handbag.

I noticed nothing, because for one of the few times in my life I wasn't being a cop. I was a big, funny-looking, blue-suited donkey and I thought I was home-run king belting them out over the fences. The reason was that I was somewhere I'd never been in my life. I was on a soapbox. Not a stage but a soapbox. A stage I could've handled. I can put on the act people want and expect, and I can still keep my eyes open and not get carried away with it, but this goddamned soapbox was something else. I was making speeches, one after another, about things that meant something to me, and all I could see was the loving gaze of my audience, and the sound of my own voice drowned out all the things that I should've been hearing and seeing.

"Maybe police departments should only recruit college graduates," Scott shrugged, coming a step closer.

"Yeah, they want us to solve crimes by these 'scientific methods,' whatever that means. And what do us cops do? We kiss ass and nod our heads and take federal funds to build computers and send cops to college and it all boils down to a cop with sharp eyes and an ability to talk to people who'll get the goddamn job done."

"Don't you think that in the age that's coming, policemen will be obsolete?" Scott's little girlfriend asked the question and she looked so wide-eyed I had to smile.

"I'm afraid not, honey," I said. "As long as there's people, there's gonna be lots of bad ones and greedy ones and weak ones."

"How can you feel that way about people and still care at all about helping them as you say you do when you arrest somebody?" she asked, shaking her head. She smiled sadly, like she felt sorry for me.

"Hell, baby, they ain't much but they're all we got. It's the only game in town!" I figured that was obvious to anybody and I started to wonder if they weren't still a little young. "By the way, are most of you social science and English majors?"

"Why do you say that?" asked the black kid, who was built like a ballplayer.

"The surveys say you are. I'm just asking. Just curious."

"I'm an engineering major," said the blond kid, who was now behind Scott, and then for the first time I was aware how close in on me these certain few were. I was becoming aware how polite they'd been to me. They were all activists and college people and no doubt had statistics and slogans and arguments to throw at me, yet I had it all my way. They just stood there nodding, smiling once in a while, and let me shoot my face off. I knew that something wasn't logical or right, but I was still intrigued with the sound of my own voice and so the fat blue maharishi said, "Anything else about police work you'd like to talk about?"

"Were you at Century City?" asked the little blonde.

"Yeah, I was there, and it wasn't anything like you read in the underground newspapers or on those edited TV tapes."

"It wasn't? I was there," said Scott.

"Well, I'm not gonna deny some people got hurt," I

said, looking from one face to another for hostility. "There was the President of the United States to protect and there were thousands of war protestors out there and I guarantee you that was no bullshit about them having sharpened sticks and bags of shit and broken bottles and big rocks. I bet I could kill a guy with a rock."

"You didn't see any needless brutality?"

"What the hell's brutality?" I said. "Most of those blue-coats out there are just lads your age. When someone spits in his face, all the goddamn discipline in the world ain't gonna stop him or any normal kid from getting that other cat's teeth prints on his baton. There's times when you just *gotta* play a little catch-up. You know what five thousand screaming people look like? Sure, we got some stick time in. Some scumbags, all they respect is force. You just gotta kick ass and collect names. Anybody with any balls woulda whaled on some of those pricks out there." Then I remembered the girl. "Sorry for the four-letter word, miss," I said as a reflex action.

"Prick is a five-letter word," she said, reminding me of the year I was living in.

Then suddenly, the blond kid behind Scott got hostile. "Why do we talk to a pig like this? He talks about helping people. What's he do besides beat their heads in, which he admits? What do *you* do in the ghettos of Watts for the black people?"

Then a middle-aged guy in a clergyman's collar and a black suit popped through the ring of young people. "I work in the eastside Chicano barrios," he announced. "What do you do for the Mexicans except exploit them?"

"What do *you* do?" I asked, getting uncomfortable at the sudden change of mood here, as several of the marchers joined the others and I was backed up against the car by fifteen or twenty people.

"I fight for the Chicanos. For brown power," said the clergyman.

"You ain't brown," I observed, growing more nervous.

"Inside I'm brown!"

"Take an enema," I mumbled, standing up straight, as I realized that things were wrong, all wrong.

Then I caught a glimpse of the black cossack hat to the left behind two girls who were crowding in to see what the yelling was all about, and I saw a hand flip a peace button at me, good and hard. It hit me in the face, the pin scratching me right under the left eye. The black guy looked at me very cool as I spun around, mad enough to charge right through the crowd.

"You try that again and I'll ding your bells, man," I said, loud enough for him to hear.

"Who?" he said, with a big grin through the moustache and goatee.

"Who, my ass," I said. "You ain't got feet that fit on a limb. I'm talking to *you*."

"You fat pig," he sneered and turned to the crowd. "He wants to arrest me! You pick out a black, that the way you do it, Mister PO-lice?"

"If anything goes down, I'm getting *you* first," I whispered, putting my left hand on the handle of my stick.

"He wants to arrest me," he repeated, louder now. "What's the charge? Being black? Don't I have any rights?"

"You're gonna get your rites," I muttered. "Your *last* rites."

"I should kill you," he said. "There's fifty braves here

and we should kill you for all the brothers and sisters you pigs murdered."

"Get it on, sucker, anytime you're ready," I said with a show of bravado because I was really scared now.

I figured that many people let loose could turn me into a doormat in about three minutes. My breath was coming hard. I tried to keep my jaw from trembling and my brain working. They weren't going to get me down on the ground. Not without a gun in my hand. I decided it wouldn't be that easy to kick *my* brains in. I made up my mind to start shooting to save myself, and I decided I'd blow up the two Black Russians, Geronimo, and Purple Legs, not necessarily in that order.

Then a hand reached out and grabbed my necktie, but it was a breakaway tie, and I didn't go with it when the hand pulled it into the crowd. At about the same time the engineering major grabbed my badge, and I instinctively brought up my right hand, holding his hand on my chest, backing up until his elbow was straight. Then I brought my left fist up hard just above his elbow and he yelped and drew back. Several other people also drew back at the unmistakable scream of pain.

"Off the pig! Off the pig!" somebody yelled. "Rip him off!"

I pulled my baton out and felt the black-and-white behind me now and they were all screaming and threatening, even the full-of-shit padre.

I would've jumped in the car on the passenger side and locked the door but I couldn't. I felt the handle and it was locked, and the window was rolled up, and I was afraid that if I fooled around unlocking it, somebody might get his ass up and charge me.

Apparently the people inside the induction center didn't know a cop was about to get his ticket cancelled, because nobody came out. I could see the cameraman fighting to get through the crowd which was spilling out on the street and I had a crazy wish that he'd make it. That's the final vanity, I guess, but I kind of wanted him to film Bumper's Last Stand.

For a few seconds it could've gone either way and then the door to my car opened and hit me in the back, scaring the shit out of me.

"Get your butt in here, Bumper," said a familiar voice, which I obeyed. The second I closed the door something hit the window almost hard enough to break the glass and several people started kicking at the door and fender of my black-and-white.

"Give me the keys," said Stan Ludlow, who worked Intelligence Division. He was sitting behind the wheel, looking as dapper as always in a dark green suit and mint-colored necktie.

I gave him the keys from my belt and he drove away from the curb as I heard something else clunk off the fender of the car. Four radio cars each containing three Metro officers pulled up at the induction center as we were leaving, and started dispersing the group.

"You're the ugliest rape victim I ever saw," said Stan, turning on Ninth Street and parking behind a plainclothes police car where his partner was waiting.

"What the hell you talking about?"

"Had, man. You just been had."

"I had a feeling something wasn't right," I said, getting sick because I was afraid to hear what I figured he was going to say. "Did they set me up?"

"Did they set you up? No, they didn't have to. You set yourself up! Christ, Bumper, you should know better than to make speeches to groups like that. What the hell made you do it?"

Stan had about fifteen years on the job and was a sergeant, but he was only about forty and except for his gray sideburns he looked lots younger. Still, I felt like a dumb little kid sitting there now. I felt like he was lots older and a damn sight wiser and took the assbite without looking at him.

"How'd you know I was speechmaking, Stan?"

"One of them is one of us," said Stan. "We had one of those guys wired with a mike. We listened to the whole thing, Bumper. We called for the Metro teams because we knew what was going to happen. Damn near didn't get to you quick enough though."

"Who were the leaders?" I was trying to save a grain or two of my pride. "The bitch in the yellow dress and the guru in the headband?"

"Hell no," said Stan, disgustedly. "Their names are John and Marie French. They're a couple of lames trying to groove with the kids. They're nothing. She's a self-proclaimed revolutionary from San Pedro and he's her husband. As a matter of fact he picked up our undercover man and drove him to the demonstration today when they were sent by the boss. French is mostly used as errand boy. He drives a VW bus and picks up everybody that needs a ride to all these peace marches. He's nothing. Why, did you have them figured for the leaders?"

"Sort of," I mumbled.

"You badmouthed them, didn't you?"

"Sort of. What about the two in the Russian hats?"

"Nobody," said Stan. "They hang around all the time with their Panther buttons and get lots of pussy, but they're nobody. Just opportunists. Professional blacks."

"I guess the guy running the show was a tall nice-looking kid named Scott?" I said, as the lights slowly turned on.

"Yeah, Scott Hairston. He's from U.C.L.A. His sister Melba was the little blonde with the peachy ass who was hanging on his arm. She was the force behind subversive club chapters starting on her high school campus when she was still a bubblegummer. Their old man, Simon Hairston's an attorney and a slippery bastard, and his brother Josh is an old-time activist."

"So the bright-eyed little baby was a goddamn viper, huh? I guess they've passed me by, Stan."

Stan smiled sympathetically and lit my cigar for me. "Look, Bumper, these kids've been weaned on this bullshit. You're just a beginner. Don't feel too bad. But for God's sake, next time don't start chipping with them. No speeches, please!"

"I must've sounded like a boob," I said, and I could feel myself flushing clear to my toes.

"It's not that so much, Bumper, but that little bitch Melba put you on tape. She always solicits casual comments from cops. Sometimes she has a concealed hand mike with a wire running up her sleeve down to a box in her handbag. She carrying a big handbag today?"

I didn't have to answer. Stan saw it in the sick look on my face.

"They'll edit your remarks, Bumper. I heard some of them from the mike *our* guy was wearing. Christ, you talked about stick time and putting teeth marks on your baton and kicking ass and collecting names."

"But all that's not how I meant it, Stan."

"That's the way your comments'll be presented—out of context. It'll be printed that way in an underground newspaper or maybe even in a daily if Simon Hairston gets behind it."

"Oooooh," I said, tilting my hat over my eyes and slumping down in my seat.

"Don't have a coronary on me, Bumper," said Stan. "Everything's going to be all right."

"All right? I'll be the laughingstock of the Department!"

"Don't worry, Melba's tapes're going to disappear."

"The undercover man?"

Stan nodded.

"Bless him," I breathed. "Which one was he? Not the kid whose arm I almost broke?"

"No," Stan laughed, "the tall black kid. I'm only telling you because we're going to have to use him as a material witness in a few days anyway, and we'll have to disclose his identity. We got secret indictments on four guys who make pretty good explosives in the basement of a North Hollywood apartment building. He's been working for me since he joined the Department thirteen months ago. We have him enrolled in college. Nice kid. Hell of a basketball player. He can't wait to wear a bluesuit and work a radio car. He's sick of mingling with all these revolutionaries."

"How do you know he can get the tape?"

"He's been practically living in Melba's skivvies for

at least six months now. He'll sleep with her tonight and that'll be it."

"Some job," I said.

"He doesn't mind that part of it," Stan chuckled. "He's anxious to see how all his friends react when they find out he's the heat. Says he's been using them as whipping boys and playing the outraged black man role for so long, they probably won't believe it till they actually see him in the blue uniform with that big hateful shield on his chest. And wait'll Melba finds out she's been balling a cop. You can bet she'll keep that a secret."

"Nobody's gonna hear about me then, huh, Stan?"

"I'll erase the tape, Bumper," said Stan, getting out of the car. "You know, in a way it worked out okay. Scott Hairston was expecting a hundred marchers in the next few hours. He didn't want trouble yet. You wrecked his game today."

"See you later, Stan," I said, trying to sound casual, like I wasn't totally humiliated. "Have a cigar, old shoe."

I was wrung out after that caper and even though it was getting late in the afternoon, I jumped on the Harbor Freeway and started driving south, as fast as traffic would permit, with some kind of half-baked idea about looking at the ocean. I was trying to do something which I usually do quite well, controlling my thoughts. It wouldn't do any good at all to stew over what happened, so I was trying to think about something else, maybe food, or Cassie, or how Glenda's jugs looked today—something good. But I was in a dark mood, and nothing good would come, so I decided to think of absolutely nothing which I can also do quite well.

I wheeled back to my beat and called the lieutenant,

telling him about the ruckus at the induction center, leaving out all the details of course, and he told me the marchers dispersed very fast and there were only a few cars still at the scene. I knew there'd hardly be any mention of this one, a few TV shots on the six o'clock news and that'd be it. I hung up and got back in my car, hoping the cameraman hadn't caught me smoking the cigar. That's another silly rule, no smoking in public, as if a cop is a Buckingham Palace guard.

SEVEN

I DROVE AROUND SOME MORE, cooling off, looking at my watch every few seconds, wanting this day to end. The noisy chatter on the radio was driving me nuts so I turned it off. Screw the radio, I thought, I never made a good pinch from a radio call. The good busts come from doing what I do best, walking and looking and talking to people.

I had a hell of an attack of indigestion going. I took four antacid tablets from the glove compartment and popped them all but I was still restless, squirming around on the seat. Cassie's three o'clock class would be finished now so I drove up Vermont to Los Angeles City College and parked out front in the red zone even though when I do that I always get a few digs from the kids or from teachers like, "You can do it but we get tickets for it." Today there was nobody in front and I didn't get any bullshit which I don't particularly mind anyway, since nobody including myself really likes authority symbols. I'm always one of the first to get my ass up when the brass tries to restrict my freedom with some idiotic rules.

I climbed the stairs leisurely, admiring the tits on some

sun-tanned, athletic-looking, ponytailed gym teacher. She
was in a hurry and took the stairs two at a time, still in her
white shorts and sneakers and white jersey that showed
all she had, and it was plenty. Some of the kids passing
me in the halls made all the usual remarks, calling me
Dick Tracy and Sheriff John, and there were a few giggles
about Marlene somebody holding some pot and then Marlene squealed and giggled. We didn't used to get snickers
about pot, and that reminded me of the only argument
concerning pot that made any sense to me. Grass, like
booze, breaks the chain and frees the beast, but does it so
much easier and quicker. I've seen it thousands of times.

Cassie was in her office with the door opened talking
to a stringy-haired bubblegummer in a micro-mini that
showed her red-flowered pantygirdle when she sat down.

"Hi," said Cassie, when she saw me in the doorway.
The girl looked at me and then back at Cassie, wondering
what the fuzz was here for.

"We'll just be a minute," said Cassie, still smiling her
clean white smile, and I nodded and walked down the hall
to the water fountain thinking how damn good she looked
in that orange dress. It was one of the twenty or so that
I'd bought her since we met, and she finally agreed with
me that she looked better in hot colors, even though she
thought it was part of any man's M.O. to like his women
in flaming oranges and reds.

Her hair was drawn back today and either way, back or
down, her hair was beautiful. It was thick brown, streaked
with silver, not gray, but real untouched silver, and her
figure was damn good for a girl her age. She was tanned
and looked more like a gym teacher than a French teacher.
She always wore a size twelve and sometimes could wear

a ten in certain full styles. I wondered if she still looked so good because she played tennis and golf or because she didn't have any kids when she was married, but then, Cruz's wife Socorro had a whole squad of kids and though she was a little overweight she still looked almost as good as Cassie. Some people just keep it all, I guess, which almost made me self-conscious being with this classy-looking woman when we went places together. I always felt like everyone was thinking, "He must have bread or she'd never be with him." But it was useless to question your luck, you just had to grab on when you had the chance, and I did. And then again, maybe I was one of those guys that's ugly in an attractive sort of way.

"Well?" said Cassie, and I turned my head and saw her standing in the doorway of her office, still smiling at me as I went over her with my eyes. The kid had left.

"That's the prettiest dress you have," I said, and I really meant it. At that moment she'd never looked better, even though some heavy wisps of hair were hanging on her cheeks and her lipstick was almost all gone.

"Why don't you admire my mind instead of my body once in a while like I do yours?" she grinned.

I followed her into the office and stepped close, intending to give her a kiss on the cheek. She surprised me by throwing her arms around my neck and kissing me long and hot, causing me to drop my hat on the floor and get pretty aroused even though we were standing in an open doorway and any minute a hundred people would walk past. When she finally stopped, she had the lazy dazzling look of a passionate woman.

"Shall we sweep everything off that damned desk?" she said in a husky voice, and for a minute or two I thought she would've. Then a bell rang and doors started opening and she laughed and sat down on her desk showing me some very shapely legs and you would never guess those wheels had been spinning for forty odd years. I plopped down in a leather chair, my mouth woolly dry from having that hot body up against me.

"Are you sure you won't come to the party tonight?" she said finally, lighting a cigarette.

"You know how I feel about it, Cassie," I said. "This is *your* night. Your friends and the students want to have you to themselves. I'll have you forever after that."

"Think you can handle me?" she asked, with a grin, and I knew from her grin she meant sexually. We had joked before about how I awoke this in her, which she said had been dormant since her husband left her seven years ago and maybe even before that, from what I knew of the poor crazy guy. He was a teacher like Cassie, but his field was chemistry.

We supposed that some of her nineteen-year-old students, as sex-obsessed as they are these days, might be making love more often than we did, but she didn't see how they could. She said it had never been like this with her, and she never knew it could be so good. Me, I've always appreciated how good it was. As long as I can remember, I've been horny.

"Come by the apartment at eleven," she said. "I'll make sure I'm home by then."

"That's pretty early to leave your friends."

"You don't think I'd sit around drinking with a bunch of educators when I could be learning at home with Officer Morgan, do you?"

"You mean I can teach a teacher?"

"You're one of the tops in your field."

"You have a class tomorrow morning," I reminded her.

"Be there at eleven."

"A lot of these teachers and students that don't have an early class tomorrow are gonna want to jive and woof a lot later than that. I think you ought to stay with them tonight, Cassie. They'd expect you to. You can't disappoint the people on your beat."

"Well, all right," she sighed, "But I won't even see you tomorrow night because I'll be dining with those two trustees. They want to give me one final look, and casually listen to my French to make sure I'm not going to corrupt the already corrupted debs at their institution. I suppose I can't run off and leave *them* either."

"It won't be long till I have you all to myself. Then *I'll* listen to your French and let you corrupt the hell out of me, okay?"

"Did you tell them you're retiring yet?" She asked the question easily, but looked me straight in the eye, waiting, and I got nervous.

"I've told Cruz," I said, "and I got a surprise for you."

"What?"

"I've decided that Friday's gonna be my last day. I'll start my vacation Saturday and finish my time while I'm on vacation. I'll be going with you."

Cassie didn't yell or jump up or look excited or anything, like I thought she would. She just went limp like her muscles relaxed suddenly, and she slipped off the desk and sat down on my lap where there isn't any too much room, and with her arms doubled around the top of my neck she started kissing me on the face and mouth and

I saw her eyes were wet and soft like her lips, and next thing I know, I heard a lot of giggling. Eight or ten kids were standing in the hall watching us through the open door, but Cassie didn't seem to hear, or didn't care. I did though because I was sitting there in my bluesuit, being loved up and getting turned on in public.

"Cassie," I gasped, nodding toward the door, and she got up, and calmly shut the door on the kids like she was ready to start again.

I stood and picked up my hat from the floor. "Cassie, this is a school. I'm in uniform."

Cassie started laughing very hard and had to sit down in the chair I'd been in, leaning back, and holding her hands over her face as she laughed. I thought how sexy even her throat was, the throat usually being the first thing to show its age, but Cassie's was sleek.

"I wasn't going to rape you," she said at last, still chuckling between breaths.

"Well, it's just that you teachers are so permissive these days, I thought you might try to do me on the desk like you said."

"Oh, Bumper," she said finally, holding her arms out, and I came over and leaned down and she kissed me eight or ten warm times all over my face.

"I can't even begin to tell you how I feel now that you're really going to do it," she said. "When you said you actually *are* finishing up this Friday, and that you told Cruz Segovia, I just went to pieces. That was relief and joy you saw on my face when I closed the door, Bumper, not passion. Well, maybe a *little* of it was."

"We've been planning all along, Cassie, you act like it was really a shock to you."

"I've had nightmares about it. I've had fantasies awake and asleep of how after I'd gone, and got our apartment in San Francisco, you'd phone me one bitter night and tell me you weren't coming, that you just could never leave your beat."

"Cassie!"

"I haven't told you this before, Bumper, but it's been gnawing at me. Now that you've told Cruz, and it's only two more days, I know it's coming true."

"I'm not married to my goddamn job, Cassie," I said, thinking how little you know about a woman, even one as close as Cassie. "You should've seen what happened to me today. I was flimflammed by a soft-nutted little kid. He made a complete ass out of me. He made me look like a *square*."

Cassie looked interested and amused, the way she always does when I tell her about my job.

"What happened?" she asked, as I pulled out my last cigar and fired it up so I could keep calm when the humiliation swept over me.

"A demonstration at the Army Induction Center. A kid, a punk-ass kid, conned me and I started blabbing off about the job. Rapping real honest with him I was, and I find out later he's a professional revolutionary, probably a Red or something, and oh, I thought I was so goddamn hip to it. I been living too much on my beat, Cassie. Too much being the Man, I guess. Believing I could outsmart any bastard that skated by. Thinking the only ones I never could really get to were the organized ones, like the bookmakers and the big dope dealers. But *sometimes* I could do things that even hurt *them*. Now there's new ones that've come along. And they have organization. And I was like a baby, they handled me so easy."

"What the hell did you *do*, Bumper?"

"Talked. I talked to them straight about things. About thumping assholes that needed thumping. That kind of thing. I made *speeches*."

"Know what?" she said, putting her long-fingered hand on my knee. "Whatever happened out there, whatever you said, I'll bet wouldn't do you or the Department a damn bit of harm."

"Oh yeah, Cassie? You should've heard me talking about when the President was here and how we busted up the riot by busting up a skull or three. I was marvelous."

"Do you know a *gentle* way to break up riots?"

"No, but we're supposed to be professional enough not to talk to civilians the way we talk in police locker rooms."

"I'll take Officer Morgan over one of those terribly wholesome, terribly tiresome TV cops, and I don't think there's a gentle way to break up riots, so I think you should stop worrying about the whole thing. Just think, pretty soon you won't have any of these problems. You'll have a real position, an important one, and people working under you."

"I got to admit, it gets me pretty excited to think about it. I bet I can come up with ways to improve plant security that those guys never dreamed of."

"Of course you can."

"No matter what I do, you pump me up," I smiled. "That's why I wanted you for my girl in spite of all your shortcomings."

"Well, you're my Blue Knight. Do you know you're a knight? You joust and live off the land."

"Yeah, I guess you might say I live off my beat, all right. 'Course I don't do much jousting."

"Just *rousting*?"

"Yeah, I've rousted a couple thousand slimeballs in my time."

"So you're my Blue Knight."

"Wait a minute, kid," I said. "You're only getting a *former* knight if you get me."

"What do you mean, 'if'?"

"It's okay to shuck about me being some kind of hero or something, but when I retire I'm just a has-been."

"Bumper," she said, and laughed a little, and kissed my hand like Glenda did. That was the second woman to kiss my hand today, I thought. "I'm not dazzled by authority symbols. It's really *you* that keeps me kissing your hands." She did it again and I've always thought that having a woman kiss your hands is just almost more than a man can take. "You're going to an important job. You'll be an executive. You have an awful lot to offer, especially to me. In fact, you have so much maybe I should share it."

"I can only handle one woman at a time, baby."

"Remember Nancy Vogler, from the English department?"

"Yeah, you want to share me with her?"

"Silly," she laughed. "Nancy and her husband were married twelve years and they didn't have any children. A couple of years ago they decided to take a boy into their home. He's eleven now."

"They adopted him?"

"No, not exactly. They're foster parents." Cassie's voice became serious. "She said being a foster parent is the most rewarding thing they've ever done. Nancy said they'd almost missed out on knowing what living is and didn't realize it until they got the boy."

Cassie seemed to be searching my face just then. Was she thinking about *my* boy? I'd only mentioned him once to her. Was there something she wanted to know?

"Bumper, after we get married and settled in our home, what would you say to *us* becoming foster parents? Not really adopting a child if you didn't want to, but being foster parents, sharing. You'd be someone for a boy to look up to and learn from."

"A kid! But I never thought about a family!"

"I've been thinking about this for a long time, and after seeing Nancy and hearing about their life, I think about how wonderful it would be for us. We're not old yet, but in ten or fifteen more years when we *are* getting old, there'd be someone else for both of us." She looked in my eyes and then down. "You may think I'm crazy, and I probably am, but I'd like you to give it some thought."

That hit me so hard I didn't know what to say, so I grinned a silly grin, kissed her on the cheek, said, "I'm end of watch in fifteen minutes. Bye, old shoe," and left.

She looked somehow younger and a little sad as she smiled and waved at me when I'd reached the stairway. When I got in my black-and-white I felt awful. I dropped two pills and headed east on Temple and cursed under my breath at every asshole that got in my way in this rush-hour traffic. I couldn't believe it. Leaving the Department after all these years and getting married was change enough, but a kid! Cassie had asked me about my ex-wife one time, just once, right after we started going together. I told her I was divorced and my son was dead and I didn't go into it any further. She never mentioned it again, never talked about kids in that way.

Damn, I thought, I guess every broad in the world should drop a foal at least once in her life or she'll never be happy. I pushed Cassie's idea out of my mind when I drove into the police building parking lot, down to the lower level where it was dark and fairly cool despite the early spring heat wave. I finished my log, gathered up my ticket books, and headed for the office to leave the log before I took off the uniform. I never wrote traffic tickets but they always issued me the ticket books. Since I made so many good felony pinches they pretty well kept their mouths shut about me not writing tickets, still, they always issued me the books and I always turned them back in just as full. That's the trouble with conformists, they'd never stop giving me those ticket books.

After putting the log in the daywatch basket I jived around with several of the young nightwatch coppers who wanted to know when I was changing to nights for the summer. They knew my M.O. too. Everybody knew it. I hated anyone getting my M.O. down too good like that. The most successful robbers and burglars are the ones who change their M.O.'s. They don't give you a chance to start sticking little colored pins in a map to plot their movements. That reminded me of a salty old cop named Nails Grogan who used to walk Hill Street.

About fifteen years ago, just for the hell of it, he started his own crime wave. He was teed off at some chickenshit lieutenant we had then, named Wall, who used to jump on our meat every night at rollcall because we weren't catching enough burglars. The way Wall figured this was that there were always so many little red pins on the pin maps for nighttime business burglaries, especially around Grogan's beat. Grogan always told me he didn't think Wall ever really read a burglary report and didn't know shit from gravy about what was going on. So a little at a time Nails started changing the pins every night before rollcall, taking the pins out of the area around his beat and sticking them in the east side. After a couple weeks of this, Wall told the rollcall what a hell of a job Grogan was doing with the burglary problem in his area, and restricted the ass chewing to guys that worked the eastside cars. I was the only one that knew what Grogan did and we got a big laugh out of it until Grogan went too far and pinned a full-blown crime wave on the east side, and Lieutenant Wall had the captain call out the Metro teams to catch the burglars. Finally the whole hoax was exposed when no one could find crime reports to go with all the little pins.

Wall was transferred to the morning watch, which is our graveyard shift, at the old Lincoln Heights jail. He retired from there a few years later. Nails Grogan never got made on that job, but Wall knew who screwed him, I'm sure. Nails was another guy that only lived a few years after he retired. He shot himself. I got a chill thinking about that, shook it off, and headed for the locker room where I took off the bluesuit and changed into my herringbone sport coat, gray slacks, and lemon yellow shirt, no tie. In this town you can usually get by without a tie anywhere you go.

Before I left, I plugged in my shaver and smoothed up a little bit. A couple of the guys were still in the locker room. One of them was an ambitious young bookworm named Wilson, who as usual was reading while sitting on the bench and slipping into his civvies. He was going to college three or four nights a week and always had a textbook tucked away in his police notebook. You'd see him in the coffee room or upstairs in the cafeteria going through it all the time. I'm something of a reader myself but I could never stand the thought of doing it because you had to.

"What're you reading?" I asked Wilson.

"Oh, just some criminal law," said Wilson, a thin young-ster with a wide forehead and large blue eyes. He was a probationary policeman, less than a year on the job.

"Studying for sergeant already?" said Hawk, a cocky, square-shouldered kid about Wilson's age, who had two years on, and was going through his badge-heavy period.

"Just taking a few classes."

"You majoring in police science?" I asked.

"No, I'm majoring in government right now. I'm think-ing about trying for law school." He didn't look right at me and I didn't think he would. This is something I've gotten used to from the younger cops, especially ones with some education, like Wilson. They don't know how to act when they're with old-timers like me. Some act salty like Hawk, trying to strut with an old beat cop, and it just looks silly. Others act more humble than they usu-ally would, thinking an old lion like me would claw their ass for making an honest mistake out of greenness. Still others, like Wilson, pretty much act like themselves, but like most young people, they think an old fart that's never even made sergeant in twenty years must be nearly illiter-ate, so they generally restrict all conversation to the basics of police work to spare you, and they generally look embarrassed like Wilson did now, to admit to you that they read books. The generation gap is as bad in this job as it is in any other except for one thing: the hazards of the job shrink it pretty fast. After a few brushes with danger, a kid pretty much loses his innocence, which is what the generation gap is really all about—innocence.

"Answer me a law question," said Hawk, putting on some flared pants. We're too GI to permit muttonchops or big moustaches or he'd surely have them. "If you commit suicide can you be prosecuted for murder?"

"Nobody ever has," Wilson smiled, as Hawk giggled and slipped on a watermelon-colored velvet shirt.

"That's only because of our permissive society," I said, and Wilson glanced at me and grinned.

"What's that book in your locker, Wilson?" I asked, nodding toward a big paperback on the top shelf.

"Guns of August."

"Oh yeah, I read that," I said. "I've read a hundred books about the First World War. Do you like it?"

"I do," he said, looking at me like he discovered the missing link. "I'm reading it for a history course."

"I read T. E. Lawrence's *Seven Pillars of Wisdom* when I was on my First World War kick. Every goddamn word. I had maps and books spread all over my pad. That little runt only weighed in at about a hundred thirty, but thirty pounds of that was brains and forty was balls. He was a boss warrior."

"A loner," Wilson nodded, really looking at me now.

"Right. That's what I dig about him. I would've liked him even better if he hadn't written it all so intimate for everyone to read. But then if he hadn't done that, I'd never have appreciated him. Maybe a guy like that finally gets tired of just enjoying it and *has* to tell it all to figure it all out and see if it means anything in the end."

"Maybe you should write your memoirs when you're through, Bumper," Wilson smiled. "You're as well known around here as Lawrence ever was in Arabia."

"Why don't you major in history?" I said. "If I went to college that'd be my meat. I think after a few courses in criminal law the rest of law school'd be a real drag, torts and contracts and all that bullshit. I could never plow through the dust and cobwebs."

"It's exciting if you like it," said Wilson, and Hawk looked a little ruffled that he was cut out of the conversation so he split.

"Maybe so," I said. "You must've had a few years of college when you came on the Department."

"Two years," Wilson nodded. "Now I'm halfway through my junior year. It takes forever when you're a full-time cop and a part-time student."

"You can tough it out," I said, lighting a cigar and sitting down on the bench, while part of my brain listened to the youngster and the other part was worrying about something else. I had the annoying feeling you get, that can sometimes be scary, that I'd been here with him before and we talked like this, or maybe it was somebody else, and then I thought, yes, that was it, maybe the cowlick in his hair reminded me of Billy, and I got an empty tremor in my stomach.

"How old're you, Wilson?"

"Twenty-six," he said, and a pain stabbed me and made me curse and rub my pot. Billy would've been twenty-six too!

"Hope your stomach holds out when you get my age. Were you in the service?"

"Army," he nodded.

"Vietnam?"

"Yeah," he nodded.

"Did you hate it?" I asked, expecting that all young people hated it.

"I didn't like the *war*. It scared hell out of me, but I didn't mind the *army* as much as I thought I would."

"That's sort of how I felt," I smiled. "I was in the Marine Corps for eight years."

"Korea?"

"No, I'm even older than that," I smiled. "I joined in forty-two, and got out in fifty, then came on the police department."

"You stayed in a long time," he said.

"Too long. The war scared me too, but sometimes peace is just as bad for a military man."

I didn't tell him the truth because it might tune him out, and the truth was that it *did* scare me, the war, but I didn't hate it. I didn't exactly like it, but I didn't hate it. It's fashionable to hate war, I know, and I wanted to hate it, but I never did.

"I swore when I left Vietnam I'd never fire another gun and here I am a cop. Figure that out," said Wilson.

I thought that was something, having him tell me that. Suddenly the age difference wasn't there. He was telling me things he probably told his young partners during lonely hours after two a.m. when you're fighting to keep awake or when you're "in the hole" trying to hide your radio car, in some alley where you can doze uncomfortably for an hour, but you never really rest. There's the fear of a sergeant catching you, or there's the radio. What if you *really* fall asleep and a hot call comes out and you miss it?

"Maybe you'll make twenty years without ever firing your gun on duty," I said.

"Have you had to shoot?"

"A few times," I nodded, and he let it drop like he should. It was only civilians who ask you, "What's it feel like to shoot someone?" and all that bullshit which is completely ridiculous, because if you do it in war or you do it as a cop, it doesn't feel like anything. If you do what has to be done, why *should* you feel anything? I never have. After the fear for your own life is past, and the adrenalin slows, nothing. But people generally can't stand truth. It makes a lousy story so I usually give them their clichés.

"You gonna stay on the job after you finish law school?"

"If I ever finish I might leave," he laughed. "But I can't really picture myself ever finishing."

"Maybe you won't want to leave by then. This is a pretty strange kind of job. It's . . . intense. Some guys wouldn't leave if they had a million bucks."

"How about you?"

"Oh, I'm pulling the pin," I said. "I'm almost gone. But the job gets to you. The way you see everyone so exposed and vulnerable. . . .And there's nothing like rolling up a good felon if you really got the instinct."

He looked at me for a moment and then said, "Rogers and I got a good two-eleven suspect last month. They cleared five holdups on this guy. He had a seven-point-six-five-millimeter pistol shoved down the back of his waistband when we stopped him for a traffic ticket. We got hinky because he was sweating and dry-mouthed when he talked to us. It's really something to get a guy like that, especially when you never know how close you came. I mean, he was just sitting there looking from Rogers to me, measuring, thinking about blowing us up. We realized it later, and it made the pinch that much more of a kick."

"That's part of it. You feel more alive. Hey, you talk like you're Bumper-ized and I didn't even break you in."

"We worked together one night, remember?" said Wilson. "My first night out of the academy. I was more scared of you than I was the assholes on the street."

"That's right, we *did* work together. I remember now," I lied.

"Well, I better get moving," said Wilson, and I was disappointed. "Got to get to school. I've got two papers due next week and haven't started them."

"Hang in there, Wilson. Hang tough," I said, as I locked my locker.

I walked to the parking lot and decided to tip a few at my neighborhood pub near Silverlake before going to Cruz's house. The proprietor was an old pal of mine who used to own a decent bar on my beat downtown before he bought this one. He was no longer on my beat of course, but he still bounced for drinks, I guess out of habit. Most bar owners don't pop for too many policemen, because they'll take advantage of it, policemen will, and they'll be so many at your watering hole you'll have to close the goddamn doors. Harry only popped for me and a few detectives he knew real well.

It was five o'clock when I parked my nineteen-fifty-one Ford in front of Harry's. I'd bought the car new and was still driving it. Almost twenty years and I only had a hundred and thirty thousand miles on her, and the same engine. I never went anywhere except at vacation time or sometimes when I'd take a trip to the river to fish. Since I met Cassie I've used the car more than I ever had before, but even with Cassie I seldom went far. We usually went to the movies in Hollywood, or to the Music Center to see light opera, or to the Bowl for a concert which was Cassie's favorite place to go, or to Dodger Stadium which was mine. Often we went out to the Strip to go dancing. Cassie was good. She had all the moves, but she couldn't get the hang of letting her body do it all. With Cassie the mind was always there. One thing I decided I wouldn't get rid of when I left L.A. was my Ford. I wanted to see just how long a car could live if you treated it right.

Harry was alone when I walked in the little knotty-pine tavern which had a pool table, a few sad booths, and a dozen bar stools. The neighborhood business was never very good. It was quiet and cool and dark in there and I was glad.

"Hi, Bumper," he said, drawing a draft beer in a frosted glass for me.

"Evening, Harry," I said, grabbing a handful of pretzels from one of the dishes he had on the bar. Harry's was one of the few joints left where you could actually get something free, like pretzels.

"How's business, Bumper?"

"Mine's always good, Harry," I said, which is what policemen always answer to that question.

"Anything exciting happen on your beat lately?" Harry was about seventy, an ugly little goblin with bony shoulder blades who hopped around behind the bar like a sparrow.

"Let's see," I said, trying to think of some gossip. Since Harry used to own a bar downtown, he knew a lot of the people I knew. "Yeah, remember Frog LaRue?"

"The little hype with the stooped-over walk?"

"That one."

"Yeah," said Harry. "I must've kicked that junkie out of my joint a million times after you said he was dealing dope. Never could figure out why he liked to set up deals in my bar."

"He got his ass shot," I said.

"What'd he do, try to sell somebody powdered sugar in place of stuff?"

"No, a narco cop nailed him."

"Yeah? Why would anybody shoot Frog? He couldn't hurt nobody but himself."

"Anybody can hurt somebody, Harry," I said. "But in this case it was a mistake. Old Frog always kept a blade on the window sill in any hotel he stayed at. And the window'd be open even in the dead of winter. That was his M.O. If someone came to his door who he thought was cops, Frog'd slit the screen and throw his dope and his outfit right out the window. One night the narcs busted in the pad when they heard from a snitch that Frog was holding, and old Froggy dumped a spoon of junk out the window. He had to slit the screen to do it and when this narc came crashing through the door, his momentum carried him clear across this little room, practically onto Frog's bed. Frog was crouched there with the blade still in his hand. The partner coming through second had his gun drawn and that was it, he put two almost in the ten ring of the goddamn bull's-eye." I put my fist on my chest just to the right of the heart to show where they hit him.

"Hope the poor bastard didn't suffer."

"Lived two days. He told about the knife bit to the detectives and swore how he never would've tried to stab a cop."

"Poor bastard," said Harry.

"At least he died the way he lived. Armload of dope. I heard from one of the dicks that at the last they gave him a good stiff jolt of morphine. Said old Frog laying there with two big holes in his chest actually looked happy at the end."

"Why in the hell don't the state just give dope to these poor bastards like Frog?" said Harry, disgustedly.

"It's the high they crave, not just feeling healthy. They build up such a tolerance you'd have to keep increasing the dose and increasing it until you'd have to give them a fix that'd make a pussycat out of King Kong. And heroin substitutes don't work with a stone hype. He wants the real thing. Pretty soon you'd be giving him doses that'd kill him anyway."

"What the hell, he'd be better off. Some of them probably wouldn't complain."

"Got to agree with you there," I nodded. "Damn straight."

"Wish that bitch'd get here," Harry mumbled, checking the bar clock.

"Who's that?"

"Irma, the goofy barmaid I hired last week. You seen her yet?"

"Don't think so," I said, sipping the beer, so cold it hurt my teeth.

"Sexy little twist," said Harry, "but a kook, you know? She'll steal your eyes out if you let her. But a good body. I'd like to break her open like a shotgun and horsefuck her."

"Thought you told me you were getting too old for that," I said, licking the foam off my upper lip, and finishing the glass, which Harry hurried to refill.

"I am, God knows, but once in a while I get this terrible urge, know what I mean? Sometimes when I'm closing up and I'm alone with her. . . .I ain't stirred the old lady for a couple years, but I swear when I'm with Irma I get the urge like a young stallion. I'm not *that* old, you know. Not by a long shot. But you know how my health's always been. Lately there's been this prostate problem. Still, when I'm around this Irma I'm awful randy. I feel like I could screw anything from a burro to a cowboy boot."

"I'll have to see this wench," I smiled.

"You won't take her away from me, will you, Bumper?"

I thought at first he was kidding and then I saw the desperate look on his face. "No, of course not, Harry."

"I really think I could make it with her, Bumper. I been depressed lately, especially with this prostate, but I could be a man again with Irma"

"Sure, Harry." I'd noticed the change coming over him gradually for the past year. He sometimes forgot to pick up bar money, which was very unusual for him. He mixed up customers' names and sometimes told you things he'd told you the last time he saw you. Mostly that, repeating things. A few of the other regular customers mentioned it when we played pool out of earshot. Harry was getting senile and it was not only sad, it was scary. It made my skin crawl. I wondered how much longer he'd be able to run the joint. I laid a quarter on the bar, and sure enough, he absently picked it up. The first time I ever bought my own drink in Harry's place.

"My old lady can't last much longer, Bumper. I ever tell you that the doctors only give her a year?"

"Yeah, you told me."

"Guy my age can't be alone. This prostate thing, you know I got to stand there and coax for twenty minutes before I can take a leak. And you don't know how lovely it is to be able to sit down and take a nice easy crap. You know, Bumper, a nice easy crap is a thing of beauty."

"Yeah, I guess so."

"I could do all right with a dame like Irma. Make me young again, Irma could." Sure.

"You try to go it alone when you get old and you'll be rotting out a coffin liner before you know it. You got to have somebody to keep you alive. If you don't, you might die without even knowing it. Get what I mean?"

"Yeah."

It was so depressing being here with Harry that I decided to split, but one of the local cronies came in.

"Hello, Freddie," I said, as he squinted through six ounces of eyeglasses into the cool darkness.

"Hi, Bumper," said Freddie, recognizing my voice before he got close enough to make me through his half-inch horn-rims. Nobody could ever mistake his twangy voice which could get on your nerves after a bit. Freddie limped over and laid both arthritic hands on the bar knowing I'd bounce for a couple drinks.

"A cold one for Freddie," I said, suddenly afraid that Harry wouldn't even know him. But that was ridiculous, I thought, putting a dollar on the bar, Harry's deterioration was only beginning. I usually bought for the bar when there were enough people in there to make Harry a little coin, trouble is, there were seldom more than three or four customers in Harry's at any one time anymore. I guess everyone runs from a man when he starts to die.

"How's business, Bumper?" asked Freddie, holding the mug in both his hands, fingers like crooked twigs.

"My business's always good, Freddie."

Freddie snuffled and laughed. I stared at Freddie for a few seconds while he drank. My stomach was burning and Harry had me spooked. Freddie suddenly looked ancient too. Christ, he probably was at least sixty-five. I'd never thought about Freddie as an older guy, but suddenly he was. Little old men they were. I had nothing in common with them now.

"Girls keeping you busy lately, Bumper?" Harry winked. He didn't know about Cassie or that I stopped chasing around after I met her.

"Been slowing down a little in that department, Harry," I said.

"Keep at it, Bumper," said Harry, cocking his head to one side and nodding like a bird. "The art of fornication is something you lose if you don't practice it. The eye muscles relax, you get bifocals like Freddie. The love muscles relax, whatta you got?"

"Maybe he is getting old, Harry," said Freddie, dropping his empty glass on its side as he tried to hand it to Harry with those twisted hands.

"Old? You kidding?" I said.

"How about you, Freddie?" said Harry. "You ain't got arthritis of the cock, have you? When was the last time you had a piece of ass?"

"About the last time you did," said Freddie sharply.

"Shit, before my Flossie got sick, I used to tear off a chunk every night. Right up till when she got sick, and I was sixty-eight years old then."

"Haw!" said Freddie, spilling some beer over the gnarled fingers. "You ain't been able to do anything but lick it for the past twenty years."

"Yeah?" said Harry, nodding fast now, like a starving little bird at a feed tray. "You know what I did to Irma here one night? Know what?"

"What?"

"I laid her right over the table there. What do you think of that, wise guy?"

"Haw. Haw. Haw," said Freddie who had been a little bit fried when he came in and was really feeling it now.

"All you can do is read about it in those dirty books," said Harry. "Me, I don't read about it, I do it! I threw old Irma right over that bar there and poured her the salami for a half hour!"

"Haw. Haw. Haw," said Freddie. "It'd take you that long to find that shriveled up old cricket dick. Haw. Haw. Haw."

"What's the sense of starting a beef?" I muttered to both of them. I was getting a headache. "Gimme a couple aspirin will you, Harry?" I said, and he shot the grinning Freddie a pissed-off look, and muttering under his breath, brought me a bottle of aspirin and a glass of water.

I shook out three pills and pushed the water away, swallowing the pills with a mouthful of beer. "One more beer," I said, "and then I gotta make it."

"Where you going, Bump? Out to hump?" Harry

leered, and winked at Freddie, forgetting he was supposed to be mad as hell.

"Going to a friend's house for dinner."

"Nice slice of tail waiting, huh?" said Harry, nodding again.

"Not tonight. Just having a quiet dinner."

"Quiet dinner," said Freddie. "Haw. Haw. Haw."

"Screw you, Freddie," I said, getting mad for a second as he giggled in his beer. Then I thought, Jesus, I'm getting loony too.

The phone rang and Harry went to the back of the bar to answer it. In a few seconds he was bitching at somebody, and Freddie looked at me, shaking his head.

"Harry's going downhill real fast, Bumper."

"I know he is, so why get him pissed off?"

"I don't mean to," said Freddie. "I just lose my temper with him sometimes, he acts so damned nasty. I heard the doctors're just waiting for Flossie to die. Any day now."

I thought of how she was ten years ago, a fat, tough old broad, full of hell and jokes. She fixed such good cold-cut sandwiches I used to make a dinner out of them at least once a week.

"Harry can't make it without her," said Freddie. "Ever since she went away to the hospital last year he's been getting more and more childish, you noticed?"

I finished my beer and thought, I've *got* to get the hell out of here.

"It happens only to people like Harry and me. When you love somebody and need them so much especially when you're old, and then lose them, that's when it happens to you. It's the most godawful thing that ever could happen to you, when your mind rots like Harry's. Better your body goes like Flossie's. Flossie's the lucky one, you know. You're lucky too. You don't love nobody and you ain't married to nothing but that badge. Nothing can ever touch you, Bumper."

"Yeah, but how about when you get too old to do the job, Freddie? How about then?"

"Well, I never thought about that, Bumper." Freddie tipped the mug and dribbled on his chin. He licked some foam off one knotted knuckle. "Never thought about that, but I'd say you don't have to worry about it. You get a little older and charge around the way you do and some-body's bound to bump you off. It might sound cold, but what the hell, Bumper, look at *that* crazy old bastard." He waved a twisted claw toward Harry still yelling in the phone. "Screwing everything with his imagination and a piece of dead skin. Look at me. What the hell, dying on your beat wouldn't be the worst way to go, would it?"

"Know why I come to this place, Freddie? It's just the most cheerful goddamn drinking establishment in Los Angeles. Yeah, the conversation is stimulating and the at-mosphere is very jolly and all."

Harry came back before I could get away from the bar. "Know who that was, Bumper?" he said, his eyes glassy and his cheeks pale. He had acne as a young man and now his putty-colored cheeks looked corroded.

"Who was it," I sighed, "Irma?"

"No, that was the hospital. I spent every cent I had, even with the hospital benefits, and now she's been put in a big ward with a million other old, dying people. And still I got to pay money for one thing or another. You know, when Flossie finally dies there ain't going to be nothing left to bury her. I had to cash in the insurance. How'll I bury old Flossie, Bumper?"

I started to say something to soothe Harry, but I heard sobbing and realized Freddie had started blubbering. Then in a second or two Harry started, so I threw five bucks on the bar for Freddie and Harry to get bombed on, and I got the hell away from those two without even saying good-bye. I've never understood how people can work in mental hospitals and old people's homes and places like that without going nuts. I felt about ready for the squirrel tank right now just being around those two guys for an hour.

EIGHT

TEN MINUTES LATER I was driving my Ford north on the Golden State Freeway and I started getting hungry for Socorro's enchiladas. I got to Eagle Rock at dusk and parked in front of the big old two-story house with the neat lawn and flower gardens on the sides. I was wondering if Socorro planted vegetables in the back this year, when I saw Cruz in the living room standing by the front window. He opened the door and stepped out on the porch, wearing a brown sport shirt and old brown slacks and his house slippers. Cruz didn't have to dress up for me, and I was glad to come here and see everyone comfortable, as though I belonged here, and in a way I did. Most bachelor cops have someplace like Cruz's house to go to once in a while. Naturally, you can get a little ding-a-ling if you live on the beat and don't ever spend some time with decent people. So you find a friend or a relative with a family and go there to get your supply of faith replenished,

I called Cruz my old roomie because when we first got out of the police academy twenty years ago, I moved into this big house with him and Socorro. Dolores was a baby, and Esteban a toddler. I took a room upstairs for over a year and helped them with their house payments until we were through paying for our uniforms and guns, and were both financially on our feet. That hadn't been a bad year and I'd never forget Socorro's cooking. She always said she'd rather cook for a man like me who appreciated her talent than a thin little guy like Cruz who never ate much and didn't really appreciate good food. Socorro was a slender girl then, twelve years younger than Cruz, nineteen years old, with two kids already, and the heavy Spanish accent of El Paso which is like that of Mexico itself. They'd had a pretty good life I guess, until Esteban insisted on joining the army and was killed two years ago. They weren't the same after that. They'd never be the same after that.

"How do you feel, *oso?*" said Cruz, as I climbed the concrete stairs to his porch. I grinned because Socorro had first started calling me *"oso"* way back in those days, and even now some of the policemen call me "bear" from Socorro's nickname.

"You hurting, Bumper?" Cruz asked. "I heard those kids gave you some trouble at the demonstration today."

"I'm okay," I answered. "What'd you hear?"

"Just that they pushed you around a little bit. *Hijo la—.* Why does a man your age get involved in that kind of stuff? Why don't you listen to me and just handle your radio calls and let those young coppers handle the militants and do the hotdog police work?"

"I answered a radio call. That's how it started. That's what I get for having that goddamn radio turned on."

"Come on in, you stubborn old bastard," Cruz grinned, holding the wood frame screen door open for me. Where could you see a wood frame screen door these days? It was an old house, but preserved. I loved it here. Cruz and I once sanded down all the woodwork in the living room, even the hardwood floor, and refinished it just as it had been when it was new.

"What're we having?" Cruz asked, brushing back his thick gray-black hair and nodding toward the kitchen.

"Well, let's see," I sniffed. I sniffed again a few times, and then took a great huge whiff. Actually I couldn't tell, because the chile and onion made it hard to differentiate, but I took a guess and pretended I knew.

"*Chile relleno, carnitas* and *cilantro* and onion. And . . . let's see . . . some enchiladas, some guacamole."

"I give up," Cruz shook his head. "The only thing you left out was rice and beans."

"Well hell, Cruz, *arroz y frijoles*, that goes without saying."

"An animal's nose."

"Sukie in the kitchen?"

"Yeah, the kids're in the backyard, some of them."

I went through the big formal dining room to the kitchen and saw Socorro, her back to me, ladling out a huge wooden spoonful of rice into two of the bowls that sat on the drainboard. She was naturally a little the worse for wear after twenty years and nine kids, but her hair was as long and black and shiny rich as ever, and though she was twenty pounds heavier, she still was a strong, lively-looking girl with the whitest teeth I'd ever seen. I snuck up behind her and tickled her ribs.

"Ay!" she said, dropping the spoon. "Bumper!"

I gave her a hug from the back while Cruz chuckled and said, "You didn't surprise him, he smelled from the door and knew just what you fixed for him."

"He's not a man, this one," she smiled, "no man ever had a nose like that."

"Just what I told him," said Cruz.

"Sit down, Bumper," said Socorro, waving to the kitchen table, which, big and old as it was, looked lost in the huge kitchen. I'd seen this kitchen when there wasn't a pathway to walk through, the day after Christmas when all the kids were young and I'd brought them toys. Kids and toys literally covered every foot of linoleum and you couldn't even see the floor then.

"Beer, Bumper?" asked Cruz, and opened two cold ones without me answering. We still liked drinking them out of the bottle, both of us, and I almost finished mine without taking it away from my mouth. And Cruz, knowing my M.O. so well, uncapped another one.

"Cruz told me the news, Bumper. I was thrilled to hear it," said Socorro, slicing an onion, her eyes glistening from the fumes.

"About you retiring right away and going with Cassie when she leaves," said Cruz.

"That's good, Bumper," said Socorro. "There's no sense hanging around after Cassie leaves. I was worried about that."

"Sukie was afraid your *puta* would seduce you away from Cassie if she was up in San Francisco and you were down here."

"*Puta?*"

"The beat," said Cruz taking a gulp of the beer. "Socorro always calls it Bumper's *puta*."

"*Cuidao!*" said Socorro to Cruz. "The children are right outside the window." I could hear them laughing, and Nacho yelled something then, and the girls squealed.

"Since you're leaving, we can talk about her can't we, Bumper?" Cruz laughed. "That beat is a *puta* who seduced you all these years."

Then for the first time I noticed from his grin and his voice that Cruz had had a few before I got there. I looked at Socorro who nodded and said, "Yes, the old *borracho*'s been drinking since he got home from work. Wants to celebrate Bumper's last dinner as a bachelor, he says."

"Don't be too rough on him," I grinned. "He doesn't get drunk very often."

"Who's drunk?" said Cruz, indignantly.

"You're on your way, *pendejo*," said Socorro, and Cruz mumbled in Spanish, and I laughed and finished my beer.

"If it hadn't been for that *puta*, Bumper would've been a captain by now."

"Oh sure," I said, going to the refrigerator and drawing two more beers for Cruz and me. "Want one, Sukie?"

"No thanks," said Socorro, and Cruz burped a couple times.

"Think I'll go outside and see the kids," I said, and then I remembered the presents in the trunk of my car that I bought Monday after Cruz invited me to dinner.

"Hey, you roughnecks," I said when I stepped out, and Nacho yelled, "Buuuum-per," and swung toward me from a rope looped over the limb of a big oak that covered most of the yard.

"You're getting about big enough to eat hay and pull a wagon, Nacho," I said. Then four of them ran toward me chattering about something, their eyes all sparkling because they knew damn well I'd never come for dinner without bringing them something.

"Where's Dolores?" I asked. She was my favorite now, the oldest after Esteban, and was a picture of what her mother had been. She was a college junior majoring in physics and engaged to a classmate of hers.

"Dolores is out with Gordon, where else?" said Ralph, a chubby ten-year-old, the baby of the family who was a terror, always raising some kind of hell and keeping everyone in an uproar.

"Where's Alice?"

"Over next door playing," said Ralph again, and the four of them, Nacho, Ralph, María, and Marta were all about to bust, and I was enjoying it even though it was a shame to make them go through this.

"Nacho," I said nonchalantly, "would you please take my car keys and get some things out of the trunk?"

"I'll help," shrieked Marta.

"I will," said María, jumping up and down, a little eleven-year-old dream in a pink dress and pink socks and black patent leather shoes. She was the prettiest and would be heartbreakingly beautiful someday.

"I'll go alone," said Nacho. "I don't need no help."

"The hell you will," said Ralph.

"You watch your language, Rafael," said María, and I had to turn around to keep from busting up at the way Ralph stuck his chubby little fanny out at her.

"Mama," said María. "Ralph did something dirty!"

"Snitch," said Ralph, running to the car with Nacho.

I strolled back into the kitchen still laughing, and Cruz and Socorro both were smiling at me because they knew how much I got a bang out of their kids.

"Take Bumper in the living room, Cruz," said Socorro. "Dinner won't be ready for twenty minutes."

"Come on, Bumper," said Cruz, taking four cold ones out of the refrigerator, and a beer opener. "I don't know why Mexican women get to be tyrants in their old age. They're so nice and obedient when they're young."

"Old age. Huh! Listen to the *viejo*, Bumper," she said, waving a wooden spoon in his direction, as we went in the living room and I flopped in Cruz's favorite chair because he insisted. He pushed the ottoman over and made me put my feet up.

"Damn, Cruz."

"Got to give you extra special treatment tonight, Bumper," he said, opening another beer for me. "You look dog tired, and this may be the last we have you for a long time."

"I'll only be living one hour away by air. You think Cassie and me aren't gonna come to L.A. once in a while? And you think you and Socorro and the kids aren't gonna come see us up there?"

"The whole platoon of us?" he laughed.

"We're gonna see each other plenty, that's for sure," I said, and fought against the down feeling that I was getting because I realized we probably would *not* be seeing each other very often at all.

"Yeah, Bumper," said Cruz, sitting across from me in the other old chair, almost as worn and comfortable as this one. "I was afraid that jealous bitch would never let you go."

"You mean my beat?"

"Right." He took several big gulps on the beer and I thought about how I was going to miss him.

"How come all the philosophizing tonight? Calling my beat a whore and all that?"

"I'm waxing poetic tonight."

"You also been tipping more than a little *cerveza*."

Cruz winked and peeked toward the kitchen where we could hear Socorro banging around. He went to an old mahogany hutch that was just inside the dining room and took a half-empty bottle of mescal out of the bottom cabinet.

"That one have a worm in it?"

"If it did I drank it," he whispered. "Don't want Sukie to see me drinking it. I still have a little trouble with my liver and I'm not supposed to."

"Is that the stuff you bought in San Luis? That time on your vacation?"

"That's it, the end of it."

"You won't need any liver you drink that stuff."

"It's good, Bumper. Here, try a throatful or two."

"Better with salt and lemon."

"Pour it down. You're the big *macho*, damn it. Drink like one."

I took three fiery gulps and a few seconds after they hit bottom I regretted it, and had to drain my bottle of beer while Cruz chuckled and sipped slowly for his turn.

"Damn," I wheezed and then the fire fanned out and my guts uncoiled and I felt good. Then in a few minutes I felt better. That was the medicine my body needed.

"They don't always have salt and lemon lying around down in Mexico," said Cruz handing me back the mescal. "Real Mexicans just mix it with saliva."

"No wonder they're such tough little bastards," I wheezed, taking another gulp, but only one this time, and handing it back.

"How do you feel now, *'mano*?" Cruz giggled, and it

made me start laughing, his silly little giggle that always started when he was half swacked.

"I feel about half as good as you," I said, and splashed some more beer into the burning pit that was my stomach. But it was a different fire entirely than the one made by the stomach acid, this was a friendly fire, and after it smoldered it felt great.

"Are you hungry?" asked Cruz.

"Ain't I always?"

"You are," he said, "you're hungry for almost everything. Always. I've often wished I was more like you."

"Like me?"

"Always feasting, on *everything*. Too bad it can't go on forever. But it can't. I'm damn glad you're getting out now."

"You're drunk."

"I am. But I know what I'm talking about, *'mano*. Cassie was sent to you. I prayed for that." Then Cruz reached in his pocket for the little leather pouch. In it was the string of black carved wooden beads he carried for luck. He squeezed the soft leather and put it away.

"Did those beads really come from Jerusalem?"

"They did, that's no baloney. I got them from a missionary priest for placing first in my school in El Paso. 'First prize in spelling to Cruz Guadalupe Segovia,' the priest said, as he stood in front of the whole school, and I died of happiness that day. I was thirteen, just barely. He got the beads in the Holy Land and they were blessed by Pius XI."

"How many kids did you beat out for the prize?"

"About six entered the contest. There were only seventy-five in the school altogether. I don't think the other five contestants spoke any English. They thought the contest would be in Spanish but it wasn't, so I won."

We both laughed at that. "I never won a thing, Cruz. You're way ahead of me." It was amazing to think of a real man like Cruz carrying those wooden beads. In this day and age!

Then the front door banged open and the living room was filled with seven yelling kids, only Dolores being absent that night, and Cruz shook his head and sat back quietly drinking his beer and Socorro came into the living room and tried to give me hell for buying all the presents, but you couldn't hear yourself over the noisy kids.

"Are these real big-league cleats?" asked Nacho as I adjusted the batting helmet for him and fixed the chin strap which I knew he'd throw away as soon as the other kids told him big leaguers don't wear chin straps.

"Look! Hot pants!" María squealed, holding them up against her adolescent body. They were sporty, blue denim with a bib, and patch pockets.

"Hot pants?" Cruz said. "Oh, no!"

"They even wear them to school, Papa. They do. Ask Bumper!"

"Ask Bumper," Cruz grumbled and drank some more beer.

The big kids were there then too, Linda, George, and Alice, all high school teenagers, and naturally I bought clothes for them. I got George a box of mod-colored long-sleeved shirts and from the look in his eyes I guess I couldn't have picked anything better.

After all the kids thanked me a dozen times, Socorro ordered them to put everything away and called us to dinner. We sat close together on different kinds of chairs at the huge rectangular oak table that weighed a ton. I know because I helped Cruz carry it in here twelve years ago when there was no telling how many kids were going to be sitting around it.

The youngest always said the prayers aloud. They crossed themselves and Ralph said grace, and they crossed themselves again and I was drooling because the *chiles rellenos* were on a huge platter right in front of me. The big chiles were stuffed with cheese and fried in a light fluffy batter, and before I could help myself, Alice was serving me and my plate was filled before any one of those kids took a thing for themselves. Their mother and father never said anything to them, they just did things like that.

"You *do* have *cilantro*," I said, salivating with a vengeance now. I knew I smelled that wonderful spice.

Marta, using her fingers, sprinkled a little extra *cilantro* over my *carnitas* when I said that, and I bit into a soft, handmade, flour tortilla crammed with *carnitas* and Socorro's own *chile* sauce.

"Well, Bumper?" said Cruz after I'd finished half a plateful which took about thirty-five seconds.

I moaned and rolled my eyeballs and everybody laughed because they knew that look so well.

"You see, Marta," said Socorro. "You wouldn't hate to cook so much if you could cook for somebody like Bumper who appreciates your work."

I grinned with a hog happy look, washing down some *chile relleno* and enchilada with three big swigs of cold beer. "Your mother is an artist!"

I finished three helpings of *carnitas*, the tender little chunks of pork which I covered with Socorro's *chile* and *cilantro* and onion. Then, after everyone was finished and there were nine pairs of brown eyes looking at me in wonder, I heaped the last three *chiles rellenos* on my plate and rolled one up with the last flour tortilla and the last few bites of *carnitas* left in the bowl, and nine pairs of brown eyes got wider and rounder.

"*Por Dios,* I thought I made enough for twenty," said Socorro.

"You did, you did, Sukie," I said, enjoying being the whole show now, and finishing it in three big bites. "I'm just extra hungry tonight, and you made it extra good, and there's no sense leaving leftovers around to spoil." With that I ate half a *chile relleno* and swallowed some beer and looked around at all the eyes, and Nacho burped and groaned. We all busted up, Ralph especially, who fell off his chair onto the floor holding his stomach and laughing so hard I was afraid he'd get sick. It was a hell of a thing when you think of it, entertaining people by being a damn glutton, just to get attention.

After dinner we cleared the table and I got roped into a game of Scrabble with Alice and Marta and Nacho with the others kibitzing, and all the time I was swilling cold beer with an occasional shot of mescal that Cruz brought out in the open now. By nine o'clock when the kids had to go to bed I was pretty well lubricated.

They all kissed me good night except George and Nacho, who shook hands, and there were no arguments about going to bed, and fifteen minutes later it was still and quiet upstairs. I'd never seen Cruz or Socorro spank any of them. Of course the older ones spanked hell out of the younger ones, I'd seen that often enough. After all, everyone in this world needs a thumping once in a while.

We took the leaf out of the table and replaced the lace tablecloth and the three of us went into the living room. Cruz was pretty well bombed out, and after Socorro complained, he decided not to have another beer. I had a cold one in my right hand, and the last of the mescal in my left.

Cruz sat next to Socorro on the couch and he rubbed his face which was probably numb as hell. He gave her a kiss on the neck.

"Get out of here," she grumbled. "You smell like a stinking wino."

"How can I smell like a wino. I haven't had any wine," said Cruz.

"Remember how we used to sit like this after dinner back in the old days," I said, realizing how much the mescal affected me, because they were both starting to look a little fuzzy.

"Remember how little and skinny Sukie was," said Cruz, poking her arm.

"I'm going to let you have it in a minute," said Socorro, raising her hand which was a raw, worn-out-looking hand for a girl her age. She wasn't quite forty years old.

"Sukie was the prettiest girl I'd ever seen," I said.

"I guess she was," said Cruz with a silly grin.

"And still is," I added. "And Cruz was the handsomest guy I ever saw outside of Tyrone Power or maybe Clark Gable."

"You really think Tyrone Power was better looking?" said Cruz, grinning again as Socorro shook her head, and to me he honestly didn't look a bit different now than he ever had, except for the gray hair. Damn him for staying young, I thought.

"Speaking of pretty girls," said Socorro, "let's hear about your new plans with Cassie."

"Well, like I told you, she was gonna go up north to an apartment and get squared away at school. Then after the end of May when Cruz and me have our twenty years, she'd fly back here and we'd get married. Now I've decided to cut it short. I'll work tomorrow and the next day and run my vacation days and days off together to the end of the month when I officially retire. That way I can leave with Cassie, probably Sunday morning or Monday and we'll swing through Las Vegas and get married on the way."

"Oh, Bumper, we wanted to be with you when you get married," said Socorro, looking disappointed.

"What the hell, at our age getting married ain't no big thing," I said.

"We love her, Bumper," said Socorro. "You're lucky, very lucky. She'll be perfect for you."

"What a looker." Cruz winked and tried to whistle, but he was too drunk.

Socorro shook her head and said, *"sinvergüenza,"* and we both laughed at him.

"What're you going to do Friday?" asked Socorro. "Just go into rollcall and stand up and say you're retiring and this is your last day?"

"Nope, I'm just gonna fade away. I'm not telling a soul and I hope you haven't said anything to anyone, Cruz."

"Nothing," said Cruz, and he burped.

"I'm just cutting out like for my regular two days off, then I'm sending a registered letter to Personnel Division and one to the captain. I'll just sign all my retirement papers and mail them in. I can give my badge and I.D. card to Cruz before I leave and have him turn them in for me so I won't have to go back at all."

"You'll have to come back to L.A. for your retirement party," said Cruz. "We're sure as hell going to want to throw a retirement party for you."

"Thanks, Cruz, but I never liked retirement parties anyway. In fact I think they're miserable. I appreciate the thought but no party for me."

"Just think," said Socorro. "To be starting a new life! I wish Cruz could leave the job too."

"You said it," said Cruz, his eyes glassy though he sat up straight. "But with all our kids, I'm a thirty-year man. Thirty years, that's a lifetime. I'll be an old man when I pull the pin."

"Yeah, I guess I'm lucky," I said. "Remember when we were going through the academy, Cruz? We thought we were old men then, running with all those kids twenty-one and twenty-two years old. Here you were thirty-one, the oldest guy in the class, and I was close behind you. Remember Mendez always called us *elefante y ratoncito*?"

"The elephant and the mouse," Cruz giggled.

"The two old men of the class. Thirty years old and I thought I knew something then. Hell, you're still a baby at that age. We were both babies."

"We were babies, *'mano*," said Cruz. "But only because we hadn't been out there yet." Cruz waved his hand toward the streets. "You grow up fast out there and learn too much. It's no damn good for a man to learn as much as you learn out there. It ruins the way you think about things, and the way you feel. There're certain things you should believe and if you stay out there for twenty years you can't believe them anymore. That's not good."

"You still believe them, don't you, Cruz?" I asked, and Socorro looked at us like we were two raving drunks, which we probably were, but we understood, Cruz and me.

"I still believe them, Bumper, because I want to. And I have Sukie and the kids. I can come home, and then the other isn't real. You've had no one to go to. Thank God for Cassie."

"I've got to go fix school lunches. Excuse me, Bumper," said Socorro, and she gave us that shake of the head which meant, it's time to leave the drunken cops to their talk. But Cruz hardly ever got drunk, and she didn't really begrudge him, even though he had trouble with his liver.

"I never could tell you how glad we were when you first brought Cassie here for dinner, Bumper. Socorro and me, we stayed awake in bed that night and talked about it and how God must've sent her, even though you don't believe in God."

"I believe in the *gods,* you know that," I grinned, gulping the beer after I took the last sip of the mescal.

"There's only one God, goddamnit," said Cruz.

"Even your God has three faces, goddamnit," I said, and gave him a glance over the top of my beer bottle, making him laugh,

"Bumper, I'm trying to talk to you seriously." And his eyes turned down at the corners like always. I couldn't woof him anymore when his eyes did that.

"Okay."

"Cassie's the answer to a prayer."

"Why did you waste all your prayers on me?"

"Why do you think, *pendejo*? You're my brother, *mi hermano*."

That made me put the beer down, and I straightened up and looked at his big eyes. Cruz was struggling with the fog of the mescal and beer because he wanted to tell me something. I wondered how in hell he had ever made the Department physical. He was barely five-eight in his bare feet, and he was so damn skinny. He'd never gained a pound, but outside of Esteban, he had the finest-looking face you would ever see.

"I didn't know you thought that much about Cassie and me."

"Of course I did. After all, I prayed her here for you. Don't you see what you were heading for? You're fifty years old, Bumper. You and some of the other old beat cops've been the *machos* of the streets all these years, but Lord, I could just see you duking it out with some young stud or chasing somebody out there and all of a sudden just lying down on that street to die. You realize how many of our classmates had heart attacks already?"

"Part of being a policeman," I shrugged.

"Not to mention some asshole blowing you up," said Cruz. "You remember Driscoll? He had a heart attack just last month and he's not nearly as fat as you, and a few years younger, and I'll bet he never does anything harder than lift a pencil. Like you today, all alone, facing a mob, like a rookie! What the hell, Bumper, you think I want to be a pallbearer for a guy two hundred and eighty pounds?"

"Two seventy-five."

"When Cassie came, I said, 'Thank God, now Bumper's got a chance.' I worried though. I knew you were smart enough to see how much woman you had, but I was afraid that *puta* had too strong a grip on you."

"Was it *you* that kept getting me assigned to the north end districts all the time? Lieutenant Hilliard kept telling me it was a mistake every time I bitched about it."

"Yeah, I did it. I tried to get you away from your beat, but I gave up. You just kept coming back down anyway and that meant nobody was patrolling the north end, so I didn't accomplish anything. I can guess what it was to you, being *el campeón* out there, having people look at you the way they do on your beat."

"Yeah, well it isn't so much," I said, nervously fidgeting with the empty bottle.

"You know what happens to old cops who stay around the streets too long."

"What?" I said, and the enchilada caught me and bit into the inside of my gut.

"They get too old to do police work and they become *characters*. That's what I'd hate to see. You just becoming an old character, and maybe getting yourself hurt bad out there before you realize you're too old. Just too old."

"I'm not that old yet. Damn it, Cruz!"

"No, not for civilian life. You have lots of good years ahead of you. But for a warrior, it's time to quit, *'mano*. I was worried about her going up there and you coming along in a few weeks. I was afraid the *puta* would get you alone when Cassie wasn't there. I'm so damn glad you're leaving with Cassie."

"So am I, Cruz," I said, lowering my voice like I was afraid to let myself hear it. "You're right. I've half thought of these things. You're right. I think I'd blow my brains out if I ever got as lonely as some I've seen, like some of those people on my beat, homeless wandering people, that don't belong anywhere. . . ."

"That's it, Bumper. There's no place for a man alone, not really. You can get along without love when you're young and strong. Some guys can, guys like you. Me, I never could. And nobody can get along without it when he gets old. You shouldn't be afraid to love, '*mano*.'"

"Am I, Cruz?" I asked, chewing two tablets because a mailed fist was beating on my guts from the inside. "Is that why I feel so unsure of myself now that I'm leaving? Is that it?"

I could hear Socorro humming as she made lunches for the entire tribe. She would write each one's name on his lunch sack and put it in the refrigerator.

"Remember when we were together in the old days? You and me and Socorro and the two kids? And how you hardly ever spoke about your previous life even when you were drunk? You only said a little about your brother Clem who was dead, and your wife who'd left you. But you really told us more, much more about your brother. Sometimes you called him in your sleep. But mostly you called someone else."

I was rocking back now, holding my guts which were throbbing, and all the tablets in my pocket wouldn't help.

"You never told us about your boy. I always felt bad that you never told *me* about him, because of how close we are. You only told me about him in your sleep."

"What did I say?"

"You'd call 'Billy,' and you'd say things to him. Sometimes you'd cry, and I'd have to go in and pick up your covers and pillow from the floor and cover you up because you'd throw them clear off the bed."

"I never dreamed about him, never!"

"How else would I know, *'mano*?" he said softly. "We used to talk a lot about it, Socorro and me, and we used to worry about a man who'd loved a brother and a son like you had. We wondered if you'd be afraid to love again. It happens. But when you get old, you've *got* to. You've got to."

"But you're safe if you *don't*, Cruz!" I said, flinching from the pain. Cruz was looking at the floor, not used to talking to me like this, and he didn't notice my agony.

"You're safe, Bumper, in one way. But in the way that counts, you're in danger. Your soul is in danger if you don't love."

"Did you believe that when Esteban was killed? Did you?"

Cruz looked up at me, and his eyes got even softer than normal and turned way down at the corners because he was being most serious. His heavy lashes blinked twice and he sighed, "Yes. Even after Esteban, and even though he was the oldest and you always feel a little something extra for the firstborn. Even after Esteban was killed I felt this to be the truth. After the grief, I knew it was God's truth. I believed it, even then."

"I think I'll get a cup of coffee. I have a stomachache. Maybe something warm. . . ."

Cruz smiled, and leaned back in his chair. Socorro was finishing the last of the lunches and I chatted with her while we warmed up the coffee. The stomachache started to fade a little.

I drank the coffee and thought about what Cruz said

which made sense, and yet, every time you get tied up to people something happens and that cord is cut, and I mean really cut with a bloody sword.

"Shall we go in and see how the old boy's doing?"

"Oh sure, Sukie," I said, putting my arm around her shoulder. Cruz was stretched out on the couch snoring.

"That's his drinking sleep. We'll never wake him up," she said. "Maybe I just better get his pillow and a blanket."

"He shouldn't be sleeping on the couch," I said. "It's drafty in this big living room." I went over to him and knelt down.

"What're you going to do?"

"Put him to bed," I said, picking him up in my arms.

"Bumper, you'll rupture yourself."

"He's light as a baby," I said, and he *was* surprisingly light. "Why the hell don't you make him eat more?" I said, following Socorro up the stairs.

"You know he doesn't like to eat. Let me help you, Bumper."

"Just lead the way, Mama. I can handle him just fine."

When we got in their bedroom I wasn't even breathing hard and I laid him on the bed, on the sheets. She had already pulled back the covers. Cruz was rattling and wheezing now and we both laughed.

"He snores awful," she said as I looked at the little squirt.

"He's the only *real* friend I ever made in twenty years. I know millions of people and I see them and eat with them and I'll miss things about all of them, but it won't be like something inside is gone, like with Cruz."

"Now you'll have Cassie. You'll be ten times closer

with her." She held my hand then. Both her hands were tough and hard.

"You sound like your old man."

"We talk about you a lot."

"Good night," I said, kissing her on the cheek. "Cassie and me are coming by before we leave to say good-bye to all of you."

"Good night, Bumper."

"Good night, old shoe," I said to Cruz in a loud voice and he snorted and blew and I chuckled and descended the stairs. I let myself out after turning out the hall light and locking the door.

When I went to bed that night I started getting scared and didn't know why. I wished Cassie was with me. After I went to sleep I slept very well and didn't dream.

THURSDAY, THE SECOND DAY

NINE

THE NEXT MORNING I worked on my badge for five minutes, and my boondockers were glistening. I was kind of disappointed when Lieutenant Hilliard didn't have an inspection, I was looking so good. Cruz looked awful. He sat at the front table with Lieutenant Hilliard and did a bad job of reading off the crimes. Once or twice he looked at me and rolled his eyes which were really sad this morning because he was so hung over. After rollcall I got a chance to talk to him for a minute.

"You look a little *crudo*," I said, trying not to smile.

"What a bastard you are," he moaned.

"It wasn't the mescal. I think you swallowed the worm."

"A complete bastard."

"Can you meet me at noon? I wanna buy you lunch."

"Don't even talk about it," he groaned, and I had to laugh.

"Okay, but save me your lunch hour tomorrow. And pick out the best, most expensive place in town. Someplace that doesn't bounce for bluecoats. That's where we're going for my last meal as a cop."

"You're actually going to *pay* for a meal on duty?"

"It'll be a first," I grinned, and he smiled but he acted like it hurt to grin.

"*Ahí te haucho,*" I said, heading for the car.

"Don't forget you have court this afternoon, '*mano,*" he said, always nagging me.

Before getting in my black-and-white I looked it over. It's always good to pull out the back seat before you leave, in case some innocent rookie on the nightwatch let one of his sneaky prisoners stash his gun down there, or a condom full of heroin, or a goddamn hand grenade. It takes so long to make a policeman out of some of these kids, nothing would surprise me. But then I reminded myself what it was like to be twenty-two. They're right in the middle of growing up, these babies, and it's awful tough growing up in that bluecoat as twenty-two-year-old Establishment symbols. Still, it chills my nuts the way they stumble around like civilians for five years or so, and let people flimflam them. Someday, I thought, I'll probably find a dead midget jammed down there behind the friggin' seat.

As soon as I hit the bricks and started cruising I began thinking about the case I had this afternoon. It was a preliminary hearing on a guy named Landry and the dicks had filed on him for being an ex-con with a gun, and also filed one count of possession of marijuana. I didn't figure to have any problems with the case. I'd busted him in January after I'd gotten information on this gunsel from a snitch named Knobby Booker, who worked for me from time to time, and I went to a hotel room on East Sixth Street on some phony pretext I couldn't completely remember until I reread the arrest report. I busted Landry in his room while he was taking a nap in the middle of the afternoon. He had about two lids of pot in a sandwich bag in a drawer by his bed to give him guts when he pulled a robbery, and a fully loaded U.S. Army forty-five automatic under his mattress. He damned near went for it when I came though the door, and I almost blew him up when he started for it. In fact, it was a Mexican standoff for a few seconds, him with his hand an inch or so under the mattress, and me crouching and coming to the bed, my six-inch Smith aimed at his upper lip, and warning about what I was going to do if he didn't pull his hand out very very slow, and he did.

Landry had gotten out on five thousand dollars' bail which some old broad put up for him. He'd been a half-assed bit actor on TV and movies a few years back, and was somewhat of a gigolo with old women. He jumped bail and was rearrested in Denver and extradited, and the arrest was now four months old. I didn't remember all the details, but of course I would read the arrest report and be up on it before I testified. The main thing of course was to hold him to answer at the prelim without revealing my informant Knobby Booker, or without even letting anyone know I *had* an informant. It wasn't too hard if you knew how.

It was getting hot and smoggy and I was already starting to sweat in the armpits. I glanced over at an old billboard on Olive Street which said, "Don't start a boy on a life of crime by leaving your keys in the car," and I snorted and farted a couple times in disgust. It's the goddamn do-gooder P.R. men, who dream up slogans like that to make everybody but the criminals feel guilty, who'll drive all real cops out of this business one of these days.

As I pulled to the curb opposite the Grand Central Market, a wino staggering down Broadway sucking on a short dog saw me, spun around, fell on his ass, dropped his bottle, and got up as though nothing happened. He started walking away from the short dog, which was rolling around on the sidewalk spilling sweet lucy all over the pavement.

"Pick up the dog, you jerk," I called to him. "I ain't gonna bust you."

"Thanks, Bumper," he said sheepishly and picked up the bottle. He waved, and hustled back down Broadway, a greasy black coat flapping around his skinny hips.

I tried to remember where I knew him from. Of course I knew him from the beat, but he wasn't just a wino face. There was something else. Then I saw through the gauntness and grime and recognized him and smiled because these days it always felt good to remember and prove to yourself that your memory is as sharp as ever.

They called him Beans. The real name I couldn't recall even though I'd had it printed up on a fancy certificate. He almost caused me to slug another policeman about ten years ago and I'd never come close to doing that before or since.

The policeman was Herb Slovin and he finally got his ass canned. Herb was fired for capping for a bail bondsman and had a nice thing going until they caught him. He was working vice and was telling everybody he busted to patronize Laswell Brothers Bail Bonds, and Slim Laswell was kicking back a few bucks to Herb for each one he sent. That's considered to be as bad as stealing, and the Department bounced his ass in a hurry after he was caught. He would've gone behind something else though if it hadn't been that. He was a hulking, cruel bastard and so horny he'd mount a cage if he thought there was a canary in there. I figured sooner or later he'd fall for broads or brutality.

It was Beans that almost caused me and Herb to tangle. Herb hated the drunk wagon. "Niggers and white garbage," he'd repeat over and over when something made him mad which was most of the time. And he called the wagon job "the N.H.I. detail." When you asked him what that stood for he'd say "No Humans Involved," and then he let out with that donkey bray of his. We were working the wagon one night and got a call on Beans because he was spread-eagled prone across San Pedro Street blocking two lanes of traffic, out cold. He'd puked and wet all over himself and didn't even wake up when we dragged him to the wagon and flipped him in on the floor. There was no problem. We both wore gloves like most wagon cops, and there were only two other winos inside. About ten minutes later when we were on East Sixth Street, we heard a ruckus in the back and had to stop the wagon and go back there and keep the other two winos from kicking hell out of Beans who woke up and was fighting mad for maybe the first time in his life. I'd busted him ten or twenty times for drunk and never had any trouble with him. You seldom have to hassle a stone wino like Beans.

They quieted down as soon as Herb opened the back door and threatened to tear their heads off, and I was just getting back in the wagon when Beans, sitting by the door, said, "Fuck you, you skin-headed jackass!" I cracked up laughing because Herb was bald, and with his long face and big yellow teeth and the way he brayed when he laughed, he *did* look like a skin-headed jackass.

Herb though, growled something, and snatched Beans right off the bench, out of the wagon into the street, and started belting him back and forth across the face with his big gloved hand. I realized from the thuds that they were sap gloves and Beans's face was already busted open and bleeding before I could pull Herb away and push him back, causing him to fall on his ass.

"You son of a bitch," he said, looking at me with a combination of surprise and bloodred anger. He almost said it like a question he was so surprised.

"He's a wino, man," I answered, and that should've been enough for any cop, especially a veteran like Herb who had twelve years on the job at that time and knew that you don't beat up defenseless winos no matter what kind of trouble they give you. That was one of the first things we learned in the old days from the beat cops who broke us in. When a man takes a swing at you or actually hits you, you have the right to kick ass, that goes without saying. It doesn't have to be tit for tat, and if some asshole gives you tit, you tat his goddamn teeth down his throat. That way, you'll save some other cop from being slugged by the same pukepot if he learns his lesson from you.

But every real cop also knows you don't beat up winos. Even if they swing at you or actually hit you. Chances are it'll be a puny little swing and you can just handcuff him and throw him in jail. Cops know very well how many fellow policemen develop drinking problems themselves, and there's always the thought in the back of your mind that there on the sidewalk, but for the gods, sleeps old Bumper Morgan.

Anyway, Herb had violated a cop's code by beating up the wino and he knew it, which probably saved us a hell of a good go right there on East Sixth Street. And I'm not at all sure it might not've ended by me getting my chubby face changed around by those sap gloves because Herb was an ex-wrestler and a very tough bastard.

"Don't you ever try that again," he said to me, as we put Beans back inside and locked the door.

"I won't, if you never beat up a drunk when you're working with me," I answered casually, but I was tense and coiled, ready to go, even thinking about unsnapping my holster because Herb looked damned dangerous at that moment, and you never know when an armed man might do something crazy. He was one of those creeps that carried an untraceable hideout gun and bragged how if he ever killed somebody he shouldn't have, he'd plant the gun on the corpse and claim self-defense. The mood was interrupted by a radio call just then, and I rogered it and we finished the night in silence. The next night Herb asked to go back to a radio car because he and I had a "personality conflict."

Shortly after that Herb went to vice and got fired, and I forgot all about that incident until about a year later on Main Street, when I ran into Beans again. That night I got into a battle with two guys I'd watched pull a pigeon drop on some old man. I'd stood inside a pawnshop and watched them through binoculars while they flimflammed him out of five hundred bucks.

They were bad young dudes, and the bigger of the two, a block-faced slob with an eighteen-inch neck was giving me a pretty good go, even though I'd already cracked two of his ribs with my stick. I couldn't finish him because the other one kept jumping on my back, kicking and biting, until I ran backward and slammed into a car and a brick wall, with him between me and the object. I did this twice and he kept hanging on and then somebody from the crowd of about twenty assholes who were gathered around enjoying the fight barreled in and tackled the little one and held him on the sidewalk until I could finish the big one by slapping him across the Adam's apple with the stick.

The other one gave up right then and I cuffed the two of them together and saw that my helper was old Beans the wino, sitting there throwing up, and bleeding from a cut eye where the little dude clawed him. I gave Beans a double sawbuck for that, and took him to a doctor, and I had the Captain's adjutant print up a beautiful certificate commending Beans for his good citizenship. Of course, I lied and said Beans was some respectable businessman who saw the fight and came to my aid. I couldn't tell them he was a down-and-out wino or they might not have done it. It was nicely framed and had Beans's real name on it, which I couldn't for the life of me remember now. I presented it to him the next time I found him bombed on East Sixth Street and he really seemed to like it.

As I remembered all this, I felt like calling him back and asking him if he still had it, but I figured he probably sold the frame for enough to buy a short dog, and used the certificate to plug the holes in his shoe. It's always best not to ask too many questions of people or to get to know them too well. You save yourself disappointment that way. Anyway, Beans was half a block away now, staggering down the street cradling the wine bottle under his greasy coat.

I took down my sunglasses which I keep stashed behind the visor in my car and settled down to cruise and watch the streets and relax even though I was too restless to really relax. I decided not to wait, but to cruise over to the school and see Cassie, who would be coming in early like she always did on Thursdays. She'd feel like I did, like everything she did these last days at school would be for the last time. But at least she knew she'd be doing similar things in another school.

I parked out front and got a few raspberries from students for parking my black-and-white in the no parking zone, but I'd be damned if I'd walk clear from the faculty lot. Cassie wasn't in her office when I got there, but it was unlocked so I sat at her desk and waited.

The desk was exactly like the woman who manned it: smart and tidy, interesting and feminine. She had an odd-shaped ceramic ashtray on one side of the desk which she'd picked up in some junk store in west L.A. There was a small, delicately painted oriental vase that held a bunch of dying violets which Cassie would replace first thing after she arrived. Under the plastic cover on the desk blotter Cassie had a screwy selection of pictures of people she admired, mostly French poets. Cassie was long on poetry and tried to get me going on haiku for a while, but I finally convinced her I don't have the right kind of imagination for poetry. My reading is limited to history and to new ways of doing police work. I liked one poem Cassie showed me about wooly lambs and shepherds and wild killer dogs. I understood that one all right.

The door opened and Cassie and another teacher, a curvy little chicken in a hot pink mini, came giggling through the door.

"Oh!" said the young broad. "Who are you?" the blue

uniform shocked her. I was sitting back in Cassie's comfortable leather-padded desk chair.

"I am the Pretty Good Shepherd," I said, puffing on my cigar and smiling at Cassie.

"Whatever that means," said Cassie, shaking her head, putting down a load of books, and kissing me on the cheek much to the surprise of her friend.

"You must be Cassie's fiancé," the friend laughed as it suddenly hit her. "I'm Maggie Carson."

"Pleased to meet you, Mágie. I'm Bumper Morgan," I said, always happy to meet a woman, especially a young one, who shakes hands, and with a firm friendly grip.

"I've heard about Cassie's policeman friend, but it surprised me, seeing that uniform so suddenly."

"We've all got our skeletons rattling, Maggie," I said. "Tell me, what've you done that makes you jump at the sight of the fuzz?"

"All right, Bumper," Cassie smiled. I was standing now, and she had me by the arm.

"I'll leave you two alone," said Maggie, with a sly wink, just as she'd seen and heard it in a thousand corny love movies.

"Nice kid," I said, after Maggie closed the door and I kissed Cassie four or five times.

"I missed you last night," said Cassie, standing there pressed up against me, smelling good and looking good in her yellow sleeveless dress. Her arms were red tan, her hair down, touching her shoulders.

"Your dinner date tonight still on?"

"Afraid so," she murmured.

"After tomorrow we'll have all the time we want together."

"Think we'll ever have all the time we want?"

"You'll get sick of seeing me hanging around the pad."

"Never happen. Besides, you'll be busy launching that new career."

"I'm more worried about the other career."

"Which one?"

"Being the kind of husband you think I'll be. I wonder if I'll be really good for you."

"Bumper!" she said, stepping back and looking to see if I meant it, and I tried a lopsided grin.

I kissed her then, as tenderly as I could, and held her. "I didn't mean it the way it came out."

"I know. I'm just a very insecure old dame."

I could've kicked my ass for blurting out something that I knew would hurt her. It was like I wanted to hurt her a little for being the best thing that ever happened, for saving me from becoming a pitiful old man trying to do a young man's work, and doing brass balls police work was definitely a young man's work. I never could've been an inside man. Never a jailer, or a desk officer, or a supply man handing out weapons to guys doing the real police work. Cassie was saving me from that nightmare. I was getting out while I was still a man alive, with lots of good years ahead. And with somebody to care about. I got a vicious gas pain just then, and I wished I wasn't standing there with Cassie so I could pop a bubble breaker.

"I guess *I'm* the silly one," said Cassie.

"If you only knew how bad I want out, Cassie, you'd stop worrying." I patted her back like I was burping her when really I was wishing I could burp myself. I could feel the bubble getting bigger and floating up in my stomach.

"All right, Bumper Morgan," she said. "Now what day are we actually leaving Los Angeles? I mean actually? As man and wife. We've got a million things to do."

"Wait till tomorrow night, me proud beauty," I answered. "Tomorrow night when we have some time to talk and to celebrate. Tomorrow night we make all the plans while having a wonderful dinner somewhere."

"In my apartment."

"Okay."

"With some wonderful champagne."

"I'll supply it."

"Police discount?"

"Naturally. My last one."

"And we celebrate tomorrow being the last day you'll ever have to put on that uniform and risk your neck for a lot of people who don't appreciate it."

"Last day I risk my neck," I nodded. "But I never did risk it for anyone but myself. I had some fun these twenty years, Cassie."

"I know it."

"Even though sometimes it's a rotten job I wouldn't wish on anyone, still, I had good times. And any risks were for Bumper Morgan."

"Yes, love."

"So get your heart-shaped fanny in gear and get your day's work done. I still got almost two days of police work left to do." I stepped away from her and picked up my hat and cigar.

"Coming by this afternoon?"

"Tomorrow."

"Tonight," she said. "I'll get away before midnight. Come to my apartment at midnight."

"Let's get some sleep tonight, baby. Tomorrow's the last day for us both on our jobs. Let's make it a good one."

"I don't like my job as well since you charged into my life, do you know that?"

"Whadda you mean?"

"The academic life. I was one of the students who never left school. I loved waddling around with a gaggle of eggheads, and then *you* had to come along so, so . . . I don't know. And now nothing seems the same."

"Come on down, kid, I like your earthy side better."

"I want you to come tonight," she said, looking me dead in the eye.

"I'd rather be with you tonight than with anyone in the world, you know that, but I really ought to go by Abd's Harem and say good-bye to my friends there. And there're a few other places."

"You mustn't disappoint people," she smiled.

"You should try not to," I said, heating up from the way she looked me in the eye just then.

"It's getting tough to make love to you lately."

"A couple more days."

"See you tomorrow," she sighed. "I think I'll jump you here in my office when I get my hands on you."

"On duty?" I frowned, and put my hat on, tipping it at a jaunty angle because, let's face it, you feel pretty good when a woman like Cassie's quivering to get you in bed.

"Good-bye, Bumper," she smiled sadly.

"Later, kid. See you later."

As soon as I cleared after leaving Cassie I got a radio call.

"One-X-L-Forty-five, One-X-L-Forty-five," said the female communications operator, "see the man at the hotel, four-twenty-five South Main, about a possible d.b."

"One-X-L-Forty-five, roger," I said, thinking this will be my last dead body call.

An old one-legged guy with all the earmarks of a reformed alky was standing in the doorway of the fleabag hotel.

"You called?" I said, after parking the black-and-white in front and taking the stick from the holder on the door and slipping it through the ring on my belt.

"Yeah. I'm Poochie the elevator boy," said the old man. "I think a guy might be dead upstairs."

"What the hell made you think so?" I said sarcastically, as we started up the stairs and I smelled the d.b. from here. The floorboards were torn up and I could see the ground underneath.

The old guy hopped up the stairs pretty quick on his one crutch without ever stopping to rest. There were about twenty steps up to the second floor where the smell could drop you and would, except that most of the tenants were bums and winos whose senses, all of them, had been killed or numbed. I almost expected the second story to have a dirt floor, the place was so crummy.

"I ain't seen this guy in number two-twelve for oh, maybe a week," said Poochie, who had a face like an ax, with a toothless puckered mouth.

"Can't you smell him?"

"No," he said, looking at me with surprise. "Can you?"

"Never mind," I said, turning right in the hallway. "Don't bother telling me where two-twelve is, I could find it with my eyes closed. Get me some coffee."

"Cream and sugar?"

"No, I mean dry coffee, right out of the can. And a frying pan."

"Okay," he said, without asking dumb questions, conditioned by fifty years of being bossed around by cops. I held a handkerchief over my nose, and opened a window in the hallway which led out on the fire escape in the alley. I stuck my head out but it didn't help, I could still smell him.

After a long two minutes Poochie came hopping back on his crutch with a frying pan and the coffee.

"Hope there's a hot plate in here," I said, suddenly thinking there might not be, though lots of the transient hotels had them, especially in the rooms used by the semipermanent boarders.

"He's got one," nodded Poochie, handing me the passkey. The key turned but the door wouldn't budge.

"I coulda told you it wouldn't open. That's why I called you. Scared old man, Herky is. He keeps a bolt on the door whenever he's inside. I already tried to get in."

"Move back."

"Going to break it?"

"Got any other suggestions?" I said, the handkerchief over my face, breathing through my mouth.

"No, I think I can smell him now."

I booted the door right beside the lock and it crashed open, ripping the jamb loose. One rusty hinge tore free and the door dangled there by the bottom hinge.

"Yeah, he's dead," said Poochie, looking at Herky who

had been dead for maybe five days, swollen and steamy in this unventilated room which not only had a hot plate, but a small gas heater that was raging on an eighty-five degree day.

"Can I look at him?" said Poochie, standing next to the bed, examining Herky's bloated stomach and rotting face. His eyelids were gone and the eyes stared silver and dull at the elevator boy who grinned toothlessly and clucked at the maggots on Herky's face and swollen sex organs.

I ran across the room and banged on the frame until I got the window open. Flies were crawling all over the glass, leaving wet tracks in the condensation. Then I ran to the hot plate, lit it, and threw the frying pan on the burner. I dumped the whole can of coffee on the frying pan, but the elevator boy was enjoying himself so much he didn't seem to mind my extravagance with his coffee. In a few minutes the coffee was burning, and a pungent smoky odor was filling the room, almost neutralizing the odor of Herky.

"You don't mind if I look at him?" asked Poochie again.

"Knock yourself out, pal," I answered, going for the door.

"Been dead a while hasn't he?"

"Little while longer and he'd have gone clear through the mattress."

I walked to the pay phone at the end of the hall on the second floor. "Come with me, pal," I called, figuring he'd roll old Herky soon as my back was turned. It's bad enough getting rolled when you're alive.

I put a dime in the pay phone and dialed operator. "Police department," I said, then waited for my dime to return as she rang the station. The dime didn't come. I looked hard at Poochie who turned away, very innocently.

"Someone stuffed the goddamn chute," I said. "Some asshole's gonna get my dime when he pulls the stuffing out later."

"Bunch of thieves around here, Officer," said Poochie, all puckered and a little chalkier than before.

I called the dicks and asked for one to come down and take the death report, then I hung up and lit a cigar, not that I really wanted one, but any smell would do at the moment.

"Is it true they explode like a bomb after a while?"

"What?"

"Stiffs. Like old Herky."

"Yeah, he'd've been all over your wallpaper pretty soon."

"Damn," said the elevator boy, grinning big and showing lots of gums, upper and lower. "Some of these guys like Herky got lots of dough hidden around," he said, winking at me.

"Yeah, well let's let him keep it. He's had it this long."

"Oh, I didn't mean we should take it."

"Course not."

"It's just that these coroner guys, they get to steal anything they find laying around."

"How long's old Herky been living here?" I asked, not bothering to find out his whole name. I'd let the detective worry about the report.

"Off and on, over five years I know of. All alone. Never even had no friends. Nobody. Just laid up there in that room sucking up the sneaky pete. Used to drink a gallon a day. I think he lived off his social security. Pay his rent, eat a little, drink a little. I never could do it myself. That's why I'm elevator boy. Can't make it on that social security."

"You ever talk to him?"

"Yeah, he never had nothing to say though. No family. Never been married. No relatives to speak of. Really alone, you know? I got me eight kids spread all over this damn country. I can go sponge off one of them ever' once in a while. Never gonna see old Poochie like that." He winked and tapped his chest with a bony thumb. "Guys like old Herky, they don't care about nobody and nobody cares about them. They check out of this world grabbing their throat and staring around a lonely hotel room. Those're the guys that swell up and pop all over your walls. Guys like old Herky." The elevator boy thought about old Herky popping, and he broke out in a snuffling croupy laugh because that was just funny as hell.

I hung around the lobby waiting for the detective to arrive and relieve me of caring for the body. While I was waiting I started examining both sides of the staircase walls. It was the old kind with a scalloped molding about seven feet up, and at the first landing there were dirty finger streaks below the molding while the rest of the wall on both sides was uniformly dirty, but unsmudged. I walked to the landing and reached up on the ledge, feeling a toilet-paper-wrapped bundle. I opened it and found a complete outfit: eyedropper, hypodermic needle, a piece of heavy thread, burned spoon, and razor blade.

I broke the eye dropper, bent the needle, and threw the hype kit in the trash can behind the rickety desk in the lobby.

"What's that?" asked the elevator boy.

"A fit."

"A hype's outfit?"

"Yeah."

"How'd you know it was there?"

"Elementary, my dear Poochie."

"That's pretty goddamn good."

The detective came in carrying a clipboard full of death reports. He was one of the newer ones, a young collegiate-looking type. I didn't know him. I talked to him for a few minutes and the elevator boy took him back to the body.

"Never catch old Poochie going it alone," he called to me with his gums showing. "Never gonna catch old Poochie busting like a balloon and plastered to your wallpaper."

"Good for you, Poochie," I nodded, taking a big breath out on the sidewalk, thinking I could still smell the dead body. I imagined that his odor was clinging to my clothes and I goosed the black-and-white, ripping off some rubber in my hurry to get away from that room.

I drove around for a while and started wondering what I should work on. I thought about the hotel burglar again and wondered if I could find Link Owens, a good little hotel creeper, who might be able to tell me something about this guy that'd been hitting us so hard. All hotel burglars know each other. Sometimes you see so many of them hanging around the lobbies of the better hotels, it looks like a thieves' convention. Then I got the code-two call to go to the station.

TEN

CODE TWO MEANS HURRY UP, and whenever policemen get that call to go to the station they start worrying about things. I've had a hundred partners tell me that: "What did I do wrong? Am I in trouble? Did something happen to the old lady? The kids?" I never had such thoughts, of course. A code-two call to go to the station just meant to me that they had some special shit detail they needed a man for, and mine happened to be the car they picked.

When I got to the watch commander's office, Lieutenant Hilliard was sitting at his desk reading the morning editorials, his millions of wrinkles deeper than usual, looking as mean as he always did when he read the cop-baiting letters to the editor and editorial cartoons which snipe at cops. He never stopped reading them though, and scowling all the way.

"Hi, Bumper," he said, glancing up. "One of the vice officers wants you in his office. Something about a bookmaker you turned for them?"

"Oh yeah, one of my snitches gave him some information yesterday. Guess Charlie Bronski needs to talk to me some more."

"Going to take down a bookie, Bumper?" Hilliard grinned. He was a hell of a copper in his day. He wore seven service stripes on his left forearm, each one signifying five years' service. His thin hands were knobby and covered with bulging blue veins. He had trouble with bone deterioration now, and walked with a cane.

"I'm a patrol officer. Can't be doing vice work. No time."

"If you've got something going with Bronski, go ahead and work on it. Vice caper or not, it's all police work. Besides, I've never seen many uniformed policemen tear off a bookmaker. That's about the only kind of pinch you've never made for me, Bumper."

"We'll see what we can do, Lieutenant," I smiled, and left him there, scowling at the editorials again, an old man that should've pulled the pin years ago. Now he'd been here too long. He couldn't leave or he'd die. And he couldn't do the work anymore, so he just sat and talked police work to other guys like him who believed police work meant throwing lots of bad guys in jail and that all your other duties were just incidental. The young officers were afraid to get close to the watch commander's office when he was in there. I've seen rookies call a sergeant out into the hall to have him approve a report so they wouldn't have to take it to Lieutenant Hilliard. He demanded excellence, especially on reports. Nobody's ever asked that of the young cops who were TV babies, not in all their lives. So he was generally avoided by the men he commanded.

Charlie Bronski was in his office with two other vice officers when I entered.

"What's up, Charlie?" I asked.

"We had some unbelievable luck, Bumper. We ran the

phone number and it comes back to an apartment on Hobart near Eighth Street, and Red Scalotta hangs around Eighth Street quite a bit when he's not at his restaurant on Wilshire. I'm betting that phone number you squeezed out of Zoot goes right into Reba McClain's pad just like I hoped. She always stays close by Red, but never too close. Red's been married happily for thirty years and has a daughter in Stanford and a son in medical school. Salt of the earth, that asshole is."

"Gave nine thousand last year to two separate churches in Beverly Hills," said one of the other vice officers, who looked like a wild young head with his collar-length hair, and beard, and floppy hat with peace and pot buttons all over it. He wore a cruddy denim shirt cut off at the shoulders and looked like a typical Main Street fruit hustler.

"And God returns it a hundredfold," said the other vice officer, Nick Papalous, a melancholy-looking guy, with small white teeth. Nick had a big Zapata moustache, sideburns, and wore orange-flowered flares. I'd worked with Nick several times before he went to vice. He was a good cop for being so young.

"You seemed pretty hot on taking a book, Bumper, so I thought I'd see if you wanted to go with us. This isn't going to be a back office, but it might lead to one, thanks to your friend Zoot. What do you say, want to come?"

"Do I have to change to civvies?"

"Not if you don't want to. Nick and Fuzzy here are going to take the door down. You and me could stiff in the call from the pay phone at the corner. Your uniform wouldn't get in the way."

"Okay, let's go," I said, anxious for a little action, glad I didn't have to take the uniform off. "Never went on a vice raid before. Do we have to synchronize our watches and all that?"

"I'll do the door," Nick grinned. "Fuzzy'll watch out the window and keep an eyeball on you and Bumper down at the pay phone on the corner. When you get the bet stiffed, Fuzzy'll see your signal and give me the okay and down goes the door."

"Kind of tough kicking, ain't it, Nick, in those crepe-soled, sneak-and-peek shoes you guys wear?"

"Damn straight, Bumper," Nick smiled. "I could sure use those size-twelve boondockers of yours."

"Thirteens," I said.

"Wish I could take down the door," said Fuzzy. "Nothing I like better than John Wayne-ing a goddamn door."

"Tell Bumper why you can't, Fuzzy," Nick grinned.

"Got a sprained ankle and a pulled hamstring," said Fuzzy, taking a few limping steps to show me. "I was off duty for two weeks."

"Tell Bumper how it happened," said Nick, still grinning.

"Freakin' fruit," said Fuzzy, pulling off the wide-brimmed hat and throwing back his long blond hair. "We got a vice complaint about this fruit down at the main library, hangs around out back and really comes on strong with every young guy he sees."

"Fat mother," said Charlie. "Almost as heavy as you, Bumper. And strong."

"Damn!" said Fuzzy, shaking his head, looking serious even though Nick was still grinning. "You shoulda seen the arms on that animal! Anyway, I get picked to operate him, naturally."

"'Cause you're so pretty, Fuzzy," said Charlie.

"Yeah, anyway, I go out there, about two in the afternoon, and hang around a little bit, and sure enough, there he is standing by that scrub oak tree and I don't know which one's the freakin tree for a couple minutes, he's so wide. And I swear I never saw a hornier fruit in my life 'cause I just walked up and said, 'Hi.' That's all, I swear."

"Come on, Fuzzy, you winked at him," said Charlie, winking at me.

"You asshole," said Fuzzy. "I swear I just said, 'Hi, Brucie,' or something like that, and this mother grabbed me. Grabbed me! In a bear hug! He pinned my arms! I was shocked, I tell you! Then he starts bouncing me up and down against his fat belly, saying, 'You're so cute. You're so cute. You're so cute.' "

Then Fuzzy stood up and started bouncing up and down with his arms up against his sides and his head bobbing. "Like this I was," said Fuzzy. "Like a goddamn rag doll bouncing, and I said, 'Y-y-y-you're u-u-u-under a-a-a-arrest,' and he stopped loving me and said, 'What?' and I said, 'YOU'RE UNDER ARREST, YOU FAT ZOMBIE!' And he threw me. Threw me! And I rolled down the hill and crashed into the concrete steps. And you know what happens then? My partner here lets him get away. He claims he couldn't catch the asshole and the guy couldn't run no faster than a pregnant alligator. My brave partner!"

"Fuzzy really wants that guy bad," Charlie grinned. "I tried to catch him, honest, Fuzzy." Then to me, "I think Fuzzy fell in love. He wanted the fat boy's phone number."

"Yuk!" said Fuzzy, getting a chill as he thought about

it. "We got a warrant for that prick for battery on a police officer. Wait'll I get him. I'll get that prick in a choke hold and lobotomize him!"

"By the way, what's the signal you use for crashing in the pad?" I asked.

"We always give it this," said Charlie, pumping his closed fist up and down.

"Double time," I smiled. "Hey, that takes me back to my old infantry days." I felt good now, getting to do something a little different. Maybe I should've tried working vice, I thought, but no, I've had lots more action and lots more variety on my beat. That's where it's at. That's where it's really at.

"Reba must have some fine, fine pussy," said Fuzzy, puffing on a slim cigar and cocking his head at Charlie. I could tell by the smell it was a ten- or fifteen-center. I'd quit smoking first, I thought.

"She's been with Red a few years now," said Nick to Fuzzy. "Wait'll you meet her. Those mug shots don't do her justice. Good-looking snake."

"You cold-blooded vice cops don't care how good-looking a broad is," I said, needling Charlie. "All a broad is to you is a booking number. I'll bet when some fine-looking whore thinking you're a trick lays down and spreads her legs, you just drop that cold badge right on top of her."

"Right on her bare tummy," said Nick. "But I'll bet Reba has more than a nice tight pussy. A guy like Scalotta could have a million broads. She must give extra good head or something."

"That's what I need, a little skull," said Fuzzy, leaning back in a swivel chair, his soft-soled shoes propped up on a desk. He was a pink-faced kid above the beard, not a day over twenty-four, I'd guess.

"A *little* skull'd be the first you ever had, Fuzzy," said Nick.

"Ha!" said Fuzzy, the cigar clenched in his teeth. "I used to have this Chinese girlfriend that was a go-go dancer. . . ."

"Come on, Fuzzy," said Charlie, "let's not start those lies about all the puss you got when you worked Hollywood. Fuzzy's laid every toadie on Sunset Boulevard three times."

"I can tell you yellow is mellow," Fuzzy leered. "This chick wouldn't ball nobody but me. She used to wet her pants playing with the hair on my chest." Fuzzy stood up then, and flexed his bicep.

Nick, always a man of few words, said, "Siddown, fruitbait."

"Anyway, Reba ain't just a good head job," said Charlie. "That's not why Scalotta keeps her. He's a leather freak and likes to savage a broad. Dresses her up in animal skins and whales the shit out of her."

"I never really believed those rumors," said Nick.

"No shit?" said Fuzzy, really interested now.

"We had a snitch tell us about it one time," said Charlie. "The snitch said Red Scalotta digs dykes and whips and Reba's his favorite. The snitch told us it's the only way Red can get it up anymore."

"He *is* an old guy," said Fuzzy seriously. "At least fifty, I think."

"Reba's a stone psycho, I tell you," said Charlie. "Remember when we busted her, Nick? How she kept talking all the way to jail about the bull daggers and how they'd chase her around the goddamn jail cell before she could get bailed out."

"That broad got dealt a bum hand," said Nick.

"Ain't got a full deck even now," Charlie agreed.

"She's scared of butches and yet she puts on dyke shows for Red Scalotta?" said Fuzzy, his bearded baby face split by a grin as he pictured it.

"Let's get it over with," said Charlie. "Then we can spend the rest of the day shooting pool in a nice cool beer bar, listening to Fuzzy's stories about all those Hollywood groupies."

Nick and Fuzzy took one vice car and I rode with Charlie in another one. It's always possible there could be more than one in the pad, and they wanted room for prisoners.

"Groovy machine, Charlie," I said, looking over the vice car which was new and air-conditioned. It was gold with mags, a stick, and slicks on the back. The police radio was concealed inside the glove compartment.

"It's not bad," said Charlie, "especially the air conditioning. Ever see air conditioning in a police car, Bumper?"

"Not the ones I drive, Charlie," I said, firing up a cigar, and Charlie tore through the gears to show me the car had some life to it.

"Vice is lots of fun, Bumper, but you know, some of the best times were when I walked with you on your beat."

"How long'd you work with me, Charlie, couple months?"

"About three months. Remember, we got that burglar that night? The guy that read the obituaries?"

"Oh yeah," I said, not remembering that it was Charlie who'd been with me. When they have you breaking in rookies, they all kind of merge in your memory, and you don't remember them very well as individuals.

"Remember? We were shaking this guy just outside the Indian beer bar near Third, and you noticed the obituary column folded up in his shirt pocket? Then you told me about how some burglars read the obituaries and then burgle the pads of the dead people after the funeral when chances are there's nobody going to be there for a while."

"I remember," I said, blowing a cloud of smoke at the windshield, thinking how the widow or widower usually stays with a relative for a while. Rotten M.O., I can't stand grave robbing. Seems like your victim ought to have some kind of chance.

"We got a commendation for that pinch, Bumper."

"We did? I can't remember."

"Of course I got one only because I was with you. That guy burgled ten or fifteen pads like that. Remember? I was so green I couldn't understand why he carried a pair of socks in his back pocket and I asked you if many of these transient types carried a change of socks with them. Then you showed me the stretch marks in the socks from his fingers and explained how they wear them for gloves so's not to leave prints. You never put me down even when I asked something that dumb."

"I always liked guys to ask questions," I said, beginning to wish Charlie'd shut up.

"Hey, Charlie," I said, to change the subject, "if we take a good phone spot today, what're the chances it could lead to something big?"

"You mean like a back office?"

"Yeah."

"Almost no chance at all. How come you're so damned anxious to take a back?"

"I don't know. I'm leaving the job soon and I never really took a big crook like Red Scalotta. I'd just like to nail one."

"Christ, I never took anyone as big as Scalotta either. And what do you mean, you're leaving? Pulling the pin?"

"One of these days."

"I just can't picture you retiring."

"*You're* leaving after twenty years aren't you?"

"Yeah, but not *you*."

"Let's forget about it," I said, and Charlie looked at me for a minute and then opened the glove compartment and turned to frequency six for two-way communication with the others.

"One-Victor-One to One-Victor-Two," said Charlie.

"One-Victor-Two, go," said Nick.

"One-Victor-One, I think it's best to park behind on the next street east, that's Harvard," said Charlie. "If anybody happens to be looking they wouldn't see you go in through the parking area in the rear."

"Okay, Charlie," said Nick, and in a few minutes we were there. Eighth Street is all commercial buildings with several bars and restaurants, and the residential north-south streets are lined with apartment buildings. We gave them a chance to get to the walkway on the second floor of the apartment house, and Charlie drove about two hundred feet south of Eighth on Harvard. We walked one block to the public telephone on the southwest corner at

Hobart. After a couple of minutes, Fuzzy leaned over a wrought iron railing on the second floor and waved.

"Let's get it on, Bumper," said Charlie, dropping in a dime. Charlie hung up after a second. "Busy."

"Zoot give you the code and all that?"

"Twenty-eight for Dandelion is the code," Charlie nodded. "This is a relay phone spot. If it was a relay call-back we might have some problems."

"What's the difference?" I asked, standing behind the phone booth so someone looking out of the apartment wouldn't see the bluesuit.

"A call-back is where the bettor or the handbook like Zoot calls the relay, that's like I'm going to do now. Then every fifteen minutes or so, the back office calls the relay and gets the bettor's number and calls the bettor himself. I think we'd have a poor chance with that kind of setup because back office clerks are sharper than some dummy sitting on the hot seat at a phone spot. Last time we took Reba McClain it was a regular relay spot where the bettor calls her and she writes the bets on a Formica board and then the back office calls every so often and she reads off the bets and wipes the Formica clean. It's better for us that way because we always try to get some physical evidence if we can move quick enough."

"The Formica?"

"Yeah," Charlie nodded. "Some guys kick in the door and throw something at the guy on the hot seat to distract him so he can't wipe the bets off. I've seen cops throw a tennis ball in the guy's face."

"Why not a baseball?"

"That's not a bad idea. You'd make a good vice cop, Bumper."

"Either way the person at the phone spot doesn't know the phone number or address of the back office?" I asked.

"Hell no. That's why I was telling you the chances are nil."

Charlie dropped the dime in again and again hung it up.

"Must be doing a good business," I said.

"Red Scalotta's relay spots always do real good," said Charlie. "I know personally of two Superior Court judges that bet with him."

"Probably some cops too," I said.

"Righteous," he nodded. "Everybody's got vices."

"Whadda you call that gimmick where the phone goes to another pad?"

"A tap out," said Charlie. "Sometimes you bust in an empty room and see nothing but a phone jack and a wire running out a window, and by the time you trace the wire down to the right apartment, the guy in the relay spot's long gone. Usually with a tap out, there's some kind of alarm hooked up so he knows when you crash in the decoy pad. Then there's a toggle relay, where a call can be laid off to another phone line. Like for instance the back office clerk dials the relay spot where the toggle switch is and he doesn't hang up. Then the bettor calls the relay and the back can take the action himself. All these gimmicks have disadvantages though. One of the main ones is that bettors don't like call-back setups. Most bettors are working stiffs and maybe on their coffee breaks they only have a few minutes to get in to their bookie, and they don't have ten or fifteen minutes to kill waiting for call-backs and all that crap. The regular relay spot with some guy or maybe some housewife earning a little extra bread by sitting on the hot seat is still the most convenient way for the book to operate."

"You get many broads at these phone spots?"

"We sure do. We get them in fronts and backs. That is, we get them in the relay phone spots as well as back offices. We hear Red Scalotta's organization pays a front clerk a hundred fifty a week and a back clerk three hundred a week. That's a good wage for a woman, considering it's tax free. A front clerk might have to go to jail once in a while but it ain't no big thing to her. The organization bails them out and pays all legal fees. Then they go right back to work. Hardly any judge is going to send someone to county jail for bookmaking, especially if she's female. And they'll never send anyone to state prison. I know a guy in the south end of town with over eighty bookmaking arrests. He's still in business."

"Sounds like a good business."

"It's a joke, Bumper. I don't know why I stay at it, I mean trying to nail them. We hear Red Scalotta's back offices gross from one to two million a year. And he probably has at least three backs going. That's a lot of bread even though he only nets eleven to sixteen percent of that. And when we take down these agents and convict them, they get a two-hundred-and-fifty-dollar fine. It's a sick joke."

"You ever get Red Scalotta himself?"

"Never. Red'll stay away from the back offices. He's got someone who takes care of everything. Once in a while we can take a front and on rare occasions a back and that's about all we can hope for. Well, let's try to duke our bet in again."

Charlie dropped in his dime and dialed the number. Then he looked excited and I knew someone answered.

"Hello," said Charlie, "this is twenty-eight for Dandelion. Give me number four in the second, five across. Give me a two-dollar, four-horse round robin in the second. The number two horse to the number four in the third to the number six in the fourth to number seven in the fifth."

Then Charlie stiffed in a few more bets for races at the local track, Hollywood Park, which is understood, unless you specify an Eastern track. Midway through the conversation, Charlie leaned out the phone booth and pumped his fist at Fuzzy, who disappeared inside the apartment building. Charlie motioned to me and I took off my hat and squeezed into the hot phone booth with him. He grinned and held the phone away from his ear, near mine.

I heard the crash over the phone, and the terrified woman scream and a second later Nick's voice came over the line and said, "Hello, sweetheart, would you care for a round robin or a three-horse parley today?"

Charlie chuckled and hung up the phone and we hopped back in the vice car and drove to the apartment house, parking in front.

When we got to the second floor, Fuzzy was smooth talking an irate landlady who was complaining about the fractured door which Nick was propping shut for privacy. A good-looking, dark-haired girl was sitting on the couch inside the apartment crying her eyes out.

"Hi, Reba," Charlie grinned as we walked in and looked around.

"Hello, Mister Bronski," she wailed, drenching the second of two handkerchiefs she held in her hands.

"The judge warned you last time, Reba," said Charlie. "This'll make your third bookmaking case. He told you you'd get those six months he suspended. You might even get a consecutive sentence on top of it."

"Please, Mister Bronski," she wailed, throwing herself face down on the couch and sobbing so hard the whole couch shook.

She was wearing a very smart jersey blouse and skirt, and a matching blue scarf was tied around her black hair. Her fair legs had a very light spattering of freckles on them. She was a fine-looking girl, very Irish.

Charlie took me in the frilly sweet-smelling bedroom where the phone was. Reba had smeared half the bets off a twelve-by-eighteen chalkboard, but the other bets were untouched. A wet cloth was on the floor where the board was dropped along with the phone.

"I'll bet she wet her pants again this time," said Charlie, still grinning as he examined the numbers and x's on the chalkboard which told the track, race, handicap position, and how much to win, place or show. The bettor's identification was written beside the bets. I noticed that K.L. placed one hell of a lot of bets, probably just before Charlie called.

"We're going to squeeze the shit out of her," Charlie whispered. "You think Zoot was shaky, wait'll you hear this broad. A real ding-a-ling."

"Go ahead," Nick was saying to someone on the phone when we came back in the living room. Fuzzy was nodding politely to the landlady and locking her out by closing the broken door and putting a chair in front of it.

"Right. Got it," said Nick, hanging up. A minute later the phone rang again.

"Hello," said Nick. "Right. Go ahead." Every few seconds he mumbled, "Yeah," as he wrote down bets. "Got it." He hung up.

"Nick's taking some bets mainly just to fuck up Scalotta," Charlie explained to me. "Some of these guys might hit, or they might hear Reba got knocked over, and then they'll claim they placed their bet and there'll be no way to prove they didn't, so the book'll have to pay off or lose the customers. That's where we get most of our tips, from disgruntled bettors. It isn't too often a handbook like Zoot Lafferty comes dancing in, anxious to turn his bread and butter."

"Mister Bronski, can I talk to you?" Reba sobbed, as Nick and then Fuzzy answered the phone and took the bets.

"Let's go in the other room," said Charlie, and we followed Reba back into the bedroom where she sat down on the soft, king-sized bed and wiped away the wet mascara.

"I got no time for bullshit, Reba," said Charlie. "You're in no position to make deals. We got you by the curlies."

"I know, Mister Bronski," she said, taking deep breaths. "I ain't gonna bullshit you. I wanna work with you. I swear I'll do anything. But please don't let me get this third case. That Judge Bowers is a bastard. He told me if I violated my probation, he'd put me in. Please, Mister Bronski, you don't know what it's like there. I couldn't do six months. I couldn't even do six days. I'd kill myself."

"You want to work for me? What could you do?"

"Anything. I know a phone number. Two numbers. You could take two other places just like this one. I'll give you the numbers."

"How do you know them?"

"I ain't dumb, Mister Bronski. I listen and I learn things. When they're drunk or high they talk to me, just like all men."

"You mean Red Scalotta and his friends?"

"Please, Mister Bronski, I'll give you the numbers, but you can't take me to jail."

"That's not good enough, Reba," said Charlie, sitting down in a violet-colored satin chair next to a messy dressing table. He lit a cigarette as Reba glanced from Charlie to me, her forehead wrinkled, chewing her lip. "That's not near good enough," said Charlie.

"Whadda you want, Mister Bronski? I'll do anything you say."

"I want the back," said Charlie easily.

"What?"

"I want one of Red's back offices. That's all. Keep your phone spots. If we take too much right away it'll burn you and I want you to keep working for Red. But I want his back office. I think you can help me."

"Oh God, Mister Bronski. Oh Mother of God, I don't know about things like that, I swear. How would I know? I'm just answering phones here. How would I know?"

"You're Red's girlfriend."

"Red has other girlfriends!"

"You're his *special* girlfriend. And you're smart. You listen."

"I don't know things like that, Mister Bronski. I swear to God and His Mother. I'd tell you if I knew."

"Have a cigarette," said Charlie, and pushed one into Reba's trembling hand. I lit it for her and she glanced up like a trapped little rabbit, choked on the smoke, then took a deep breath, and inhaled down the right pipe. Charlie let her smoke for a few seconds. He had her ready to break, which is what you want, and you shouldn't wait, but she was obviously a ding-a-ling and you had to improvise when your subject is batty. He was letting her unwind, letting her get back a little confidence. Just for a minute.

"You wouldn't protect Red Scalotta if it meant your ass going to jail, would you, Reba?"

"Hell no, Mister Bronski, I wouldn't protect my mother if it meant that."

"Remember when I busted you before? Remember how we talked about those big hairy bull dykes you meet in jail? Remember how scared you were? Did any of them bother you?"

"Yes."

"Did you sleep in jail?"

"No, they bailed me out."

"What about after you get your six months, Reba? Then you have to sleep in jail. Did you see any dildoes in jail?"

"What's that?"

"Phony dicks."

"I hate those things," she shuddered.

"How would you like to wake up in the middle of the night with two big bull dykes working on you? And what's more, how would you feel if you really started *liking* it? It happens all the time to girls in jail. Pretty soon you're a stone butch, and then you might as well cut off that pretty hair, and strap down those big tits, because you're not a woman anymore. Then you can lay up in those butch pads with a bunch of bull daggers and a pack of smelly house cats and drop pills and shoot junk because you can't stand yourself."

"Why're you doing this to me, Mister Bronski?" said Reba, starting to sob again. She dropped the cigarette on the carpet and I picked it up and snuffed it. "Why do men like to hurt? You all hurt!"

"Does Red hurt you?" asked Charlie calmly, sweating a little as he lit another cigarette with the butt of the last one.

"Yes! He hurts!" she yelled, and Fuzzy stuck his head in the door to see what the shouting was about, but Charlie motioned him away while Reba sobbed.

"Does he make you do terrible things?" asked Charlie, and she was too hysterical to see he was talking to her like she was ten years old.

"Yes, the bastard! The freaky bastard. He hurts me! He likes to hurt! That fucking old freak!"

"I'll bet he makes you do things with bull daggers," said Charlie, glancing at me, and I realized I broke him in right. He wasn't a guy to only stick it in halfway.

"He *makes* me do it, Mister Bronski," said Reba. "I don't enjoy it, I swear I don't. I hate to do it with a woman. I wasn't raised like that. It's a terrible sin to do those things."

"I'll bet you don't like taking action for him either. You hate sitting on this hot seat answering the phones, don't you?"

"I *do* hate it, Mister Bronski. I *do* hate it. He's so goddamn cheap. He just won't give me money for anything. He makes me always work for it. I have to do those things with them two or three nights a week. And I have to sit here in this goddamn room and answer those goddamn phones and every minute I know some cop might be ready to break down the door and take me to jail. Oh, please help me, Mister Bronski."

"Stop protecting him then," said Charlie.

"He'll kill me, Mister Bronski," said Reba, and her pretty violet eyes were wide and round and her nostrils were flared, and you could smell the fear on her.

"He won't kill you, Reba," said Charlie soothingly. "You won't get a jacket. He'll never know you told me. We'll make it look like someone else told."

"No one else *knows*," she whispered, and her face was dead white.

"We'll work it out, Reba. Stop worrying, we know how to protect people that help us. We'll make it look like someone else set it up. I promise you, he'll never know you told."

"Tell me you swear to God you'll protect me."

"I swear to God I'll protect you."

"Tell me you swear to God I won't go to jail."

"We've got to book you, Reba. But you know Red'll bail you out in an hour. When your case comes up I'll personally go to Judge Bowers and you won't go to jail behind that probation violation."

"Are you a hundred percent sure?"

"I'm almost a hundred percent sure, Reba. Look, I'll talk for you myself. Judges are always ready to give people another chance, you know that."

"But that Judge Bowers is a bastard!"

"I'm a hundred percent sure, Reba. We can fix it."

"You got another cigarette?"

"Let's talk first. I can't waste any more time."

"If he finds out, I'm dead. My blood'll be on you."

"Where's the back?"

"I only know because I heard Red one night. It was after he'd had his dirty fun with me and a girl named Josie that he brought with him. She was as sick and filthy as Red. And he brought another guy with him, a Jew named Aaron something."

"Bald-headed guy, small, glasses and a gray moustache?"

"Yeah, that's him," said Reba.

"I know of him," said Charlie, and now he was squirming around on the velvet chair, because he had the scent, and I was starting to get it too, even though I didn't know who in the hell Aaron was.

"Anyway, this guy Aaron just watched Josie and me for a while and when Red got in bed with us, he told Aaron to go out in the living room and have a drink. Red was high as a kite that night, but at least he wasn't mean. He didn't hurt me. Can I please have that cigarette, Mister Bronski?"

"Here," said Charlie, and his hand wasn't quite as steady, which is okay, because that showed that good information could still excite him.

"Tastes good," said Reba, dragging hard on the cigarette. "Afterwards, Red called a cab for Josie and sent her home, and him and Aaron started talking and I stayed in the bedroom. I was supposed to be asleep, but like I say, I'm not dumb, Mister Bronski, and I always listen and try to learn things.

"Aaron kept talking about the 'laundry,' and at first I didn't get it even though I knew that Red was getting ready to move one of his back offices. And even though I never saw it, or any other back office, I knew about them from talking to bookie agents and people in the business. Aaron was worrying about the door to the laundry and I figured there was something about the office door being too close to the laundry door, and Aaron tried to argue Red into putting another door in the back near an alley, but Red thought it would be too suspicious.

"That was all I heard, and then one day, when Red was taking me to his club for dinner, he said he had to stop by to pick up some cleaning and he parks by this place near Sixth and Kenmore, and he goes in a side door and comes out after a few minutes and says his suits weren't ready. Then I noticed the sign on the window. It was a Chinese laundry." Reba took two huge drags, blowing one through her nose as she drew on the second one.

"You're a smart girl, Reba," said Charlie.

"I ain't guaranteeing this is the right laundry, Mister Bronski. In fact, I ain't even sure the laundry they were talking about had anything to do with the back office. I just *think* it did."

"I think you're right," said Charlie.

"You got to protect me, Mister Bronski. I got to live with him, and if he knows, I'll die. I'll die in a bad way, a *real* bad way, Mister Bronski. He told me once what he did to a girl that finked on him. It was thirty years ago, and he talked about it like it was yesterday, how she screamed and screamed. It was so awful it made me cry. You got to protect me!"

"I will, Reba. I promise. Do you know the address of the laundry?"

"I know," she nodded. "There were some offices or something on the second floor, maybe like some business offices, and there was a third floor but nothing on the windows in the third floor."

"Good girl, Reba," Charlie said, taking out his pad and pencil for the first time, now that he didn't have to worry about his writing breaking the flow of the interrogation.

"Charlie, give me your keys," I said. "I better get back on patrol."

"Okay, Bumper, glad you could come." Charlie nipped me the keys. "Leave them under the visor. You know where we park?"

"Yeah, I'll see you later."

"I'll let you know what happens, Bumper."

"See you, Charlie. So long, kid," I said to Reba.

"Bye," she said, wiggling her fingers at me like a little girl.

ELEVEN

IT WAS OKAY driving back to the Glass House in the vice car because of the air conditioning. Some of the new black-and-whites had it, but I hadn't seen any yet. I turned on the radio and switched to a quiet music station and lit a cigar. I saw the temperature on the sign at a bank and it said eighty-two degrees. It felt hotter than that. It seemed awfully muggy.

After I crossed the Harbor Freeway I passed a large real estate office and smiled as I remembered how I cleaned them out of business machines one time. I had a snitch tell me that someone in the office bought several office machines from some burglar, but the snitch didn't know who bought them or even who the burglar was. I strolled in the office one day during their lunch hour when almost everyone was out and told them I was making security checks for a burglary prevention program the police department was sponsoring. A cute little office girl with a snappy fanny took me all around the place and I checked their doors and windows and she helped me write down the serial number of every machine in the place so that the police department would have a record if they were ever stolen. Then as soon as I got back to the station, I phoned Sacramento and gave them the numbers and found that thirteen of the nineteen machines had been stolen in various burglaries around the greater Los Angeles area. I went back with the burglary dicks and impounded them along with the office manager. IBM electric typewriters are just about the hottest thing going right now. Most of the machines are sold by the thieves to "legitimate" businessmen who, like everyone else, can't pass up a good buy.

It was getting close to lunch time and I parked the vice car at the police building and picked up my black-and-white, trying to decide where to have lunch. Olvera Street was out, because I'd had Mexican food with Cruz and Socorro last night. I thought about Chinatown, but I'd been there Tuesday, and I was just about ready to go to a good hamburger joint I know of when I thought about Odell Bacon. I hadn't had any bar-b-que for a while, so I headed south on Central Avenue to the Newton Street area and the more I thought about some bar-b-que the better it sounded and I started salivating.

I saw a Negro woman get off a bus and walk down a residential block from Central Avenue and I turned on that street for no reason, to get over to Avalon. Then I saw a black guy on the porch of a whitewashed frame house. He was watching the woman and almost got up from where he was sitting until he saw the black-and-white. Then he pretended to be looking at the sky and sat back, a little too cool, and I passed by and made a casual turn at the next block and then stomped down and gave her hell until I got to the first street north. Then I turned east again, south on Central, and finally made the whole block, deciding to come up the same street again. It was an old scam around here for purse snatchers to find a house where no one was home and sit on the stoop of the house near a bus stop, like they lived at the pad, and when a broad walked by, to run out, grab the purse, and then cut through the yard to the next street where a car would be stashed. Most black women around here don't carry purses. They carry their money in their bras out of necessity, so you don't see that scam used too much anymore, but I would've bet this guy was using it now. And this woman had a big brown leather purse. You just don't get suspicious of a guy when he approaches you from the porch of a house in your own neighborhood.

I saw the woman in mid-block and I saw the guy walking behind her pretty fast, I got overanxious and pushed a little too hard on the accelerator, instead of gliding along the curb, and the guy turned around, saw me, and cut to his right through some houses. I knew there'd be no sense going after him. He hadn't done anything yet, and besides, he'd lay up in some backyard like these guys always do and I'd never find him. I just went on to Odell Bacon's Bar-b-que, and when I passed the woman I glanced over and smiled, and she smiled back at me, a pleasant-looking old ewe. There were white sheep and black sheep and there were wild dogs and a few Pretty Good Shepherds. There'd be one sheep herder less after tomorrow, I thought.

I could smell the smoky meat a hundred yards away. They cooked it in three huge old-fashioned brick ovens. Odell and his brother Nate were both behind the counter when I walked in. They wore sparkling white cook's uniforms and hats and aprons even though they served the counter and watched the register and didn't have to do the cooking anymore. The place hadn't started to fill up for lunch yet. Only a few white people ate there, because they're afraid to come down here into what is considered the ghetto, and right now there were only a couple customers in the place and I was the only paddy. Everyone in South L.A. knew about Bacon's bar-b-que though. It was the best soul food and bar-b-que restaurant in town.

"Hey, Bumper," said Nate, spotting me first. "What's happening man?" He was the youngest, about forty, coffee brown. He had well-muscled arms from working construction for years before he came in as Odell's partner.

"Nothin to it, Nate," I grinned. "Hi, Odell."

"Aw right, Bumper," said Odell, and smiled big. He was a round-faced fat man. "I'm aw right. Where you been? Ain't seen you lately."

"Slowing down," I said. "Don't get around much these days."

"That'll be the day," Nate laughed. "When ol' Bumper can't git it on, it ain't worth gittin."

"Some gumbo today, Bumper?" asked Odell.

"No, think I'll have me some ribs," I said, thinking the gumbo did sound good, but the generous way these guys made it, stuffed full of chicken and crab, it might spoil me for the bar-b-que and my system was braced for the tangy down-home sauce that was their specialty, the like of which I'd never had anywhere else.

"Guess who I saw yestiday, Bumper?" said Odell, as he boxed up some chicken and a hot plate of beef, french fries, and okra for a take-out customer.

"Who's that?"

"That ponk you tossed in jail that time, 'member? That guy that went upside ol' Nate's head over a argument about paying his bill, and you was just comin' through the door and you rattled his bones but good. 'Member?"

"Oh yeah, I remember. Sneed was his name. Smelled like dogshit."

"That's the one," Nate nodded. "Didn't want him as a customer no how. Dirty clothes, dirty body, dirty mouf."

"Lucky you didn't get gangrene when that prick hit you, Nate," I said.

"Ponk-ass bastard," said Nate, remembering the punch that put him out for almost five minutes. "He come in the other day. I recognized him right off, and I tol' him to git his ass out or I'd call Bumper. He musta 'membered the name, 'cause he got his ass out wif oney a few cuss words."

"He remembered me, huh?" I grinned as Odell set down a cold glass of water, and poured me a cup of coffee without asking. They knew of course that I didn't work Newton Street Station and they only bounced for the Newton Street patrol car in the area, but after that Sneed fight, they always fed *me* free too, and in fact, always tried to get me to come more often. But I didn't like to take advantage. Before that, I used to come and pay half price like any uniformed cop could do.

"Here come the noonday rush," said Nate, and I heard car doors slam and a dozen black people talking and laughing came in and took the large booths in the front. I figured them for teachers. There was a high school and two grade schools close by and the place was pretty full by the time Nate put my plate in front of me. Only it wasn't a plate, it was a platter. It was always the same. I'd ask for ribs, and I'd get ribs, a double portion, and a heap of beef, oozing with bar-b-que sauce, and some delicious fresh bread that was made next door, and an ice-cream scoop of whipped butter. I'd sop the bread in the bar-b-que and either Nate or Odell would ladle fresh hot bar-b-que on the platter all during the meal. With it I had a huge cold mound of delicious slaw, and only a few fries because there wasn't much room for anything else. There just was no fat on Odell's beef. He was too proud to permit it, because he was almost sixty years old and hadn't learned the new ways of cutting corners and chiseling.

After I got over the first joy of remembering exactly how delicious the beef was, one of the waitresses started helping at the counter because Odell and Nate were swamped. She was a buxom girl, maybe thirty-five, a little bronzer than Nate, with a modest natural hairdo, which I like, not a way-out phony Afro. Her waist was very small for her size and the boobs soared out over a flat stomach. She knew I was admiring her and didn't seem to mind, and as always, a good-looking woman close by made the meal perfect.

"Her name's Trudy," said Odell, winking at me, when the waitress went to the far end of the counter. His wink and grin meant she was fair game and not married or anything. I used to date another of his waitresses once in a while, a plump, dusky girl named Wilma who was a thirty-two year old grandmother. She finally left Odell's and got married for the fourth time. I really enjoyed being with her. I taught her the swim and the jerk and the boogaloo when they first came out. I learned them from my Madeleine Carroll girlfriend.

"Thanks, Odell," I said. "Maybe next time I come in I'll take a table in her section."

"Anythin' funny happen lately, Bumper?" asked Nate after he passed some orders through to the kitchen.

"Not lately. . . . Let's see, did I ever tell you about the big dude I stopped for busting a stop sign out front of your place?"

"Naw, tell us," said Odell, stopping with a plate in his hand.

"Well, like I say, this guy blew the stop sign and I chased him and brought him down at Forty-first. He's a giant, six-feet-seven maybe, heavier than me. All muscle. I ran a make on him over the radio while I'm writing a ticket. Turns out there's a traffic warrant for his arrest."

"Damn," said Nate, all ears now. "You had to fight him?"

"When I tell him there's this warrant he says, 'Too bad, man, I just ain't going to jail.' Just that cool he said it. Then he steps back like he's ready."

"Guddamn," said Odell.

"So then it just comes to me, this idea. I walk over to the police car and pick up the radio and say in a loud voice, 'One-X-L-Forty-five requesting an ambulance at Forty-first and Avalon.' The big dude, he looks around and says, 'What's the ambulance for?' I say, 'That's for you, asshole, if you don't get in that car.'

"So he gets in the car and halfway to jail he starts chuckling, then pretty soon he really busts up. 'Man,' he says, 'You really flimflammed my ass. This is the first time I ever laughed my way to jail.'"

"Gud-damn, Bumper," said Odell. "You're somethin' else. Guddamn." Then they both went off laughing to wait on customers.

I finished the rest of the meat, picked the bones, and

sopped up the last of the bread, but I wasn't happy now. In fact, it was depressing there with a crowd of people and the waitresses rushing around and dishes clattering, so I said good-bye to Nate and Odell. Naturally, I couldn't tip them even though they personally served me, so I gave two bucks to Nate and said, "Give it to Trudy. Tell her it's an advance tip for the good service she's gonna give me next time when I take a table in her section."

"I'll tell her, Bumper," Nate grinned as I waved and burped and walked out the door.

As I was trying to read the temperature again over a savings and loan office, the time flashed on the marquee. It was one-thirty, which is the time afternoon court always convenes. It dawned on me that I'd forgotten I had to be at a preliminary hearing this afternoon!

I cursed and stomped on it, heading for the new municipal court annex on Sunset, near the Old Mission Plaza, and then I slowed down and thought, what the hell, this is the last time I'll ever go to court on duty. I may get called back to testify after I'm retired, but this'll be the last time *on duty* as a working cop, and I'd never been late to court in twenty years. So what the hell, I slowed down and cruised leisurely to the court building.

I passed one of the Indian bars on Main Street, and saw two drunken braves about to duke it out as they headed for the alley in back, pushing and yelling at each other. I knew lots of Payutes and Apaches and others from a dozen Southwest tribes, because so many of them ended up downtown here on my beat. But it was depressing being with them. They were so defeated, those that ended up on Main Street, and I was glad to see them in a fistfight once in a while. At least that proved they could strike back a little bit, at something, even if it was at another drunken tribal brother. Once they hit my beat they were usually finished, or maybe long before they arrived here. They'd become winos, and many of the women, fat five-dollar whores. You wanted to pick them up, shake them out, send them somewhere, in some direction, but there didn't seem to be anywhere an Indian wanted to go. They were hopeless, forlorn people. One old beat cop told me they could break your heart if you let them.

I saw a Gypsy family walking to a rusty old Pontiac in a parking lot near Third and Main. The mother was a stooped-over hag, filthy, with dangling earrings, a peasant blouse, and a full red skirt hanging lopsided below her knees. The man walked in front of her. He was four inches shorter and skinny, about my age. A very dark unshaven face turned my way, and I recognized him. He used to hang around downtown and work with a Gypsy dame on pigeon drops and once in a while a Jamaican switch. The broad was probably his old lady, but I couldn't remember the face just now. There were three kids following: a dirty, beautiful teenage girl dressed like her mother, a ragtag little boy of ten or so, and a curly-haired little doll of four who was dressed like mama also.

I wondered what kind of scam they were working on now, and I tried to think of his name and couldn't, and I wondered if he'd remember me. As late as I was for court, I pulled to the curb.

"Hey, just a minute," I called.

"What, what, what?" said the man. "Officer, what's the problem? What's the problem? Gypsy boy. I'm just a Gypsy boy. You know me don't you, Officer? I talked with you before, ain't I? We was just shopping, Officer. Me and my babies and my babies' mother."

"Where're your packages?" I asked, and he squinted from the bright sunshine and peered into the car from the passenger side. His family all stood like a row of quail, and watched me.

"We didn't see nothing we liked, Officer. We ain't got much money. Got to shop careful." He talked with his hands, hips, all his muscles, especially those dozen or so that moved the mobile face, in expressions of hope and despair and honesty. Oh, what honesty.

"What's your name?"

"Marcos. Ben Marcos."

"Related to George Adams?"

"Sure. He was my cousin, God rest him."

I laughed out loud then, because every Gypsy I'd ever talked to in twenty years claimed he was cousin to the late Gypsy king.

"I know you don't I, Officer?" he asked, smiling then, because I had laughed, and I didn't want to leave because I enjoyed hearing the peculiar Hit to the Gypsy speech, and I enjoyed looking at his unwashed children who were exceptionally beautiful, and I wondered for the hundredth time whether a Gypsy could ever be honest after centuries of living under a code which praised deceit and trickery and theft from all but other Gypsies. Then I was sad because I'd always wanted to really know the Gypsies. That would be the hardest friendship I would ever make, but I had it on my list of things to accomplish before I die. I knew a clan leader named Frank Serna, and once I went to his home in Lincoln Heights and ate dinner with a houseful of his relatives, but of course they didn't talk about things they usually talked about, and I could tell by all the nervous jokes that having an outsider and especially a cop in the house was a very strange thing for the clan. Still, Frank asked me back, and when I had time I was going to work on breaking into the inner circle and making them trust me a little because there were Gypsy secrets I wanted to know. But I could never hope to do it without being a cop, because they'd only let me know them if they first thought I could do them some good, because all Gypsies lived in constant running warfare with cops. It was too late now, because I would *not* be a cop, and I would *never* get to learn the Gypsy secrets.

"We can go now, Officer?" said the Gypsy, holding his hands clasped together, in a prayerful gesture. "It's very hot for my babies' mama here in the sun."

I looked at the Gypsy woman then, looked at her face and she was *not* a hag, and not as old as I first thought. She stood much taller now and glared at me because her man was licking my boots and I saw that she had once been as pretty as her daughter, and I thought of how I had so often been accused of seeing good things in all women, even ones who were ugly to my partners, and I guessed it was true, that I exaggerated the beauty of all women I knew or ever saw. I wondered about that, and I was wallowing in depression now.

"Please, sir. Can we go now?" he said, the sweat running down the creases in his face, and on his unwashed neck.

"Go your way, Gypsy," I said, and dug out from the curb, and in a few minutes I was parked and walking in the court building.

TWELVE

BEEN WAITING FOR YOU, Bumper," said the robbery detective, a wrinkled old-timer named Miles. He had been a robbery detective even before I came on the job and was one of the last to still wear a wide-brimmed felt hat. They used to be called the "hat squad," and the wide felt hat was their trademark, but of course in recent years no one in Los Angeles wore hats like that. Miles was a stubborn old bastard though, he still wore his, and a wide-shouldered, too-big suit coat with two six-inch guns, one on each hip, because he was an old robbery detective and the hat squad legend demanded it and other policemen expected it.

"Sorry I'm late, Miles," I said.

"That's okay, the case just got sent out to Division Forty-two. Can you handle this by yourself? I got another prelim in Forty-three and a couple of rookie arresting officers for witnesses. If I ain't in there to tell this young D.A. how to put on his case, we might lose it."

"Sure, I'll handle it. Am I the only witness?"

"You and the hotel manager."

"Got the evidence?"

"Yeah, here it is." Miles pulled a large manila envelope out of his cheap plastic briefcase and I recognized the evidence tag I had stuck on there months ago when I made the arrest.

"The gun's in there and the two clips."

"Too bad you couldn't file a robbery."

"Yeah, well like I explained to you right after that caper, we were lucky to get what we did."

"You filed an eleven-five-thirty too, didn't you?"

"Oh yeah. Here's the pot, I almost forgot." Miles reached back in the briefcase and pulled out an analyzed-evidence envelope with my seal on it that contained the marijuana with the chemist's written analysis on the package.

"How many jobs you figure this guy for?"

"I think I told you four, didn't I?"

"Yeah."

"Now we think he done six. Two in Rampart and four here in Central."

"It's a shame you couldn't make him on at least one robbery."

"You're telling me. I had him in a regular show-up and I had a few private mug-shot show-ups, and I talked and coaxed and damn near threatened my victims and witnesses and the closest I could ever come was one old broad that said he *looked* like the bandit."

"Scumbag really did a good job with makeup, huh?"

"Did a hell of a job," Miles nodded. "Remember, he was an actor for a while and he did a hell of a good job with paint and putty. But shit, the M.O. was identical, the way he took mom and dad markets. Always asked for a case of some kind of beer they were short of and when they went in the back for the beer, boom, he pulled the forty-five automatic and took the place down."

"He ever get violent?"

"Not in the jobs in Central. I found out later he pistol-whipped a guy in one of the Rampart jobs. Some seventy-year-old grocery clerk decided he was Wyatt Earp and tried to go for some fucked-up old thirty-two he had stashed under the counter. Landry really laid him open. Three times across the eyes with the forty-five. He blinded him. Old guy's still in the hospital."

"His P.O. going to violate him?"

"This asshole has a rabbit's foot. He finished his parole two weeks before you busted him. Ain't that something else? Two weeks!"

"Well, I better get in there," I said. "Some of these deputy D.A.'s get panicky when you're not holding their hands. You get a special D.A. for this one?"

"No. It's a dead bang case. You got him cold. Shouldn't be any search and seizure problems at all. And even though we know this guy's a good robber, we ain't got nothing on him today but some low-grade felonies, ex-con with a gun and possession of pot."

"Can't we send him back to the joint with his record?"

"We're going to try. I'll stop in the courtroom soon as I can. If you finish before me, let me know if you held him to answer."

"You got doubts I'll hold him?" I grinned, and headed for the courtroom, feeling very strange as I had all day. The last time I wore a bluesuit into a courtroom, I thought.

This courtroom was almost empty. There were only three people in the audience, two older women, probably the kind that come downtown and watch criminal trials for fun, and a youngish guy in a business suit who was obviously a witness and looked disgusted as hell about being here. Since these courtrooms are for preliminary hearings only, there was no jury box, just the judge's bench and witness box, the counsel tables, the clerk's desk, and a small desk near the railing for the bailiff.

At least I'll be through hassling with this legal machinery, I thought, which cops tend to think is designed by a bunch of neurotics because it seems to go a hundred miles past the point where any sane man would've stopped. After a felony complaint is filed, the defendant is arraigned and then has a preliminary hearing which amounts to a trial. This takes the place of a grand jury indictment and it's held to see if there's good enough cause to bind him over to superior court for trial, and then he's arraigned again in superior court, and later has a trial. Except that in between there're a couple of hearings to set aside what you've done already. In capital cases there's a separate trial for guilt and another for penalty, so that's why celebrated California cases drag on for years until they cost so much that everybody gives up or lets the guy cop to a lesser included offense.

We have a very diligent bunch of young public defenders around here who, being on a monthly salary and not having to run from one good paying client to another, will drive you up a wall defending a chickenshit burglary like it was the Sacco-Vanzetti trial. The D.A.'s office has millions of very fine crimes to choose from and won't issue a felony complaint unless they're pretty damned sure they can get a conviction. But then, there aren't that many real felony convictions, because courts and prisons are so overcrowded. A misdemeanor plea is accepted lots of times even from guys with heavyweight priors.

All this would make Los Angeles a frustrating place to be a cop if it weren't for the fact that the West in general is not controlled by the political clubhouse, owing to the fact that our towns are so sprawling and young. This means that in my twenty years I could bust *any* deserving son of a bitch, and I never got bumrapped except once when I booked an obnoxious French diplomat for drunk driving after he badmouthed me. I later denied to my bosses that he told me of his diplomatic immunity.

But in spite of all the bitching by policemen there's one thing you can't deny: it's still the best system going, and even if it's rough on a cop, who the hell would want to walk a beat in Moscow or Madrid, or anywhere in between? We gripe for sympathy but most of us know that a cop's never going to be loved by people in general, and I say if you got to have lots of love, join the fire department.

I started listening a little bit to the preliminary hearing that was going on. The defendant was a tall, nice-looking guy named John Trafford, about twenty-seven years old, and his pretty woman, probably his wife, was in the courtroom. He kept turning and making courageous gestures in her direction which wasn't particularly impressing Judge Martha Bedford, a tough, severe-looking old girl who I had always found to be a fair judge, both to the people and the defense. There was a fag testifying that this clean-cut-looking young chap had picked him up in a gay bar and gone to the fag's pad, where after an undescribed sex act the young defendant, who the fag called Tommy, had damn near cut his head off with a kitchen knife. And then he ransacked the fruit's pad and stole three hundred blood-soaked dollars which were found in his pocket by two uniformed coppers who shagged him downtown at Fifth and Main where he later illegally parked his car.

The defense counsel was badgering the fruit, an effeminate little man about forty years old, who owned a photography studio, and the fruit wasn't without sympathy for the defendant as he glanced nervously at his friend "Tommy," and I thought this was darkly humorous and typical. Weak people need people so much they'd forgive anything. I didn't think the defense counsel was succeeding too well in trying to minimize the thing as just another fruitroll, since the hospital record showed massive transfusions and a hundred or so sutures needed to close up the neck wounds of the fruit.

The young defendant turned around again and shot a long sad glance at pretty little mama who looked brave, and after Judge Redford held him to answer on the charges of attempted murder and robbery, his lawyer tried to con her into a bail reduction because the guy had never been busted before except once for wife beating.

Judge Redford looked at the defendant then, staring at his handsome face and calm eyes, and I could tell she wasn't listening to the deputy D.A. who was opposing the bail reduction and recounting the savagery of the cutting. She was just looking at the young dude and he was looking at her. His blond hair was neatly trimmed and he wore a subdued pin-striped suit.

Then she denied the motion for bail reduction, leaving the huge bail on this guy and I was sure she saw what I saw in his face. He was one to be reckoned with. You could see the confidence and intelligence in his icy expression. And power. There's real power you can feel when it's in a guy like this and it even gave me a chill. You can call him a psychopath or say that he's evil, but whatever he is, he's the deadly Enemy, and I wondered how many other times his acts ended in blood. Maybe it was him that ripped the black whore they dug out of a garbage pile on Seventh Street last month, I thought.

You've got to respect the power to harm in a guy like him, and you've got to be scared by it. It sure as hell scared Her Honor, and after she refused to lower the bail he smiled a charming boyish smile at her and she turned away. Then he looked at his teary wife again and smiled at her, and then he felt me watching and I caught his eye and felt *myself* smiling, and my look was saying: I know you. I know you very well. He looked at me calmly for a few seconds, then his eyes sort of glazed over and the deputy led him out of court. Now that I knew he hung around downtown, I thought, I'd be watching for that boy on my beat.

The judge left the bench and the deputy D.A., a youngster whose muttonchops and moustache didn't fit, started reading the complaint to get ready for my case.

Timothy Landry, my defendant, was led in by a deputy sheriff. A deputy public defender was handling the case since Landry was not employed, even though Miles figured he'd stolen ten thousand or so.

He was a craggy-looking guy, forty-four years old, with long, dyed black hair that was probably really gray, and a sallow face that on some guys never seems to get rosy again after they do some time in the joint. He had the look of an ex-con all over him. His bit movie parts were mostly westerns, a few years back, right after he got out of Folsom.

"Okay, Officer," said the young D.A., "where's the investigator?"

"He's busy in another court. I'm Morgan, the arresting officer. I'm handling the whole thing. Dead bang case. You shouldn't have any problems."

He probably had only a few months' experience. They stick these deputy D.A.'s in the preliminary hearings to give them instant courtroom experience handling several cases a day, and I figured this one hadn't been here more than a couple months. I'd never seen him before and I spent lots of time in court because I made so many felony pinches.

"Where's the other witness?" asked the D.A., and for the first time I looked around the courtroom and spotted Homer Downey, who I'd almost forgotten was subpoenaed in this case. I didn't bother talking with him to make sure he knew what he'd be called on to testify to, because his part in it was so insignificant you almost didn't need him at all, except as probable cause for me going in the hotel room on an arrest warrant.

"Let's see," muttered the D.A. after he'd talked to Downey for a few minutes. He sat down at the counsel table reading the complaint and running his long fingers through his mop of brown hair. The public defender looked like a well-trimmed ivy-leaguer, and the D.A., who's theoretically the law and order guy, was mod. He even wore round granny glasses.

"Downey's the hotel manager?"

"Right," I said as the D.A. read my arrest report.

"On January thirty-first, you went to the Orchid Hotel

at eight-two-seven East Sixth Street as part of your routine duties?"

"Right. I was making a check of the lobby to roust any winos that might've been hanging around. There were two sleeping it off in the lobby and I woke them up intending to book them when all of a sudden one of them runs up the stairs, and I suddenly felt I had more than a plain drunk so I ordered the other one to stay put and I chased the first one. He turned down the hall to the right on the third floor and I heard a door close and was almost positive he ran into room three-nineteen."

"Could you say if the man you chased was the defendant?"

"Couldn't say. He was tall and wore dark clothes. That fleabag joint is dark even in the daytime, and he was always one landing ahead of me."

"So what did you do?"

"I came back down the stairs, and found the first guy gone. I went to the manager, Homer Downey, and asked him who was living in room three-nineteen, and he showed me the name Timothy Landry on the register, and I used the pay telephone in the lobby and ran a warrant check through R and I and came up with a fifty-two-dollar traffic warrant for Timothy Landry, eight-twenty-seven East Sixth Street. Then I asked the manager for his key in case Landry wouldn't open up and I went up to three-nineteen to serve the warrant on him."

"At this time you thought the guy that ran in the room was Landry?"

"Sure," I said, serious as hell.

I congratulated myself as the D.A. continued going over the complaint because that wasn't a bad story now that I went back over it again. I mean I felt I could've done better, but it wasn't bad. The truth was that a half hour before I went in Landry's room I'd promised Knobby Booker twenty bucks if he turned something good for me, and he told me he tricked with a whore the night before in the Orchid Hotel and that he knew her pretty good and she told him she just laid a guy across the hall and had seen a gun under his pillow while he was pouring her the pork.

With that information I'd gone in the hotel through the empty lobby to the manager's room and looked at his register, after which I'd gotten the passkey and gone straight to Landry's room where I went in and caught him with the gun and the pot. But there was no way I could tell the truth and accomplish two things: protecting Knobby, and convicting a no-good dangerous scumbag that should be back in the joint. I thought my story was very good.

"Okay, so then you knew there was a guy living in the room and he had a traffic warrant out for his arrest, and you had reason to believe he ran from you and was in fact hiding in his room?"

"Correct. So I took the passkey and went to the room and knocked twice and said, 'Police officer.'"

"You got a response?"

"Just like it says in my arrest report, counsel. A male voice said, 'What is it?' and I said, 'Police officer, are you Timothy Landry?' He said, 'Yeah, what do you want?' and I said, 'Open the door, I have a warrant for your arrest.'"

"Did you tell him what the warrant was for?"

"Right, I said a traffic warrant."

"What did he do?"

"Nothing. I heard the window open and knew there

was a fire escape on that side of the building, and figuring he was going to escape, I used the passkey and opened the door."

"Where was he?"

"Sitting on the bed by the window, his hand under the mattress. I could see what appeared to be a blue steel gun barrel protruding a half inch from the mattress near his hand, and I drew my gun and made him stand up where I could see from the doorway that it *was* a gun. I hand-cuffed the defendant and at this time informed him he was under arrest. Then in plain view on the dresser I saw the waxed-paper sandwich bag with the pot in it. A few minutes later, Homer Downey came up the stairs, and joined me in the defendant's room and that was it."

"Beautiful probable cause," the D.A. smiled. "And real lucky police work."

"Real luck," I nodded seriously. "Fifty percent of good police work is just that, good luck."

"We shouldn't have a damn bit of trouble with Chimel or any other search and seizure cases. The contraband narcotics was in plain view, the gun was in plain view, and you got in the room legally attempting to serve a warrant. You announced your presence and demanded admittance. No problem with eight-forty-four of the penal code."

"Right."

"You only entered when you felt the man whom you held a warrant for was escaping?"

"I didn't hold the warrant," I reminded him. "I only knew about the existence of the warrant."

"Same thing. Afterwards, this guy jumped bail and was rearrested recently?"

"Right."

"Dead bang case."

"Right."

After the public defender was finished talking with Landry he surprised me by going to the rear of the courtroom and reading my arrest report and talking with Homer Downey, a twitchy little chipmunk who'd been manager of the Orchid for quite a few years. I'd spoken to Homer on maybe a half-dozen occasions, usually like in this case, to look at the register or to get the passkey.

After what seemed like an unreasonably long time, I leaned over to the D.A. sitting next to me at the counsel table. "Hey, I thought Homer was the people's witness. He's grinning at the P.D. like he's a witness for the defense."

"Don't worry about it," said the D.A. "Let him have his fun. That public defender's been doing this job for exactly two months. He's an eager beaver."

"How long you been going it?"

"Four months," said the D.A., stroking his moustache, and we both laughed.

The P.D. came back to the counsel table and sat with Landry, who was dressed in an open-throat, big-collared, brown silk shirt, and tight chocolate pants. Then I saw an old skunk come in the courtroom. She had hair dyed like his, and baggy pantyhose and a short skirt that looked ridiculous on a woman her age, and I would've bet she was one of his girlfriends, maybe even the one he jumped bail on, who was ready to forgive. I was sure she was his baby when he turned around and her painted old kisser wrinkled in a smile. Landry looked straight ahead, and the bailiff in the court was not as relaxed as he usually was with an in-custody felony prisoner sitting at the counsel table. He too figured Landry for a bad son of a bitch, you could tell.

Landry smoothed his hair back twice and then seldom moved for the rest of the hearing.

Judge Redford took the bench again and we all quieted down and came to order.

"Is your true name Timothy G. Landry?" she asked the defendant, who was standing with the public defender.

"Yes, Your Honor."

Then she went into the monotonous reading of the rights even though they'd been read to Landry a hundred times by a hundred cops and a dozen other judges, and she explained the legal proceeding to him which *he* could have explained to *her*, and I looked at the clock, and finally, she tucked a wisp of straight gray hair behind her black hornrimmed glasses and said, "Proceed."

She was a judge I always liked. I remembered once in a case where I'd busted three professional auto thieves in a hot Buick, she'd commended me in court. I'd stopped these guys cruising on North Broadway through Chinatown and I knew, *knew* something was wrong with them and something wrong with the car when I noticed the *rear* license plate was bug-spattered, but the license, the registration, the guy's driver's license, everything checked out. But I felt it and I knew. And then I looked at the identification tag, the metal tag on the door post with the spot-welded rivets, and I stuck my fingernail under it and one guy tried to split, and only stopped when I drew the six-inch and aimed at his back and yelled, "Freeze, asshole, or name your beneficiary."

Then I found that the tag was not spot-welded on, but was glued, and I pulled it off and later the detectives made the car as a Long Beach stolen. Judge Bedford said it was good police work on my part.

The D.A. was ready to call his first witness, who was Homer Downey, and who the D.A. needed to verify the fact that he rented the room to Landry, in case Landry later at trial decided to say he was just spending the day in a friend's pad and didn't know how the gun and pot got in there. But the P.D. said, "Your Honor, I would move at this time to exclude all witnesses who are not presently being called upon to testify."

I expected that. P.D.'s always exclude all witnesses. I think it's the policy of their office. Sometimes it works pretty well for them, when witnesses are getting together on a story, but usually it's just a waste of time.

"Your Honor, I have only two witnesses," said the D.A., standing up. "Mr. Homer Downey and Officer Morgan the arresting officer, who is acting as my investigating officer. I would request that he be permitted to remain in the courtroom."

"The investigating officer will be permitted to remain, Mr. Jeffries," she said to the public defender. "That doesn't leave anyone we can exclude, does it?"

Jeffries, the public defender, blushed because he hadn't enough savvy to look over the reports to see how many witnesses there were, and the D.A. and I smiled, and the D.A. was getting ready to call old Homer when the P.D. said, "Your Honor, I ask that if the arresting officer is acting as the district attorney's investigating officer in this case, that he be instructed to testify first, even if it's out of order, and that the other witness be excluded."

The D.A. with his two months' extra courtroom

experience chuckled out loud at that one. "I have no objection, Your Honor," he said.

"Let's get on with it, then," said the judge, who was getting impatient, and I thought maybe the air-conditioner wasn't working right because it was getting close in there.

She said, "Will the district attorney please have his other witness rise?"

After Downey was excluded and told to wait in the hall the D.A. finally said, "People call Officer Morgan," and I walked to the witness stand and the court clerk, a very pleasant woman about the judge's age, said, "Do you solemnly swear in the case now pending before this court to tell the truth, the whole truth, and nothing but the truth, so help you God?"

And I looked at her with my professional witness face and said, "Yes, I do."

That was something I'd never completely understood. In cases where I wasn't forced to embellish, I always said, "I do," and in cases where I was fabricating most of the probable cause, I always made it more emphatic and said, "*Yes*, I do." I couldn't really explain that. It wasn't that I felt guilty when I fabricated, because I didn't feel guilty, because if I hadn't fabricated, many many times, there were people who would have been victimized and suffered because I wouldn't have sent half the guys to the joint that I sent over the years. Like they say, most of the testimony by all witnesses in a criminal case is just lyin' and denyin'. In fact, everyone expects the *defense* witnesses to "testilie" and would be surprised if they didn't.

"Take the stand and state your name, please," said the clerk.

"William A. Morgan, M-O-R-G-A-N."

"What is your occupation and assignment?" asked the D.A.

"I'm a police officer for the City of Los Angeles assigned to Central Division."

"Were you so employed on January thirty-first of this year?"

"Yes, sir."

"On that day did you have occasion to go to the address of eight-twenty-seven East Sixth Street?"

"Yes, sir."

"At about what time of the day or night was that?"

"About one-fifteen p.m."

"Will you explain your purpose for being at that location?"

"I was checking for drunks who often loiter and sleep in the lobby of the Orchid Hotel, and do damage to the furniture in the lobby."

"I see. Is this lobby open to the public?"

"Yes, it is."

"Had you made drunk arrests there in the past?"

"Yes, I had. Although usually, I just sent the drunks on their way, my purpose being mainly to protect the premises from damage."

"I see," said the D.A., and my baby blues were getting wider and rounder and I was polishing my halo. I worked hard on courtroom demeanor, and when I was a young cop, I used to practice in front of a mirror. I had been told lots of times that jurors had told deputy D.A.'s that the reason they convicted a defendant was that Officer Morgan was so *sincere* and honest-looking.

Then I explained how I chased the guy up the stairs and saw him run in room three-nineteen, and how naturally I was suspicious then, and I told how Homer showed me the register and I read Timothy Landry's name. I phoned R and I and gave them Landry's name and discovered there was a traffic warrant out for his arrest, and I believed he was the man who had run in three-nineteen. I wasn't worried about what Homer would say, because I *did* go to his door to get the passkey of course, and I *did* ask to see the register, and as far as Homer knew about the rest of it, it was the gospel.

When I got to the part about me knocking on the door and Landry answering and telling me he was Timothy Landry, I was afraid Landry was going to fly right out of his chair. That was his first indication I was embellishing the story a bit, and the part about the window opening could have been true, but the bastard snorted so loud when I said the gun was sticking out from under the mattress, that the P.D. had to poke him in the ribs and the judge shot him a sharp look.

I was sweating a little at that point because I was pissed off that a recent case made illegal the search of the premises pursuant to an arrest. Before this, I could've almost told the whole truth, because I would've been entitled to search the whole goddamn room which only made good sense. Who in the hell would waste four hours getting a search warrant when you didn't have anything definite to begin with, and couldn't get one issued in the first place?

So I told them how the green leafy substance resembling marijuana was in plain view on the dresser, and Landry rolled his eyes up and smacked his lips in disgust because I got the pot out of a shoe box stashed in the closet. The P.D. didn't bother taking me on *voir dire* for my opinion that the green leafy substance was pot, because I guessed he figured I'd made a thousand narcotics arrests, which I had.

In fact, the P.D. was so nice to me I should've been warned. The D.A. introduced the gun and the pot and the P.D. stipulated to the chemical analysis of the marijuana, and the D.A. introduced the gun as people's exhibit number one and the pot as people's number two. The P.D. never objected to anything on direct examination and my halo grew and grew until I must've looked like a bluesuited monk, with my bald spot and all. The P.D. never opened his mouth until the judge said, "Cross," and nodded toward him.

"Just a few questions, Officer Morgan," he smiled. He looked about twenty-five years old. He had a very friendly smile.

"Do you recall the name on the hotel register?"

"Objection, Your Honor," said the D.A. "What name, what are we . . ."

The judge waved the D.A. down, not bothering to sustain the objection as the P.D. said, "I'll rephrase the question, Your Honor. Officer, when you chased this man up the stairs and then returned to the manager's apartment did you look at the name on the register or did you ask Mr. Downey who lived there?"

"I asked for the register."

"Did you read the name?"

"Yes, sir."

"What was the name?"

"As I've testified, sir, it was the defendant's name, Timothy G. Landry."

"Did you then ask Mr. Downey the name of the man in three-nineteen?"

"I don't remember if I did or not. Probably not, since I read the name for myself."

"What was the warrant for, Officer? What violation?"

"It was a vehicle code violation, counsel. Twenty-one four-fifty-three-A, and failure to appear on that traffic violation."

"And it had his address on it?"

"Yes, sir."

"Did you make mention of the warrant number and the issuing court and the total bail and so forth on your police report?"

"Yes, sir, it's there in the report," I said, leaning forward just a little, just a hint. Leaning was a sincere gesture, I always felt.

Actually it was two hours after I arrested Landry that I discovered the traffic warrant. In fact, it was when I was getting ready to compose a plausible arrest report, and the discovery of a traffic warrant made me come up with this story.

"So you called into the office and found out that Timothy G. Landry of that address had a traffic warrant out for his arrest?"

"Yes, sir."

"Did you use Mr. Downey's phone?"

"No, sir, I used the pay phone in the hall."

"Why didn't you use Mr. Downey's phone? You could've saved a dime." The P.D. smiled again.

"If you dial operator and ask for the police you get your dime back anyway, counsel. I didn't want to bother Mr. Downey further, so I went out in the hall and used the pay phone."

"I see. Then you went back upstairs with the key Mr. Downey gave you?"

"Yes, sir."

"You knocked and announced yourself and made sure the voice inside was Timothy Landry, for whom you had knowledge that a warrant existed?"

"Yes, sir. The male voice said he was Timothy Landry. Or rather he said yes when I asked if he was Timothy Landry." I turned just a little toward the judge, nodding my head ever so slightly when I said this. Landry again rolled his eyeballs and slumped down in his seat at that one.

"Then when you heard the window opening and feared your traffic warrant suspect might escape down the fire escape, you forced entry?"

"I used the passkey."

"Yes, and you saw Mr. Landry on the edge of the bed as though getting ready to go out the window?"

"Yes, that's right."

"And you saw a metal object protruding from under the mattress?"

"I saw a blue metal object that I was sure was a gun barrel, counsel," I corrected him, gently.

"And you glanced to your right and there in plain view was the object marked people's two, the sandwich bag containing several grams of marijuana?"

"Yes, sir."

"I have no further questions of this witness," said the P.D., and now I was starting to worry a little, because he just went over everything as though he were the D.A. on direct examination. He just made our case stronger by giving me a chance to tell it again.

What the hell? I thought, as the judge said, "You may step down."

I sat back at the counsel table and the D.A. shrugged at my questioning look.

"Call your next witness," said the judge, taking a sip of water, as the bailiff got Homer Downey from the hall. Homer slouched up to the stand, so skinny the crotch of his pants was around his knees. He wore a dirty white shirt for the occasion and a frayed necktie and the dandruff all over his thin brown hair was even visible from the counsel table. His complexion was as yellow and bumpy as cheese pizza.

He gave his name, the address of the Orchid Hotel, and said he had been managing the place for three years. Then the D.A. asked him if I contacted him on the day of the arrest and looked at his register and borrowed his passkey, and if some ten minutes later did he come to the defendant's room and see me with the defendant under arrest, and how long had the defendant lived there, and did he rent the room to the defendant and only the defendant, and did all the events testified to occur in the city and county of Los Angeles, and Homer was a fairly good talker and a good witness, also very sincere, and was finished in a few minutes.

When direct examination was finished the public defender stood up and started pacing like in the Perry Mason shows and the judge said, "Sit down, counsel," and he apologized and sat down like in a real courtroom, where witnesses are only approached by lawyers when permission is given by the judge and where theatrical stuff is out of the question.

"Mister Downey, when Officer Morgan came to your

door on the day in question, you've testified that he asked to see your register, is that right?"

"Yes."

"Did he ask you who lived in three-nineteen?"

"Nope, just asked to see the register."

"Do you remember whose name appeared on the register?"

"Sure. His." Downey pointed at Landry, who stared back at him.

"By him, do you mean the defendant in this case? The man on my right?"

"Yes."

"And what's his name?"

"Timothy C. Landowne."

"Would you repeat that name, please, and spell it?"

My heart started beating hard then, and the sweat broke out and I said to myself, "Oh no, oh no!"

"Timothy C. Landowne. T-I-M . . ."

"Spell the last name please," the P.D. smiled and I got sick.

"Landowne. L-A-N-D-O-W-N-E."

"And the middle initial was C as in Charlie?"

"Yes, sir."

"Are you sure?"

"Sure I'm sure. He's been staying at the hotel for four, five months now. And he even stayed a couple months last year."

"Did you ever see the name Timothy G. Landry on any hotel records? That's L-A-N-D-R-Y?"

"No."

"Did you ever see the name anywhere?"

"No."

I could feel the D.A. next to me stiffen as he finally started to catch on.

"Did you at any time tell Officer Morgan that the man in three-nineteen was named Timothy G. Landry?"

"No, because that's not his name as far as I know, and I never heard that name before today."

"Thank you, Mister Downey," said the public defender, and I could feel Landry, grinning with his big shark teeth, and I was trying hard to come up with a story to get out of this. I knew at that moment, and admitted to myself finally and forever, that I should've been wearing my glasses years before this, and could no longer do police work or anything else without them, and if I hadn't been so stupid and had my glasses on, I would've seen that the name on that register was a half-assed attempt at an alias on the part of Landry, and even though the traffic warrant was as good as gold and really belonged to him, I couldn't possibly have got the right information from R and I by giving the computer the wrong name. And the judge would be sure of that in a minute because the judge would have the defendant's make sheet. And even as I was thinking it she looked at me and whispered to the court clerk who handed her a copy of the make sheet and nowhere in his record did it show he used an alias of Landowne. So I was trapped, and then Homer nailed the coffin tight.

"What did the officer do after you gave him the key?"

"He went out the door and up the stairs."

"How do you know he went up the stairs?"

"The door was open just a crack. I put my slippers on in a hurry because I wanted to go up there too so's not to miss the action. I thought something might happen, you know, an arrest and all."

"You remember my talking to you just before this hearing and asking you a few questions, Mister Downey?"

"Yes, sir."

"Do you remember my asking you about the officer using the pay phone in the lobby to call the police station?"

"Yes, sir," he said, and I had a foul taste in my mouth and I was full of gas and had branding iron indigestion pains and no pills for them.

"Do you remember what you said about the phone?"

"Yes, sir, that it didn't work. It'd been out of order for a week and I'd called the phone company, and in fact I was mad because I thought maybe they came the night before when I was out because they promised to come, and I tried it that morning just before the officer came and it was still broke. Buzzed real crazy when you dropped a dime in."

"Did you drop a dime in that morning?"

"Yes, sir. I tried to use it to call the phone company and it didn't matter if I dialed or not, it made noises so I used my own phone."

"You could *not* call out on that phone?"

"Oh no, sir."

"I suppose the phone company would have a record of your request and when they finally fixed the phone?"

"Objection, Your Honor," said the D.A. weakly. "Calls for a conclusion."

"Sustained," said the judge, looking only at me now, and I looked at Homer just for something to do with my eyes.

"Did you go upstairs behind the officer?" asked the P.D. again, and now the D.A. had slumped in his chair and was tapping with a pencil, and I'd passed the point of nervous breathing and sweat. Now I was cold and thinking, thinking about how to get out of this and what I would say if they recalled me to the stand, if either of them recalled me, and I thought the defense might call me because I was *their* witness now, they owned me.

"I went upstairs a little bit after the officer."

"What did you see when you got up there?"

"The officer was standing outside Mister Landowne's room and like listening at the door. He had his hat in his hand and his ear was pressed up to the door."

"Did he appear to see you, or rather, to look in your direction?"

"No, he had his back to my end of the hall and I decided to peek from around the corner, because I didn't know what he was up to and maybe there'd be a big shootout or something, and I could run back down the stairs if something dangerous happened."

"Did you hear him knock on the door?"

"No, he didn't knock."

"Objection," said the D.A. "The witness was asked . . ."

"All right," said the judge, holding her hand up again as the D.A. sat back down.

"Did you ever *hear* the officer knock?" the judge asked the witness.

"No, sir," said Homer to the judge, and I heard a few snickers from the rear of the court, and I thanked the gods that there were only a few spectators and none of them were cops.

"Did the officer say anything while you were there observing?" asked the P.D.

"Nothing."

"How long did you watch him?"

"Two, three minutes, maybe longer. He knelt down and tried to peek in the keyhole, but I had them all plugged two years ago because of hotel creepers and peeping toms."

"Did you . . . strike that, did the officer say anything that you could hear while you were climbing the stairway?"

"I never heard him say nothing," said Homer, looking bewildered as hell, and noticing from my face that something was sure as hell wrong and I was very unhappy.

"Then what did he do?"

"Used the key. Opened the door."

"In what way? Quickly?"

"I would say careful. He like turned the key slow and careful, and then he pulled out his pistol and then he seemed to get the bolt turned, and he kicked open the door and jumped in the room with the gun out front."

"Could you hear any conversation then?"

"Oh yeah," he giggled, through gapped, brown-stained teeth. "The officer yelled something to Mister Landowne."

"What did he say? His *exact* words if you remember."

"He said, 'Freeze asshole, you move and you're wallpaper.' "

I heard all three spectators laugh at that one, but the judge didn't think it was funny and neither did the D.A., who looked almost as sick as I figure I looked.

"Did you go in the room?"

"Yes, sir, for a second."

"Did you see anything unusual about the room?"

"No. The officer told me to get out and go back to my room so I did."

"Did you notice if anything was on the dresser?"

"I didn't notice."

"Did you hear any other conversation between the officer and the defendant?"

"No."

"Nothing at all?"

"The officer warned him about something."

"What did he say?"

"It was about Mister Landowne not trying anything funny, something like that. I was walking out."

"What did he say?"

"Well, it's something else not exactly decent."

"We're grown up. What did he say?"

"He said, 'You get out of that chair and I'll shove this gun so far up your ass there'll be shit on the grips.' That's what he said. I'm sorry." Homer turned red and giggled nervously and shrugged at me.

"The defendant was sitting in a chair?"

"Yes."

"Was it his own gun the officer was talking about?"

"Objection," said the D.A.

"I'll rephrase that," said the P.D. "Was the officer holding his own gun in his hand at that time?"

"Yes, sir."

"Did you see the other gun at that time?"

"No, I never saw no other gun."

The P.D. hesitated for a long, deadly silent minute and chewed on the tip of his pencil, and I almost sighed out loud when he said, "I have no further questions," even though it was much too late to feel relieved.

"I have a question," said Judge Bedford, and she pushed her glasses up over a hump on her thin nose and said,

"Mister Downey, did you happen to go into the lobby any time that morning *before* the officer arrived?"

"No."

"You never went out or looked out into the lobby area?"

"Well, only when the officer drove up in front. I saw the police car parked in front, and I was curious and I started out the door and then I saw the officer climbing the front steps of the hotel and I went back inside to put a shirt and shoes on so's to look presentable in case he needed some help from me."

"Did you look into the lobby?"

"Well, yes, it's right in front of my door, ma'am."

"Who was in the lobby?"

"Why, nobody."

"Could you see the entire lobby? All the chairs? Everywhere in the lobby area?"

"Why sure. My front door opens right on the lobby and it's not very big."

"Think carefully. Did you see two men sleeping anywhere near the lobby area?"

"There was nobody there, Judge."

"And where was the officer when you were looking into the empty lobby?"

"Coming in the front door, ma'am. A couple seconds later he came to my door and asked about the room and looked at the register like I said."

My brain was burning up now like the rest of me, and I had an idiotic story ready when they recalled me about how I'd come in the lobby once and then got out and come in again when Homer saw me and thought it was the first entry. And I was prepared to swear the phone worked, because what the hell, anything was possible with telephone problems. And even if that bony-assed, dirty little sneak followed me up the stairs, maybe I could convince them I called to Landry *before* Downey got up there, and what the hell, Downey didn't know if the marijuana was on the dresser or in the closet, and I was trying to tell myself everything would be all right so I could keep the big-eyed honest look on my kisser because I needed it now if ever in my life.

I was waiting to be recalled and I was ready even though my right knee trembled and made me mad as hell, and then the judge said to the public defender and the D.A., "Will counsel please approach the bench?"

Then I knew it was all over and Landry was making noises and I could feel the shark grin as his head was turned toward me. I just stared straight ahead like a zombie and wondered if I'd walk out of this courtroom in handcuffs for perjury, because anybody in the world could see that dumb shit Homer Downey was telling the stone truth and didn't even know what the P.D. was doing to me.

When they came back to the table after talking with the judge, the D.A. smiled woodenly at me and whispered, "It was the name on the register. When the public defender realized that Homer didn't know Landry's real name, he asked him about the register. It was the register that opened it all up for him. She's going to dismiss the case. I don't know what to advise you, Officer. I've never had anything like this happen before. Maybe I should call my office and ask what to do if . . ."

"Would you care to offer a motion to dismiss, Mister Jeffries?" asked the judge to the public defender, who jumped to his feet and did just that, and then she dismissed the case, and I hardly heard Landry chuckling all over the place and I knew he was shaking hands with that baby-faced little python that defended him. Then Landry leaned over the public defender and said, "Thanks, stupid," to me, but the P.D. told him to cool it. Then the bailiff had his hand on my shoulder and said, "Judge Redford would like to see you in her chambers," and I saw the judge had left the bench and I walked like a toy soldier toward the open door. In a few seconds I was standing in the middle of this room, and facing a desk where the judge sat looking toward the wall which was lined with bookcases full of law books. She was taking deep breaths and thinking of what to say.

"Sit down," she said, finally, and I did. I dropped my hat on the floor and was afraid to stoop down to pick it up I was so dizzy.

"In all my years on the bench I've never had that happen. Not like that. I'd like to know why you did it."

"I want to tell you the truth," I said and my mouth was leathery. I had trouble forming the words. My lips popped from the dryness every time I opened my mouth. I had seen nervous suspects like that thousands of times when I had them good and dirty, and they knew I had them.

"Maybe I should advise you of your constitutional rights before you tell me anything," said the judge, and she took off her glasses and the bump on her nose was more prominent. She was a homely woman and looked smaller here in her office, but she looked stronger too, and aged.

"The hell with my rights!" I said suddenly. "I don't give a damn about my rights, I want to tell you the truth."

"But I intend to have the district attorney's office is-

sue a perjury complaint against you. I'm going to have
that hotel register brought in, and the phone company's
repairman will be subpoenaed and so will Mister Downey
of course, and I think you'll be convicted."

"Don't you even care about what I've got to say?" I
was getting mad now as well as scared, and I could feel
the tears coming to my eyes, and I hadn't felt anything
like this since I couldn't remember when.

"What can you say? What can anyone say? I'm awfully disappointed. I'm sickened in fact." She rubbed her
eyes at the corners for a second and I was busting and
couldn't hold on.

"*You're* disappointed? *You're* sickened? What the hell
do you think I'm feeling at this minute? I feel like you got
a blowtorch on the inside of my guts and you won't turn
it off and it'll never be turned off, that's what I feel, Your
Honor. Now can I tell the God's truth? Will you at least
let me tell it?"

"Go ahead," she said, and lit a cigarette and leaned
back in the padded chair and watched me.

"Well, I have this snitch, Your Honor. And I've got to
protect my informants, you know that. For his own personal safety, and so he can continue to give me information. And the way things are going in court nowadays with
everyone so nervous about the defendant's rights, I'm
afraid to even mention confidential informants like I used
to, and I'm afraid to try to get a search warrant because
the judges are so damn hinky they call damn near every
informant a material witness, even when he's not. So in
recent years I've started . . . exploring ways around."

"You've started lying."

"Yes, I've started lying! What the hell, I'd hardly ever

convict any of these crooks if I didn't lie at least a little bit. You know what the search and seizure and arrest rules are like nowadays."

"Go on."

Then I told her how the arrest went down, exactly how it went down, and how I later got the idea about the traffic warrant when I found out he had one. And when I was finished, she smoked for a good two minutes and didn't say a word. Her cheeks were eroded and looked like they were hacked out of a rocky cliff. She was a strong old woman from another century as she sat there and showed me her profile and finally she said, "I've seen witnesses lie thousands of times. I guess every defendant lies to a greater or lesser degree and most defense witnesses stretch hell out of the truth, and of course I've seen police officers lie about probable cause. There's the old hackneyed story about feeling what appeared to be an offensive weapon like a knife in the defendant's pocket and reaching inside to retrieve the knife and finding it to be a stick of marijuana. That one's been told so many times by so many cops it makes judges want to vomit. And of course there's the furtive movement like the defendant is shoving something under the seat of the car. That's always good probable cause for a search, and likewise that's overdone. Sure, I've heard officers lie before, but nothing is black and white in this world and there are degrees of truth and untruth, and like many other judges who feel police officers cannot possibly protect the public these days, I've given officers the benefit of the doubt in probable cause situations. I never really believed a Los Angeles policeman would *completely* falsify his entire testimony as you've done today. That's why I feel sickened by it."

"I didn't falsify it all. He had the gun. It *was* under the mattress. He *had* the marijuana. I just lied about where I found it. Your Honor, he's an active bandit. The robbery dicks figure him for six robberies. He's beaten an old man and blinded him. He's . . ."

She held up her hand and said, "I didn't figure he was using that gun to stir his soup with, Officer Morgan. He has the look of a dangerous man about him."

"You could see it too!" I said. "Well . . ."

"Nothing," she interrupted. "That means nothing. The higher courts have given us difficult law, but by God, it's the law!"

"Your Honor," I said slowly. And then the tears filled my eyes and there was nothing I could do. "I'm not afraid of losing my pension. I've done nineteen years and over eleven months and I'm leaving the Department after tomorrow, and officially retiring in a few weeks, but I'm not afraid of losing the money. That's not why I'm asking, why I'm *begging* you to give me a chance. And it's not that I'm afraid to face a perjury charge and go to jail, because you can't be a crybaby in this world. But Judge, there are people, policemen, and other people, people on my beat who think I'm something special. I'm one of the ones they really look up to, you know? I'm not just a character, I'm a hell of a cop!"

"I know you are," she said. "I've noticed you in my courtroom many times."

"You have?" Of course I'd been in her courtroom as a witness before, but I figured all bluecoats looked the same to blackrobes. "Don't get down on us, Judge Bedford. Some coppers don't lie at all, and others only lie a little like you said. Only a few like me would do what I did."

"Why?"

"Because I care, Your Honor, goddamnit. Other cops put in their nine hours and go home to their families twenty miles from town and that's it, but guys like me, why I got nobody and I want nobody. I do my living on my beat. And I've got things inside me that make me do these things against my better judgment. That proves I'm dumber than the dumbest moron on my beat."

"You're not dumb. You're a clever witness. A very clever witness."

"I never lied that much before, Judge. I just thought I could get away with it. I just couldn't read that name right on that hotel register. If I could've read that name right on the register I never would've been able to pull off that traffic warrant story and I wouldn't've tried it. And I probably wouldn't be in this fix, and the reason I couldn't really see that name and only assumed it must've been Landry is because I'm fifty years old and farsighted, and too stubborn to wear my glasses, and kidding myself that I'm thirty and doing a young man's job when I can't cut it anymore. I'm going out though, Judge. This clinches it if I ever had any doubts. Tomorrow's my last day. A knight. Yesterday somebody called me a Blue Knight. Why do people say such things? They make you think you're really something and so you got to win a battle every time out. Why should I care if Landry walks out of here? What's it to *me?* Why do they *call* you a knight?"

She looked at me then and put the cigarette out and I'd never in my life begged anyone for anything, and never licked anyone's boots. I was glad she was a woman because it wasn't quite so bad to be licking a woman's boots, not *quite* so bad, and my stomach wasn't only burning now, it was hurting in spasms, like a big fist was pounding inside in a jerky rhythm. I thought I'd double over from the pain in a few minutes.

"Officer Morgan, you fully agree don't you that we can call off the whole damn game and crawl back in primeval muck if the orderers, the enforcers of the law, begin to operate outside it? You understand that there could be no civilization, don't you? You know, don't you, that I as well as many other judges am terribly aware of the overwhelming numbers of criminals on those streets whom you policemen must protect us from? You cannot always do it and there are times when you are handcuffed by court decisions that presume the goodness of people past all logical presumption. But don't you think there are judges, and yes, even defense attorneys, who sympathize with you? Can't you see that you, you policemen of all people, must be more than you are? You must be patient and above all, honest. Can't you see if you go outside the law regardless of how absurd it seems, in the name of enforcing it, that we're all doomed? Can you see these things?"

"Yes. Yes, I know, but old Knobby Booker doesn't know. And if I had to name him as my snitch he might get a rat jacket and somebody might rip him off. . . ." And now my voice was breaking and I could hardly see her because it was all over and I knew I'd be taken out of this courtroom and over to the county jail. "When you're alone out there on that beat, Your Honor, and everyone knows you're the Man. . . . The way they look at you . . . and how it feels when they say, 'You're a champ, Bumper. You're a warlord. You're a Knight, a Blue Knight. . . .'" And then I could say no more and said no more that day to that woman.

The silence was buzzing in my ears and finally she said, "Officer Morgan, I'm requesting that the deputy district attorney say nothing of your perjured testimony in his report to his office. I'm also going to request the public defender, the bailiff, the court reporter and the clerk, not to reveal what happened in there today. I want you to leave now so I can wonder if I've done the right thing. We'll never forget this, but we'll take no further action."

I couldn't believe it. I sat for a second, paralyzed, and then I stood up and wiped my eyes and walked toward the door and stopped and didn't even think to thank her, and looked around, but she was turned in her chair and watching the book stacks again. When I walked through the courtroom, the public defender and the district attorney were talking quietly and both of them glanced at me. I could feel them look at me, but I went straight for the door, holding my stomach, and waiting for the cramps to subside so I could think.

I stepped into the hall and remembered vaguely that the gun and narcotics evidence were still in the courtroom, and then thought the hell with it, I had to get out in the car and drive with the breeze in my face before the blood surging through my skull blew the top of my head off.

I went straight for Elysian Park around the back side, got out of the car, filled my pockets with acid eaters from the glove compartment, and climbed the hill behind the reservoir. I could smell eucalyptus, and the dirt was dry and loose under my shoes. The hill was steeper than I thought and I was sweating pretty good after just a few minutes of walking. Then I saw two park peepers. One had binoculars to see the show better. They were watching the road down below where couples sit in their cars at any hour of the day or night under the trees and make love.

"Get outta my park, you barfbags," I said, and they turned around and saw me standing above them. They both were middle-aged guys. One of them, with fishbelly pale skin, wore orange checkered pants and a yellow turtleneck and had the binoculars up to his face. When I spoke he dropped them and bolted through the brush. The other guy looked indignant and started walking stiff-legged away like a cocky little terrier, but when I took a few steps toward him, cursing and growling, he started running too, and I picked up the binoculars and threw them at him, but missed and they bounced off a tree and fell in the brush. Then I climbed the hill clear to the top and even though it was smoggy, the view was pretty good. By the time I flopped on the grass and took off my Sam Browne and my hat, the stomach cramps were all but gone. I fell asleep almost right away and slept an hour there on the cool grass.

THIRTEEN

WHEN I WOKE UP, the world tasted horrible and I popped an acid eater just to freshen my mouth. I laid there on my back for a while and looked up at a blue-jay scampering around on a branch.

"Did you shit in my mouth?" I said, and then wondered what I'd been dreaming about because I was sweaty even though it was fairly cool here. A breeze blowing over me felt wonderful. I saw by my watch it was after four and I hated to get up but of course I had to. I sat up, tucked in my shirt, strapped on the Sam Browne and combed back my hair which was tough to do, it was so wild and wiry. And I thought, I'll be glad when it all falls out and then I won't have to screw around with it anymore. It was hell sometimes when even your hair wouldn't obey you. When you had no control over anything, even your goddamn hair. Maybe I should use hair spray, I thought, like these pretty young cops nowadays. Maybe while I still had some hair I should get those fifteen-dollar haircuts and ride around in a radio car all day, spraying my hair instead of booking these scumbags, and then I could stay out of trouble, then no judge could throw me in jail for perjury, and disgrace me, and ruin everything I've done for twenty years, and ruin everything they all think about me, all of them, the people on the beat.

One more day and it's over, thank Christ, I thought, and half stumbled down the hill to my car because I still wasn't completely awake.

"One-X-L-Forty-five, One-X-L-Forty-five, come in," said the communications operator, a few seconds after I started the car. She sounded exasperated as hell, so I guess she'd been trying to get me. Probably a major crisis, like a stolen bicycle, I thought.

"One-X-L-Forty-five, go," I said disgustedly into the mike.

"One-X-L-Forty-five, meet the plainclothes officer at the southeast corner of Beverly and Vermont in Rampart Division. This call has been approved by your watch commander."

I rogered the call and wondered what was going on and then despite how rotten I felt, how disgusted with everything and everybody, and mostly this miserable crummy job, despite all that, my heart started beating a little bit harder, and I got a sort of happy feeling bubbling around inside me because I knew it had to be Charlie Bronski. Charlie must have something, and next thing I knew I was driving huckety-buck over Temple, slicing through the heavy traffic and then bombing it down Vermont, and I spotted Charlie in a parking lot near a market. He was standing beside his car looking hot and tired and mad, but I knew he had something or he'd never call me out of my division like this.

"About time, Bumper," said Charlie, "I been trying to

reach you on the radio for a half hour. They told me you left court a long time ago."

"Been out for investigation, Charlie. Too big to talk about."

"Wonder what *that* means," Charlie smiled, with his broken-toothed, Slavic, hard-looking grin. "I got something so good you won't believe it."

"You busted Red Scalotta!"

"No, no, you're dreaming," he laughed. "But I got the search warrant for the back that Reba told us about."

"How'd you do it so fast?"

"I don't actually have it yet. I'll have it in fifteen minutes when Nick and Fuzzy and the Administrative Vice team get here. Nick just talked to me on the radio. Him and Fuzzy just left the Hall of Justice. They got the warrant and the Ad Vice team is on the way to assist."

"How the hell did you do it, Charlie?" I asked, and now I'd forgotten the judge, and the humiliation, and the misery, and Charlie and me were grinning at each other because we were both on the scent. And when a real cop gets on it, there's nothing else he can think about. Nothing.

"After we left Reba I couldn't wait to get started on this thing. We went to that laundry over near Sixth and Kenmore. Actually, it's a modern dry cleaning and laundry establishment. They do the work on the premises and it's pretty damned big. The building's on the corner and takes in the whole ground floor, and I even saw employees going up to the second floor where they have storage or something. I watched from across the street with binoculars and Fuzzy prowled around the back alley and found the door Reba said Aaron was talking about."

"Who in the hell is Aaron, Charlie?"

"He's Scalotta's think man. Aaron Fishman. He's an accountant and a shrewd organizer and he's got everything it takes but guts, so he's a number two man to Scalotta. I never saw the guy, I only heard about him from Ad Vice and Intelligence. Soon as Reba described that little Jew I knew who she was talking about. He's Scalotta's link with the back offices. He protects Red's interests and hires the back clerks and keeps things moving. Dick Reemey at Intelligence says he doesn't think Red could operate without Aaron Fishman. Red's drifting away from the business more and more, getting in with the Hollywood crowd. Anyway, Fuzzy, who's a nosy bastard, went in the door to the laundry and found a stairway that was locked, and a door down. He went down and found a basement and an old vented furnace and a trash box, and he started sifting through and found a few adding machine tapes all ending in fives and zeros, and he even found a few charred pieces of owe sheets and a half-burned scratch sheet. I'll bet Aaron would set fire to his clerk if he knew he was that careless."

Charlie chuckled for a minute and I lit a cigar and looked at my watch.

"Don't worry about the time, Bumper, the back office clerks don't leave until an hour or so past the last post. He's got to stay and figure his tops."

"Tops?"

"Top sheets. This shows each agent's code and lists his bettors and how much was won and lost."

"Wonder how Zoot Lafferty did today?" I laughed.

"Handbooks like Zoot get ten percent hot or cold, win or lose," said Charlie. "Anyway, Fuzzy found a little evidence to corroborate Reba, and then came the most unbelievable tremendous piece of luck I ever had in this job. He's crawling around down there in the basement like a rat, picking up burned residue, and next thing he sees is a big ugly guy standing stone still in the dark corner of the basement. Fuzzy almost shit his pants and he didn't have a gun or anything because you don't really need weapons when you're working books. Next thing, this guy comes toward him like the creature from the black lagoon and Fuzzy said the door was behind the guy and just as he's thinking about rushing him with his head down and trying to bowl him over on his ass, the giant starts talking in a little-boy voice and says, 'Hello, my name is Bobby. Do you know how to fix electric trains?'

"And next thing Fuzzy knows this guy leads him to a little room in the back where there's a bed and a table and Fuzzy has to find a track break in a little electric train set that Bobby's got on his table, and all the time the guy's standing there, his head damn near touching the top of the doorway he's so big, and making sure Fuzzy fixes it."

"Well, what . . ."

"Lemme finish," Charlie laughed. "Anyway, Fuzzy gets the train fixed and the big ox starts banging Fuzzy on the back and shoulders out of sheer joy, almost knocking Fuzzy's bridgework loose, and Fuzzy finds out this moron is the cleanup man, evidently some retarded relative of the owner of the building, and he lives there in the basement and does the windows and floors and everything in the place.

"There're some offices on the second floor with a

completely different stairway, Fuzzy discovers, and this locked door is the only way up to this part of the third floor except for the fire escape in back and the ladder's up and chained in place. This giant, Bobby, says that the third floor is all storage space for one of the offices on the second floor except for 'Miss Terry's place,' and then he starts telling Fuzzy how he likes Miss Terry and how she brings him pies and good things to eat every day, so Fuzzy starts pumping him and Bobby tells him how he hardly ever goes in Miss Terry's place, but he washes the windows once in a while and sometimes helps her with something. And with Fuzzy prodding, he tells about the wooden racks where all the little yellow cards are with the numbers. Those're the ABC professional-type markers of course, and he tells about the adding machine, two adding machines, in fact, and when Fuzzy shows him the burned National Daily Reporter, Bobby says, yeah, those are always there. In short, he completely describes an elite bookmaking office right up to the way papers are bundled and filed."

"You used this Bobby for your informant on the search warrant affidavit?"

"Yeah. I didn't have to mention anything about Reba. According to the affidavit, we got the warrant solely on the basis of this informant Bobby and our own corroborative findings."

"You'll have to use the poor guy in court?"

"He'll certainly have to be named," said Charlie.

"How old a guy is he?"

"I don't know, fifty, fifty-five."

"Think they'll hurt him?"

"Why should they? He doesn't even know what he's

doing. They can see that. They just fucked up, that's all. Why should they hurt a dummy?"

"Because they're slimeballs."

"Well, you never know," Charlie shrugged. "They might. Anyway, we got the warrant, Bumper. By God, I kept my promise to you."

"Thanks, Charlie. Nobody could've done better. You got anybody staked on the place?"

"Milburn. He works in our office. We'll just end up busting the broad, Terry. According to the dummy she's the only one ever comes in there except once in a while a man comes in, he said. He couldn't remember what the man looked like. This is Thursday. Should be a lot of paper in that back office. If we get enough of the records we can hurt them, Bumper."

"A two-hundred-and-fifty-dollar fine?" I sniffed.

"If we get the right records we can put Internal Revenue on them. They can tax ten percent of gross for the year. And they can go back as far as five years. That hurts, Bumper. That hurts even a guy as big as Red Scalotta, but it's tough to pull it off."

"How're you going in?"

"We first decided to use Bobby. We can use subterfuge to get in if we can convince the court that we have information that this organization will attempt to destroy records. Hell, they all do that. Fuzzy thought about using Bobby to bang on the lower door to the inside stairway and call Terry and have Terry open the door which she can buzz open. We could tell Bobby it's a game or something, but Nick and Milburn voted us down. They thought when we charged through the door and up the steps through the office door and got Terry by the ass, old

Bobby might decide to end the game. If he stopped playing I imagine he'd be no more dangerous than a brahma bull. Anyway, Nick and Milburn were afraid we'd have to hurt the dummy so they voted us down."

"So how'll you do it?"

"We borrowed a black policewoman from Southwest Detectives. We got her in a blue dungaree apron suit like the black babes that work pressing downstairs. She's going to knock on the downstairs door and start yelling something unintelligible in a way-out suede dialect, and hope Terry buzzes her in. Then she's going to walk up the steps and blab something about a fire in the basement and get as close to Terry as she can, and we hope she can get right inside and get her down on the floor and sit on her because me and Nick'll be charging up that door right behind her. The Administrative Vice team'll follow in a few minutes and help us out since they're the experts on a back-office operation. You know, I only took one back office before so this'll be something for me too."

"Where'll I be?"

"Well, we got to hide you with your bluesuit, naturally, so you can hang around out back, near the alley behind the solid wood fence on the west side. After we take the place I'll open the back window and call you and you can come on in and see the fruits of your labor with Zoot Lafferty."

"What'll you do about getting by your star witness?"

"The dummy? Oh, Fuzzy got stuck with that job since he's Bobby's best pal," Charlie chuckled. "Before any of us even get in position Fuzzy's going in to get Bobby and walk him down the street to the drugstore for an ice cream sundae."

"One-Victor-One to Two, come in," said a voice over frequency six.

"That's Milburn at the back office," said Charlie, hurrying to the radio.

"Go, Lem," said Charlie over the mike.

"Listen, Charlie," said Milburn. "A guy just went in that doorway outside. It's possible he could've turned left into the laundry, I couldn't tell, but I think he made a right to the office stairway."

"What's he look like, Lem?" asked Charlie.

"Caucasian, fifty-five to sixty, five-six, hundred fifty, bald, moustache, glasses. Dressed good. I think he parked one block north and walked down because I saw a white Cad circle the block twice and there was a bald guy driving and looking around like maybe for heat."

"Okay, Lem, we'll be there pretty quick," said Charlie, hanging up the mike, red-faced and nodding at me without saying anything.

"Fishman," I said.

"Son of a bitch," said Charlie. "Son of a bitch. He's there!"

Then Charlie got on the mike and called Nick and the others, having trouble keeping his voice low and modulated in his excitement, and it was affecting me and my heart started beating. Charlie told them to hurry it up and asked their estimated time of arrival.

"Our E.T.A. is five minutes," said Nick over the radio.

"Jesus, Bumper, we got a chance to take the office and Aaron Fishman at the same time! That weaselly lit-

tle cocksucker hasn't been busted since the depression
days!"

I was still happy as hell for Charlie, but looking at it
realistically, what the hell was there to scream about?
They had an idiot for an informant, and I didn't want
to throw cold water, but I knew damn well the search
warrant stood a good chance of being traversed, especially if Bobby was brought into court as a material witness and they saw his I.Q. was less than par golf. And
if it wasn't traversed, and they convicted the clerk and
Fishman, what the hell would happen to them, a two-
hundred-fifty-dollar fine? Fishman probably had four
times that much in his pants pocket right now. And I
wasn't any too thrilled about I.R.S. pulling off a big case
and hitting them in the bankbook, but even if they did,
what would it mean? That Scalotta couldn't buy a new
whip every time he had parties with sick little girls like
Reba? Or maybe Aaron Fishman would have to drive his
Cad for two years without getting a new one? I couldn't
see anything to get ecstatic about when I considered
it all. In fact, I was feeling lower by the minute, and
madder. I prayed Red Scalotta would show up there too
and maybe try to resist arrest, even though my common
sense told me nothing like that would ever happen, but
if it did . . .

"There should be something there to destroy the
important records," said Charlie, puffing on a cigarette
and dancing around impatiently waiting for Nick and the
others to drive up.

"You mean like flash paper? I've heard of that," I
said.

"They sometimes use that, but mostly in fronts," said

Charlie. "You touch a flame or a cigarette to it and it goes up in one big flash and leaves no residue. They also got this dissolving paper. You drop it in water and it dissolves with no residue you can put under a microscope. But sometimes in backs they have some type of small furnace they keep charged where they can throw the real important stuff. Where the hell is that Nick?"

"Right here, Charlie," I said, as the vice car sped across the parking lot. Nick and Fuzzy and the Negro policewoman were inside and another car was following with the two guys from Administrative Vice.

Everybody was wetting their pants when they found out Aaron Fishman was in there, and I marveled at vice officers, how they can get excited about something that is so disappointing, and depressing, and meaningless, when you thought about it. And then Charlie hurriedly explained to the Ad Vice guys what a uniformed cop was doing there, saying it started out as my caper. I knew one of the Ad Vice officers from when he used to work Central Patrol and we jawed and made plans for another five minutes, and finally piled into the cars.

We turned north on Catalina from Sixth Street before getting to Kenmore and then turned west and came down Kenmore from the north. The north side of Sixth Street is all apartment buildings and to the south is the Miracle Mile, Wilshire Boulevard. Sixth Street itself is mostly commercial buildings. Everybody parked to the north because the windows were painted on the top floor of the building on this side. It was the blind side, and after a few minutes everybody got ready when Fuzzy was seen through binoculars skipping down the sidewalk with Bobby, who even from this distance looked like

Gargantua. With the giant gone the stronghold wasn't quite so impregnable.

In a few minutes they were all hustling down the sidewalk and I circled around the block on foot and came in behind the wooden fence and I was alone and sweating in the sunshine, wondering why the hell I wanted this so bad, and how the organization would get back on its feet, and another of Red's back offices would just take as much of the action as it could until a new back could be set up, and Aaron would get his new Cad in two years. And he and Red would be free to enjoy it all and maybe someone like me would be laying up in the county jail for perjury in the special tank where they keep policemen accused of crimes, because a policeman put in with the regular pukepots would live probably about one hour at best.

This job didn't make sense. How could I have told myself for twenty years that it made any sense at all? How could I charge around that beat, a big blue stupid clown, and pretend that anything made any sense at all? Judge Redford *should've* put me in jail, I thought. My brain was boiling in the sunshine, the sweat running in my eyes and burning. That would've been a consistent kind of lunacy at least. What the hell are we doing here like this?

Then suddenly I couldn't stand it there alone, my big ass only partly hidden by the fence, and I walked out in the alley and over to the fire escape of the old building. The iron ladder was chained up like an ancient fearsome drawbridge. A breach of fire regulation to chain it up, I thought, and I looked around for something to stand on, and spotted a trash can by the fence which I emptied and turned upside down under the ladder. And then in a minute I was dangling there like a fat sweaty baboon, tearing my pants on the concrete wall, scuffing my shoes, panting, and finally sobbing, because I couldn't get my ass up there on a window ledge where I could then climb over the railing on the second floor.

I fell back once, clear to the alley below. I fell hard on my shoulder, and thought if I'd been able to read that hotel register I'd never have been humiliated like that, and I thought of how I was of no value whatever to this operation which was in itself of no value because if I couldn't catch Red Scalotta and Aaron Fishman by the rules, then they would put *me* in jail. And I sat on my ass there in the alley, panting, my hands red and sore and my shoulder hurting, and I thought then, if I go to the dungeon and Fishman goes free, then *I'm* the scumbag and *he's* the Blue Knight, and I wondered how he would look in my uniform.

Then I looked up at that ladder and vowed that I'd die here in this alley if I didn't climb that fire escape. I got back on the trash can and jumped up, grabbing the metal ladder and feeling it drop a little until the chain caught it. Then I shinnied up the wall again, gasping and sobbing out loud, the sweat like vinegar in my eyes, and got one foot up and had to stop and try to breathe in the heat. I almost let go and thought how that would make sense too if I fell head first now onto the garbage can and broke my fat neck. Then I took a huge breath and knew if I didn't make it now I never would make it, and I heaved my carcass up, up, and then I was sitting on the window ledge and surprisingly enough I still had my hat on and I hadn't lost my gun. I was perched there on the ledge in a pile of birdshit, and a fat gray pigeon sat on the fire escape railing over me. He cooed and looked at me gasping and grimacing and wondered if I was dangerous.

"Get outta here, you little prick," I whispered, when he crapped on my shoulder. I swung my hat at him and he squawked and flew away.

Then I dragged myself up carefully, keeping most of my weight on the window ledge, and I was on the railing and then I climbed over and was on the first landing of the fire escape where I had to rest for a minute because I was dizzy. I looked at my watch and saw that the police-woman should be about ready to try her flimflam now, so, dizzy or not, I climbed the second iron ladder.

It was steep and long to the third floor, one of those almost vertical iron ladders like on a ship, with round iron hand railings. I climbed as quietly as I could, taking long deep breaths. Then I was at the top and was glad I wouldn't have to make the steep descent back down. I should be walking out through the back office if every-thing went right. When Charlie opened the back door to call to me, I'd be standing right here watching the door instead of crouched in some alley. And if I heard any doors breaking, or any action at all, I'd kick in the back door here, and maybe *I'd* be the first one inside the place, and maybe I'd do something else that could land me in jail, but the way I felt this moment, maybe it would be worth it because twenty years didn't mean a goddamn thing when Scalotta and Fishman could wear *my* uniform and I could wear jail denims with striped patch pockets and lay up there in the cop's tank at the county jail.

Then I heard a crash and I knew the scam hadn't worked because this was a door breaking far away, way down below, which meant they'd had to break in that first door, run up those steps clear to the third floor and break in the other door, and then I found myself kicking on the back door which I didn't know was steel reinforced with a heavy bar across it. It wouldn't go, and at that moment I didn't know how sturdy they had made it and I thought it was a regular door and I was almost crying as I kicked it because I couldn't even take down a door anymore and I couldn't do *anything* anymore. But I kicked, and kicked, and finally I went to the window on the left and kicked right through it, cutting my leg. I broke out the glass with my hands and I lost my hat and cut my forehead on the glass and was raging and yelling something I couldn't remember when I stormed through that room and saw the terrified young woman and the trembling bald little man by the doorway, their arms full of boxes. They looked at me for a second and then the woman started screaming and the man went out the door, turned right and headed for the fire escape with me after him. He threw the bar off the steel door and was back out on the fire escape, a big cardboard box in his arms crammed with cards and papers, and he stopped on the landing and saw how steep that ladder was. He was holding tight to the heavy box and he turned his back to the ladder and gripped the box and was going to try to back down the iron stairs when I grabbed him with my bloody hands and he yelled at me as two pigeons flew in our faces with a whir and rattle of wings.

"Let me go!" he said, the little greenish sacs under his eyes bulging. "You ape, let me go!"

And then I don't know if I just let him go or if I put pressure against him. I honestly don't know, but it doesn't really make any difference, because pulling away from me like he was, and holding that box like Midas's gold, I knew exactly what would happen if I just suddenly did what he was asking.

So I don't know for sure if I shoved him or if I just released him, but as I said, the result would've been the same, and at this moment in my life it was the only thing that made the slightest bit of sense, the only thing I could do for any of it to make any sense at all. He would never wear my bluesuit, never, if I only did what he was asking. My heart was thumping like the pigeon's wing, and I just let go and dropped my bleeding hands to my sides.

He pitched backward then, and the weight of the box against his chest made him fall head first, clattering down the iron ladder like an anchor being dropped. He was screaming and the box had broken open and markers and papers were flying and sailing and tumbling through the air. It *did* sound like an anchor chain feeding out, the way he clattered down. On the landing below where he stopped, I saw his dentures on the first rung of the ladder not broken, and his glasses on the landing, broken, and the cardboard box on top of him so you could hardly see the little man doubled over beneath it. He was quiet for a second and then started whimpering, and finally sounded like a pigeon cooing.

"What happened, Bumper?" asked Charlie, running out on the fire escape, out of breath.

"Did you get all the right records, Charlie?"

"Oh my God, what happened?"

"He fell."

"Is he dead?"

"I don't think so, Charlie. He's making a lot of noises."

"I better call for an ambulance," said Charlie. "You better stay here."

"I intend to," I said, and stood there resting against the railing for five minutes watching Fishman. During that time, Nick and Charlie went down and unfolded him and mopped at his face and bald head, which was broken with huge lacerations.

Charlie and me left the others there and drove slowly in the wake of the screaming ambulance which was taking Fishman to Central Receiving Hospital.

"How bad is your leg cut?" asked Charlie, seeing the blood, a purple wine color when it soaks through a policeman's blue uniform.

"Not bad, Charlie," I said, dabbing at the cuts on my hands.

"Your face doesn't look bad. Little cut over your eye."

"I feel fine."

"There was a room across from the back office," said Charlie. "We found a gas-fed burn oven in there. It was fired up and vented through the roof. They would've got to it if you hadn't crashed through the window. I'm thankful you did it, Bumper. You saved everything for us."

"Glad I could help."

"Did Fishman try to fight you or anything?"

"He struggled a little. He just fell."

"I hope the little asshole dies. I'm thinking what he

means to the organization and what he is, and I hope the little asshole dies, so help me God. You know, I thought you pushed him for a minute. I thought you did it and I was glad."

"He just fell, Charlie."

"Here we are, let's get you cleaned up," said Charlie, parking on the Sixth Street side of Central Receiving where a doctor was going into the ambulance that carried Fishman. The doctor came out in a few seconds and waved them on to General Hospital where there are better surgical facilities.

"How's he look, doctor?" asked Charlie, as we walked through the emergency entrance.

"Not good," said the doctor.

"Think he'll die?" asked Charlie.

"I don't know. If he doesn't, he may wish he had."

The cut on my leg took a few stitches but the ones on my hands and face weren't bad and just took cleaning and a little germ killer. It was almost seven o'clock when I finished my reports telling how Fishman jerked out of my grasp and how I got cut.

When I left, Charlie was dictating his arrest report to a typist.

"Well, I'll be going now, Charlie," I said, and he stopped his dictation and stood up and walked with me a little way down the hall and looked for a second like he was going to shake hands with me.

"Thanks, Bumper, for everything. This is the best vice pinch I've ever been in on. We got more of their records than I could've dreamed of."

"Thanks for cutting me in on it, Charlie."

"It was *your* caper."

"Wonder how Fishman's doing?" I said, getting a sharp pain and feeling a bubble forming. I popped two tablets.

"Fuzzy called out there about a half hour ago. Couldn't find out much. I'll tell you one thing, I'll bet Red Scalotta has to get a new accountant and business advisor. I'll bet Fishman'll have trouble adding two-digit numbers after this."

"Well, maybe it worked out right."

"Right? It was more than that. For the first time in years I feel like maybe there *is* some justice in the world, and even though they fuck over you and rub it in your face and fuck over the law itself, well, now for the first time I feel like maybe there's other hands in it, and these hands'll give you some justice. I feel like the hand of God pushed that man down those stairs."

"The hand of God, huh? Yeah, well I'll be seeing you, Charlie. Hang in there, old shoe."

"See you, Bumper," said Charlie Bronski, his square face lit up, eyes crinkled, the broken tooth showing.

The locker room was empty when I got there, and after I sat down on the bench and started unlacing my boondockers, I suddenly realized how sore I was. Not the cuts from the glass, that was nothing. But my shoulder where I fell in that alley, and my arms and back from dangling there on that fire escape, when I couldn't do what any young cop could do—pull my ass up six feet in the air. And my hands were blistered and raw from hanging there and from clawing at the concrete wall trying to get that boost. Even my ass was sore, deep inside, the muscles of both cheeks, from kicking against that steel reinforced door and bouncing off it like a tennis ball, or maybe in my case like a lumpy medicine ball. I was very very sore all over.

In fifteen minutes I'd gotten into my sport coat and slacks, and combed my hair as best I could, which just means rearranging what resembles a bad wiring job, and slipped on my loafers, and was driving out of the parking lot in my Ford. The gas pains were gone, and no indigestion. Then I thought of Aaron Fishman again, folded over, his gouged head twisted under the puny little body with the big cardboard box on top. But I stopped that nonsense right there, and said, no, no, you won't haunt my sleep because it doesn't matter a bit that I made you fall. I was just the instrument of some force in this world that, when the time is right, screws over almost every man, good or bad, rich or poor, and usually does it just when the man can bear it least.

FOURTEEN

IT WAS DARK NOW, and the spring night, and the cool breeze, even the smog, all tasted good to me. I rolled the windows down to suck up the air, and jumped on the Hollywood Freeway, thinking how good it would be at Abd's Harem with a bunch of happy Arabs.

Hollywood was going pretty good for a Thursday night, Sunset and Hollywood Boulevards both being jammed with cars, mostly young people, teeny boppers who've literally taken over Hollywood at night. The place has lost the real glamour of the forties and early fifties. It's a kid's town now, and except for a million hippies, fruits and servicemen, that's about all you see around the Strip and the main thoroughfares. It's a very depressing place for that reason. The clubs are mostly bottomless skin houses and psychedelic joints, but there're still some places you can go, some excellent places to eat.

I'd come to know Yasser Hafiz and the others some ten or twelve years ago when I was walking my beat on Main Street. One night at about two a.m., I spotted a paddy hustler taking a guy up the back stairs of the Marlowe Hotel, a sleazy Main Street puke hole used by whores and fruits and paddy hustlers. I was alone because my partner, a piss-poor excuse for a cop named Syd Bacon, was laying up in a hotel room knocking a chunk off some bubble-assed taxi dancer he was going with. He was supposed to meet me back on the beat at one-thirty but never showed up.

I hurried around the front of the hotel that night and went up the other stairway and hid behind the deserted clerk's desk, and when the paddy hustler and his victim came that way down the hall, I jumped inside the small closet at the desk. I was just in time because the paddy hustler's two partners came out of a room two doors down and across the hall.

They were whispering, and one of them faded down the front stairway to watch the street. The second walked behind the desk, turned the lamp on and pretended to be reading a newspaper he carried with him. They were black of course. Paddy hustling was always a Negro flimflam and that's where the name came from, but lately I've seen white hustlers using this scam on other paddies.

"Say, brother," said the hustler who was with the paddy. I left the door open a crack and saw the paddy was a well-dressed young guy, bombed out of his skull, weaving around where he stood, trying hard to brush his thick black hair out of his eyes. He'd lost his necktie somewhere, and his white dress shirt was stained from booze and unbuttoned.

"Wha's happening blood?" said the desk clerk, putting down his paper.

"Alice in tonight?" said the first one, acting as the procurer. He was the bigger of the two, a very dark-skinned guy, tall and fairly young.

"Yeah, she's breathin' fire tonight," said the other one. He was young too. "Ain't had no man yet and that bitch is a nymphomaniac!"

"Really," said the procurer. "Really."

"Let's go, I'm ready," said the paddy, and I noticed his Middle East accent.

"Jist a minute, man," said his companion. "That whore is fine pussy, but she is a stone thief, man. You better leave the wallet with the desk clerk."

"Yeah, I kin put it in the safe," said the bored-looking guy behind the desk. "Never tell when that whore might talk you into a all-night ride and then rob your ass when you falls asleep."

"Right, brother," said the procurer.

The paddy shrugged and took out his wallet, putting it on the desk.

"Better leave the wristwatch and ring too," warned the desk clerk.

"Thank you," the paddy nodded, obeying the desk clerk, who removed an envelope from under the counter, which he had put there for the valuables.

"Kin I have my five dollars now?" asked the first man. "And the clerk'll take the five for Alice and three for the room."

"All right," said the paddy, unsteadily counting out thirteen dollars for the two men.

"Now you go on in number two-thirty-seven there," said the desk clerk, pointing to the room where the first one had come out. "I'll buzz Alice's room and she be in there in 'bout five minutes. And baby, you better hold on 'cause she move like a steam drill."

The paddy smiled nervously and staggered down the hall, opening the door and disappearing inside.

"Ready, blood?" grinned the desk clerk.

"Le's go," said the big one, chuckling as the clerk turned off the lamp.

I'd come out of the closet without them seeing, and stood at the desk now, with my Smith pointed at the right eyeball of the desk clerk. "Want a room for the night, gentlemen?" I said. "Our accommodations ain't fancy, but it's clean and we can offer two very square meals a day."

The procurer was the first to recover, and he was trying to decide whether to run or try something more dangerous. Paddy hustlers didn't usually carry guns, but they often carried blades or crude saps of some kind. I aimed at his eyeball to quiet down his busy mind. "Freeze, or name your beneficiary," I said.

"Hey, Officer, wha's happenin'?" said the desk clerk with a big grin showing lots of gold. "Where you come from?"

"Down the chimney. Now get your asses over there and spread-eagle on the wall!"

"Sheee-it, this is a humbug, we ain't done nothin'," said the procurer.

"Shit fuck," grumbled the desk clerk.

This was in the days when we still believed in wall searches, before so damn many policemen got shot or thumped by guys who practiced coming out of that spread-eagled position. I abandoned it a few years before the Department did, and I put hot suspects on their knees or bellies. But at this time I was still using the wall search.

"Move your legs back, desk clerk!" I said to the smaller

one, who was being cute, barely leaning forward. He only shuffled his feet a few inches so I kicked him hard behind the right knee and he screamed and did what I told him. The scream brought the paddy out.

"Is something wrong?" asked the paddy who was half-undressed, trying to look sober as possible.

"I'm saving you from being flimflammed, asshole," I said. "Get your clothes on and come out here." He just stood there gaping. Then I yelled, "Get dressed, stupid!" my gun in my left hand still pointing at the spread-eagled paddy hustlers, and my handcuffs in my right hand getting ready to cuff the two hustlers together, and my eyes drilling the dipshit victim who stood there getting ready to ask more dumb questions. I didn't see or hear the third paddy hustler, a big bull of a kid, who'd crept up the front stairway when he heard the ruckus. If he'd been an experienced hustler instead of a youngster he'd have left the other two and gone his way. But being inexperienced, he was loyal to his partners, and just as I was getting ready to kick the paddy in the ass to get him moving, two hundred pounds falls on my back and I'm on the floor fighting for my gun and my life with all three hustlers.

"Git the gun, Tyrone!" yelled the desk clerk to the kid. "Jist git the *gun!*"

The procurer was cursing and hitting me in the face, head, and neck, anywhere he could, and the desk clerk was working on my ribs while I tried to protect myself with my left arm. All my thoughts were on the right arm, and hand, and the gun in the hand, which the kid was prying on with both his strong hands. For a few seconds everything was quiet, except for the moans and breathing and muffled swearing of the four of us, and then the kid was winning and almost had the gun worked loose when I heard a godawful Arab war cry and the paddy cracked the desk clerk over the head with a heavy metal ashtray.

Then the paddy was swinging it with both hands and I ducked my head, catching a glancing blow on the shoulder that made me yelp and which left a bruise as big as your fist. The fourth or fifth swing caught the procurer in the eyes and he was done, laying there holding his bleeding face and yelling, "YOW, YOW, YOW," like somebody cut his nuts off.

The kid lost his stomach at this point and said, "Aw right, aw right, aw right," raising his hands to surrender and scooting back on his ass with his hands in the air until he backed against the wall.

I was so sick and trembling I could've vomited and I was ready to kill all three of them, except that the desk clerk and the procurer looked half-dead already. The kid was untouched.

"Stand up," I said to the kid, and when he did, I put my gun in the holster, reached for my beavertail, and sapped him across the left collarbone. That started him yelling and bitching, and he didn't stop until we got him to the hospital, which made me completely disgusted. Up until then I had some respect for him because he was loyal to his friends and had enough guts to jump a cop who had a gun in his hand. But when he couldn't suffer in silence, he lost my respect. I figured this kind of crybaby'd probably make a complaint against me for police brutality or something, but he never did.

"What can I do, sir?" asked the paddy after I had the three hustlers halfway on their feet. I was trying to stay on mine as I leaned against the desk and covered them with the gun. This time I kept my eyes open.

"Go downstairs and put a dime in the pay phone and dial operator," I panted, still not sure how sober he was, even though he damn near decapitated all of us. "Ask for the police and tell them an officer needs assistance at the Marlowe Hotel, Fifth and Main."

"Marlowe Hotel," said the paddy. "Yes, sir."

I never found out what he said over the phone, but he must've laid it on pretty good because in three minutes I had patrol units, vice cops, felony cars, and even some dicks who rolled from the station. There were more cops than tenants at the Marlowe and the street out front was lined with radio cars, their red lights glowing clear to Sixth Street.

The paddy turned out to be Yasser's oldest son, Abd, the one the Harem was named for, and that was how I got to know them. Abd stayed with me for several hours that night while I made my reports, and he seemed like a pretty good guy after he had a dozen cups of coffee and sobered up. He had a very bad recollection of the whole thing when we went to court against the paddy hustlers, and he ended up testifying to what I told him happened before we went in the courtroom. That part about saving my ass, he never did remember, and when I drove him home to Hollywood after work that night, in gratitude for what he did for me, he took me in the house, woke up his father, mother, uncle, and three of his brothers to introduce me and tell them that I saved him from being robbed and killed by three bandits. Of course he never told them the whole truth about how the thing went down in a whorehouse, but that was okay with me, and since he really thought *I* saved *him* instead of the other way around, and since he really enjoyed having been saved even though it didn't happen, and making me the family hero, what the hell, I let him tell it the way he believed it happened so as not to disappoint them.

It was about that time that Yasser and his clan had moved here from New York where they had a small restaurant. They had pooled every cent they could lay hands on to buy the joint in Hollywood, liquor license and all, and had it remodeled and ready to open. We sat in Yasser's kitchen that night, all of us, drinking *arak* and wine, and then beer, and we all got pretty zonked except Abd who was sick, and I picked out the name for the new restaurant.

It's a corny name, I know, but I was drunk when I picked it and I could've done better. But by then I was such a hero to them they wouldn't have changed it for anything. They insisted on me being a kind of permanent guest of Abd's Harem. I couldn't pay for a thing in there and that's why I didn't come as often as I wanted to.

I drove in the parking lot in back of Abd's Harem instead of having the parking lot attendant handle the Ford, and I came in through the kitchen.

"*Al-salām 'alaykum, Baba,*" I said to Yasser Hafiz Hammad, a squat, completely bald old man with a heavy gray moustache, who had his back to me as he mixed up a huge metal bowlful of *kibbi* with clean powerful hands which he dipped often in ice water so the *kibbi* wouldn't stick to them.

"Bumper! *Wa-'alaykum al-salām,*" he grinned through the great moustache. He hugged me with his arms, keeping his hands free, and kissed me on the mouth. That was something I couldn't get over about Arabs. They didn't usually kiss women in greeting, only men.

"Where the hell you keep yourself, Bumper?" he said, dipping a spoon in the raw kibbi for me to sample it. "We don't see you much no more."

"Delicious, *Baba*," I said.

"Yes, but is it ber-fect?"

"It's ber-fect, *Bubba*."

"You hungry, eh, Bumper?" he said, returning to the *kibbi* and making me some little round balls which he knew I'd eat raw. I liked raw *kibbi* every bit as good as baked, and *kibbi* with yogurt even better.

"You making *labaneeyee* tonight, *Baba?*"

"Sure, Bumper. Damn right. What else you want? *Sfeeha? Bamee?* Anything you want. We got lots of dish tonight. Bunch of Lebanese and Syrian guys in the banquet room. Ten entrées they order special. Son of a bitch, I cook all goddamn day. When I get rest, I coming out and have a goddamn glass of *arak* with you, okay?"

"Okay, *Baba*," I said, finishing the *kibbi* and watching Yasser work. He kneaded the ground lamb and cracked wheat and the onion and cinnamon and spices, after dipping his hands in the ice water to keep the mixture pliable. This *kibbi* was well stuffed with pine nuts and the meat was cooked in butter and braised. When Yasser got it all ready he spread the *kibbi* over the bottom of a metal pan and the *kibbi* stuffing over the top of that, and another layer of *kibbi* on top of that. He cut the whole pan into little diamond shapes and then baked it. Now I couldn't decide whether to have the *kibbi* with yogurt or the baked *kibbi*. What the hell, I'll have them both, I thought. I was pretty hungry now.

"Look, Bumper," said Yasser Hafiz, pointing to the little footballs of *kibbi* he'd been working on all day. He'd pressed hollows into the center and stuffed them with lamb stuffing and was cooking them in a yogurt sauce.

Yeah, I'll have both, I thought. I decided to go in and start on some appetizers. I was more than hungry all of a sudden and not quite so tired, and all I could think of was the wonderful food of Abd's Harem.

Inside, I spotted Ahmed right away, and he grinned and waved me to a table near the small dance area where one of his dancers could shove her belly in my face. Ahmed was tall for an Arab, about thirty years old, the youngest of Yasser's sons, and had lived in the States since he was a kid. He'd lost a lot of the Arab ways and didn't kiss me like his father and his uncles did, when the uncles were here helping wait tables or cooking on a busy weekend night.

"Glad you could come tonight, Bumper," said Ahmed with a hint of a New York accent, since his family had lived there several years before coming to Los Angeles. When he talked to the regular customers though, he put on a Middle East accent for show.

"Think I'll have some appetizers, Ahmed. I'm hungry tonight."

"Good, Bumper, good," said Ahmed, his dark eyes crinkling at the corners when he grinned. "We like to see you eat." He clapped his hands for a good-looking, red-haired waitress in a harem girl's outfit, and she came over to the table.

Abd's Harem was like all Middle East restaurants, but bigger than most. There were Saracen shields on the wall, and scimitars, and imitation Persian tapestries, and the booths and tables were dark and heavy, leather-padded, and studded with hammered bronzework. Soothing Arab music drifted through the place from several hidden speakers.

"Bring Bumper some lamb tongue, Barbara. What else would you like, Bumper?"

"A little *humos tahini,* Ahmed."

"Right. *Humos* too, Barbara."

Barbara smiled at me and said, "A drink, Bumper?"

"All right, I'll have *arak.*"

"If you'll excuse me, Bumper," said Ahmed, "I've got to take care of the banquet room for the next hour. Then I'll join you and we'll have a drink together."

"Go head on, kid," I nodded. "Looks like you're gonna have a nice crowd."

"Business is great, Bumper. Wait'll you see our new belly dancer."

I nodded and winked as Ahmed hurried toward the banquet room to take care of the roomful of Arabs. I could hear them from where I sat, proposing toasts and laughing. They seemed pretty well lubricated for so early in the evening.

The appetizers were already prepared and the waitress was back to my table in a few minutes with the little slices of lamb's tongue, boiled and peeled and seasoned with garlic and salt, and a good-sized dish of *humos*, which makes the greatest dip in the world. She gave me more *humos* than any of the paying customers get, and a large heap of the round flat pieces of warm Syrian bread covered with a napkin. I dipped into the *humos* right away with a large chunk of the Syrian bread and almost moaned out loud it was so delicious. I could taste the sesame seeds even though they were ground into the creamy blend of garbanzo beans, and I poured olive oil all over it, and dipped lots of oil up in my bread. I could also taste the clove and crushed garlic and almost forgot the lamb tongue I was enjoying the *humos* so much.

"Here's your *arak*, Bumper," said Barbara, bringing me the drink and another dish of *humos* a little smaller than the first. "Yasser says not to let you ruin your dinner with the tongue and *humos*."

"No chance, kid," I said, after swallowing a huge mouthful of tongue and bread. I gulped some *arak* so I could talk. "Tell *Baba* I'm as hungry as a tribe of Bedouins and I'll eat out his whole kitchen if he's not careful."

"And as horny as a herd of goats?"

"Yeah, tell him that too," I chuckled. That was a standing joke between Yasser and Ahmed and me that all the girls had heard.

Now that the starvation phase was over I started to feel pain in my leg and shoulder. I poured some water into the clear *arak*, turning it milky. I glanced around to make sure no one could see and I loosened up my belt and smiled to myself as I smelled the food all through the place. I nibbled now, and tried not to be such a crude bastard, and I sipped my *arak*, getting three refills from Barbara who was a fast and good waitress. Then the pain started to go away.

I saw Ahmed running between kitchen, bar, and banquet room, and I thought that Yasser was lucky to have such good kids. All his sons had done well, and now the last one was staying in the business with him. The Arab music drifted softly through the place and mingled with the food smell, and I was feeling damn warm now. In about an hour the band would be here, a three-piece Armenian group who played exotic music for the belly dancer that I was anxious to see. Ahmed really knew his dancers.

"Everything okay, Bumper?" Ahmed called in an Arab accent since other customers were around.

"Okay," I grinned, and he hurried past on one of his trips to the kitchen.

I was starting to sway with the sensual drums and I was feeling much better, admiring the rugs hanging on the walls, and other Arabian Nights decorations like water pipes that kids used now for smoking dope, and the swords up high enough on the walls so some drunk couldn't grab them and start his own dance. Abd's Harem was a very good place, I thought. Really an oasis in the middle of a tacky, noisy part of Hollywood which was generally so phony I couldn't stand it.

I noticed that Khalid, one of Yasser's brothers, was helping in the bar tonight. I figured as soon as he saw me I'd get another big hairy kiss.

"Ready, Bumper?" said Barbara, smiling pretty, and padding quietly up to my table with a huge tray on a food cart.

"Yeah, yeah," I said, looking at the dishes of baked *kibbi*, *kibbi* with yogurt, stuffed grape leaves and a small skewer of shish kebab.

"Yasser said to save room for dessert, Bumper," said Barbara as she left me there. I could think of nothing at times like these, except the table in front of me, and I waged a tough fight against myself to eat slowly and savor it, especially the grape leaves which were a surprise for me, because Yasser doesn't make them all the time. I could taste the mint, fragrant and tangy in the yogurt that I ladled over the grape leaves, pregnant with lamb and rice, succulent parsley, and spices. Yasser added just the right amount of lemon juice for my taste.

After a while, Barbara returned and smiled at me as I sat sipping my wine, at peace with the world.

"Some pastry, Bumper? *Baklawa?*"

"Oh no, Barbara," I said, holding my hand up weakly. "Too rich. No *baklawa*, no."

"All right," she laughed. "Yasser has something special for you. Did you save a little room?"

"Oh no," I said painfully, as she took away the cartload of empty plates.

Arabs are so friendly and hospitable, and they like so much to see me eat, I would've hated to do something horrible like upchucking all his hard work. My belly was bulging so much I had to move the chair back two inches, and my shirt was straining to pop open. I thought of Fat-stuff in the old "Smilin' Jack" cartoon strip and remembered how I used to laugh at the poor bastard always popping his buttons, when I was young and slim.

A few minutes later Barbara came back with an oversized sherbet glass.

"*Moosh moosh!*" I said. "I haven't had *moosh moosh* for a year."

Barbara smiled and said, "Yasser says that Allah sent you tonight because Yasser made your favorite dessert today and thought about you."

"*Moosh moosh!*" I said as Barbara left me, and I scooped up a mouthful and let it lay there on my tongue, tasting the sweet apricot and lemon rind, and remembering how Yasser's wife, Yasmine, blended the apricot and lemon rind and sugar, and folded the apricot puree into

the whipped cream before it was chilled. They all knew
it was my very favorite. So I ended up having two more
cups of *moosh moosh* and then I was really through. Barbara cleared the table for the last time and Ahmed and
Yasser both joined me for ten minutes.

There's an Arab prayer which translates something
like, "Give me a good digestion, Lord, and something to
digest." It was the only prayer I ever heard that I thought
made a lot of sense, and I thought that if I believed in God
I wouldn't lay around begging from Him and mumbling a
lot of phony promises. This particular Arab prayer said all
I'd say to Him, and all I'd expect of Him, so even though
I didn't believe, I said it before and after I ate dinner in
Abd's Harem. Sometimes I even said it at other times.
Sometimes even at home I said it.

When the Armenians arrived, I was happy to see the
oud player was old Mr. Kamian. He didn't often play at
Abd's Harem anymore. His grandsons Berge and George
were with him, and anyone could see they were his grandsons, all three being tall, thin, with hawk noses and dark-
rimmed blazing eyes. Berge would play the violin and
George, the youngest, a boy not yet twenty, would play
the *darbuka* drums. It was just a job to the two young
ones. They were good musicians, but it was old Kamian
I would hear as he plucked and stroked those *oud* strings
with the quill of an eagle feather. It's a lute-like instrument and has no frets like a guitar. Yet the old man's fingers knew exactly where to dance on that *oud* neck, so
fast it was hard to believe. It gave me goose bumps and
made it hard to swallow when I saw that old man's slender, brittle-looking fingers dart over those twelve strings.

Once I was there in the afternoon when they were rehearsing new dancers, and old Kamian was telling Armenian tales to Berge's children. I sat there hidden behind a beaded curtain and heard Kamian tell about the fiery horses of Armenia, and pomegranates full of pearls and rubies, and about Hazaran-Bulbul, the magic nightingale of a thousand songs. He made me feel like a kid that day listening to him, and ever since, when I hear him play the *oud*, I could almost climb aboard one of those fiery horses.

Another time when I was here late at night listening to Mr. Kamian play, his oldest son Leon sat with me drinking scotch and told me the story of his father, how he was the only survivor of a large family which totaled, cousins and all, half of a village that was massacred by Turkish soldiers. Mr. Kamian was fifteen years old then, and his body was left in a big ditch with those of his parents, brothers, sisters, everyone in his entire world.

"The thing that saved him that day was the *smell* of death," said Leon, who spoke five languages, English with only a slight accent, and like all Armenians, loved to tell stories. "As he lay there, my father wanted to be dead with the others. It wasn't the sight or idea of death that made him drag himself up and out of that ditch, it was the smell of rotting bodies which at last was the only unbearable thing, and which drove him to the road and away from his village forever.

"For almost a year he wandered, his only possession an *oud* which he rescued from a plundered farmhouse. One night when he was huddling alone in the wilderness like Cain, feeling like the only human being left on earth, he became very angry that God would let this happen, and like the child he was, he *demanded* a sign from Him, and he waited and listened in the darkness, but he heard only the wind howling across the Russian steppes. Then he wondered how he could ever have believed in a God who would let this happen to Armenia. His tiny Christian island in a sea of Islam. There was no sign, so he strummed the *oud* and sang brave songs into the wind all that night.

"The very next night the boy was wandering through a village much like his had been, and of course he passed hundreds of starving refugees on the road. He took off from the road to find a place to sleep in the trees where someone wouldn't kill him just to steal the *oud*. There in the woods he saw a black sinister shape rising from the ground, and the first thing the boy thought was that it was a *dev*, one of those fearsome Armenian ogres his *nany* used to tell him about. He raised the flimsy *oud* like it was an ax and prepared to defend himself. Then the dark form took shape and spoke to him in Armenian from beneath a ragged cloak, 'Please, do you have something to eat?'

"The boy saw a child in the moonlight, covered with sores, stomach bloated, barely able to walk. Her teeth were loose, eyes and gums crusted, and a recently broken nose made it hard for her to breathe. He examined her face and saw that at no time could that face have been more than homely, but now it was truly awful. He spoke to her a few moments and found she was thirteen years old, a wandering refugee, and he remembered the proud and vain demand he had made of God the night before. He began to laugh then, and suddenly felt stronger. He couldn't stop laughing and the laughter filled him with strength. It alarmed the girl, and he saw it, and finally he said, 'The God of Armenians has a sense of humor. How can you doubt someone with a sense of humor like His? You're to come with me, my little *dev.*'

" 'What do you want of me, sir?' she asked, very frightened now.

" 'What do I want of you?' he answered softly. 'Look at you. What do you have to offer? Everything has been taken from you and everything has been done to you. What could anyone in the world possibly want of you now? Can you think of what it is, the thing I want?'

" 'No, sir.'

" 'There is only one thing left. To *love* you, of course. We're good for no more than this. Now come with me. We're going to find *our* Armenia.'

"She went with the half-starved, wild-eyed boy. They survived together and wandered to the Black Sea, somehow got passage, and crossed on foot through Europe, through the war and fighting, ever westward to the Atlantic, working, having children. Finally, in 1927, they and five children, having roamed half the world, arrived in New York, and from force of habit more than anything, kept wandering west, picking up jobs along the way until they reached the Pacific Ocean. Then my mother said, 'This is as far as we go. This ocean is too big.' And they stopped, had four more children, sixty-one grandchildren, and so far, ten great grandchildren, more than forty with the Kamian name that would not die in the ditch in Armenia. Most of his sons and grandsons have done well, and he still likes to come here sometimes once a week and play his *oud* for a few people who understand."

So that was the story of old Kamian, and I didn't doubt any of it, because I've known a lot of tough bastards in my time that could've pulled off something like that, but the thing that amazed me, that I couldn't really understand, is how he could've taken the little girl with him that night. I mean he could've helped her, sure. But he purposely *gave* himself to her that night. After what he'd already been through, he up and *gave* himself to somebody! That was the most incredible thing about Mr. Kamian, that, and how the hell his fingers knew exactly where to go on that *oud* when there were no frets to guide them.

"You eat plenty, Bumper?" asked Yasser, who came to the table with Ahmed, and I responded by giving him a fat-cat grin and patting him on the hand, and whispering "*Shukran*" in a way that you would know meant thanks without knowing Arabic.

"Maybe you'll convert me, feeding me like that. Maybe I'll become a Moslem," I added.

"What you do during Ramadan when you must fast?" laughed Yasser.

"You see how *big* Abd's kids?" said Yasser, lifting his apron to reach for his wallet, and laying some snapshots on me that I pretended I could see.

"Yeah, handsome kids," I said, hoping the old man wouldn't start showing me all his grandkids. He had about thirty of them, and like all Arabs, was crazy about children.

Ahmed spoke in Arabic that had to do with the banquet room, and Yasser seemed to remember something.

"Scoose me, Bumper," said the old boy, "I come back later, but I got things in the kitchen."

"Sure, *Baba*," I said, and Ahmed smiled as he watched his father strut back to the kitchen, the proud patriarch of a large family, and the head of a very good business, which Abd's Harem certainly was.

"How old is your father now?"

"Seventy-five," said Ahmed. "Looks good, doesn't he?"

"Damn good. Tell me, can he still eat like he used to, say ten, fifteen years ago?"

"He eats pretty well," Ahmed laughed. "But no, not like he used to. He used to eat like you, Bumper. It was a joy to watch him eat. He says food doesn't taste quite the same anymore."

I started getting gas pains, but didn't pop a tablet because it would be rude for Ahmed to see me do that after I'd just finished such a first-rate dinner.

"It'd be a terrible thing for your appetite to go," I said. "That'd be almost as bad as being castrated."

"Then I never want to get *that* old, Bumper," Ahmed laughed, with the strength and confidence of only thirty years on this earth. "Of course there's a third thing, remember, your digestion? Got to have that, too."

"Oh yeah," I said. "Got to have digestion or appetite ain't worth a damn."

Just then the lights dimmed, and a bluish spot danced around the small bandstand as the drums started first. Then I was amazed to see Laila Hammad run out to the floor, in a gold-and-white belly dancer's costume, and the music picked up as she stood there, chestnut hair hanging down over her boobs, fingers writhing, and working the *zils*, those little golden finger cymbals, hips swaying as George's hands beat a blood-heating rhythm on the *darbuka*. Ahmed grinned at me as I admired her strong golden thighs.

"How do you like our new dancer?"

"Laila's your dancer?"

"Wait'll you see her," said Ahmed, and it was true, she really was something. There was art to the dancing, not just lusty gyrations, and though I'm no judge of belly dancing, even I could see it.

"How old is she now?" I said to Ahmed, watching her mobile stomach, and the luxurious chestnut hair, which was all her own, and now hung down her back and then streamed over her wonderful-looking boobs.

"She's nineteen," said Ahmed, and I was very happy to see how good-looking she'd turned out.

Laila had worked as a waitress here for a few years, even when she was much too young to be doing it, but she always looked older, and her father, Khalil Hammad, was a cousin of Yasser's, who lingered for years with cancer, running up tremendous hospital bills before he finally died. Laila was a smart, hard-working girl, and helped support her three younger sisters. Ahmed once told me Laila never really knew her mother, an American broad who left them when they were little kids. I'd heard Laila was working in a bank the last couple years and doing okay.

You could really see the Arab blood in Laila now, in the sensual face, the nose a little too prominent but just suiting her, and in the wide full mouth, and glittering brown eyes. No wonder they were passionate people, I thought, with faces like that. Yes, Laila was a jewel, like a fine half-Arab mare with enough American blood to give good height and those terrific thighs. I wondered if Ahmed had anything going with her. Then Laila started "sprinkling salt" as the Arabs say. She revolved slowly on the ball of one bare foot, jerking a hip to each beat of the *darbuka*. And if there'd been a small bag of salt tied to the throbbing hip, she would've made a perfect ring of salt on the floor around her. It's a hot, graceful move, not hard at all. I do it myself to hardrock music.

When Laila was finished with her dance and ran off the floor and the applause died down I said, "She's beautiful, Ahmed. Why don't you con her into marrying you?"

"Not interested," said Ahmed, shaking his head. He leaned over the table and took a sip of wine before speaking. "There're rumors, Bumper. Laila's supposed to be whoring."

"I can't believe that," I said, remembering her again as a teenage waitress who couldn't even put her lipstick on straight.

"She left her bank job over a year ago. Started belly dancing professionally. You never knew her when she was a real little tot. I remember when she was three years old and her aunts and uncles taught her to dance. She was the cutest thing you ever saw. She was a smart little girl."

"Where did you hear she was tricking?"

"In this business you hear all about the dancers," said Ahmed. "You know, she's one of the few belly dancers in town that's really an Arab, or rather, half-Arab. She's no cheapie, but she goes to bed with guys if they can pay the tariff. I hear she gets two hundred a night."

"Laila's had a pretty tough life, Ahmed," I said. "She had to raise little sisters. She never had time to be a kid herself."

"Look, I'm not blaming her, Bumper. What the hell, I'm an American. I'm not like the old folks who wait around on the morning after the wedding to make sure there's blood on the bridal sheets. But I have to admit that whoring bothers me. I'm just not that Americanized, I guess. I used to think maybe when Laila got old enough . . . well, it's too late now. I shouldn't have been so damn busy these last few years. I let her get away and now . . . it's just too late."

Ahmed ordered me another drink, then excused himself, saying he'd be back in a little while. I was starting to feel depressed all of a sudden. I wasn't sure if the talk about Laila set it off or what, but I thought about her selling her ass to these wealthy Hollywood creeps. Then I thought about Freddie and Harry, and Poochie and Herky, and Timothy G. for goddamn Landry, but that was too depressing to think about. Suddenly for no reason I thought about Esteban Segovia and how I used to worry that he really would become a priest like he wanted to be when he returned from Vietnam, instead of a dentist like I always wanted him to be. That dead boy was about Laila's age when he left. Babies. Nobody should die a baby.

All right, Bumper, I said to myself, let's settle down to some serious drinking. I called Barbara over and ordered a double scotch on the rocks even though I'd mixed my drinks too much and had already more than enough.

After my third scotch I heard a honey-dipped voice say, "Hi, Bumper."

"Laila!" I made a feeble attempt at getting up, as she sat down at my table, looking smooth and cool in a modest white dress, her hair tied back and hanging down one side, her face and arms the color of a golden olive.

"Ahmed told me you were here, Bumper," she smiled, and I lit her cigarette, liberated women be damned, and called Barbara over to get her a drink.

"Can I buy you a drink, kid?" I asked. "It's good to

see you all grown up, a big girl and all, looking so damn gorgeous."

She ordered a bourbon and water and laughed at me, and I knew for sure I was pretty close to being wiped out. I decided to turn it off after I finished the scotch I held in my hand.

"I was grown up last time you saw me, Bumper," she said, grinning at my clownish attempts to act sober. "All men appreciate your womanhood better when they see your bare belly moving for them."

I thought about what Ahmed had told me, and though it didn't bother me like it did Ahmed, I was sorry she had to do it, or that she *thought* she had to do it.

"You mean that slick little belly was moving for ol' Bumper?" I said, trying to kid her like I used to, but my brain wasn't working right.

"Sure, for you. Aren't you the hero of this whole damned family?"

"Well how do you like dancing for a living?"

"It's as crummy as you'd expect."

"Why do you do it?"

"You ever try supporting two sisters on a bank teller's wage?"

"Bullshit," I said too loud, one elbow slipping out from under me. "Don't give me that crybaby stuff. A dish like you, why you could marry any rich guy you wanted."

"Wrong, Bumper. I could screw any rich guy I wanted. And get paid damn well for it."

"I wish you wouldn't talk like that, Laila."

"You old bear," she laughed, as I rubbed my face which had no feeling whatsoever. "I know Ahmed told you I'm a whore. It just shames the hell out of these Arabs. You know how subtle they are. Yasser hinted around the other day that maybe I should change my name now that I'm show biz. Hammad's too ordinary, he said. Maybe something more American. They're as subtle as a boot in the ass. How about Feinberg or Goldstein, Bumper? I'll bet they wouldn't mind if I called myself Laila Feinberg. That'd explain my being a whore to the other Arabs, wouldn't it? They could start a rumor that my mother was a Jew."

"What the hell're you telling *me* all this for?" I said, suddenly getting mad. "Go to a priest or a headshrinker, or go to the goddamn mosque and talk to the Prophet, why don't you? I had enough problems laid on me today. Now you?"

"Will you drive me home, Bumper? I do want to talk to you."

"How many more performances you got to go?" I asked, not sure I could stay upright in my chair if I had another drink.

"I'm through. Marsha's taking my next one for me. I've told Ahmed I'm getting cramps."

I found Ahmed and said good-bye while Laila waited for me in the parking lot. I tipped Barbara fifteen bucks, then I staggered into the kitchen, thanked Yasser, and kissed him on the big moustache while he hugged me and made me promise to come to his house in the next few weeks.

Laila was in the parking lot doing her best to ignore two well-dressed drunks in a black Lincoln. When they saw me staggering across the parking lot in their direction the driver stomped on it, laid a patch of rubber, and got the hell out.

"Lord, I don't blame them," Laila laughed. "You

look wild and dangerous, Bumper. How'd you get those scratches on your face?"

"My Ford's right over there," I said, walking like Frankenstein's monster so I could stay on a straight course.

"The same old car? Oh, Bumper." She laughed like a kid and she put my arm around her and steered me to my Ford, but around to the passenger side. Then she patted my pockets, found my keys, got them, pushed me in, and closed the door after me.

"Light-fingered broad," I mumbled. "You ever been a hugger-mugger?"

"What was that, Bumper?" she said, getting behind the wheel and cranking her up.

"Nothing, nothing," I mumbled, rubbing my face again.

I dozed while Laila drove. She turned the radio on and hummed, and she had a pretty good voice too. In fact, it put me to sleep, and she had to shake me awake when we got to her pad.

"I'm going to pour you some muddy Turkish coffee and we're going to talk," she said, helping me out of the Ford, and for a second the sidewalk came up in my eyes, but I closed them and stood there and everything righted itself.

"Ready to try the steps, Bumper?"

"As I'll ever be, kid."

"Let's get it on," she said, my arm around her wide shoulders, and she guided me up. She was a big strong girl. Ahmed was nuts, I thought. She'd make a hell of a wife for him or *any* young guy.

It took some doing but we reached the third floor of her apartment building, a very posh place, which was actually three L-shaped buildings scattered around two Olympic-sized pools. Mostly catered to swinging singles which reminded me of the younger sisters.

"The girls home?" I asked.

"I live alone during the school year, Bumper. Nadia lives in the dorm at U.S.C. She's a freshman. Dalai boards at Ramona Convent. She'll be going to college next year."

"Ramona Convent? I thought you were a Moslem."

"I'm nothing."

We got in the apartment and Laila guided me past the soft couch, which looked pretty good to sleep on, and dumped me in a straight-backed kitchen chair after taking off my sport coat and hanging it in a closet.

"You even wear a gun off duty?" she asked as she ladled out some coffee and ran some water from the tap.

"Yeah," I said, not knowing what she was talking about for a minute, I was so used to the gun. "This job makes you a coward. I don't even go out without it in this town anymore, except to Harry's bar or somewhere in the neighborhood."

"If I saw all the things you have, maybe I'd be afraid to go out without one too," she shrugged.

I didn't know I was dozing again until I smelled Laila there shaking me awake, a tiny cup of Turkish coffee thick and dark on a saucer in front of me. I smelled her sweetness and then I felt her cool hand again and then I saw her wide mouth smiling.

"Maybe I should spoon it down your throat till you get sober."

"I'm okay," I said, rubbing my face and head.

I drank the coffee as fast as I could even though it

scalded my mouth and throat. Then she poured me another, and I excused myself, went to the head, took a leak, washed my face in cold water, and combed my hair. I was still bombed when I came back, but at least I wasn't a zombie.

Laila must've figured I was in good enough shape. "Let me turn on some music, Bumper, then we can talk."

"Okay." I finished the second cup almost as fast as the first and poured myself a third.

The soft stirring song of an Arab girl singer filled the room for a second and then Laila turned down the volume. It's a wailing kind of plaintive sound, almost like a chant at times, but it gets to you, at least it did to me, and I always conjured up mental pictures of the Temple of Karnak, and Giza, and the streets of Damascus, and a picture I once saw of a Bedouin on a pink granite cliff in the blinding sun looking out over the Valley of the Kings. I saw in his face that he knew more about history, even though he was probably illiterate, than I ever would, and I promised myself I'd go there to die when I got old. If I ever *did* get old, that is.

"I still like the old music," Laila smiled, nodding toward the stereo set. "Most people don't like it. I can put on something else if you want."

"Don't touch it," I said, and Laila looked in my eyes and seemed glad.

"I need your help, Bumper."

"Okay, what is it?"

"I want you to talk to my probation officer for me."

"You're on probation? What for?"

"Prostitution. The Hollywood vice cops got three of us in January. I pleaded guilty and was put on probation."

"Whadda you want me to do?"

"I wasn't given *summary* probation like my lousy thousand-dollar lawyer promised. I got a tough judge and I have to report to a P.O. for two years. I want to go somewhere and I need permission."

"Where you going?"

"Somewhere to have a baby. I want to go somewhere, have my baby, adopt it out, and come back."

She saw the "Why me? Why in the hell me?" look in my eyes.

"Bumper, I need you for this. I don't want my sisters to know anything. Nothing, you hear? They'd only want to raise the baby and for God's sake, it's hard enough making it in this filthy world when you know who the hell your two parents are and have them to raise you. I've got a plan and you're the only one my whole damned tribe would listen to without questions. They trust you completely. I want you to tell Yasser and Ahmed and all of them that you don't think I should be dancing for a living, and that you have a friend in New Orleans who has a good-paying office job for me. And then tell the same thing to my P.O. and convince her it's the truth. Then I'll disappear for seven or eight months and come back and tell everyone I didn't like the job or something. They'll all get mad as blazes but that'll be it."

"Where the hell you going?"

"What's it matter?" she shrugged. "Anywhere to have the kid and farm it out. To New Orleans. Wherever."

"You're not joining the coat hanger corps are you?"

"An abortion?" she laughed. "No, I figure when you make a mistake you should have the guts to at least see it through. I won't shove it down a garbage disposal. I was raised an Arab and I can't change."

"You got any money?"

"I've got thirteen thousand in a bank account. I'd like you to handle it for me and see that the girls have enough to get them through the summer while they're living here in my apartment. If everything goes right I'll be back for a New Year's Eve party with just you and me and the best bottle of scotch money can buy."

"Will you have enough to live on?" I asked, knowing where she got the thirteen thousand.

"I've got enough," she nodded.

"Listen, goddamnit, don't lie to me. I'm not gonna get involved if you're off somewhere selling your ass in a strange town with a foal kicking around in your belly."

"I wouldn't take any chances," she said, looking deep in my eyes again. "I swear it. I've got enough in another account to live damn well for the whole time I'll be gone. I'll show you my bankbooks. And I can afford to have the kid in a good hospital. A private room if I want it."

"Wow!" I said, getting up, light-headed and dizzy. I stood for a second and shuffled into the living room, dropping on the couch and laying back. I noticed that the red hose on Laila's crystal and gold narghile was uncoiled. Those pipes are fine decorator items but they never work right unless you stuff all the fittings with rags like Laila's was. I often smoked mint-flavored Turkish tobacco with Yasser. Laila smoked hashish. There was a black-and-white mosaic inlaid box setting next to the narghile. The lid was open and it was half full of hash, very high-grade, expensive, shoe-leather hash, pressed into dark flat sheets like the sole of your shoe.

Laila let me alone and cleared the kitchen table. What a hell of a time. First the decision to retire. And after I told Cassie, everything seemed right. And then Cassie wants a kid! And a goddamn pack of baby Bolsheviks make an ass out of me. Humiliate me! Then perjury, for chrissake. I felt like someone was putting out cigars on the inside of my belly, which was so hard and swollen I couldn't see my knees unless I sat up straight. But at least I got a back office, even if I did almost die in the pigeon shit.

"What a day," I said when Laila came in and sat down on the end of the couch.

"I'm sorry I asked you, Bumper."

"No, no, don't say that. I'll do it. I'll help you."

She didn't say anything, but she got up and came over and sat on the floor next to me, her eyes wet, and I'll be a son of a bitch if she didn't kiss my hand!

Laila got up then, and without saying anything, took my shoes off, and I let her lift my legs up and put them on the couch. I felt like a beached walrus laying there like that, but I was still swacked. In fact, I felt drunker now laying down, and I was afraid the room would start spinning, so I wanted to start talking. "I had a miserable goddamn day."

"Tell me about it, Bumper," said Laila, sitting there on the floor next to me and putting her cool hand on my hot forehead as I loosened my belt. I knew I was gone for the night. I was in no shape to get up, let alone drive home. I squirmed around until my sore shoulder was settled against a cushion.

"Your face and hands are cut and your body's hurting."

"Guess I can sleep here, huh?"

"Of course. How'd you get hurt?"

"Slipped and fell off a fire escape. Whadda you think about me retiring, Laila?"

"Retiring? Don't be ridiculous. You're too full of hell."

"I'm in my forties, goddamnit. No, I might as well level with you. I'll be fifty this month. Imagine that. When I was born Warren G. Harding was a new President!"

"You're too alive. Forget about it. It's too silly to think about."

"I was sworn in on my thirtieth birthday, Laila. Know that?"

"Tell me about it," she said, stroking my cheek now, and I felt so damn comfortable I could've died.

"You weren't even born then. That's how long I been a cop."

"Why'd you become a cop?"

"Oh, I don't know."

"Well, what did you do *before* you became a cop?"

"I was in the Marine Corps over eight years."

"Tell me about it."

"I wanted to get away from the hometown, I guess. There was nobody left except a few cousins and one aunt. My brother Clem and I were raised by our grandmother, and after she died, Clem took care of me. He was a ripper, that bastard. Bigger than me, but didn't look anything like me. A handsome dog. Loved his food and drink and women. He owned his own gas station and just before Pearl Harbor, in November it was, he got killed when a truck tire blew up and he fell back into the grease pit. My brother Clem died in a filthy grease pit, killed by a goddamn tire! It was ridiculous. There was nobody else I gave a damn about so I joined the Corps. Guys actu-

ally *joined* in those days, believe it or not. I got wounded
twice, once at Saipan and then in the knees at Iwo, and it
almost kept me off the Department. I had to flimflam the
shit out of that police surgeon. You know what? I didn't
hate war. I mean, why not admit it? I didn't hate it."

"Weren't you ever afraid?"

"Sure, but there's something about danger I like, and
fighting was something I could do. I found that out right
away and after the war I shipped over for another hitch
and never did go back to Indiana. What the hell, I never
had much there anyway. Billy was here with me and I had
a job I liked."

"Who's Billy?"

"He was my son," I said, and I heard the air-conditioner
going and I knew it was cool, because Laila looked so
crisp and fresh, and yet my back was soaked and the
sweat was pouring down my face and slipping beneath
my collar.

"I never knew you were married, Bumper."

"It was a hundred years ago."

"Where's your wife?"

"I don't know. Missouri, I think. Or dead maybe. It's
been so long. She was a girl I met in San Diego, a farm
girl. Lots of them around out here on the coast during
the war. They drifted out to find defense work, and some
of them boozed it too much. Verna was a pale, skinny
little thing. I was back in San Diego from my first trip
over. I had my chest full of ribbons and had a cane because my first hit was in the thigh. That's one reason my
legs aren't worth a shit today, I guess. I picked her up in
a bar and slept with her that night and then I started coming by whenever I got liberty and next thing you know,

before I ship out, she says she's knocked up. I had the feeling so many guys get, that they're gonna get bumped off, that their number's up, so we got drunk one night and I took her to a justice of the peace in Arizona and married her. She got an allotment and wrote me all the time and I didn't think too much about her till I got hit the second time and went home for good. And there she was, with my frail, sickly Billy. William's my real name, did you know that?"

"No, I didn't."

"So anyway, I screwed up, but just like you said, Laila, there was no sense anybody else suffering for it so I took Verna and Billy and we got a decent place to stay in Oceanside, and I thought, what the hell, this is a pretty fair life. So I reenlisted for another hitch and before long I was up for master sergeant. I could take Verna okay. I mean I gotta give her credit, after Billy came she quit boozing and kept a decent house. She was just a poor dumb farm girl but she treated me and Billy like champs, I have to admit. I was lucky and got to stay with Headquarters Company, Base, for five years, and Billy was to me, like . . . I don't know, standing on a granite cliff and watching all the world from the Beginning until Now, and for the first time there was a reason for it all. You understand?"

"Yes, I think so."

"You won't believe this, but when he was barely four years old he printed a valentine card for me. He could print and read at four years old, I swear it. He asked his mother how to make the words and then he composed it himself. It said, 'Dad. I love you. Love, Billy Morgan.' Just barely four years old. Can you believe that?"

"Yes, I believe you, Bumper."

"But like I said, he was a sickly boy like his mother, and even now when I tell you about him, I can't picture him. I put him away mentally, and it's not possible to picture how he looked, even if I try. You know, I read where only schizophrenics can control subconscious thought, and maybe I'm schizoid, I don't doubt it. But I can do it. Sometimes when I'm asleep and I see a shadow in a dream and the shadow is a little boy wearing glasses, or he has a cowlick sticking up in the back, I wake up. I sit straight up in my bed, wide awake. I *cannot* picture him either awake or asleep. You're smart to adopt out your kid, Laila."

"When did he die?"

"When he was just five. Right after his birthday, in fact. And it shouldn't have surprised me really. He was anemic and he had pneumonia twice as a baby, but still, it *was* a surprise, you know? Even though he was sick so long, it was a surprise, and after that, Vern seemed dead too. She told me a few weeks after we buried him that she was going home to Missouri and I thought it was a good idea so I gave her all the money I had and I never saw her again.

"After she left, I started drinking pretty good, and once, on weekend liberty, I came to L.A. and got so drunk I somehow ended up at El Toro Marine Base with a bunch of other drunken jarheads instead of at Camp Pendleton where I was stationed. The M.P.'s at the gate let the other drunks through, but of course my pass was wrong, so they stopped me. I was mean drunk then, and confused as hell, and I ended up swinging on the two M.P.'s.

"I can hardly remember later that night in the El Toro brig. All I really recall was two brig guards, one black guy and one white guy, wearing khaki pants and skivvy shirts, dragging me off the floor of the cell and taking me in the head where they worked me over with billies and then to the showers to wash off the blood. I remember holding onto the faucets with my head in the sink for protection, and the billies landing on my arms and ribs and kidneys and the back of my head. That was the first time my nose was ever broken."

Laila was still stroking my face and listening. Her hands felt cool and good.

"After that, they gave me a special courtmartial, and after all the M.P.'s testified, my defense counsel brought out a platoon or so of character witnesses, and even some civilians, wives of the marines who lived near Verna and Billy and me. They all talked about me, and Billy, and how extra smart and polite he was. Then the doctor who treated me in the brig testified as a defense witness that I was unbalanced at the time of the fight and not responsible for my actions, even though he had no psychiatric training. My defense counsel got away with it and when it was over I didn't get any brig time. I just got busted to buck sergeant.

"Is it hot in here, Laila?"

"No, Bumper," she said, stroking my cheek with the back of her fingers.

"Well, anyway, I took my discharge in the spring of nineteen-fifty and fooled around a year and finally joined the Los Angeles Police Department."

"Why did you do it, Bumper? The police force?"

"I don't know. I was good at fighting, I guess that's why. I thought about going back in the Corps when Korea broke out, and then I read something that said, 'Policemen are soldiers who act alone,' and I figured that was the only thing I hated about the military, that you couldn't act alone very much. And as a cop I could do it all myself, so I became a cop."

"You never heard from Verna?" asked Laila quietly, and suddenly I was cold and damp and getting chills laying there.

"About six years after I came on the job I got a letter from a lawyer in Joplin. I don't know how he found me. He said she'd filed for divorce and after that I got the final papers. I paid his fee and sent her about five hundred I'd saved, to get her started. I always hoped maybe she found some nice working stiff and went back to the farm life. She was one who couldn't make it by herself. She'd have to love somebody and then of course she'd have to suffer when something took them away from her, or maybe when they left on their own. She'd never learn you gotta suffer *alone* in this world. I never knew for sure what happened to her. I didn't try to find out because I'd probably just discover she was a wino and a streetwalking whore and I'd rather think otherwise."

"Bumper?"

"What?"

"Please take my bed tonight. Go in and shower and take my bed. You're dripping wet and you'll get sick if you stay here on the couch."

"I'll be okay. You should see some of the places I've slept. Just give me a blanket."

"Please."

She began trying to lift me and that almost made me laugh out loud. She was a strong girl, but no woman was about to raise Bumper Morgan, two hundred and seventy-five pounds anytime, and almost three hundred this night with all of me cold dead weight from the booze.

"Okay, okay," I grumbled, and found I wasn't too drunk when I stood up. I made my way to her bedroom, stripped, and jumped in the shower, turning it on cold at the end. When I was through I dried in her bath towel which smelled like woman, took the wet gauze bandage off my leg, and felt better than I had all day. I rinsed my mouth with toothpaste, examined my meat-red face and red-webbed eyes, and climbed in her bed naked, which is the only way to sleep, winter or summer.

The bed smelled like her too, or rather it smelled like woman, since all women are pretty much the same to me. They all smell and feel the same. It's the essence of womanhood, that's the thing I need.

I was dozing when Laila came in and tiptoed to the shower and it seemed like seconds later when she was sitting on the bed in a sheer white nightgown whispering to me. I smelled lilac, and then woman, and I came to with her velvet mouth all over my face.

"What the hell?" I mumbled, sitting up.

"I touched you tonight," said Laila. "You told me things. Maybe for the first time in years, Bumper, I've really touched another person!" She put her hand on my bare shoulder.

"Yeah, well that's enough touching for one night," I said, disgusted with myself for telling her all those personal things, and I took her hand off my shoulder. Now I'd have to fly back to L.A. in a couple of weeks to set this thing up with Laila and her family. Everyone was complicating my life lately.

"Bumper," she said, drawing her feet up under her and

laughing pretty damn jolly for this time of night. "Bumper, you're wonderful. You're a wonderful old panda. A big blue-nosed panda. Do you know your nose is blue?"

"Yeah, it gets that way when I drink too much," I said, figuring she'd been smoking hash, able to see right through the nightie at her skin which was now exactly the color of apricots. "I had too many blood vessels busted too many times there on my nose."

"I want to get under the covers with you, Bumper."

"Look, kid," I said. "You don't owe me a goddamn thing. I'll be glad to help you flimflam your family."

"You've let me touch you, Bumper," she said, and the warm wide velvet mouth was on me again, my neck and cheek, and all that chestnut hair was covering me until I almost couldn't think about how ridiculous this was.

"Goddamnit," I said, holding her off. "This is a sickening thing you're doing. I knew you since you were a little girl. Damn it, kid, I'm an old bag of guts and you're still just a little child to me. This is unnatural!"

"Don't call me kid. And don't try to stop me from having you."

"*Having* me? You're just impressed by cops. I'm a father symbol. Lots of young girls feel like that about cops."

"I hate cops," she answered, her boobs wobbling against my arms, which were getting tired. "It's you I want because you're more man than I've ever had my hands on."

"Yeah, I'm about six cubic yards," I said, very shaky.

"That's not what I meant," she said, her hands going over me, and she was kissing me again and I was doing everything I could to avoid the pleasures of a thousand and one nights.

"Listen, I couldn't if I wanted to," I groaned. "You're just too young, I just couldn't do it with a kid like you."

"Want to bet?"

"Don't, Laila."

"How can a man be so aware and be so square," she smiled, standing up and slipping off the nightie.

"It's just the bluesuit," I said with a voice gone hoarse and squeaky. "I probably look pretty sharp to you in my uniform."

Laila busted up then, falling on the bed and rolling on her stomach, laughing for a good minute. I smiled weakly, staring at her apricot ass and those thunder thighs, thinking it was over. But after she stopped laughing she smiled at me softer than ever, whispered in Arabic, and crept under the sheet.

FRIDAY,
THE LAST DAY

FIFTEEN

I WOKE UP Friday morning with a terrible hangover. Laila
was sprawled half on top of me, a big smooth naked doe,
which was the reason I woke up. After living so many
years alone I don't like sleeping with anyone. Cassie, who
I made love to maybe a hundred times, had never slept
with me, not all night. We'd have to get twin beds, Cassie
and me. I just can't stand to be too close to anybody for
too long.

Laila didn't wake up and I took my clothes into the
living room and dressed, leaving a note that said I'd get in
touch in a week or so, to work out the details of handling
her bank account and dumping a load of snow on Yasser
and the family.

Before I left I crept back into the bedroom to look at
her this last time. She was sprawled on her stomach, sleek
and beautiful.

"*Salām*, Laila," I whispered. "A thousand *salāms*, little
girl."

I very carefully made my way down the stairs of
Laila's apartment house to my car parked in front, and
I felt a little better when I got out on the road with the

window down driving onto the Hollywood Freeway on a windy, not too smoggy day.

Then I thought for a few minutes about how it had been with Laila and I was ashamed because I always prided myself on being something more than the thousands of ugly old slimeballs you see in Hollywood with beautiful young babies like her. She did it because she was grateful and neurotic and confused and I took advantage. I'd always picked on someone my own size all my life, and now I was no better than any other horny old fart.

I went home and had a cold shower and a shave and I felt more or less human after some aspirin and three cups of coffee that started the heartburn going for the day. I wondered if after a few months of retirement my stomach might begin to rebuild itself, and who knows, maybe I'd have digestive peace.

I got to the Glass House a half hour early and by the time I shined my black high-top shoes, buffed the Sam Browne, hit the badge with some rouge and a cloth, I was sweating a little and feeling much improved. I put on a fresh uniform since the one from yesterday was covered with blood and birdshit. When I pinned on the gleaming shield and slid the scarred baton through the chrome ring on my Sam Browne I felt even better.

At rollcall Cruz was sitting as usual with the watch commander, Lieutenant Hilliard, at the table in front of the room, and Cruz glanced at me several times like he expected me to get up and make a grand announcement that this was my last day. Of course I didn't, and he looked a little disappointed. I hated to disappoint anyone, especially Cruz, but I wasn't going out with a trumpet blare. I really wanted Lieutenant Hilliard to hold an inspection this morning, my last one, and he did. He limped down the line and said my boondockers and my shield looked like a million bucks and he wished some of the young cops looked half as sharp. After inspection I drank a quart or so from the water fountain and I felt better yet.

I meant to speak to Cruz about our lunch date, but Lieutenant Hilliard was talking to him so I went out to the car, and decided to call him later. I fired up the black-and-white, put my baton in the holder on the door, tore off the paper on my writing pad, replaced the old hot sheet, checked the back seat for dead midgets, and drove out of the station. It was really unbelievable. The *last time*.

After hitting the bricks, I cleared over the air, even though I worried that I'd get a burglary report or some other chickenshit call before I could get something in my stomach. I couldn't stand the idea of anything heavy just now so I turned south on San Pedro and headed for the dairy, which was a very good place to go for hangover cures, at least it always was for me. It was more than a dairy, it was the plant and home office for a dairy that sold all over Southern California, and they made very good specialty products like cottage cheese and buttermilk and yogurt, all of which are wonderful for hangovers if you're not too far gone. I waved at the gate guard, got passed into the plant, and parked in front of the employee's store, which wasn't opened yet.

I saw one of the guys I knew behind the counter setting up the cash register and I knocked on the window.

"Hi, Bumper," he smiled, a young guy, with deep-set green eyes and a mop of black hair. "What do you need?"

"Plasma, pal," I said, "but I'll settle for yogurt."

"Sure. Come on in, Bumper," he laughed, and I passed through, heading for the tall glass door to the cold room where the yogurt was kept. I took two yogurts from the shelf, and he gave me a plastic spoon when I put them on the counter.

"That all you're having, Bumper?" he asked, as I shook my head and lifted the lid and spooned out a half pint of blueberry which I finished in three or four gulps and followed with a lime. And finally, what the hell, I thought, I grabbed another, French apple, and ate it while the guy counted his money and said something to me once or twice which I nodded at, and I smiled through a mouthful of cool creamy yogurt that was coating my stomach, soothing me, and making me well.

"Never saw anyone put away yogurt like that, Bumper," he said after I finished.

I couldn't remember this young guy's name, and wished like hell they wore their names on the gray work uniform because I always like to make a little small talk and call someone by name when he's feeding me. It's the least you can do.

"Could I have some buttermilk?" I asked, after he threw the empty yogurt containers in a gleaming trash can behind the counter. The whole place sparkled, being a dairy, and it smelled clean, and was nice and cool.

"Why sure, Bumper," he said, leaving the counter and coming back with a pint of cold buttermilk. Most of the older guys around the dairy wouldn't bring me a pint container, and here I was dying of thirst from the booze. Rather than say anything I just tipped it up and poured it down, only swallowing three times to make him realize his mistake.

"Guess I should've brought you a quart, huh?" he said after I put the milk carton down and licked my lips.

I smiled and shrugged and he went in the back, returning with a quart.

"Thanks, pal," I said. "I'm pretty thirsty today." I tipped the quart up and let it flow thick and delicious into my mouth, and then I started swallowing, but not like before, more slowly. When I finished it I was really fit again. I was well. I could do anything now.

"Take a quart with you?" he said. "Would you like more yogurt or some cottage cheese?"

"No thanks," I said. I don't believe in being a hog like some cops I've worked with. "Gotta get back to the streets. Friday mornings get pretty busy sometimes."

I really should've talked a while. I knew I should, but I just didn't feel like it. It was the first time this guy ever served me so I said the thing that all policemen say when they're ninety percent sure what the answer will be.

"How much do I owe you?"

"Don't mention it," he said, shaking his head. "Come see us anytime, Bumper."

While driving out the main gate of the dairy, I fired up a fresh cigar which I knew couldn't possibly give me indigestion because my stomach was so well coated I could eat tin cans and not notice.

Then I realized that was the last time I'd ever make my dairy stop. Damn, I thought, everything I do today will be for the last time. Then I suddenly started hoping I'd get some routine calls like a burglary report or maybe a family dispute which I usually hated refereeing. I wouldn't even mind writing a traffic ticket today.

It would've been something, I thought, really something to have stayed on the job after my twenty years. You have your pension in the bag then, and you own your own mortgage, having bought and paid for them with twenty years' service. Regardless of what you ever do or don't do you have a forty percent pension the rest of your life, from the moment you leave the Department. Whether you're fired for pushing a slimeball down the fire escape, or whether you're booked for lying in court to put a scumbag where he ought to be, or whether you bust your stick over the hairy little skull of some college brat who's tearing at your badge and carrying a tape recorder at a demonstration, no matter what you do, they got to pay you that pension. If they have to, they'll mail those checks to you at San Quentin. Nobody can take your pension away. Knowing that might make police work even a little *more* fun, I thought. It might give you just a little more push, make you a little more aggressive. I would've liked to have done police work knowing that I owned my own mortgage.

As I was cruising I picked a voice out of the radio chatter. It was the girl with the cutest and sexiest voice I ever heard. She was on frequency thirteen today, and she had her own style of communicating. She didn't just come on the horn and answer with clipped phrases and impersonal "rogers." Her voice would rise and fall like a song, and getting even a traffic accident call from her, which patrol policemen hate worst because they're so tedious, was somehow not quite so bad. She must've been hot for some cop in unit Four-L-Nine because her voice came in soft and husky and sent a shiver through me when she said, "Foah-L-Ninah, rrrrrrraj-ahh!"

Now that's the way to roger a call, I thought. I was

driving nowhere at all, just touring the beat, looking at people I knew and ones I didn't know, trying not to think of all the things I'd never do out here. I was trading them for things I'd *rather* do, things any sane man would rather do, like be with Cassie and start my new career and live a civilized normal life. Funny I should think of it as *civilized*, that kind of life. That was one of the reasons I'd always wanted to go to North Africa to die.

I always figured kind of vaguely that if somebody didn't knock me off and I lasted say thirty years, I'd pull the pin then because I could never do my kind of police work past sixty. I really thought I could last that long though. I thought that if I cut down on the groceries and the drinking and the cigars, maybe I could last out here on the streets until I was sixty. Then I'd have learned almost all there was to learn here. I'd know all the secrets I always wanted to know and I'd hop a jet and go to the Valley of the Kings and look out there from a pink granite cliff and see where all *civilization* started, and maybe if I stayed there long enough and didn't get drunk and fall off a pyramid, or get stomped to death by a runaway camel, or ventilated by a Yankee-hating Arab, maybe if I lasted there long enough, I'd find out the last thing I wanted to know: whether *civilization* was worth the candle after all.

Then I thought of what Cruz would say if I ever got drunk enough to tell him about this. He'd say, "'*Mano*, let yourself love, and give yourself away. You'll get your answer. You don't need a sphinx or a pink granite cliff.'"

"Hi, Bumper," a voice yelled, and I turned from the glare of the morning sun and saw Percy opening his pawnshop.

"Hi, Percy," I yelled back, and slowed down to wave.

He was a rare animal, an honest pawnbroker. He ran hypes and other thieves out of his shop if he even suspected they had something hot. And he always demanded good identification from a customer pawning something. He was an honest pawnbroker, a rare animal.

I remembered the time Percy gave me his traffic ticket to take care of because this was the first one he'd ever gotten. It was for jaywalking. He didn't own a car. He hated them and took a bus to the shop every day. I just couldn't disillusion old Percy by letting him know that I couldn't fix a ticket, so I took it and paid it for him. It's practically impossible to fix a ticket anymore in this town. You have to know the judge or the City Attorney. Lawyers take care of each other of course, but a cop can't fix a ticket. Anyway, I paid it, and Percy thought I fixed it and wasn't disappointed. He thought I was a hell of a big man.

Another black-and-white cruised past me going south. The cop driving, a curly-haired kid named Nelson, waved, and I nodded back. He almost rear-ended a car stopped at the red light because he was looking at some chick in hot pants going into an office building. He was a typical young cop, I thought. Thinking of pussy instead of police work. And just like all these cats, Nelson loved talking about it. I think they all love talking about it these days more than they love doing it. That gave me a royal pain in the ass. I guess I've had more than my share in my time. I've had some good stuff for an ugly guy, but by Maggie's muff, I never talked about screwing a dame, not with anybody. In my day, a guy was unmanly if he did that. But your day is over after this day, I reminded myself, and swung south on Grand.

Then I heard a Central car get a report call at one of

the big downtown hotels and I knew the hotel burglar
had hit again. I'd give just about anything, I thought, to
catch that guy today. That'd be like quitting after your
last home run, like Ted Williams. A home run your last
time up. That'd be something. I cruised around for twenty
minutes and then drove to the hotel and parked behind
the black-and-white that got the call. I sat there in my car
smoking a cigar and waited another fifteen minutes until
Clarence Evans came out. He was a fifteen-year cop, a tall
stringbean who I used to play handball with before my
ankles got so bad.

We had some good games. It's especially fun to play
when you're working nightwatch and you get up to the
academy about one a.m. after you finish work, and play
three hard fast games and take a steam bath. Except Evans didn't like the steam bath, being so skinny. We always took a half case of beer with us and drank it up after
we showered. He was one of the first Negroes I worked
with as a partner when L.A.P.D. became completely inte-
grated several years ago. He was a good copper and he liked
working with me even though he knew I always preferred
working alone. On nightwatch it's comforting sometimes
to have someone riding shotgun or walking beside you.
So I worked with him and lots of other guys even though
I would've rather had a one-man beat or an "L" car that
you work alone, "L" for lonesome. But I worked with him
because I never could disappoint anyone that wanted to
work with me that bad, and it made the handball playing
more convenient.

Then I saw Clarence coming out of the hotel carrying his report notebook. He grinned at me, came walk-

ing light-footed over to my car, opened the door and sat down.

"What's happening, Bumper?"

"Just curious if the hotel creeper hit again, Clarence."

"Took three rooms on the fifth floor and two on the fourth floor," he nodded.

"The people asleep?"

"In four of them. In the other one, they were down in the bar."

"That means he hit before two a.m."

"Right."

"I can't figure this guy," I said, popping an antacid tablet. "Usually he works in the daytime but sometimes in the early evening. Now he's hitting during the night when they're in and when they're not in. I never heard of a hotel burglar as squirrelly as this guy."

"Maybe that's it," said Evans. "A squirrel. Didn't he try to hurt a kid on one job?"

"A teddy bear. He stabbed the hell out of a big teddy bear. It was all covered up with a blanket and looked like a kid sleeping."

"That cat's a squirrel," said Evans.

"That would explain why the other hotel burglars don't know anything," I said, puffing on the cigar and thinking. "I never did think he was a pro, just a lucky amateur."

"A lucky looney," said Evans. "You talked to all your snitches?" He knew my M.O. from working with me. He knew I had informants, but like everyone else he didn't know how many, or that I paid the good ones.

"I talked to just about everyone I know. I talked to a hotel burglar who told me he'd already been approached by three detectives and that he'd tell us if he knew anything, because this guy is bringing so much heat on all the hotels he'd like to see us get him."

"Well, Bumper, if anybody lucks onto the guy I'm betting you will," said Evans, putting on his hat and getting out of the car.

"Police are baffled but an arrest is imminent," I winked, and started the car. It was going to be a very hot day.

I was given a report call at Pershing Square, an injury report. Probably some pensioner fell off his soapbox and was trying to figure how he could say there was a crack in the sidewalk and sue the city. I ignored the call for a few minutes and let her assign it to another unit. I didn't like to do that. I always believed you should handle the calls given to you, but damn it, I only had the rest of the day and that was it, and I thought about Oliver Horn and wondered why I hadn't thought about him before. I couldn't waste time on the report call so I let the other unit handle it and headed for the barbershop on Fourth Street.

Oliver was sitting on a chair on the sidewalk in front of the shop. His ever-present broom was across his lap, and he was dozing in the sunshine.

He was the last guy in the world you would ever want to die and come back looking like. Oliver was built like a walrus with one arm cut off above the elbow. It was done maybe forty years ago by probably the worst surgeon in the world. The skin just flapped over and hung there. He had orange hair and a big white belly covered with orange hair. He long ago gave up trying to keep his pants up, and usually they barely gripped him below the gut so that his belly button was always popping out at you. His shoelaces were untied and destroyed from stepping on them because it was too hard to tie them one-handed, and he had a huge lump on his chin. It looked like if you squeezed it, it'd break a window. But Oliver was surprisingly clever. He swept out the barbershop and two or three businesses on this part of Fourth Street, including a bar called Raymond's where quite a few ex-cons hung out. It was close to the big hotels and a good place to scam on the rich tourists. Oliver didn't miss anything and had given me some very good information over the years.

"You awake, Oliver?" I asked.

He opened one blue-veined eyelid. "Bumper, how's it wi'choo?"

"Okay, Oliver. Gonna be a hot one again today."

"Yeah, I'm gettin' sticky. Let's go in the shop."

"Don't have time. Listen, I was just wondering, you heard about this burglar that's been ripping us downtown here in all the big hotels for the past couple months?"

"No, ain't heard nothin'."

"Well, this guy ain't no ordinary hotel thief. I mean he probably ain't none of the guys you ordinarily see around Raymond's, but he might be a guy that you would *sometimes* see there. What the hell, even a ding-a-ling has a drink once in a while, and Raymond's is convenient when you're getting ready to rape about ten rooms across the street."

"He a ding-a-ling?"

"Yeah."

"What's he look like?"

"I don't know."

"How can I find him then, Bumper?"

"I don't know, Oliver. I'm just having hunches now. I think the guy's done burglaries before. I mean he knows how to shim doors and all that. And like I say, he's a little

dingy. I think he's gonna stab somebody before too long.
He carries a blade. A *long* blade, because he went clear
through a mattress with it."

"Why'd he stab a mattress?"

"He was trying to kill a teddy bear."

"You been drinkin', Bumper?"

I smiled, and then I wondered what the hell I was doing here because I didn't know enough about the burglar
to give a snitch something to work with. I was grabbing
at any straw in the wind so I could hit a home run before
walking off the field for the last time. Absolutely pathetic
and sickening, I thought, ashamed of myself.

"Here's five bucks," I said to Oliver. "Get yourself a
steak."

"Jeez, Bumper," he said, "I ain't done nothin' for it."

"The guy carries a long-bladed knife and he's a psycho and lately he takes these hotels at any goddamn hour
of the day or night. He just might go to Raymond's for
a drink sometime. He just might use the restroom while
you're cleaning up and maybe he'll be tempted to look
at some of the stuff in his pockets to see what he stole.
Or maybe he'll be sitting at the bar and he'll pull a pretty
out of his pocket that he just snatched at the hotel, or
maybe one of these sharp hotel burglars that hangs out at
Raymond's will know something, or say something, and
you're always around there. Maybe anything."

"Sure, Bumper, I'll call you right away I hear anything
at all. Right away, Bumper. And you get any more clues
you let me know, hey, Bumper?"

"Sure, Oliver, I'll get you a good one from my clues
closet."

"Hey, that's aw right," Oliver hooted. He had no teeth

in front, upper or lower. For a long time he had one upper tooth in front.

"Be seeing you, Oliver."

"Hey, Bumper, wait a minute. You ain't told me no funny cop stories in a long time. How 'bout a story?"

"I think you heard them all."

"Come on, Bumper."

"Well, let's see. I told you about the seventy-five-year-old nympho I busted over on Main that night?"

"Yeah, yeah," he hooted, "tell me that one again. That's a good one."

"I gotta go, Oliver, honest. But say, did I ever tell you about the time I caught the couple in the back seat up there in Elysian Park in one of those maker's acres?"

"No, tell me, Bumper."

"Well, I shined my light in there and here's these two down on the seat, the old boy throwing the knockwurst to his girlfriend, and this young partner I'm with says, 'What're you doing there?' And the guy gives the answer ninety percent of the guys do when you catch them in that position: 'Nothing, Officer.' "

"Yeah, yeah," said Oliver, his shaggy head bobbing.

"So I say to the guy, 'Well, if *you* ain't doing anything, move over there and hold my flashlight and lemme see what *I* can do.' "

"Whoooo, that's funny," said Oliver. "Whoooo, Bumper."

He was laughing so hard he hardly saw me go, and I left him there holding his big hard belly and laughing in the sunshine.

I thought about telling Oliver to call Central Detectives instead of me, because I wouldn't be here after today, but what the hell, then I'd have to tell him *why* I wouldn't be here, and I couldn't take another person telling me why I should or should not retire. If Oliver ever called, somebody'd tell him I was gone, and the information would eventually get to the dicks. So what the hell, I thought, pulling back into the traffic and breathing exhaust fumes. It would've been really something though, to get that burglar on this last day. Really something.

I looked at my watch and thought Cassie should be at school now, so I drove to City College and parked out front. I wondered why I didn't feel guilty about Laila. I guess I figured it wasn't really my fault.

Cassie was alone in the office when I got there. I closed the door, flipped my hat on a chair, walked over, and felt that same old amazement I've felt a thousand times over how well a woman fits in your arms, and how soft they feel.

"Thought about you all night," she said after I kissed her a dozen times or so. "Had a miserable evening. Couple of bores."

"You thought about me all night, huh?"

"Honestly, I did." She kissed me again. "I still have this awful feeling something's going to happen."

"Every guy that ever went into battle has that feeling."

"Is that what our marriage is going to be, a battle?"

"If it is, you'll win, baby. I'll surrender."

"Wait'll I get you tonight," she whispered. "You'll surrender all right."

"That green dress is gorgeous."

"But you still like hot colors better?"

"Of course."

"After we get married I'll wear nothing but reds and oranges and yellows. . . ."

"You ready to talk?"

"Sure, what is it?"

"Cruz gave me a talking-to—about you."

"Oh?"

"He thinks you're the greatest thing that ever happened to me."

"Go on," she smiled.

"Well . . ."

"Yes?"

"Damn it, I can't go on. Not in broad daylight with no drink in me. . . ."

"What did you talk about, silly?"

"About you. No, it was more about me. About things I need and things I'm afraid of. Twenty years he's my friend and suddenly I find out he's a damned intellectual."

"What do you need? What're you afraid of? I can't believe you've ever been afraid of anything."

"He knows me better than you know me."

"That makes me sad. I don't want anyone knowing you better than I do. Tell me what you talked about."

"I don't have time right now," I said, feeling a gas bubble forming. Then I lied and said, "I'm on the way to a call. I just had to stop for a minute. I'll tell you all about it tonight. I'll be at your pad at seven-thirty. We're going out to dinner, okay?"

"Okay."

"Then we'll curl up on your couch with a good bottle of wine."

"Sounds wonderful," she smiled, that clean, hot, female smile that made me kiss her.

"See you tonight," I whispered.

"Tonight," she gasped, and I realized I was crushing her. She stood in the doorway and watched me all the way down the stairs.

I got back in the car and dropped two of each kind of pill and grabbed a handful from the glove compartment and shoved them in my pants pockets for later.

As I drove back on the familiar streets of the beat I wondered why I couldn't talk to Cassie like I wanted. If you're going to marry someone you should be able to tell her almost anything about yourself that she has a right to know.

I pulled over at a phone booth then and called Cruz at the station. Lieutenant Hilliard answered and in a couple seconds I heard Cruz's soft voice, "Sergeant Segovia?" He said it like a question,

"Hello, Sergeant Segovia, this is future former Officer Morgan, what the hell you doing besides pushing a pencil and shuffling paper?"

"What're you doing besides ignoring your radio calls?"

"I'm just cruising around this miserable beat thinking how great it'll be not to have to do it anymore. You decided where you want me to take you for lunch?"

"You don't have to take me anywhere."

"Look, goddamnit, we're going to some nice place, so if you won't pick it, I will."

"Okay, take me to Seymours."

"On my beat? Oh, for chrissake. Look, you just meet me at Seymour's at eleven-thirty. Have a cup of coffee but don't eat a damn thing because we're going to a place I know in Beverly Hills."

"That's a long way from your beat, all right."

"I'll pick you up at Seymour's."

"Okay, *'mano, ahí te huacho.*"

I chuckled after I hung up at that Mexican slang because *watching* for me is exactly what Cruz always did when you stop and think about it. Most people say, "I'll be seeing you," because that's what they do, but Cruz, he always watched for me. It felt good to have old sad-eye watching for me.

SIXTEEN

I GOT BACK IN MY CAR and cruised down Main Street, by the parking lot at the rear of the Pink Dragon. I was so sick of pushing this pile of iron around that I stopped to watch some guys in the parking lot.

There were three of them and they were up to something. I parked the car and backed up until the building hid me. I got out and walked to the corner of the building, took my hat off, and peeked around the corner and across the lot.

A skinny hype in a long-sleeved blue shirt was talking to another brown-shirted one. There was a third one with them, a little T-shirt who stood a few steps away. Suddenly Blue-shirt nodded to Brown-shirt, who walked up and gave something to little T-shirt, who gave Brown-shirt something back, and they all hustled off in different directions. Little T-shirt was walking toward me. He was looking back over his shoulder for cops, and walking right into one. I didn't feel like messing around with a narco bust but this was too easy. I stepped in the hotel doorway and when T-shirt walked past, squinting into the sun, I reached out, grabbed him by the arm, and jerked him inside. He was just a boy, scared as hell. I shoved him face forward into the wall, and grabbed the hip pocket of his denims.

"What've you got, boy? Bennies or reds? Or maybe you're an acid freak?"

"Hey, lemme go!" he yelled.

I took the bennies out of his pocket. There were six rolls, five in a roll, held together by a rubber band. The day of ten-benny rolls was killed by inflation.

"How much did they make you pay, kid?" I asked, keeping a good grip on his arm. He didn't look so short up close, but he was skinny, with lots of brown hair, and young, too young to be downtown scoring pills in the middle of the morning.

"I paid seven dollars. But I won't ever do it again if you'll lemme go. Please lemme go."

"Put your hands behind you, kid," I said, unsnapping my handcuff case.

"What're you doing? Please don't put those on me. I won't hurt you or anything."

"I'm not afraid of you hurting me," I laughed, chewing on a wet cigar stump that I finally threw away. "It's just that my wheels are gone and my ass is too big to be chasing you all over these streets." I snapped on one cuff and brought his palms together behind his back and clicked on the other, taking them up snug.

"How much you say you paid for the pills?"

"Seven dollars. I won't never do it again if you'll lemme go, I swear." He was dancing around, nervous and scared, and he stepped on my right toe, scuffing up the shine.

"Careful, damn it."

"Oh, I'm sorry. Please lemme go. I didn't mean to step on you."

"Those cats charged you way too much for the pills," I said, as I led him to the radio car.

"I know you won't believe me but it's the first time I ever bought them. I don't know *what* the hell they cost."

"Sure it is."

"See, I knew you wouldn't believe me. You cops don't believe nobody."

"You know all about cops, do you?"

"I been arrested before. I know you cops. You all act the same."

"You must be a hell of a heavyweight desperado. Got a ten-page rap sheet, I bet. What've you been busted for?"

"Running away. Twice. And you don't have to put me down."

"How old are you?"

"Fourteen."

"In the car," I said, opening the front door. ""And don't lean back on the cuffs or they'll tighten."

"You don't have to worry, I won't jump out," he said as I fastened the seat belt over his lap.

"I ain't worrying, kid."

"I got a name. It's Tilden," he said, his square chin jutting way out.

"Mine's Morgan."

"My first name's Tom."

"Mine's Bumper."

"Where're you taking me?"

"To Juvenile Narcotics."

"You gonna book me?"

"Of course."

"What could I expect," he said, nodding his head disgustedly. "How could I ever expect a cop to act like a human being."

"You shouldn't even expect a human being to act like a human being. You'll just get disappointed."

I turned the key and heard the click-click of a dead battery. Stone-cold dead without warning.

"Hang loose, kid," I said, getting out of the car.

"Where could *I* go?" he yelled, as I lifted the hood to see if someone had torn the wires out. That happens once in a while when you leave your black-and-white somewhere that you can't keep an eye on it. It looked okay though. I wondered if something was wrong with the alternator. A call box was less than fifty feet down the sidewalk so I moseyed to it, turning around several times to keep an eye on my little prisoner. I called in and asked for a garage man with a set of booster cables and was told to stand by for about twenty minutes and somebody'd get out to me. I thought about calling a sergeant since they carry booster cables in their cars, but I decided not to. What the hell, why be in a rush today? What was there to prove now? To anyone? To myself?

Then I started getting a little hungry because there was a small diner across the street and I could smell bacon and ham. The odor was blowing through the duct in the front of the place over the cooking stoves. The more I sniffed the hungrier I got, and I looked at my watch and thought, what the hell. I went back and unstrapped the kid.

"What's up? Where we going?"

"Across the street."

"What for? We taking a bus to your station or something?"

"No, we gotta wait for the garage man. We're going across the street so I can eat."

"You can't take me in there looking like this," said the kid, as I led him across the street. His naturally rosy cheeks were lobster-red now. "Take the handcuffs off."

"Not a chance. I could never catch a young antelope like you.

"I swear I won't run."

"I know you won't, with your hands cuffed behind you and me holding the chain."

"I'll die if you take me in there like a dog on a leash in front of all those people."

"Ain't nobody in there you know, kid. And anybody that might be in there's been in chains himself, probably. Nothing to be embarrassed about."

"I could sue you for this."

"Oh *could* you?" I said, holding the door and shoving him inside.

There were only three counter customers, two con guys, and a wino drinking coffee. They glanced up for a second and nobody even noticed the kid was cuffed. I pointed toward a table at the rear.

"Got no waitress this early, Bumper," said T-Bone, the proprietor, a huge Frenchman who wore a white chef's hat and a T-shirt, and white pants. I'd never seen him in anything else.

"We need a table, T-Bone," I said, pointing to the kid's handcuffs.

"Okay," said T-Bone. "What'll you have?"

"I'm not too hungry. Maybe a couple over-easy eggs and some bacon, and a few pieces of toast. And oh, maybe some hash browns. Glass of tomato juice. Some coffee. And whatever the kid wants."

"What'll you have, boy?" asked T-Bone, resting his huge hairy hands on the counter and grinning at the boy, with one gold and one silver front tooth. I wondered for the first time where in the hell he got a silver crown like that. Funny I never thought of that before. T-Bone wasn't a man you talked to. He only used his voice when it was necessary. He just fed people with as few words as possible.

"How can I eat anything?" said the kid. "All chained up like a convict or something." His eyes were filling up and he looked awful young just then.

"I'm gonna unlock them," I said. "Now what the hell you want? T-Bone ain't got all day."

"I don't know what I want."

"Give him a couple fried eggs straight up, some bacon, and a glass of milk. You want hash browns, kid?"

"I guess so."

"Give him some orange juice too, and an order of toast. Make it a double order of toast. And some jam."

T-Bone nodded and scooped a handful of eggs from a bowl by the stove. He held four eggs in that big hand and cracked all four eggs one at a time without using the other hand. The kid was watching it.

"He's got some talent, hey, kid?"

"Yeah. You said you were taking these off."

"Get up and turn around," I said, and when he did I unlocked the right cuff and fastened it around the chrome leg of the table so he could sit there with one hand free.

"Is this what you call taking them off?" he said. "Now I'm like an organ grinder's monkey on a chain!"

"Where'd you ever see an organ grinder? There ain't been any grinders around here for years."

"I saw them on old TV movies. And that's what I look like."

"Okay, okay, quit chipping your teeth. You complain more than any kid I ever saw. You oughtta be glad to be getting some breakfast. I bet you didn't eat a thing at home this morning."

"I wasn't even *at* home this morning."

"Where'd you spend the night?"

He brushed back several locks of hair from his eyes with a dirty right hand, "I spent part of the night sleeping in one of those all-night movies till some creepy guy woke me up with his cruddy hand on my knee. Then I got the hell outta there. I slept for a little while in a chair in some hotel that was open just down the street."

"You run away from home?"

"No, I just didn't feel like sleeping at the pad last night. My sis wasn't home and I just didn't feel like sitting around by myself."

"You live with your sister?"

"Yeah."

"Where's your parents?"

"Ain't got none."

"How old's your sister?"

"Twenty-two."

"Just you and her, huh?"

"Naw, there's always somebody around. Right now it's a stud named Slim. Big Blue always got somebody around."

"That's what you call your sister? Big Blue?"

"She used to be a dancer, kind of. In a bar. Topless. She

went by that name. Now she's getting too fat in the ass so she's hustling drinks at the Chinese Garden over on Western. You know the joint?"

"Yeah, I know it."

"Anyway, she always says soon as she loses thirty pounds she's going back to dancing which is a laugh because her ass is getting wider by the day. She likes to be called Big Blue so even *I* started calling her that. She got this phony dyed-black hair, see. It's almost blue."

"She oughtta wash your clothes for you once in a while. That shirt looks like a grease rag."

"That's 'cause I was working on a car with my next door neighbor yesterday. I didn't get a chance to change it." He looked offended by that crack. "I wear clothes clean as anybody. And I even wash them and iron them myself."

"That's the best way to be," I said, reaching over and unlocking the left cuff.

"You're taking them off?"

"Yeah. Go in the bathroom and wash your face and hands and arms. And your neck."

"You sure I won't go out the window?"

"Ain't no window in that john," I said. "And comb that mop outta your face so somebody can see what the hell you look like."

"Ain't got a comb."

"Here's mine," I said, giving him the pocket comb.

T-Bone handed me the glasses of juice, the coffee, and the milk while the kid was gone, and the bacon smell was all over the place now. I was wishing I'd asked for a double order of bacon even though I knew T-Bone would give me an extra big helping.

I was sipping the coffee when the kid came back in. He was looking a hundred percent better even though his neck was still dirty. At least his hair was slicked back and his face and arms up to the elbow were nice and clean. He wasn't a handsome kid, his face was too tough and craggy, but he had fine eyes, full of life, and he looked you right in your eye when he talked to you. That's what I liked best about him.

"There's your orange juice," I said.

"Here's your comb."

"Keep it. I don't even know why I carry it. I can't do anything with this patch of wires I got. I'll be glad when I get bald."

"Yeah, you couldn't look no worse if you was bald," he said, examining my hair.

"Drink your orange juice, kid."

We both drank our juice and T-Bone said, "Here, Bumper," and handed a tray across the counter, but before I could get up the kid was on his feet and grabbed the tray and laid everything out on the table like he knew what he was doing.

"Hey, you even know what side to put the knife and fork on," I said.

"Sure. I been a busboy. I done all kinds of work in my time."

"How old you say you are?"

"Fourteen. Well, almost fourteen. I'll be fourteen next October."

When he'd finished he sat down and started putting away the chow like he was as hungry as I thought he was. I threw one of my eggs on his plate when I saw two weren't going to do him, and I gave him a slice of my toast. He was a first-class eater. That was something else I liked about him.

While he was finishing the last of the toast and jam, I went to the door and looked across the street. A garage attendant was replacing my battery. He saw me and waved that it was okay. I waved back and went back inside to finish my coffee.

"You get enough to eat?" I asked.

"Yeah, thanks."

"You sure you don't want another side of bacon and a loaf or two of bread?"

"I don't get breakfasts like that too often," he grinned.

When we were getting ready to leave I tried to pay T-Bone.

"From you? No, Bumper."

"Well, for the kid's chow, then." I tried to make him take a few bucks.

"No, Bumper. You don't pay nothin'."

"Thanks, T-Bone. Be seeing you," I said, and he raised a huge hand covered with black hair, and smiled gold and silver. And I almost wanted to ask him about the silver crown because it was the last time I'd have a chance.

"You gonna put the bracelets back on?" asked the boy, as I lit a cigar and patted my stomach and took a deep sniff of morning smog.

"You promise you won't run?"

"I swear. I hate those damn things on my wrists. You feel so helpless, like a little baby."

"Okay, let's get in the car," I said, trotting across the street with him to get out of the way of the traffic.

"How many times you come downtown to score?" I asked before starting the car.

"I never been downtown alone before. I swear. And I didn't even hitchhike. I took a bus. I was even gonna take a bus back to Echo Park. I didn't wanna run into cops with the pills in my pocket."

"How long you been dropping bennies?"

"About three months. And I only tried them a couple times. A kid I know told me I could come down here and almost any guy hanging around could get them for me. I don't know why I did it."

"How many tubes you sniff a day?"

"I ain't a gluehead. It makes guys crazy. And I never sniffed paint, neither."

Then I started looking at this kid, really looking at him. Usually my brain records only necessary things about arrestees, but now I found myself looking really close and listening for lies. That's something else you can't tell the judge, that you'd bet your instinct against a polygraph. I *knew* this boy wasn't lying. But then, I seemed to be wrong about everything lately.

"I'm gonna book you and release you to your sister. That okay with you?"

"You ain't gonna send me to Juvenile Hall?"

"No. You wanna go there?"

"Christ, no. I gotta be free. I was scared you was gonna lock me up. Thanks. Thanks a lot. I just gotta be free. I couldn't stand being inside a place like that with everybody telling you what to do."

"If I ever see you downtown scoring pills again, I'll make sure you go to the Hall."

The kid took a deep breath. "You'll never see me again, I swear. Unless you come out around Echo Park."

"As a matter of fact, I don't live too far from there."

"Yeah? I got customers in Silverlake and all around Echo Park. Where do you live?"

"Not far from Bobby's drive-in. You know where that is? All the kids hang around there."

"Sure I do. I work with this old guy who's got this pickup truck and equipment. Why don't you let us do your yard? We do front and back, rake, trim, weed and everything for eight bucks."

"That's not too bad. How much you get yourself?"

"Four bucks. I do all the work. The old guy just flops in the shade somewhere till I'm through. But I need him because of the truck and stuff."

This kid had me so interested I suddenly realized we were just sitting there. I put the cigar in my teeth and turned the key. She fired right up and I pulled out in the traffic. But I couldn't get my mind off this boy.

"Whadda you do for fun? You play ball or anything?"

"No, I like swimming. I'm the best swimmer in my class, but I don't go out for the team."

"Why not?"

"I'm too busy with girls. Look." The boy took out his wallet and showed me his pictures. I glanced at them while turning on Pico, three shiny little faces that all looked the same to me.

"Pretty nice," I said, handing the pictures back.

"*Real* nice," said the kid with a wink.

"You look pretty athletic. Why don't you play baseball? That used to be my game."

"I like sports I can do by myself."

"Don't you have any buddies?"

"No, I'm more of a ladies' man."

"I know what you mean, but you can't go through this world by yourself. You should have some friends."

"I don't need nobody."

"What grade you in?"

"Eighth. I'll sure be glad to get the hell out of junior high. It's a ghoul school."

"How you gonna pass if you cut classes like this?"

"I don't ditch too often, and I'm pretty smart in school, believe it or not. I just felt rotten last night. Sometimes when you're alone a lot you get feeling rotten and you just wanna go out where there's some people. I figured, where am I gonna find lots of people? Downtown, right? So I came downtown. Then this morning I felt more rotten from sleeping in the creepy movie so I looked around and saw these two guys and asked them where I could get some bennies and they sold them to me. I really wanted to get high, but swear to God, I only dropped bennies a couple times before. And one lousy time I dropped a red devil and a rainbow with some guys at school, and that's all the dope I ever took. I don't really dig it, Officer. Sometimes I drink a little beer."

"I'm a beer man myself, and you can call me Bumper."

"Listen, Bumper, I meant it about doing your yard work. I'm a hell of a good worker. The old man ain't no good, but I just stick him away in a corner somewheres and you should see me go. You won't be sorry if you hire us."

"Well, I don't really have a yard myself. I live in this apartment building, but I kind of assist the manager and he's always letting the damn place go to hell. It's mostly planted in ivy and ice plant and junipers that he lets get pretty seedy-looking. Not too much lawn except little squares of grass in front of the downstairs apartments."

"You should see me pull weeds, Bumper. I'd have that ice plant looking alive and green in no time. And I know how to take care of junipers. You gotta trim them a little, kind of shape them. I can make a juniper look soft and trim as a virgin's puss. How about getting us the account? I could maybe give you a couple bucks kickback."

"Maybe I'll do that."

"Sure. When we get to the police station, I'll write out the old man's name and phone number for you. You just call him when you want us to come. One of these days I'm getting some business cards printed up. It impresses hell out of people when you drop a business card on them. I figure we'll double our business with a little advertising and some business cards."

"I wouldn't be surprised."

"This the place?" The kid looked up at the old brown brick station. I parked in the back.

"This is the place," I said. "Pretty damned dreary, huh?"

"It gives me the creepies."

"The office is upstairs," I said, leading him up and inside, where I found one of the Juvenile Narcotics officers eating lunch.

"Hi, Bumper," he said.

"What's happening, man," I answered, not able to think of his name. "Got a kid with some bennies. No big thing. I'll book him and pencil out a quick arrest report."

"Worthwhile for me talking to him?"

"Naw, just a little score. First time, he claims. I'll take care of it. When should I cite him back in?"

"Make it Tuesday. We're pretty well up to the ass in cite-ins."

"Okay," I said, and nodded to another plainclothes officer who came in and started talking to the first one.

"Stay put, kid," I said to the boy and went to the head. After I came out, I went to the soft drink machine and got myself a Coke and one for the boy. When I came back in he was looking at me kind of funny.

"Here's a Coke," I said, and we went in another office which was empty. I got a booking form and an arrest report and got ready to start writing.

He was still looking at me with a little smile on his face.

"What's wrong?" I said.

"Nothing."

"What're you grinning at?"

"Oh, was I grinning? I was just thinking about what those two cops out there said when you went to the john."

"What'd they say?"

"Oh, how you was some kind of cop."

"Yeah," I mumbled as I put my initial on a couple of the bennies so I could recognize them if the case went to court. I knew it wouldn't though. I was going to request that the investigator just counsel and release him.

"You and your sister're gonna have to come in Tuesday morning and talk to an investigator."

"What for?"

"So he can decide if he ought to C-and-R you, or send you to court."

"What's C and R? Crush and rupture?"

"Hey, that's pretty good," I chuckled. He was a spunky

little bastard. I was starting to feel kind of proud of him. "C and R means counsel and release. They almost always counsel and release a kid the first time he's busted instead of sending him to juvenile court."

"I told you I been busted twice for running away. This ain't my first fall."

"Don't worry about it. They're not gonna send you to court."

"How do you know?"

"They'll do what I ask."

"Those juvies said you was really some kind of cop. No wonder I got nailed so fast."

"You were no challenge," I said, putting the bennies in an evidence envelope and sealing it.

"I guess not. Don't forget to lemme give you the old guy's name and phone number for the yard work. Who you live with? Wife and kids?"

"I live alone."

"Yeah?"

"Yeah."

"I might be able to give you a special price on the yard-work. You know, you being a cop and all."

"Thanks, but you should charge your full price, son."

"You said baseball was your game, Bumper?"

"Yeah, that's right." I stopped writing for a minute because the boy seemed excited and was talking so much.

"You like the Dodgers?"

"Yeah, sure."

"I always wanted to learn about baseball. Maury Wills is a Dodger, ain't he?"

"Yeah."

"I'd like to go to a Dodger game sometime and see Maury Wills."

"You never been to a big league game?"

"Never been. Know what? There's this guy down the street. Old fat fart, maybe even older than you, and fatter even. He takes his kid to the school yard across the street all day Saturday and Sunday and hits fly balls to him. They go to a game practically every week during baseball season."

"Yeah?"

"Yeah, and know what the best part of it is?"

"What?"

"All that exercise is really good for the old man. That kid's doing him a *favor* by playing ball with him."

"I better call your sister," I said, suddenly getting a gas bubble and a burning pain at the same time. I was also getting a little light-headed from the heat and because there were ideas trying to break through the front of my skull, but I thought it was better to leave them lay right now. The boy gave me the number and I dialed it.

"No answer, kid," I said, hanging up the phone.

"Christ, you gotta put me in Juvenile Hall if you don't find her?"

"Yeah, I do."

"You can't just drop me at the pad?"

"I can't."

"Damn. Call Ruby's Playhouse on Normandie. That joint opens early and Slim likes to hang out there sometimes. Damn, not the Hall!"

I got Ruby's Playhouse on the phone and asked for Sarah Tilden, which he said was her name.

"Big Blue," said the boy. "Ask for Big Blue."

"I wanna talk to Big Blue," I said, and then the bartender knew who I was talking about.

A slurred young voice said, "Yeah, who's this?"

"This is Officer Morgan, Los Angeles Police, Miss Tilden. I've arrested your brother downtown for possession of dangerous drugs. He had some pills on him. I'd like you to drive down to thirteen-thirty Georgia Street and pick him up. That's just south of Pico Boulevard and west of Figueroa." After I finished there was a silence on the line for a minute and then she said, "Well, that does it. Tell the little son of a bitch to get himself a lawyer. I'm through."

I let her go on with the griping a little longer and then I said, "Look, Miss Tilden, you'll have to come pick him up and then you'll have to come back here Tuesday morning and talk to an investigator. Maybe they can give you some advice."

"What happens if I don't come pick him up?" she said.

"I'd have to put him in Juvenile Hall and I don't think you'd want that. I don't think it would be good for him."

"Look, Officer," she said. "I wanna do what's right. But maybe you people could help me somehow. I'm a young woman, too goddamn young to be saddled with a kid his age. I can't raise a kid. It's too hard for me. I got a lousy job. Nobody should expect me to raise a kid brother. I been turned down for welfare even, how do you like that? If I was some nigger they'd gimme all the goddamn welfare I wanted. Look, maybe it would be best if you *did* put him in Juvenile Hall. Maybe it would be best for him. It's *him* I'm thinking of, you see. Or maybe you could put him in one of those foster homes. Not like a criminal, but someplace where somebody with lots of time can watch over him and see that he goes to school."

"Lady, I'm just the arresting officer and my job is to get him home right now. You can talk about all this crap to the juvenile investigator Tuesday morning, but I want you down here in fifteen minutes to take him home. You understand me?"

"Okay, okay, I understand you," she said. "Is it all right if I send a family friend?"

"Who is it?"

"It's Tommy's uncle. His name's Jake Pauley. He'll bring Tommy home."

"I guess it'll be okay."

After I hung up, the kid was looking at me with a lopsided smile. "How'd you like Big Blue?"

"Fine," I said, filling in the boxes on the arrest report. I was sorry I had called her in front of the kid, but I wasn't expecting all that bitching about coming to get him.

"She don't *want* me, does she?"

"She's sending your uncle to pick you up."

"I ain't got no uncle."

"Somebody named Jake Pauley."

"Hah! Old Jake baby? Hah! He's some uncle."

"Who's he? One of her friends?"

"They're friendly all right. She was shacked up with him before we moved in with Slim. I guess she's going back to Jake. Jesus, Slim'll cut Jake wide, deep, and often."

"You move around a lot, do you?"

"*Do* we? I been in seven different schools. Seven! But, I guess it's the same old story. You probably hear it all the time."

"Yeah, I hear it all the time."

I tried to get going on the report again and he let me write for a while but before I could finish he said, "Yeah, I been meaning to go to a Dodger game. I'd be willing to pay the way if I could get somebody with a little baseball savvy to go with me."

Now in addition to the gas and the indigestion, I had a headache, and I sat back with the booking slip finished and looked at him and let the thoughts come to the front of my skull, and of course it was clear as water that the gods conspire against me, because here was this boy. On my last day. Two days after Cassie first brought up the thing that's caused me a dozen indigestion attacks. And for a minute I was excited as hell and had to stand up and pace across the room and look out the window.

Here it is, I thought. Here's the thing that puts it all away for good. I fought an impulse to call Cassie and tell her about him, and another impulse to call his sister back and tell her not to bother sending Jake baby, and then I felt dizzy on top of the headache. I looked down at my shield and without willing it I reached down and touched it and my sweaty finger left a mark on the brass part which this morning had been polished to the luster of gold. The finger mark turned a tarnished orange before my eyes, and I thought about trading my gold and silver shield for a little tinny retirement badge that you can show to old men in bars to prove what you used to be, and which could never be polished to a luster that would reflect sunlight like a mirror.

Then the excitement I'd felt for a moment began to fade and was replaced with a kind of fear that grew and almost smothered me until I got hold of myself. This was too much. This was all *much* too much. Cassie was one terrible responsibility, but I needed her. Cruz told me. Socorro told me. The elevator boy in the death room of the hotel told me. The old blubbering drunks in Harry's bar told me. I needed her. Yes, maybe, but I didn't need this other kind of responsibility. I didn't need *this* kind of cross. Not me. I walked into the other room where the juvenile officer was sitting.

"Listen, pal," I said. "This kid in here is waiting for his uncle. I explained the arrest to his sister and cited her back. I gotta meet a guy downtown and I'm late. How about taking care of him for me and I'll finish my reports later."

"Sure, Bumper. I'll take care of it," he said, and I wondered how calm I looked.

"Okay, kid, be seeing you," I said, passing through the room where the boy sat. "Hang in there, now."

"Where you going, Bumper?"

"Gotta hit the streets, kid," I said, trying to grin. "There's crime to crush."

"Yeah? Here's the phone number. I wrote it down on a piece of paper for you. Don't forget to call us."

"Yeah, well, I was thinking, my landlord is a cheap bastard. I don't think he'd ever go for eight bucks. I think you'd be better off not doing his place anyway. He probably wouldn't pay you on time or anything."

"That's okay. Give me your address, we'll come by and give you a special price. Remember, I can kick back a couple bucks."

"No, it wouldn't work out. See you around, huh?"

"How 'bout us getting together for a ball game, Bumper? I'll buy us a couple of box seats."

"I don't think so. I'm kind of giving up the Dodgers."

"Wait a minute," he said, jumping to his feet. "We'll do your gardening for four dollars, Bumper. Imagine that! Four dollars! We'll work maybe three hours. You can't beat that."

"Sorry, kid," I said, scuttling for the door like a fat crab.

"Why did you ever mention it then? Why did you ever say 'maybe'?"

I can't help you, boy, I thought. I don't have what you need.

"Goddamn you!" he yelled after me, and his voice broke. "You're just a cop! Nothing but a goddamn cop!"

I got back in the car feeling like someone kicked me in the belly and I headed back downtown. I looked at my watch and groaned, wondering when this day would end.

At the corner of Pico and Figueroa I saw a blind man with a red-tipped cane getting ready to board a bus. Some do-gooder in a mod suit was grabbing the blind man's elbow and aiming him, and finally the blind man said something to the meddler and made his own way.

"That's telling him, Blinky," I said under my breath. "You got to do for yourself in this world or they'll beat you down. The gods are strong, lonesome bastards and *you* got to be too."

SEVENTEEN

AT ELEVEN-FIFTEEN I was parking in front of Seymour's to meet Cruz. His car was there but I looked in the window and he wasn't at the counter. I wondered where he could be. Then I looked down the block and saw three black-and-whites, two detective cars, and an ambulance.

Being off the air with the kid I hadn't heard a call come out, and I walked down there and made my way through a crowd of people that was forming on the sidewalk around the drugstore. Just like everybody else, I was curious.

"What's happening, Clarence?" I said to Evans, who was standing in front of the door.

"Didn't you hear, Bumper?" said Evans, and he was sweating and looked sick, his coffee-brown face working nervously every-which way, and he kept looking around everywhere but at me.

"Hear what?"

"There was a holdup. A cop walked in and got shot," said a humpbacked shine man in a sailor's hat, looking up at me with an idiotic smile.

My heart dropped and I felt the sick feeling all policemen get when you hear that another policeman was shot.

"Who?" I asked, worrying that it might've been that young bookworm, Wilson.

"It was a sergeant," said the hunchback.

I looked toward Seymour's then and I felt the blood rush to my head.

"Let me in there, Clarence," I said.

"Now, Bumper, No one's allowed in there and you can't do anything. . . ."

I shoved Evans aside and pushed on the swinging aluminum doors, which were bolted.

"Bumper, please," said Evans, but I pulled away from him and slammed my foot against the center of the two doors, driving the bolt out of the aluminum casing.

The doors flew open with a crash and I was inside and running through a checkstand toward the rear of the big drugstore. It seemed like the store was a mile long and I ran blind and light-headed, knocking a dozen hair spray cans off a shelf when I barreled around a row of display counters toward the popping flashbulbs and the dozen plainclothesmen who were huddled in groups at the back of the store.

The only uniformed officer was Lieutenant Hilliard and it seemed like I ran for fifteen minutes to cover the eighty feet to the pharmacy counter where Cruz Segovia lay dead.

"What the hell . . ." said a red-faced detective I could barely see through a watery mist as I knelt beside Cruz, who looked like a very young boy sprawled there on his back, his hat and gun on the floor beside him and a frothy blood puddle like a scarlet halo fanning out around him from a through-and-through head shot. There was one red glistening bullet hole to the left of his nose and one in his chest which was surrounded by wine-purple bloodstains on the blue uniform. His eyes were open and he was looking right at me. The corneas were not yet dull or cloudy and the eyes were turned down at the corners, those large eyes more serious and sad than ever I'd seen them, and I knelt beside him in his blood and whispered, " 'Mano! 'Mano! 'Mano! Oh, Cruz!"

"Bumper, get the hell out of there," said the bald detective, grabbing my arm, and I looked up at him, seeing a very familiar face, but still I couldn't recognize him.

"Let him go, Leecher. We got enough pictures," said another plainclothesman, older, who was talking to Lieutenant Hilliard. He was one I should know too, I thought. It was so strange. I couldn't remember any of their names, except my lieutenant, who was in uniform.

Cruz looked at me so serious I couldn't bear it. And I reached in his pocket for the little leather pouch with the beads.

"You mustn't take anything from him," Lieutenant Hilliard said in my ear with his hand on my shoulder. "Only the coroner can do that, Bumper."

"His beads," I muttered. "He won them because he was the only one who could spell English words. I don't want them to know he carries beads like a nun."

"Okay, Bumper, okay," said Lieutenant Hilliard, patting my shoulder, and I took the pouch. Then I saw the box of cheap cigars spilled on the floor by his hand. And there was a ten-dollar bill there on the floor.

"Give me that blanket," I said to a young ambulance attendant who was standing there beside his stretcher, white in the face, smoking a cigarette.

He looked at me and then at the detectives.

"Give me that goddamn blanket," I said, and he handed the folded-up blanket to me, which I covered Cruz with after I closed his eyes so he couldn't look at me like that. *"Ahí te huacho,"* I whispered. "I'll be watching for you, *'mano*." Then I was on my feet and heading toward the door, gulping for breath.

"Bumper," Lieutenant Hilliard called, running painfully on his bad right leg and holding his hip.

I stopped before I got to the door.

"Will you go tell his wife?"

"He came in here to buy me a going-away present," I said, feeling a suffocating pressure in my chest.

"You were his best friend. You should tell her."

"He wanted to buy me a box of cigars," I said, grabbing him by the bony shoulder. "Damn him, I'd never smoke those cheap cigars. Damn him!"

"All right, Bumper. Go to the station. Don't try to work anymore today. You go on home. We'll take care of the notification. You take care of yourself."

I nodded and hurried out the door, looking at Clarence Evans but not understanding what he said to me. I got in the car and drove up Main Street, tearing my collar open to breathe, and thought about Cruz lying frail and naked and unprotected there in the morgue and thinking how they'd desecrate him, how they'd stick that turkey skewer in him for the liver temperature, and how they'd put a metal rod in the hole in his face for the bullet angle, and I was so damned glad I'd closed his eyes so he wouldn't be watching all that.

"You see, Cruz," I said, driving over Fourth Street with no idea where I was going. "You see? You almost had me convinced, but you were all wrong. I was right."

"You shouldn't be afraid to love, *'mano*," Cruz answered, and I slammed on my brakes when I heard him and I almost slid through the red light. Someone leaned on his horn and yelled at me.

"You're safe, Bumper, in one way," said Cruz in his gentle voice, "but in the way that counts, you're in danger. Your soul is in danger if you don't love."

I started when the light was green but I could hardly see.

"Did you believe that when Esteban was killed? Did you?"

"Yes, I knew it was the God's truth," he said, and his sad eyes turned down at the corners and this time I *did* blow a red light and I heard tires squeal and I turned right going the wrong way on Main Street and everyone was honking horns at me but I kept going to the next block and then turned left with the flow of traffic.

"Don't look at me with those goddamn turned-down eyes!" I yelled, my heart thudding like the pigeon's wing. "You're wrong, you foolish little man. Look at Socorro. Look at your children. Don't you see now, you're wrong? Damn those eyes!"

Then I pulled into an alley west of Broadway and got out of the car because I suddenly couldn't see at all now and I began to vomit. I threw it all up, all of it. Someone in a delivery truck stopped and said something but I waved him off and heaved and heaved it all away.

Then I got back in the car and the shock was wearing off. I drove to a pay phone and called Cassie before she left her office. I crowded in that phone booth doubled over by stomach cramps and I don't really know everything I said to her except that Cruz was dead and I wouldn't be going with her. Not now, not ever. And then there was lots of crying on the other end of the line and talking back and forth that didn't make any sense, and finally I heard myself say, "Yes, yes, Cassie. You go on. Yes, maybe I'll feel different later. Yes. Yes. Yes. Yes. You go on. Maybe I'll see you there in San Francisco. Maybe someday I'll feel different. Yes."

I was back in my car driving, and I knew I'd have to go to Socorro tonight and help her. I wanted to bury Cruz as soon as possible and I hoped she would want to. And now, gradually at first, and then more quickly, I felt as though a tremendous weight was lifted from my shoulders and there was no sense analyzing it, but there it was. I felt somehow light and free like when I first started on my beat. "There's nothing left now but the *puta*. But she's not a *puta*, *'mano*, she's not!" I said, lying to both of us for the last time, "You couldn't tell a whore from a bewitching lady. I'll keep her as long as I can, Cruz, and when I can't keep her anymore she'll go to somebody that can. You can't blame her for that. That's the way the world is made." And Cruz didn't answer my lie and I didn't see his eyes. He was gone. He was like Herky now, nothing more.

I began thinking of all the wandering people: Indians, Gypsies, Armenians, the Bedouin on that cliff where I'd never go, and now I knew the Bedouin saw nothing more than sand out there in that valley.

And as I thought these things I turned to my left and I was staring into the mouth of the Pink Dragon. I passed the Dragon by and drove on toward the station, but the further I drove, the more the anger welled up in me, and the anger mixed with the freedom I felt, so that for a while I felt like the most vigorous and powerful man on earth, a real *macho*, Cruz would've said. I turned around and headed back to the Dragon. This was the day for the Dragon to die, I thought. I could make Marvin fight me, and the others would help him. But no one could stand up to me and at last I'd destroy the Dragon.

Then I glanced down at my shield and saw that the smog had made the badge hideous. It was tarnished, and smeared with a drop of Cruz's blood. I stopped in front of Rollo's and went inside.

"Give it a fast buff, Rollo. I'm in a hurry."

"You know there ain't a single blemish on this badge," Rollo sighed.

"Just shine the goddamn badge."

He glanced up with his faded eyes, then at my trousers, at my wet bloody knees, and he bent silently over the wheel.

"There you are, Bumper," he said when he finished it.

I held the badge by the pin and hurried outside.

"Be careful, Bumper," he called. "Please be careful."

Passing by Rollo's store front I saw the distorted reflection in the folds of the plastic sun covering. I watched the reflection and had to laugh at the grotesque fat policeman who held the four-inch glittering shield in front of him as he lumbered to his car. The dark blue uniform was dripping sweat and the fat policeman opened the burning white door and squeezed his big stomach behind the wheel.

He settled in his saddle seat and jammed the nightstick under the seat cushion next to him, pointed forward.

Then he fastened his shield to his chest and urged the machine westward. The sun reflecting off the hood blinded him for a moment, but he flipped down the visor and drove west to the Pink Dragon.

"Now I'll kill the Dragon and drink its blood," said the comic blue policeman. "In the *front* door, down the Dragon's throat."

I laughed out loud at him because he was good for no more than this. He was disgusting and pathetic and he couldn't help himself. He needed no one. He sickened me. He only needed glory.

ABOUT THE AUTHOR

Joseph Wambaugh, a former LAPD detective sergeant, is the *New York Times* bestselling author of sixteen prior works of fiction and nonfiction, many of which have been adapted for the big and small screen, including *The Onion Field* and *The Choirboys*. He is a Grand Master of the Mystery Writers of America and lives in Southern California.

From Joseph Wambaugh,

the master of the cop thriller,

comes his most gripping,

sensational novel ever . . .

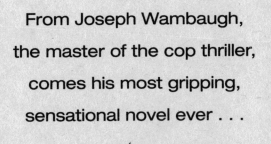

Please turn this page

for a preview

HOLLYWOOD CROWS

Available in hardcover

CHAPTER 1

"DUDE, YOU BETTER drop that *long* knife," the tall, sun-tanned cop said. At Hollywood Station they called him "Flotsam" by virtue of his being a surfing enthusiast.

His shorter partner, also with a major tan, hair even more suspiciously blond and sun streaked, dubbed "Jetsam" for the same reason, said, sotto voce, "Bro, that ain't a knife. That's a bayonet, in case you can't see too good. And why didn't you check out a Taser and a beanbag gun from the kit room, is what I'd like to know. That's what the DA's office and fid are gonna ask if we have to light him up. Like, 'Why didn't you officers use nonlethal force?' Like, 'Why'd that Injun have to bite the dust when you coulda captured him alive?' That's what they'll say."

"I thought you checked them out and put them in the trunk. You walked toward the kit room."

"No, I went to the john. And you were too busy ogling Ronnie to know where I was at," Jetsam said. "Your head was somewheres else. You gotta keep your mind in the game, bro."

Everyone on the midwatch at Hollywood Station knew

that Jetsam had a megacrush on Officer Veronica "Ronnie" Sinclair and got torqued when Flotsam or anybody else flirted with her. In any case, both surfer cops considered it sissified to carry a Taser on their belts.

Referring to section 5150 of the Welfare and Institutions Code, which all cops used to describe a mental case, Flotsam whispered, "Maybe this fifty-one-fifty's trashed on PCP, so we couldn't taze him anyways. He'd swat those darts outta him like King Kong swatted the airplanes. So just chill. He ain't even giving us the stink eye. He just maybe thinks he's a wooden Indian or something."

"Or maybe we're competing with a bunch of other voices he's hearing and they're scarier," Jetsam observed. "Maybe we're just echoes."

They'd gotten nowhere by yelling the normal commands to the motionless Indian, a stooped man in his early forties, only a decade older than they were but with a haggard face, beaten down by life. And while the cops waited for the backup they'd requested, they'd begun speaking to him in quiet voices, barely audible in the unlit alley over the traffic noise on Melrose Avenue. It was there that 6-X-46 had chased and cornered him, a few blocks from Paramount Studios, from where the code 2 call had come.

The Indian had smashed a window of a boutique to steal a plus-size gold dress with a handkerchief hemline and a red one with an empire waist. He'd squeezed into the red dress and walked to the Paramount main gate, where he'd started chanting gibberish and, perhaps prophetically, singing "Jailhouse Rock" before demanding admittance from a startled security officer who had dialed 9-1-1.

"These new mini-lights ain't worth a shit," Jetsam said,

referring to the small flashlights that the LAPD bought
and issued to all officers ever since a widely viewed video-
taped arrest showed an officer striking a combative black
suspect with his thirteen-inch aluminum flashlight, which
caused panic in the media and in the police commission
and resulted in the firing of the Latino officer.

After this event, new mini-flashlights that couldn't
cause harm to combative suspects unless they ate them
were ordered and issued to new recruits. Everything was
fine with the police commission and the cop critics except
that the high-intensity lights set the rubber sleeves on fire
and almost incinerated a few rookies before the Department recalled all of those lights and ordered these new
ten-ouncers.

Jetsam said, "Good thing that cop used flashlight therapy instead of smacking the vermin with a gun. We'd all
be carrying two-shot derringers by now."

Flotsam's flashlight seemed to better illuminate the
Indian, who stood staring up white-eyed at the starless
smog-shrouded sky, his back to the graffiti-painted wall
of a two-story commercial building owned by Iranians,
leased by Vietnamese. The Indian may have chosen the
red dress because it matched his flip-flops. The gold dress
lay crumpled on the asphalt by his dirt-encrusted feet,
along with the cut-offs he'd been wearing when he'd done
the smash-and-grab.

So far, the Indian hadn't threatened them in any way.
He just stood like a statue, his breathing shallow, the
bayonet held down against his bare left thigh, which was
fully exposed. He'd sliced the slit in the red dress clear up
to his flank, either for more freedom of movement or to
look more provocative.

"Dude," Flotsam said to the Indian, holding his Glock nine in the flashlight beam so the Indian could observe that it was pointed right at him, "I can see that you're spun out on something. My guess is you been doing crystal meth, right? And maybe you just wanted an audition at Paramount and didn't have any nice dresses to wear to it. I can sympathize with that too. I'm willing to blame it on Oscar de la Renta or whoever made the fucking things so alluring. But you're gonna have to drop that *long* knife now or pretty soon they're gonna be drawing you in chalk on this alley."

Jetsam, whose nine was also pointed at the ponytailed Indian, whispered to his partner, "Why do you keep saying *long* knife to this zombie instead of bayonet?"

"He's an Indian," Flotsam whispered back. "They always say *long* knife in the movies."

"That refers to us white men!" Jetsam said. "We're the fucking *long* knives!"

"Whatever," said Flotsam. "Where's our backup, anyhow? They coulda got here on skateboards by now."

When Flotsam reached tentatively for the pepper-spray canister on his belt, Jetsam said, "Uncool, bro. Liquid Jesus ain't gonna work on a meth-monster. It only works on cops. Which you proved the time you hit *me* with act-right spray instead of the 'roided-up primate I was doing a death dance with."

"You still aggro over that?" Flotsam said, remembering how Jetsam had writhed in pain after getting the blast of OC spray full in the face while they and four other cops swarmed the hallucinating bodybuilder who was paranoid from mixing recreational drugs with steroids. "Shit happens, dude. You can hold a grudge longer than my ex-wife."

In utter frustration, Jetsam finally said quietly to the Indian, "Bro, I'm starting to think you're running a game on us. So you either drop that bayonet right now or the medicine man's gonna be waving chicken claws over your fucking ashes."

Taking the cue, Flotsam stepped forward, his pistol aimed at the Indian's pustule-covered face, damp with sweat on this warm night, eyes rolled back, features strangely contorted in the flashlight beams. And the tall cop said just as quietly, "Dude, you're circling the drain. We're dunzo here."

Jetsam put his flashlight in his sap pocket, nowadays a cell-phone pocket, since saps had become LAPD artifacts, extended his pistol in both hands, and said to the Indian, "Happy trails, pard. Enjoy your dirt nap."

That did it. The Indian dropped the bayonet and Flotsam said, "Turn and face the wall and interlace your fingers behind your head!"

The Indian turned and faced the wall, but he obviously did not understand "interlace."

Jetsam said, "Cross your fingers behind your head!"

The Indian crossed his middle fingers over his index fingers and held them up behind his head.

"No, dude!" Flotsam said. "I didn't ask you to make a fucking wish, for chrissake!"

"Never mind!" Jetsam said, pulling the Indian's hands down and cuffing them behind his back.

Finally the Indian spoke. He said, "Do you guys have a candy bar I could buy from you? I'll give you five dollars for a candy bar."

When Jetsam was walking the Indian to their car, the prisoner said, "Ten. I'll give you ten bucks. I'll pay you when I get outta jail."

After stopping at a liquor store to buy their meth-addled, candy-craving arrestee a Nutter Butter, they drove him to Hollywood Station and put him in an interview room, cuffing one wrist to a chair so he could still eat his candy. The night-watch D2, a lazy sensitivity-challenged detective known as "Compassionate" Charlie Gilford, was annoyed at being pulled away from shows like *American Idol,* which he watched on a little TV he kept concealed in the warren of work cubicles the size of airline restrooms, where he sat for hours on a rubber donut. He loved to watch the panels brutalize the hapless contestants.

The detective was wearing a short-sleeved, wrinkled white shirt and one of his discount neckties, a dizzying checkerboard of blues and yellows. Everyone said his ties were louder than Mötley Crüe, and even older. Charlie got fatigued listening to the story of the window smash on Melrose, the serenade to the guard at Paramount Studios' main gate, the foot chase by the surfer cops, and the subsequent eerie confrontation, all of which Flotsam described as "weird."

He said to them, "Weird? This ain't weird." And then he uttered the phrase that one heard every night around the station when things seemed too surreal to be true: "Man, this is fucking Hollywood!" After that, there was usually no need for further comment.

But Charlie decided to elaborate: "Last year the mid-watch busted a goony tweaker totally naked except for a pink tutu. He was waving a samurai sword on Sunset

Boulevard when they took him down. That was weird. This ain't shit."

When he spotted the acronym for American Indian Movement tattooed on the prisoner's shoulder, he touched it with a pencil and said, "What's that mean, chief? Assholes in Moccasins?"

The Indian just sat munching on the Nutter Butter, eyes shut in utter bliss.

Then the cranky detective sucked his teeth and said to the arresting officers, "And by the way, you just had to feed him chocolate, huh? This tweaker don't have enough speed bumps?"

To the Indian he said, "Next time you feel like breaking into show business, take a look in the mirror. With that mug, you only got one option. Buy a hockey mask and try singing 'Music of the Night.'"

"I'll give you twenty bucks for another Nutter Butter," the Indian finally said to Compassionate Charlie Gilford. "And I'll confess to any crime you got."

Nathan Weiss, called Hollywood Nate by the other cops because of his obsession, recently waning, to break into the movie business, had left Watch 5, the midwatch, eight months earlier, shortly after the very senior sergeant known as the Oracle had died of a massive heart attack there on the police Walk of Fame in front of Hollywood Station. Nothing was the same on the midwatch after they lost the Oracle. Hollywood Nate had been pulled out of trouble, usually involving women, and spared from disciplinary action more than once by the grizzled forty-six-year veteran supervisor, who had died just short of his sixty-ninth birthday.

Everyone said it was fitting that the Oracle had died on that Walk, where stars honoring Hollywood Division officers killed on duty were embedded in marble and brass just as they were for movie stars on Hollywood Boulevard. The Oracle had been *their* star, an anachronism from another era of policing, from long before the Rodney King riots and Rampart Division evidence-planting scandal. Long before the LAPD had agreed to a Department of Justice "consent decree" and gotten invaded by federal judges and lawyers and politicians and auditors and overseers and media critics. Back when the cops could be guided by proactive leaders, not reactive bureaucrats more fearful of the federal overseers and local politicians than of the street criminals. The day after the Oracle died, Nathan Weiss had gone to temple, the first time in fifteen years, to say Kaddish for the old sergeant.

All of them, street cops and supervisors, were now smothered in paperwork designed to prove that they were "reforming" a police force of more than ninety-five hundred souls who ostensibly needed reforming because of the actions of half a dozen convicted cops from both incidents combined. Hundreds of sworn officers had been taken from street duties to manage the paper hurricane resulting from the massive "reformation." The consent decree hanging over the LAPD was to expire in two more years, but they'd heard that before and knew it could be extended. Like the war in Iraq, it seemed that it would never end.

The Oracle had been replaced by a university-educated twenty-eight-year-old with a degree in political science who'd rocketed almost to the top of the promotion list with little more than six years of experience, not to mention overcoming disadvantages of race and gender. Sergeant Jason Treakle was a white male, and that wasn't helpful in the diversity-obsessed city of Los Angeles, where fifty-five languages were spoken by students in the school district.

Hollywood Nate called Sergeant Treakle's roll call speeches a perfect meld of George Bush's garbled syntax and the tin ear of Al Gore. During those sessions Nate could hear cartilage crackling from all the chins bouncing off chests as the troops failed to stay awake and upright. He'd hated the rookie sergeant's guts the first time they'd met, when Sergeant Treakle criticized Nate in front of the entire assembly for referring to Officer Ronnie Sinclair as a "very cool chick." Ronnie took it as a compliment, but Sergeant Treakle found it demeaning and sexist.

Then, during an impromptu inspection, he'd frowned upon Hollywood Nate's scuffed shoes. He'd pointed at Nate's feet with an arm that didn't look long enough for his body, saying the shoes made Nate look "unkempt," and suggested that Nate try spit-shining them. Sergeant Treakle was big on spit shines, having spent six months in the ROTC at his university. Because of his knife-blade mouth, the cops soon referred to him as "Chickenlips."

Hollywood Nate, like his idol, the Oracle, had always worn ordinary black rubber-soled shoes with his uniform. He liked to needle the cops who wore expensive over-the-ankle boots to look more paramilitary but then experienced sweaty feet, foot fungus, and diminished running speed. Nate would ask them if their spit-shined boots made it easier to slog through all the snow and ice storms on Sunset and Hollywood Boulevards.

And Hollywood Nate had given up suggesting that field

training officers stop making the new P1 probationers call
them sir or ma'am, as most did. The more rigid and GI of
the FTOs seemed to be those who'd never served in the
military and they wouldn't think of letting their probies
wear the gung-ho boots before finishing their eighteen-
month probation. Nate would privately tell the rookies to
forget about boots, that their feet would thank them for
it. And Nate never forgot that the Oracle had never spit-
shined his shoes.

Before the midwatch hit the streets, every cop would
ritually touch the picture of the Oracle for luck, even
new officers who'd never known him. It hung on the wall
by the door of the roll call room. In the photo their late
sergeant was in uniform, his retro gray crew cut freshly
trimmed, smiling the way he'd always done, more with
his smart blue eyes than with his mouth. The brass plate
on the frame simply said:

THE ORACLE
APPOINTED: FEB 1960
END-OF-WATCH: AUG 2006
SEMPER COP

Hollywood Nate, like all the others, had tapped the
picture frame before leaving roll call on the first evening
he'd met his new sergeant. Then he'd gone straight downstairs to the watch commander's office and asked to be re-
assigned to the day watch, citing a multitude of personal
and even health reasons, all of them lies. It had seemed to
Nate that an era had truly ended. The Oracle—the kind

of cop Nate told everyone he had wanted to be when he grew up—had been replaced by a politically correct, paper-shuffling little putz with dwarfish arms, no lips, and a shoe fetish.

At first, Hollywood Nate wasn't fond of Watch 2, the early day watch, certainly not the part where he had to get up before 5 A.M. and speed from his one-bedroom apartment in the San Fernando Valley to Hollywood Station, change into his uniform, and be ready for 0630 roll call. He didn't like that at all. But he did like the hours of the 3/12 work shift. On Watch 2, the patrol officers worked three twelve-hour days a week during their twenty-eight-day deployment periods, making up one day at the end. That gave Nate four days a week to attend cattle calls and harangue casting agents, now that he'd earned enough vouchers to get his Screen Actors Guild card, which he carried in his badge wallet right behind his police ID.

So far, he'd gotten only one speaking part, two lines of dialogue, in a TV movie that was co-produced by an over-the-hill writer/director he'd met during one of the red carpet events at the Kodak Center, where Nate was tasked with crowd control. Nate won over that director by body blocking an anti-fur protester in a sweaty tank top before she could shove one of those "I'd Rather Go Naked" signs at the director's wife, who was wearing a faux-mink stole.

Nate sealed the deal and got the job when he told the hairy protester he'd hate to see *her* naked and added, "If wearing fur is a major crime, why don't you scrape those pits?"

The movie was about mate-swapping yuppies, and Nate was typecast as a cop who showed up after one of the husbands beat the crap out of his cheating spouse. The battered wife was scripted to look at the hawkishly handsome, well-muscled cop whose wavy dark hair was just turning silver at the temples, and wink at him with her undamaged eye.

To Nate, there didn't seem to be much of a story and he was given one page of script with lines that read: "Good evening, ma'am. Did you call the police? What can I do for you that isn't immoral?"

During that one-day gig, the grips and gaffers and especially the craft services babe who provided great sandwiches and salads all told Nate that this was a "POS" movie that might never reach the small screen at all. After she'd said it, Nate knew that his initial impression had been correct: It was a piece of shit, for sure. Hollywood Nate Weiss was already thirty-six years old, with fifteen years on the LAPD. He needed a break. He needed an agent. He didn't have time left in his acting life to waste on pieces of shit.

On the morning after the midwatch surfer cops busted the wooden Indian, Nate Weiss was assigned to a one-man day-watch report car known as a U-boat, which responded to report-writing calls instead of those that for safety reasons required a pair of officers. At 8:30 A.M. Nate did what he always did when he caught a U-boat assignment: He went to Farmers Market at Third and Fairfax for a coffee break.

The fact that Farmers Market was a couple of blocks out of Hollywood Division didn't bother him much. It was a small peccadillo that the Oracle would always forgive. Nate loved everything about that old landmark: the tall clock tower, the stalls full of produce, the displays of fresh fish and meat, the shops and ethnic eateries. But mostly he loved the open-air patios where people gathered this time of morning for cinnamon rolls, fresh-baked muffins, French toast, and other pastries.

Nate ordered a latte and a bagel, taking a seat at a small empty table close enough to eavesdrop on the "artistes' table." He'd started doing it after he'd overheard them talking about pitching scripts to HBO and getting financing for small indie projects and doing lunch with a famous agent from CAA who one of them said was a schmuck—all topics of fascination to Hollywood Nate Weiss.

By now, he was almost able to recognize them from their voices without looking at them directly. There was the features director who, due to Hollywood ageism, complained that he couldn't even get arrested at the studios. Ditto for three former screenwriters who were regulars at the table, as well as for a former TV producer. A dozen or more of these would come and go, all males, the average age being seventy-plus, far too old for the youth-obsessed entertainment business that had nurtured them.

A formerly famous painter and sculptor, wearing a trademark black beret, wasn't selling so well these days either. Nate heard him tell the others that when his wife asks him what he wants for dinner, his usual response is, "Get off my back, will ya?" Then the painter added, "But don't feel sorry for us. We're getting used to living in our car."

A former TV character actor wearing a safari jacket from Banana Republic, whose face was familiar to Nate, stood up and informed the others he had to leave and make an important call to a VP in development at Universal to discuss a script he'd been deciding whether or not to accept.

After he'd gone, the director said, "The poor schlemiel. I'll bet he gets a 'Please leave a message' recording from the VP at Universal. That's who he discusses the project with—a machine. Probably has to call back a hundred and thirty-five times to get his whole pitch into the VP's voice mail."

"I've suspected he's calling the number for highway information when he pretends to be talking to HBO," the painter said, clucking sadly.

"He never was any good, even in his prime," the director said. "Thought he was a method actor. They'd run out of money doing retakes. Twenty tics a take on average."

"If he had more of a name, they could paint him like a whore and let him do arthritis and Geico commercials, like the rest of those has-beens," said the has-been TV producer.

"And women?" one of the screenwriters said. "He thinks we believe his daffy seduction stories. Instead of another face-lift, the old bastard should have his balls stapled to his thigh to keep them from dropping in the toilet."

"He could do it without anesthetic," said the oldest of the screenwriters. "At his age it's a dead zone down there."

All of the geezers, who tended to talk over one another in multiple conversations, went silent for a moment when a stunning young woman paused to look into a nearby shop that sold glassware and candles. She wore a canary cotton jersey accented by hyacinth stitching, and $400 second-skin jeans, and stood nearly six feet tall in her Jimmy Choo lilac suede pumps. She had a full, pouty upper lip, and butterscotch blonde hair so luxurious it fanned across her shoulder when she turned to look at a glass figurine and then fell back perfectly into place when she continued walking. Her amazing hair gleamed when spangled sunlight pierced the covered patio and provided honey-colored highlights.

The codgers sighed and snuffled and did everything but drool before resuming their conversations. Nate watched her walk out toward the parking lot. Her remarkable body said Pilates loud and clear, and he could see she wasn't wearing a bra. There in Hollywood, and even in Beverly Hills, Nate Weiss had not seen many showstoppers like her.

By then, Nate was ready to go back to work. It was getting depressing listening to the old guys railing about ageism, knowing in their hearts they'd never work again. He'd noticed that always around 9:30 A.M., they'd get up one by one and make excuses to leave, for important calls from directors, or for appointments with agents, or to get back to scripts they were polishing. Nate figured they all just went home to sit and stare at phones that never rang. It gave him a chill to think that he might be looking at Nathan Weiss a few decades from now.

Nate strolled to the parking lot thirty yards behind the beauty with the butterscotch hair, wanting to see what she drove. He figured her for a Beverly Hills hottie in an Aston Martin with a vanity license plate, compliments of a bucks-up husband or sugar daddy who drove a stately Rolls Phantom. It was almost disappointing when she got into a red BMW sedan instead of something really expensive and exotic.

Impulsively, he jotted down her license number, and when he got back to his black-and-white, ran a DMV check and saw that she lived in the Hollywood Hills, off Laurel Canyon Boulevard in the development called Mt. Olympus, where realtors claimed there were more Italian cypress trees per acre than anywhere else on earth. Her address surprised him a bit. There were lots of well-to-do foreign nationals on Mt. Olympus: Israelis, Iranians, Arabs, Russians, and Armenians, and others from former Soviet bloc countries, some of whom had been suspects or victims in major crimes. A few of the residents reportedly owned banks in Moscow, and it was not uncommon to see young adults driving Bentleys, and teenagers in BMWs and Porsches.

Around the LAPD it was said that mobbed-up former Soviets were more dangerous and cruel than the Sicilian gangsters ever were back in the day. Just five months earlier, two Russians had been sentenced to death in Los Angeles Superior Court for kidnapping and murder. They'd suffocated or strangled four men and one woman in a $1.2 million ransom scheme.

Mt. Olympus was pricey, all right, but not the crème de la crème of local real estate, and Nate thought that the area didn't suit her style. Luckily, it was in Hollywood Division and he'd often patrolled the streets up there. He figured it was unlikely that this Hills bunny would ever need a cop, but after finally getting his SAG card, Hollywood Nate Weiss was starting to believe that maybe anything was possible.

At 6 P.M. that day, after the midwatch had cleared with communications and was just hitting the streets, and Nate

Weiss was an hour from end-of-watch, the electronic beep sounded on the police radio and the PSR's voice said to a midwatch unit, "All units in the vicinity and Six-X-Seventy-six, a jumper at the northeast corner, Hollywood and Highland. Six-X-Seventy-six, handle code three."

Hollywood Nate in his patrol unit—which everyone at LAPD called their "shop" because of the identifying shop numbers on the front doors and roof—happened to be approaching the traffic light west at that intersection. He'd been gazing at the Kodak Center and dreaming of red carpets and stardom when the call came out. He saw the crowd of tourists gathering, looking up at a building twelve stories high, with an imposing green cupola. Even several of the so-called Street Characters who hustled tourists in the forecourt of Grauman's Chinese Theatre were jaywalking or running along the Walk of Fame to check out the excitement.

Superman was there, of course, and the Hulk, but not Spider-Man, who was in jail. Porky Pig waddled across the street, followed by Barney the dinosaur and three of the Beatles, the fourth staying behind to guard the karaoke equipment. Everyone was jabbering and pointing up at the top of the vacant building, formerly a bank, where a young man in walking shorts, tennis shoes, and a purple T-shirt with "Just Do It" across the front sat on the roof railing, a dozen stories above the street below.

In the responding unit were Veronica Sinclair and Catherine Song, both women in their early thirties who, as far as Nate was concerned, happened to be among the better cops on midwatch. Cat was a sultry Korean American whose hobby was volleyball and whose feline grace made her name a perfect fit. Nate, who had been trying unsuccessfully to date her for nearly a year, loved Cat's raven hair, cut in a retro bob like the girls in the 1930s movies that he had in his film collection. Cat was a divorced mother of a two-year-old boy.

Ronnie Sinclair had been at Hollywood Station for less than a year, but she'd been a heartthrob from the first moment she'd arrived. She was a high-energy brunette with a very short haircut that worked, given her small, tight ears and well-shaped head. She had pale blue eyes, great cheekbones, and a bustline that made all the male cops pretend they were admiring the shooting medals hanging on her shirt flap. The remarkable thing about her was that her childless marriages had been to two police officers named Sinclair who were distant cousins, so Flotsam and Jetsam called her Sinclair Squared. Most of the midwatch officers over the age of thirty were single but had been divorced at least once, including the surfer cops and Hollywood Nate.

The two women were met at the open door of the vacant building by an alarm company employee who said, "I don't know yet how he got in. Probably broke a window in the back. The elevator still works."

Ronnie and Cat hurried inside to the elevators, Nate right behind them. And all three stood waiting for the elevator, trying to be chatty to relieve the gathering tension.

"Why aren't you circling the station about now?" Ronnie said, looking at her watch. "You're almost end-of-watch and there must be a starlet waiting."

Nate looked at his own watch and said, "I still have, let's see, forty-seven minutes to give to the people of Los Angeles. And who needs starlets when I have such talent surrounding me?"

When Nate, whose womanizing was legendary at Hollywood Station, shot her his Groucho leer, Ronnie said, "Forget it, Nate. Ask me for a date sometime when you're a star and can introduce me to George Clooney."

That caused Hollywood Nate to whip out his badge wallet and proudly remove the SAG card tucked right underneath his police ID, holding it up for Ronnie and Cat to see.

Ronnie looked at it and said, "Even O.J. has one of those."

Cat said, "Sorry, Nate, but my mom wants me to date and marry a rich Buddhahead lawyer next time, not some oh-so-cute, round-eyed actor like you."

"Someday you'll both want me to autograph an eight-by-ten head shot for you," Nate said, pleased that Cat thought he was cute, more pleased that she'd called him an actor. "Then I'll be the one playing hard to get."

During the ride up in the elevator they didn't speak anymore, growing tense even though the location of the jumper call, here in the heart of Hollywood tourism, made it likely that it was just a stunt by some publicity junkie. The three cops were trying their best not to take it too seriously. Until they climbed to the observation deck encircling the cupola and saw him, shirtless now, straddling a railing with arms outstretched, tennis shoes pressed together, head slightly bowed in the crucifixion pose. This, as tourists, hustlers, tweakers, pickpockets, cartoon characters, and various Hollywood crazies were standing down below, yelling at him to stop being a chickenshit and jump for Jesus.

"Oh, shit!" Cat said, speaking for all of them.

The three cops walked very slowly toward him and he

turned around on the railing to face them, wobbling precariously, making onlookers down below either scream or cheer. His sandy, shoulder-length hair was blowing in his face, and his eyes behind wire-rimmed glasses were even more pale blue than Ronnie's. In fact, she thought he looked a lot like her cousin Bob, a drummer in a rock band. Maybe it was that, but she took the lead and the others let her have it.

She smiled at him and said, "Hey, whadda you say you come on down here and let's talk."

"Stay where you are," he said.

She held up her hands, palms forward, and said, "Okay, okay, I'm cool with that. But how about coming down now?"

"You're going to kill me, aren't you?" he said.

"Of course not," Ronnie said. "I just wanna talk to you. What's your name? They call me Ronnie."

He did not respond, so she said, "Ronnie is short for Veronica. A lot of people see my name somewhere and think I'm a guy."

Still he did not respond, so she said, "Do you have a nickname?"

"Tell them to go," he said, pointing at Nate and Cat. "I know they want to kill me."

Ronnie turned around, but the others had immediately retreated to the door when they heard his demand, Cat saying, "Be careful, Ronnie!"

Then Ronnie said to him, "See, they've gone."

"Take off your gun belt," he said. "Or I'll jump."

"Okay!" Ronnie said, unfastening her Sam Browne and lowering it to her feet, close enough to grab for it.

"Step away from the gun," he said. "I know you want to kill me."

"Why would I kill you?" Ronnie said, taking a single step toward him. "You're getting ready to kill yourself. You see, that wouldn't make sense, would it? No, I don't wanna kill you. I wanna help you. I know I can if you'll just get down from that railing and talk to me."

"Do you have a cigarette?" he said, and for a few seconds he swayed in the wind, and Ronnie sucked in a lungful of air, then let it out slowly.

"I don't smoke," she said, "but I can have my partner find you a cigarette. Her name's Cat. She's very nice and I bet you'd like her a lot."

"Never mind," he said. "I don't need a cigarette. I don't need anything."

"You need a friend," Ronnie said. "I'd like to be that friend. I have a cousin who looks just like you. What's your name?"

"My name's Randolph Bronson and I'm not crazy," he said. "I know what I'm doing."

"I don't think you're crazy, Randolph," Ronnie said, and now she could feel sweat running down her temples, and her hands felt slimy. "I just think you're feeling sad and need someone to talk to. That's why I'm here. To talk to you."

"Do you know what it's like to be called crazy? And schizophrenic?" he asked.

"Tell me about it, Randolph," Ronnie said, walking another step closer until he said, "Stop!"

"I'm sorry!" she said. "I'll stay right here if it makes you feel better. Tell me about your family. Who do you live with?"

"I'm a burden to them," he said. "A financial burden. An emotional burden. They won't be sorry to see me gone."

After six long minutes of talking, Ronnie Sinclair was fairly certain that the young man was ready to surrender. She found out that he was nineteen years old and had been treated for mental illness most of his life. Ronnie believed that she had him now, that she could talk him down from the railing. She was addressing him as "Randy" by the time backup arrived on the street, including a rescue ambulance and the fire department, whose engine only served to clog traffic. Still no crisis negotiator from Metropolitan Division had arrived.

And the first supervisor to show up at the scene was Sergeant Jason Treakle, who'd been on a suck-up mission to buy two hamburgers and an order of fries for the night-watch lieutenant. Sergeant Treakle had gotten a brainstorm the moment he'd heard the call. The idea actually made him say "Wow!" aloud, though he was alone in the car. Then he looked at the bag of burgers next to him, turned on his light bar, and sped to the location of the jumper call.

The young sergeant had recently read about an attempted suicide where a jumper had been talked down by a crisis negotiator who'd bought him a sandwich that they shared while talking at length about the people, real and imagined, who were tormenting him. The crisis negotiator had gotten her photo in the *L.A. Times* and had done several tv interviews.

When the midwatch supervisor ascended to the tower, carrying the bag of burgers, and brushed past Cat Song and Hollywood Nate, Cat said, "Sergeant Treakle, wait! Ronnie's talking to the guy. Wait, please."

Hollywood Nate said, "Don't go out there, Sergeant."

The sergeant said, "Don't tell me my job, Weiss."

Nate Weiss, who had several years in age and job experience on his former supervisor, said, "Sergeant, nobody should *ever* bust in on a suicide standoff. This might be Hollywood but this is not a movie, and there's no air bag down there."

"Thanks for your wise counsel," Sergeant Treakle said with a chilly glance at Nate. "I'll keep it in mind if you ever become my boss."

Ronnie turned and saw him striding confidently along the deck and said, "Sergeant! Go back, please! Let me handle—"

The anguished moan from Randolph Bronson made her spin around. He was staring at the uniformed sergeant with the condescending smile and the bulging paper bag in his hand, into which he was reaching.

The boy's pale eyes had gotten huge behind the eyeglasses. Then he looked at Ronnie and said, "He's going to kill me!"

And he was gone. Just like that.

The screams from the crowd, a gust of wind, and Cat's and Nate's shouts all prevented Ronnie from hearing her own cry as she lunged forward and gaped over the railing. She saw him bounce once on the pavement. Several bluesuits immediately began holding back the most morbid of the boulevard onlookers.

A few minutes later, there were a dozen more uniforms in the lobby of the building who observed Ronnie Sinclair, eyes glistening, yelling curses into the face of Ser-

geant Jason Treakle, who had gone pale and didn't know
how to respond to his subordinate.

Ronnie didn't remember what she'd yelled, but Cat
later said, "You started dropping F-bombs and it was
beautiful. There's nothing Treakle can do about it, because now he knows he was dead wrong. And now that
kid is just plain dead."

When they got out to the street, they were amazed to
see that Randolph Bronson's wire-rimmed glasses were
still affixed to his face and only one lens was broken. He
had not blown apart, as some of them do, but there was a
massive pool of blood.

Cat put an arm around Ronnie's shoulder, squeezed it,
and said, "Gimme the keys to our shop. Let me drive us
to the station."

Ronnie handed Cat the car keys without objection.

Compassionate Charlie Gilford, who never missed a
newsworthy incident, especially with carnage involved,
arrived in time to observe them picking up the body, and
he offered his usual on-scene commentary.

The lanky veteran detective sucked his teeth and said
to the body snatcher driving the coroner's van, "So, one
of our patrol sergeants thought he could keep this looney tune from a back flip by feeding him a meal, right?
Man, this is fucking Hollywood! Everybody knows you
can walk a couple blocks to Musso and Frank's and dine
with movie stars on comfort food. And Wolfgang Puck's
got a joint right inside the Kodak Center with some of
the trendiest eats in town. But what does our ass-wipe
sergeant do to cheer up a depressed wack job? He brings

the dude a fucking Big Mac! No wonder the fruitloop jumped."

Later that night, Compassionate Charlie Gilford saw Ronnie Sinclair in the report room massaging her temples, waiting for the interrogation from Force Investigation Division, knowing that this one would be handled just like an officer-involved shooting.

The detective said merrily, "I hear you really carpet bombed Chickenlips Treakle, Ronnie. Hollywood Nate told me you wouldn't hear *that* many 'motherfuckers' at a Chris Rock concert. Way to go, girl!"

mjg

"Blisteringly funny police procedural."
—*New York Times Book Review*

DON'T MISS JOSEPH WAMBAUGH'S
CLASSIC NOVEL

THE NEW CENTURIONS

Ex-cop turned #1 *New York Times* bestselling
writer Joseph Wambaugh forged a new
kind of literature with his great early police
procedurals. Here in his classic debut novel,
Wambaugh presents a stunning, raw, and
unforgettable depiction of life behind the thin
blue line.

Available wherever books are sold from
Grand Central Publishing